Two action-packed novels of the American frontier

Signet Brand Double Westerns:

THE LONE RIFLE

and

BARRANCA

The Lone Rifle

and

Barranca

by

Gordon D. Shirreffs

A SIGNET BOOK from
NEW AMERICAN LIBRARY
TIMES MIRROR

Published by
THE NEW AMERICAN LIBRARY
OF CANADA LIMITED

NAL books are also available at discounts in bulk quantity for industrial or sales-promotional use. For details, write to Premium Marketing Division, New American Library, Inc., 1301 Avenue of the Americas, New York, New York 10019.

Originally appeared in paperback as separate volumes published by The New American Library

First Printing, Double Western Edition, May, 1978

1 2 3 4 5 6 7 8 9

SIGNET, SIGNET CLASSICS, MENTOR, PLUME AND MERIDIAN BOOKS are published in Canada by The New American Library of Canada Limited, Scarborough, Ontario

PRINTED IN CANADA

COVER PRINTED IN U.S.A.

The Lone Rifle

CHAPTER ONE

The dry prairie wind had shifted as the sun moved westward across the Kansas plains. The clear morning sky had become dotted with slowly drifting clouds that threw fleeting shadows on the rolling, grassy terrain. To the north a shimmering heat haze had begun to form over the valley of the Smoky Hill River. A dun-colored mass drifted northwesterly across a wide, shallow valley south of the valley of the Smoky Hill, raising a thin cloud of bitter yellowish dust that settled on the cured buffalo grass like a great shaggy blanket.

The lone horseman reined his bay to a halt and then slid from the saddle. He carefully lifted the heavy, long-barreled Sharps rifle from its saddle slings and fitted the ten-power Vollmer rifle-telescope to the mounts atop the Sharps barrel. He padded softly up the sandy slope and lay bellyflat behind a clump of soapweed, removing his dusty hat before he raised his head above the lip of the low ridge. A fleeting grin passed across his brown face. *"Cibolo!"* he said. The wind had shifted just as he had predicted it would with the coming of the greater heat of the July day. It was now blowing from the vast herd of grazing buffalo directly toward him.

Miles Flint slid down out of sight and levered open the breechblock of the heavy rifle, placing a big paper-patched cartridge into the chamber of the converted Sharps, closing the breechblock, and setting the hammer at half cock. He carefully checked the rifle telescope, cleaning the good German lens with a camel's-hair brush. He bellied up the slope again and placed the *bois d'arc* buffalo sticks just between two clumps of soapweed, separating them to place the rifle barrel in the upper crotch of the sticks. He rested the butt of the rifle on the ground and lighted a cigar. He drew in a few deep breaths of the smoke and then tossed the cigar down the slope to a bare patch of the sandy soil, watching the thin smoke waver upward and then drift with the wind. He nodded, then placed a score of fat-bellied brass .45-120-550 cartridges on a flat rock close to hand. Miles unfastened his big, cloth-covered canteen and placed it beside the rock.

The wind was a little variable but blowing almost directly from the herd toward Miles. He would need no windage. He studied the herd through the powerful rifle 'scope. An old cow stood fifty yards closer to him than the rest of the herd, a good two hundred and fifty yards from Miles's "stand." He wanted to work closer, but there was no cover between him and the herd. Miles knelt on the slope, gripped the buffalo sticks with his left hand just below the crotch of the sticks, and sighted on the unsuspecting cow. He used the upper crosshairs, then slowly took up the trigger slack. He took in a deep breath, held it, then let out half of it. He settled the upper crosshairs for a lung shot and squeezed off. The rifle roared, spitting flame and smoke; driving powerfully back into the hollow of his shoulder. He peered through the smoke that blew back into his lean face. The cow had been hit. She moved ahead a few feet, then suddenly went down on her foreknees. The bulls nearest her raised their heads at the smell of the blood and moved closer, sniffing at her. One of the younger bulls hooked at her with his horns. Miles nodded. They were more interested in her than they were in the cause of her strange behavior.

Miles reloaded. From now on it would be heart or neck shots to cause quick death. He fired swiftly, almost casually, but each of his actions was that of the skilled professional. The smoking, empty brass hulls tinkled against the flat rock. A fresh round was slid into the chamber. A moment's hesitation and the Sharps roared. Each heavy slug struck its mark. The herd was getting nervous, raising their shaggy heads and sniffing the wind, but they held their ground until the sixth buffalo went down; then they began to mill a little. The bulls moved out to the flanks of the herd, the cows nuzzled the calves inside the protective ring.

Miles slid down the slope and poured water down the smoking barrel to clean the fouling. It looked like a damned good stand. He needed four more hides for that day's work. An excellent stand that morning had enabled him to get twenty-five hides from a smaller herd. His skilled Canuck skinners were still hard at work on them on a fork of the Smoky Hill where he had set up his camp, beyond a westward ridge and downwind of the bigger herd. Thirty-five a day was Miles Flint's quota. He had set it for himself in his four years of buffalo hunting. It was a good day's work for both Miles and his skinners—no more, no less.

He eased back up the slope and settled his rifle in the sticks.

As he did so he noted a thin wraith of dust beyond the eastward ridge of the shallow valley. He narrowed his gray eyes. He had thoroughly scouted that area the evening before and had seen no buffalo for miles. As far as he knew, no herd had moved into the area during the day, and it wasn't likely they had done so. He was at least twenty miles from the nearest camp of buffalo hunters. It wouldn't be Indians—they wouldn't advertise their approach like that. They were seen only when they wanted to be seen.

Miles fired again and dropped a massive bull. The herd was restless but holding its ground. Miles shifted his tobacco chew and spat to one side, eyeing that dust cloud. It was getting closer. If it was a buffalo herd—and he was almost positive that it couldn't be—they were moving far too fast for the normal movement of a herd from one grazing area to another. He rubbed his lean jaw and studied the dust. It was moving directly toward the herd he was working on. If the oncoming herd panicked the herd in the valley, they'd likely drive right down toward Miles's skinning camp on Smoky Hill Fork.

He downed a cow and a young bull. The herd began to drift to the north, rather than to the west, heading upwind as usual for the ridge that separated the valley from the valley of the Smoky Hill. Miles spat out his chew and stood up. It wasn't like buffalo to move toward higher ground, even upwind, unless they were frightened.

The dust swirled up thicker and thicker. Miles dropped to his knees and placed an ear close to the ground. His face tightened, and an uneasy feeling stirred his guts. A steady tremor came to him through the great sounding board of the earth. Something was moving toward the great buffalo herd; something moving on thousand of hooves and moving fast—too damned fast! It was likely another herd, maybe stampeded by some damned fool playing at being a buffalo runner, a menace to every other hunter in the area.

Miles picked up his cartridges, slung his canteen, snapped together the buffalo sticks, and grabbed his rifle. It was time to move and stand not upon the order of his going. After casing the 'scope, he put the rifle in the slings. He swung up on the bay and turned eastward, a puzzled look on his lean face. He touched the bay with his heels and rode along the ridge crest, keeping out of sight of the herd as much as possible. Maybe they wouldn't be panicked and stampeded by the oncoming herd, and he could make a stand the next morning within close proximity to his skinning camp. The dust was swirling up thicker and thicker. If the running herd stampeded the valley herd and the combined herds drove west toward the fork of the Smoky Hill, there would be hell to pay and no pitch hot.

The bay tossed its head and whinnied sharply. Miles patted his neck. "You don't like it either, hey, boy?" he said quietly.

The dust was driving down into the valley now, swirling over the nervous herd. Slowly they turned away from the north ridge and swung uneasily at a fast walk toward the west, leaving the humped carcasses of their dead. The bulls swung out to cover the flanks of the herd, the cows and calves held within their protection. Dust rose from their thudding hooves to mingle with the sweeping dust of the oncoming herd, thickening on the freshening wind.

Miles quirted the bay down the side of the low ridge into the valley and then let the bay run free. It was faster, although infinitely more dangerous, to cut across the face of the oncoming herd. The herd was beginning to move faster, humping awkwardly up and down, clumped close together and shaking the ground with the impact of thousands of hooves. Miles freed his converted Remington six-shooter from its sheath. Five rounds of .44 soft-nose slugs could drop as many buffalo at extremely close range, but Miles prayed to God it wouldn't come to that.

The bay's hooves drummed on the harder ground of the valley floor, drowned out by the ominous thundering of the buffalo herd. The buffalo were running free now with their deceptive, awkward style, covering the ground at a rapid pace. The bay drew from the deep well of his stamina and kept well ahead of the herd. They reached the low rise at the west end of the valley. Miles looked back over his shoulder. Something had topped the eastern ridge. A great mass of movement, shrouded in swirling yellowish dust, pouring down into the valley on the heels of the last of the buffalo herd, blotting out the prairie grass until the whole valley was filled from one side to the other. The slanting rays of the sun shone on sweat-glistening hides of myriad colors and on the tremendous spreading horns of the beasts.

Miles stared in disbelief. "Longhorns!" he yelled. He plied the braided quirt with all his strength.

He began to yell as soon as he saw the distant camp, placed just beyond the dotted carcasses of the buffalo he had killed from his first stand that day. Most of them had been flayed of their heavy pelts, the naked bloody flesh of the carcasses shining greasily under the sun's rays. Thick clouds of buzzing flies swarmed around. The sun also glinted from the clear, shallow waters of the fork just beyond the pitched tents and Red River carts and the remuda of mules and horses. A thin wraith of smoke rose from the cookfire. Some of the Canucks were pegging out the green hides on the level ground north of the camp for curing under the hot sun.

Miles thrust the heavy Remington upward and fired three times, the big pistol bucking back hard into the fork of his hand. He saw the faces of the skinners turn toward him. Big Tom, the Negro cocinero, looked up from his cookfire. "Stampede!" screamed Miles at the top of his voice. He knew he couldn't be heard; the buffalo had already topped the rise behind him, ramrodded on by the longhorns behind them, a moving mass of living flesh, of death on the hoof for any living thing that stood in its way.

There was no time to save any equipment. Everything had to be sacrificed to get those four men free from the shaggy, dusty death that was roaring toward them at a speed almost approaching that of a horse. Everything must go. Hides, carts, tents, supplies, gear, and weapons. *Everything!* One of the skinners fought to free the mules from a cart harness, and another skinner ran out toward the picketed mules and horses.

"No! No!" screamed Miles.

A horn of the herd had swung in toward the fork, eating up yardage between themselves and the picketed animals. One after the other the mules and horses jerked free, the picket pins flying through the dusty air. In a moment one skinner was gone beneath the pounding, sharp-edged hoofs.

The man at the cart mounted a mule, but the frightened beast, smelling the herd, buckjumped and then sunfished, pitching off his unwanted rider. The skinner sprinted futilely toward the creek. Big Tom came out of a tent, hugging something to his chest. He ran for the lone tree that stood at the edge of the fork and began to clamber up it, impeded by his heavy burden. The buffalo herd swirled around a knoll just beyond Miles, that created a vacuum in the mass of frightened animals, and then they thundered over the campsite, raising a pall of dust that blotted everything from sight except the sunshot reflection from the horns of the beasts.

There was nothing else Miles could do but try to save his own life. The bay could outrun them just so long. Miles reined in the bay, flipped open the loading gate of the hot Remington, and rammed in four rounds just in time to slide from the saddle and face the onrushing herd. He raised the pistol like a duelist and fired at the nearest bull, about fifty feet away. The impetus of the bull and the weight of the herd behind him tumbled fifteen hundred pounds of dead buffalo almost at Miles's feet. He fired again, dropping a big cow behind the bull. The bay tugged at the reins wrapped around Miles's left arm and spoiled his third shot, but the fourth shot dropped a young bull that was veering in toward Miles. The shaggy shoulder butted the bay aside, and the tip of a horn lightly raked Miles's sweating face. He emptied the Remington just in time for the thundering herd to pass around the tumbled buffalo, leaving a narrow V of open space where Miles held on to the rearing, plunging bay.

Miles tied his scarf across the eyes of the bay, feeling the strong body shiver in panic. The herd smashed past. The heat and dust of it seemed to fill the whole world. Miles buried his face in the bay's mane and prayed as he had not prayed since he was a Union soldier at Gettysburg the day the Texans had nearly swept clear over Little Round Top.

The dust was a living thing, coating Miles's face, filtering into his nose and eyes, coating his tongue, and burning his sweating flesh. The heat sickened him, and the ground trembled spasmodically beneath his feet, heaving and rocking, or so it seemed, as the minutes ticked past, mounting into a quarter, a half, and then into a full hour. It seemed to Miles that the stampede would never end. Once he risked a glance at the pounding masses streaming past the dusty blockade of flesh he had flung down before him and he saw that these were longhorns passing now, their great horns clashing and clacking together. The smell of them was different, too, and the heat of the massed bodies almost blistered his face.

Then he sensed, rather than noticed, a slackening in the onrushing masses. He raised his head, peering red-eyed through the swirling dust. Stragglers pounded past, and once he thought he heard a man yell; he hoped to God it was one of his men. The dust hung thick as a pall over the fork and the ground still trembled, but the stampede had passed Miles. Not a scrap of vegetation showed on the trampled ground. Over it all hung the stench of dust, heavy droppings of the frightened buffaloes and cattle, and the acrid smell of the beasts.

A sustained bellowing came to him from the ridge, and more longhorns pounded into the valley, their great shining horns catching the light of the sun through the dust. Somewhere within the dust pall arose a familiar sound. The piercing rebel yell came again and a horseman pounded past on the flank of the herd, muffled to the eyes in his bandana, Mex hat pulled low, driving his racing buckskin against the leaders of the herd, forcing them to turn ever northward toward the ridge beyond which lay the Smoky Hill. Other riders smashed through the dust, whooping and yelling, working the tons of moving flesh toward the ridge with professional skill. A handgun cracked again and again.

Miles slowly pulled his sweat-soaked scarf from his burning face. He wiped the dusty layers from his face and neck and then drank deeply of the tepid water in his canteen. He filled his hat and let the shivering bay drink from it. The wet hat felt gratefully cool against Miles's burning head. He slowly took a cigar and bit off the end in a savage snap of his jaws, lighting the weed with a thumbnail-snapped lucifer. His glacial gray eyes remained on that damnable herd that had driven the buffalo into a stampede. "Gawddamn them and their damned cows!" he spat out.

Miles reloaded the Remington and sheathed it. It was characteristic of him that he checked the heavy Sharps before he led the bay toward the fork. Gone were the clear, purling waters. Gone were the tules and the lone tree. Gone were the camp, hides, Red River carts, horses, and mules. *Gone were the four men. . . .*

It was almost impossible to tell where the prairie left off and the fork began, for both banks were a trampled mass of churned mud and water. It was almost impossible to tell where the camp had been, for the lone tree that had marked it had vanished. The ground still trembled, but the buffalo herd was now moving over a distant rise, leaving a shroud of bitter dust hanging in the air, shot through with sun rays, glistening golden against the dust. To the north, closer to the Smoky Hill, moved the mass of longhorns, now at a more sober pace, bellowing thirstily as they caught the scent of the water, clashing their great horns, some of which spread as much as seven feet across on the full-grown *ladinos*. Several horsemen were loping after the buffalo herd to round up the longhorns that had stampeded the buffalo and then joined in their maddened rush over the defenseless camp.

Miles shifted his cigar and looked up to see the white tilts of wagons rising above the eastern ridge, swaying and pitching as the mule teams pulled them down into the valley, while the whiplashes of the muleskinners popped like skirmishing fire. It was a big spread, judging by the number of wagons and the many horsemen that rode with the herd.

Miles watered the bay and walked back toward the spot where he thought the camp had been. Thousands of sharp-edged hooves, weighed down by tons of buffalo meat and beef, had cut and recut the ground until it was one indistinguishable mass, pocked like the surface of the moon, only a thousand times over in miniature. It was as though the herd had meant to smash the banks of the fork and everything on them back into the basic elements of Mother Earth.

Miles shoved back his hat. "Jesus God," he said softly and not irreverently. "They never had a chance." A bitter loneliness winged invisibly out of the dusty air to settle like a harpy on Miles's broad shoulders. He had worked with those four men for over four years, paying all the expenses and sharing fifty-fifty with them, when the average skinner got two bits a hide. He had faced other stampedes with them, prairie flash floods, a blue norther or two, prairie fires, the "red buffalo" of the Plains, marauding bands of Comanches, Kiowas, Cheyennes, and thieving Pawnees. A rather ill-assorted but harmonious group, with three laughing Canucks and one big Missouri nigger who had been as close to being a real friend as Miles Flint, Illinois born and bred, had ever had. "Jesus God," he said softly again. The shock had not yet worn off to give way to the bitter hate that would surely come.

He knelt in the mire and picked up a scrap of buckskin that had a few blue, pink, and white seed beads clinging to it—likely a sleeve garter worn by one of the Canucks. He paced slowly through the mud. Here he found a splintered bit of the lone tree where Big Tom had pitifully sought shelter. Here he found a shattered wedge of the grindstone used to sharpen the skinning knives. There was something else in the mud, startingly white against the darkness . . . the bones of a man's arm and part of the hand still partly clothed in bloody scraps of dark-skinned flesh. The pitiful relic, all that was recognizable of Big Tom, lay across a battered rectangle of brass-mounted wood. Miles pried the heavy box out of the mud. The lid was cracked clean through, but the contents were safe enough, likely shielded by Big Tom's body as he fell before the pounding hooves. He opened the lid and looked down upon his valued set of reloading tools; bullet mold, tool for decapping and recapping the spent brass shells, a swage for bullet resizing, and a bullet seater, plus other odds and ends for keeping his Sharps in prime condition as well as for fashioning the reloads for it. Big Tom had carried the box from the tent, thinking of it first, before he had thought of himself, for he had known how much Miles valued it.

Miles closed the lid and looked down at the bones. "Odd," he said quietly. "His bones are the same color as a white man's."

The stampeded herd was a low rumble of thunder to the west. The longhorns had slowed to a fast walk toward the waters of the Smoky Hill, the wagons trailing along behind them out of the swirling dust. Three horsemen were riding swiftly toward the lone man who stood in the mud and blood beside the fork.

"Yuh all right, mistah?" yelled one of the riders.

Miles did not answer. His big brown hand slid down to the worn walnut grip of his Remington. It had killed men before and it would kill men again. Texans most likely. He spat at the thought of Texans.

Two of the riders spurred forward, scattering gobs of mud from beneath their horses' hoofs. The thick beard of one of them moved in the wind of his passage. The third rider had slowed his mount to a walk, keeping his eyes on Miles.

It was then Miles noted that it wasn't a slim man at all, but a woman, riding sidesaddle, wearing a Confederate-gray full-skirted riding habit.

"Are you all right, sir?" asked the bearded man in a deep, almost melodious voice, certainly not the tone of a Texan. Sounded like an educated man, a rarity amongst Texans, or at least so Miles thought.

Miles looked coldly at the bearded man. "You've wiped out my camp," he said in a flat voice.

"I assure you it was not intentional, sir. My name is Jonas Carlisle, trail driver."

Miles studied the man. He had said "trail driver" as though it were an honor, an accolade bestowed only on the richly deserving. "Intentional?" said Miles softly. "You stampeded thousands of buffalo over my camp because of your cursed longhorns. No word of warning. Where was your scout? Your trail boss? Your points? Surely you don't drive thousands of longhorns through open country like this without an advance party of some kind. One man could have warned you of those buffalo and the fact that my camp was here on the fork."

The other man, much younger, leaned forward in his saddle and looked at Miles with cold blue eyes. His tone was Texas, with all its faults and virtues, when he spoke. "He *said* it wasn't intentional, mistah. Mistah Carlisle means what he says."

Miles knew he was dealing with a breed of man entirely different from Jonas Carlisle. He had met such men as this young Texan in other places and at other times, mostly in violence, peering through the swirling gunsmoke with the deadly whistling of the minie balls playing a threnody to the deeper cracking of the rifles.

"Yuh hear what I say, mistah?" said the Texan as softly as he could speak, but there was honed steel beneath the softness of it, like the whetted edge of a bowie knife.

Carlisle held up a hand. "Enough, Cotton," he said. "This gentleman has a right to be angry. I assure you, sir, we had no knowledge of buffalo hunters being out here in the Smoky Hill country."

Miles relighted his cigar, watching Cotton through the flare of the match and the smoke. "The name is Miles Flint," he said. "Buffalo hunters don't usually advertise where they are. Buffalo can panic easily enough as it is. A blowing leaf, a howling coyote, a careless shot can do it." Cotton's hard blue eyes held Miles's cold gray eyes just long enough for the quick measuring, quite often the only measuring a man could have of another before the more deadly measuring began over the cold, metal eye of a gun muzzle.

"I'll gladly pay for all damages," said Carlisle.

Miles nodded. "I knew you'd say that. Does your damned payment allow for the lives of four good men?"

The Texan shifted in his saddle, looking down at the last earthly relic of Big Tom. "Well, anyways," he said out of the side of his mouth, "one of them was a niggah, wasn't he? Lookit the meat on them bones."

Miles looked at the Texan. "Maybe he was a better man than you are, Texan," he said with studied insult.

The Texan went whitefaced as the deadly verbal glove struck at him. His right hand dropped to his pistol butt.

"Enough of this!" snapped Jonas Carlisle. His tone had changed, too. He was no gunslinger, no Texas fighting cock, no killing machine like the two men who faced each other in front of him, but there was steel in his tone; the steel of a man used to responsibility, used to giving orders and having them obeyed. "Cotton, you keep out of this! Mister Flint has reason to be angry. *You* do *not!*"

Cotton opened and closed his mouth, never taking his eyes from Miles. Those glacial eyes seemed to go over Miles inch by inch, taking stock, enough to imprint Miles Flint forever in his memory. Miles knew right then and there that Cotton would never forget what Miles had said . . . ever.

"Go back to the herd," said Carlisle to the Texan. "Get some of the boys. Go after those beeves that followed the buffalo herd. I want them back at the Smoky Hill by dusk."

Cotton nodded, touching the brim of his hat. He spurred his dun toward the fork, his long, white-blond hair flowing as he rode, his back ramrod-straight.

"Is he the trail boss?" asked Miles. "Or do you handle that chore yourself, Mister Carlisle?"

"He is not the trail boss, Mister Flint. Nor do I handle that chore. Beck Sterret is trail boss. Another Texan. One of the best, if not the *best* in the business."

"The best trail boss or the best Texan?" said Miles, almost idly.

"Both," said the woman as she reined in her mare beside Jonas Carlisle.

Miles took off his hat and removed the cigar from his mouth to look into the loveliest eyes he had seen in years—soft, lustrous brown, a velvety coloring that seemed to hold something deeply beneath it. Deep, oh so very deep . . .

"My wife, Lorena," said Carlisle with ill-concealed pride. "This gentleman is Mister Flint, Lorena."

She was at least fifteen years younger than her husband, slim as a girl, and even the riding habit could not conceal her womanly features. Nature had been more than kind to

Lorena Carlisle. Miles's appreciation of Jonas Carlisle as a man of taste moved up a few notches. "Lorena," said Miles quietly. "I've heard that name before."

She smiled quickly. "Around the campfiahs of the Army of no'the'n Virginia, perhaps, Mistah Flint?" she said softly, *proudly*. Texas pride, to be admired or hated, depending on one's viewpoint.

Miles nodded. "A lovely, haunting song, 'Lorena'," he said.

"You are a Confederate veteran then?" she asked expectantly. "Perhaps a Kentuckian or Missourian?"

Miles shook his head. "We heard them singing that song many times around their campfires at night," he said. His eyes held hers and could not look away.

A flitting shade of coolness crossed the oval loveliness of her face, and her eyes hardened a little, like dark amber, but they still held him.

Carlisle looked about on the trampled, muddy ground. "I can repay you for your material losses," he said with genuine feeling. "But I can never repay you for the fine men you have lost."

Miles looked up at him. "It is not your debt to repay."

Carlisle narrowed his eyes. "I do not understand, Mister Flint."

Miles looked toward the drifting dust of the distant cattle herd, now at the Smoky Hill, slaking their prodigious thirst after the long trail miles. The man responsible for the deaths of Miles's employees and friends was there with the herd, holding to his responsibility for the herd, not thinking of the men who had died because he had not kept a scout or point out ahead of his herd. That, too, was his responsibility.

Miles nodded. "You're a long way from railhead," he said. "Where are you driving them?"

The answer struck Miles like the blow of a fist. "Montana," said Carlisle quietly.

"That's loco!" said Miles.

"Nelson Story did it."

"Over six years ago," said Miles.

"With a handful of Texans," said Lorena proudly.

Miles turned and looked up into that proud, lovely face. "And split-breech Remingtons the Sioux had never run into before, plus at least *one* Yankee."

Carlisle looked at Miles with a trace of amusement on his bearded face. "I've never heard of any Yankee being with that drive except Story himself," he said.

Miles placed a hand on his heavy Sharps. "He had a Yankee meat hunter with him," he said.

"You?" asked the trail driver.

Miles nodded. "All the way north from Fort Laramie," he said.

Carlisle slapped a heavy hand on his thigh. "By God!" he said. He looked quickly at Lorena. "Sorry," he added. "What will you do now, Mister Flint?"

"Quien sabe? My hides are gone. My skinners and cocinero are gone. I'm wiped out except for my horse and rifle. I'll likely head back to Dodge for supplies, carts, wagons, skinners, and suchlike."

Carlisle leaned forward in his saddle. "I'll repay you for all your losses, as I said before. I cannot repay you for the men. Would you consider hunting for me on this drive?"

Miles shook his head. "You'll never get through," he said. "Red Cloud stands in the way. The Bozeman Trail is closed. No white man living can get past Red Cloud, leastways no man driving a herd of longhorns and trailing a bunch of wagons and a *woman*."

She seemed to start a little, as though he had struck a soft spot. He had gotten home to her at least. Damn her and her beauty and her overweening Texas conceit!

"I mean to get through," said Carlisle in a distant voice. "There is a great future in Montana. I have land there, a great deal of land in the best cattle country in the world. Story broke the way, and now the Sioux have closed it. Well, they cannot stand in the way of our progress. They cannot stand in *my* way, Mister Flint! They have closed the way, but someone must reopen it. *I* am that man! It is my destiny!"

Miles picked up the reins of his bay. "Alexander the Great had a destiny. So did Julius Caesar and Napoleon Bonaparte. Not too long ago Jeff Davis and Bobby Lee had a destiny. Something stood in their way. Do not trifle with destiny, Mister Carlisle. It has a mean habit of turning on a man."

Carlisle's mouth worked a little through his thick chestnut beard. The faraway look faded from his deep eyes. "Can I offer you the hospitality of my camp on the Smoky Hill?"

Miles nodded shortly. "You can."

"Ride with us, then."

Miles shook his head. "Ride on," he said over his shoulder. "I'll be along later."

Carlisle and his lovely young wife rode on, looking back from a low knoll toward the destroyed camp and the man who still stood there. Miles Flint stood with hat in hand and bowed head.

"He is praying for his dead, Jonas," she said.

Jonas Carlisle's eyes were half closed. "He has prayed for his dead before," he said, "in many places—on the battlefields of the war and out here on the Great Plains. He will accept their loss as he has accepted the loss of others." Carlisle touched his horse with his spurs. "I have a destiny to the north," he added, almost as though talking to himself again. "And somehow I know that the destiny of that man, and mine, are inextricably bound together."

They rode on in the late-afternoon sunshine toward the wraith of dust above the distant Smoky Hill. Once Lorena looked back, but Miles was gone, riding to the west. She did not answer her husband, but she knew. *She knew* . . .

CHAPTER TWO

Miles Flint rode in from the velvety darkness to the west toward the glow of the campfires.

The mingled odors of bacon, bannock and beans, and strong coffee drifted along the quiet river, mingled with the pungent smell of the fires of buffalo chips, the *bois de vache,* or "wood of the cow." There was little wood along that stretch of the Smoky Hill. As Miles reached the faintly lighted rim of the firelight wash, sun-bronzed men, their hair hanging almost to their shoulders, raised their faces from the steaming mugs of coffee to look thoughtfully at the big Yankee they had heard about after the herd had been bedded for the night. They knew of his loss, but they had also listened to the terse words of Jess Morser, nicknamed "Cotton" because of his ash-white hair. The big Yankee's insult would not be forgotten. The man would have to be measured, and if he was found wanting . . .

Firelight reflected from the faded white tilts of the three fine Studebaker wagons that had been drawn apart from the chuckwagon and the supply wagons to form part of a square, the open side facing the Smoky Hill and a copse of stunted willows. Somewhere in the bottoms a mule bawled from the remuda.

Miles looked toward the herd, a great patch of darkness on the lighter ground beyond the river. They would likely move out before dawn, heading for the Republican. He swung down from the tired bay and led it toward the Studebakers. A startling sound reached him, and he stopped short. A woman had laughed from within the wagon square, and the sound of it drove a shaft of loneliness into him that touched the deep well of his sorrow. Ruth, his girl wife, had laughed like that. Shortly after the war, fever had stilled her laughter forever. The sound of woman's laughter now haunted him.

"Stop wheah yuh are," a harsh voice said in the darkness.

Miles looked toward the tall man who detached himself from the shadows of one of the wagons and moved quickly toward Miles. "I wasn't moving," said Miles.

The tall man grounded a long-barreled rifle. "Yuh ride late," he said.

"I was looking for some of my boys," said Miles. "Maybe you heard what happened to them? You Texans made a clean sweep."

"Cotton said yuh had a loose mouth." The Texan spat to one side. "Yuh keep talkin' like thet, mistah, and mebbe you'll have a comeuppance with some of us boys."

"A pleasure," said Miles. "I'll put you on the list."

"The name is Starr. Cass Starr."

The challenge hung in the quiet air. Miles looked steadily at the tall man.

"Yuh ridin' along to the Bozeman with us, mistah?" said Starr.

"I'm not sure," said Miles.

The Texan shifted his rifle. "I'm mebbe lookin' forward to it."

Miles led the bay on. He looked back. "How many men with this corrida?"

"Thirty."

"How many Texans?"

"Twenty."

Miles smiled. "Fair odds for one Yankee," he said.

Starr raised his head. "Why, gawddamn yuh!" he snapped.

"Is that you, Mister Flint?" Jonas Carlisle called out. His broad form was outlined against the firelight.

Miles could almost feel the savage hatred of the Texan behind him as he walked toward the trail driver. Nothing mattered at that moment to Miles Flint. There was a savagery within him, too, a cold, killing savagery that could only be sated by the blood of the man who had caused the destruction of his camp.

"We have saved some dinner for you, Mister Flint," said Jonas.

"I'll take care of my horse first," said Miles.

"A beautiful animal," said Carlisle. He lighted a cigar. "We thought you had left for Dodge."

Miles looked over his shoulder toward the west. "I had a hope that some of them might have survived."

"And now you do not."

Miles shook his head. He unsaddled the bay, rubbed him down, and then led him to the river, where he picketed him near the willows. Miles washed in the river. Now and then he heard the trail hands laughing around their fires near the chuckwagon, the center of any trail camp. It meant nothing to them that Miles's whole life had been blotted out in a matter of minutes because of their carelessness. Most of them had seen too much violent death to worry about the deaths of three Canucks and a nigger.

He picked up his rifle and walked toward the Studebakers. He saw Lorena before he entered the shifting circle of firelight. She was seated on a folding stool, dressed in a gingham dress almost like those worn by the gaunt emigrant women of the Oregon Trail, but there was a difference. This dress had likely not been sewed by her slim hands. It was fitted exquisitely to her form. Her dark hair had been swept up and fastened with a blood-red ribbon, and as she looked toward Miles the firelight sparkled from her dark eyes and deftly touched her full, soft lips with a red brush. She looked like a painting, except for the quick pulse in the hollow of her lovely throat, encircled with a black velvet ribbon held by a tiny diamond pin. It was almost as though she had been expecting him, knowing full well he would come . . . that he would *have* to come.

"A plate for Mister Flint, Pomp!" called out Jonas Carlisle. He looked at Miles. "Will you have whiskey, sir?"

"I can use it," said Miles.

"Bourbon or rye?"

Miles smiled. "Rye is a Westerner's drink," he said. He leaned his rifle against a wagon and hung his 'scope case from it.

Pomp, a small, fast-moving Negro with a tinge of gray in his dark wool, unfolded a table, deftly spread a cloth on it, placed *silverware,* not crude cutlery, on the cloth, set a filled plate on the table, then vanished again, only to reappear with the glass of rye. "Coffee, suh?" he said.

"Later, please, Pomp," said Miles.

Carlisle paced back and forth, sucking on his cigar, as though eager to have Miles finish his meal so that he could talk with him. Now and again he walked down toward the river, locked his arms behind his broad back, and stared thoughtfully to the north, where the ice-chip stars stippled the dark sky. It was then that Miles would raise his head to see Lorena looking directly at him, and her eyes did not shift when he looked deep into them. Yet she wasn't bold or wanton. How many men had she looked at that way?

"Why do you hunt buffalo, Mistah Flint?" she asked at last.

He looked up at her. "It's a living," he said.

"It's more than just that, isn't it?"

He nodded. "I'm my own boss. This is good country. A man is not penned within four walls. The wind and the sky are walls and roof enough for any man."

"Not *any* man," she said.

He looked at her and then away. It was disquieting, and yet he knew she was no bitch in heat.

"How many buffalo have you killed?" she asked as she accepted a cup of coffee from Pomp.

"I have never kept count, Mrs. Carlisle. I have averaged about twenty to forty a day for weeks on end, four years in all."

"And you intend to keep on?"

He nodded. "I want no other life. Not right now, at least."

"Jonas says you buffalo runners will kill yourselves out of business."

Miles shrugged. "It's inevitable. If I don't kill them, someone else will."

"And then what happens?"

He placed knife and fork on his plate and pushed it back. He drained his glass and felt for a cigar.

"Pomp!" said Jonas from behind Miles. "A cigar for Mister Flint!"

The little Negro appeared like the genie out of the legendary lantern, cigar box opened, a flint lighter in his other hand. Miles selected a long nine, and Pomp lighted it, then vanished.

Jonas sat down and placed heavy hands on his thighs. "You said Red Cloud would stand in the way. Did you mean that?"

Miles blew a smoke ring. "He does," he said dryly.

Spurs chimed softly and musically from behind Miles. "Indians," said a flat, toneless voice. "All they evah do is beg for sugah, tobacco, whiskey, and a wo-haw or two. A taste of powdersmoke will drive them off like gnats befo' a smudge fiah."

Miles turned slowly to see a man, perhaps half a head shorter than himself but every bit as broad-shouldered and muscular, standing in the opening between two of the wagons. There wasn't an ounce of fat on his tough frame, although he had six to seven years of age on Miles. There was a cold grayness about the man, from dusty gray hat to dark hair shot with gray at the sides to gray eyes almost disfiguring in their lightness against the darkness of his skin and thick dragoon mustache. This was a man who expected nothing but hardship and violence in his life. A fighting man from the looks of him, and the weak be damned.

Jonas stood up. "Beck, this gentleman is Miles Flint, the buffalo runner whose camp we inadvertently destroyed this afternoon. Mister Flint, this gentleman is Beckwith Sterret, my trail boss." There was a note of pride in Carlisle's voice as he mentioned Sterret.

Miles took the cigar from his mouth and stood up to face the trail boss. "I didn't find any of my men, Mister Sterret," he said quietly. He made no effort to extend a hand, nor did Sterret make a move to offer his. There was a coldness between them, perhaps a faint prophecy of death in the future.

Sterret rubbed his dusty jaw. "Three or fo' thousand buffalo and several hundred stampedin' longhorns don't let much stand in the way, Mistah Flint," said Sterret. There was no note of apology in his flat, even voice. No sorrow. Nothing of pity, of remorse, not even superficially, for the four men who had died because of his carelessness. Yet it was somehow just what Miles had expected.

"Those buffalo wouldn't have stampeded if you had diverted the herd in time," said Miles.

"We were on the way to watah, Mistah Flint," said the Texan. "We made twenty-five waterless miles today."

"And those cows couldn't wait another half hour by diversion past the buffalo," said Miles coldly.

Sterret raised his head. "It's my job to handle the herd," he said as though that excused everything else.

Miles nodded. "How many beeves did *you* lose, Mister Sterret?"

"Not a dam' one, Mistah Flint." He looked at Lorena. "Beggin' yore pardon, ma'am."

"I thought as much," said Miles.

For a moment they stood there studying each other, then Sterret looked at Jonas. "Herd is well bedded, Mistah Carlisle," he said as though nothing had happened between him and Miles. "I kep' the stampeded bunch this side of the river. We can cross them in the mornin'. I don't want the rest of the herd to be disturbed by them plowin' acrost the river."

"Fine," said Jonas. "Whiskey, Beck?"

"Don't mind if I do."

Miles sat down. Pomp had refilled his glass, and the little servant brought a glass to the trail boss. Sterret hunkered down on his heels and stared moodily into the fire, as though Miles

Flint had ceased to exist or at least to occupy his thoughts.

Jonas sat down. "Perhaps we can deal with Red Cloud, Mister Flint," he suggested.

Miles looked up from his rye. "Call me Miles," he said.

"Miles, then."

"I would be willing to deal with him," said Jonas thoughtfully.

"Deal, hell!" said Beck. "We can drive them like cattle."

"These are Teton Sioux," said Miles. "No one drives *them*."

"I thought Red Cloud was an Oglala," said Jonas.

"He is," said Miles. "The Teton Sioux is composed of the Oglalas, Baulés, Hunkpapas, Sans Arcs, Miniconjous, Wahpetons, and the Sihasapas. The Tetons form about half of the Sioux nation."

"Nation?" said Sterret. He spat to one side. "Yuh talk as if they were *white* men."

Jonas looked at his trail boss. "Please, Beck," he said. "Miles has had experience with these people. It may be of inestimable value to us."

Beck stood up and drained his glass. He looked sideways at Miles. "What did yuh have, Flint, a blanket dictionary?"

Jonas flushed. "Go check the night herders, Beck," he said.

"I'm the *trail boss*," said Sterret.

Jonas stood up slowly and looked at the Texan. Miles again caught the strength of Jonas Carlisle. A man used to authority and to giving orders.

Sterret pulled down the brim of his hat. "We pull out at first light," he said. He walked off, his spurs chiming softly.

Jonas sat down. "I apologize for him," he said. He narrowed his eyes as he saw the look on Miles's hawk face.

Miles sipped his liquor. "There is no need for that. I would not accept a personal apology from that man under any circumstances."

Lorena knew now why this lobo of a man had come into their camp, and it was not for food, warmth, or shelter. A cold feeling came over her, and she shivered in the night air.

"Get Mrs. Carlisle a shawl, Pomp," said Jonas. He looked at Miles. "Continue about the Sioux, if you please, sir."

Miles blew a smoke ring. "Red Cloud got riled during the war," he said. "Miners crossed into Montana from Idaho. Helena, Bozeman, and Virginia City sprang up like mushrooms. The Army wanted to build a road from Fort Laramie through the Powder River and Big Horn countries of Wyoming and then west across Montana as a shortcut from the East to the goldfields."

"The Bozeman Trail!" said Jonas.

"Exactly," said Miles.

"That is all Sioux coountry, is it not?" asked Lorena as Pomp draped the shawl about her shapely shoulders.

"They had driven the Crows from it," said Miles. He relighted his cigar and looked into the dying fire as though conjuring up the picture. "The Sioux and the Northern Cheyenne claimed the white man was frightening the buffalo. So they held the Powder River valley and the surrounding country, filled with buffalo, as an everlasting supply of meat and hides."

"They kill only what they need," she said.

Jonas looked at her. "They stand in the way," he said.

"It sounds so cruel, Jonas."

"It is progress," he said flatly.

Miles watched Pomp refill the rye glass. "Some Sioux chiefs signed a treaty for the new Army road. The Bozeman Trail. But they were only subchiefs. Red Cloud and many other chiefs did not sign. The Army went ahead anyway. Red Cloud captured some soldiers and civilian workers, held them prisoner for two weeks, and then released them because his young men had threatened to kill them." He looked at Jonas. "Red Cloud said, 'I shall stand in the trail.' "

"And is he?" said Lorena.

"Yes," said Miles.

"It is said that he came to Fort Laramie to deal with the Army," said Jonas.

"He did," said Miles. "The road was being built. Fort Reno had been built on the Powder River one hundred and seventy-five miles from Fort Laramie. Goldseekers were already pushing up the Bozeman Trail. Nothing could stop them. They had the 'white man's sickness,' according to the Sioux. We call it gold fever. Red Cloud would not sell his hunting grounds. The Army kept on anyway. They began to build Fort Phil Kearny fifty miles northwest of Fort Reno, on Piney Fork of Lodge Pole Creek in the Big Horn Mountains. Red Cloud began to gather his strength. Spotted Tail of the Brulés joined him with his warriors. About a hundred miles beyond Fort Kearny the Army built Fort C. F. Smith. Red Cloud countered by trying to enlist his bitter enemies, the Crows, against the whites in an all-out war. The Crows refused. But in time Fort Phil Kearny was virtually under siege. The Army had its fort, but it was useless—Red Cloud *had* barred the Bozeman."

"Nelson Story got through," said Lorena. "You were with him."

"God alone knows how we got through," said Miles. Memories flooded back to him. "The Army refused to let Story pass with his thousands of Texas cattle, a handful of Texans, and one lone Yankee." He smiled wryly. "With the luck of a genius, or a fool, whichever way one looks at it, Story got through to the Gallatin."

"My country," said Jonas.

"And the Bozeman Trail?" said Lorena.

Miles looked at her. Her loveliness struck him again. "The Army was forced to abandon the Big Horn country. Forts Smith, Kearny, and Reno were burned by the Indians while the retreating soldiers were still within sight of the smoke. It was a defeat for the Army. There are no soldiers in that country now. In exchange Red Cloud agreed to let the building of the Union Pacific go unchallenged. He has kept his word on that."

"And do you not think we can make it, Miles?" said Jonas.

"No," said Miles flatly. "Drive your herd back to the railhead and sell it. There is money in trail driving that way. All you'll find on the Bozeman Trail is death and the loss of everything. The time is not yet for trail herds to follow the way of Nelson Story."

The firelight played on Jonas's strong bearded face as he paced back and forth. There was no fear on his face. "Montana is my destiny," he said. "There the grass is knee-deep and the water plentiful and sweet. There are sheltered valleys along the Gallatin for thousands of head of good beeves. The government allowed me a great grant there for services rendered, and I plan to add more land to it. I mean to build an empire there, Miles."

"You'll have to get there first," said Miles dryly.

"I mean to." Jonas stopped pacing and looked directly at Miles. "You'll join us?"

"No."

Lorena shifted a little in her seat and adjusted her shawl. She shot a quick glance at Miles and then flushed a little as he saw her.

Miles stood up. "I can ride north for a time with you. The buffalo will be drifting north to get the cured grass. I can resupply at Fort Leavenworth."

Jonas smiled. "Thanks, Miles."

Miles bowed a little to Lorena. "Evenin', ma'am," he said.

She nodded her shapely head and watched the two men walk toward the river.

Jonas stopped at the edge of the river. "One thing, Miles, I must say. My men are Texans for the most part. Almost all of them are Confederate veterans. They are tough as rawhide and bowie steel. They obey me and work hard for me because I pay top wages and treat them squarely. They know I am of Yankee stock, but I give them no cause for quarrel on that account."

"The war is over," said Miles. "They lost. It's about time they faced the truth."

Jonas inspected the glowing end of his cigar. "These men are not to be trifled with. I have seen swift and killing gunplay for less than what passed between you and Cotton this afternoon, and Beck Sterret as well."

"I lost four friends out there today," said Miles.

"You cannot blame all of us for that."

"I can blame one man," said Miles.

Jonas nodded. "I see. It's like that, then."

"It's like that," repeated Miles.

"Good night," said Miles. He watched the trail driver walk toward the dying firelight. Lorena rose to meet him. He placed an arm around her slim waist and walked her to the nearest wagon and helped her in. He walked back to the fire, staring into the ash-covered embers.

Miles made his bunk. He pulled off his moccasins and sat there watching Jonas until the firelight was gone. A lamp flared up in the Studebaker where Lorena was. Miles saw the broad shadow of Jonas cast upon the tilt by the yellow light of the lantern. Then the lamp flicked out.

CHAPTER THREE

The smoke of the cookfire rose thin and threadlike against the first faint traces of dawn in the eastern sky, but already the air was thickening with dust as the smaller herd on the south bank was pushed across the shallow river, the "swimmers," or lead cows, splashing willingly into the cool water, eyes wide and staring, horns glistening wetly. The drivers had eaten in shifts while it was still dark. Already, across the Smoky Hill, the point riders were shaping up the herd, while the swing and flank riders were "crowding" the herd into the trail formation, with much shouting and popping of rawhide lashes.

The first mounts of the day had been selected from the remuda of over ninety horses, some of them half broken and all of them lively. The wrangler, helped by a few hands, had formed a fence of ropes between two supply wagons and had held the remuda there while each herder had selected his mount and roped it. Before the first true light of dawn exploded silently in the east, the herd was one unit again and the point was a good mile and a half up the trail, led by Old Brimstone, the ten-year-old steer who had an uncanny way of picking the best trail. Ernie Masland had told Miles over a cup of Arbuckle's best that Jonas Carlisle had paid aplenty for Old Brimstone back in Texas.

Miles saddled his bay as the wagons rolled toward the ford. Float logs were lashed along the sides but proved to be unnecessary, for the water hardly rose above the level of the wagon beds. The remuda splashed past, driven by the wrangler and his helper, the two youngest hands in the Carlisle corrida. The dust rose thickly from the trail to meet the light of the dawn. Miles slung his cased 'scope and heavy Sharps to the saddle and then lighted a cigar, watching the smooth efficiency of the corrida, ramrodded by Beck Sterret, who had been up before the cocinero. The man missed nothing.

Two horses were ground-reined near the last of the Studebakers. Jonas Carlisle walked to one of them and turned to give Lorena a hand into the sidesaddle, arranging her riding habit skirt so that it fell in full folds, revealing only the tips of her tiny riding boots. He reached up and patted her face, then mounted himself and rode toward Miles.

Miles mounted and waited for the trail driver.

Jonas drew rein. "Where will you ride today?" he asked.

Miles shrugged. *"Quien sabe?* Out of the dust. I thought perhaps antelope steaks would go good tonight."

Jonas smiled. "Capital!" He placed a hand on his cantle roll and looked back at Lorena. "Keep her company for a while, like a good fellow." He touched his horse with his spurs and rode into the river, his eyes on his valued herd and not on his valued wife. The thought was that of Miles Flint.

The dawn wind was whipping her riding-habit skirts and her dark hair as he rode toward her. She placed a little gloved hand against her hair and hastily adjusted it with hairpins, a gesture so utterly feminine and concentrated that it brought another pang of piercing memory to Miles.

"Are you riding with me, Miles?" she said.

"I had hoped to."

She smiled quickly. "It does get lonely," she said. "I can't stand to ride in those wagons."

"We can cross upstream. There is another ford there, and the dust is downwind."

They rode knee to knee toward the ford. Miles entered the water first to test the depth, then beckoned to her. Her mare splashed into the water. The two horses struggled out on the far bank. The herd was still there, coming into clear view in the gathering light of the day. The two "point" riders controlled the lead, with the upwind side handled by Cass Starr, the *segundo*, second-in-command to the trail boss. Along the sides of the strung-out herd were first the "swing" and then the "flank" riders, with the "drag" riders closing up the rear, eating dust, gathering in the strays, driving on the stragglers. The remuda trotted along upwind of the herd, with the wagons upwind of them. Already the chuckwagon was gaining on the rest of the wagons, so that the cocinero could have coffee and cold fare ready at the noon halt. The whole formation was efficient and safe enough in Kansas, but along the Bozeman they'd have to tighten up or Jonas would find painted warriors cutting in on his horses, wagons, cattle, and perhaps even his woman.

The sun flared up, touching the prairie with golden light, changing the dull pewter of the Smoky Hill into a quick burst of silver, glinting from the wet hides of the cattle that had crossed the river that morning and reflecting from the polished horns of the herd.

"Where did you meet Nelson Story?" asked Lorena.

Miles looked at her with a start. He had been preoccupied with the drive and the coming of the summer day. "Fort Laramie," he said.

"Were you a soldier then?"

"No, but I had been scouting the Powder River country for the Army."

"Why did Nelson Story drive to Montana?" she asked.

"He had made a strike on a placer claim near Summit, at the head of Alder Gulch, or what is now Virginia City. He knew he could make a killing by trail driving north from Texas to Missouri, now that he had capital. With one companion he rode from Virginia City right through the Sioux country with forty thousand dollars in his jeans. He bought his beef in Texas and drove it north toward Missouri, but the Kansas Jayhawkers wanted two dollars a head toll. Thousands of head of cattle were backed up near Baxter Springs because the Texas trail drivers had cattle aplenty and no money at all. Those who tried to drive through met death and defeat. More than a quarter of a million steers were backed up south of the Missouri line when Story got there."

She looked at him. "And that was when he decided to try for Montana?"

Miles nodded. "He had already driven his herd of three thousand head five hundred miles. He knew Montana could use beef on the hoof. So he pointed his herd west and then north, aiming for Montana, twenty-one hundred miles away and right through the heart of the Sioux country."

"So you rode with him."

He grinned. "I could hardly let one Yankee take the chances he was taking."

"Against the Sioux?"

He grinned again. "No, against the Texans who were riding with him."

"That isn't fair!" she cried.

"I won't apologize," he said.

"But how did you get through the Sioux country?"

"God only knows. We could have cut southwest from Fort Laramie to the Oregon Trail, then over the divide into Idaho, then recrossing north into Virginia City. But it meant crossing two high mountain passes. The season was getting on. The passes might be blocked with snow. The Bozeman Trail, dangerous as it was, was lower and about two hundred and fifty miles shorter. We pointed them north, Mrs. Carlisle."

"Please call me Lorena," she said.

He looked into those eyes, and his senses seemed to swim a little. "Lorena, then," he said quietly.

"When did you see the Indians, Miles?"

"Oh, they were always around, although we saw them only when they wanted to be seen." He would not mention the charred areas they had passed along the Bozeman, with rust-scaled wagon iron lying in thick ashes and other more gruesome things lying about. She would likely see them soon enough if Jonas Carlisle had his way.

The sun rose higher, fashioning the dry heat of the day. The sky was as yet cloudless, stained only by the thick trail dust that rose high to be tattered by the wind.

"We taught the Sioux a lesson with the rolling-block, breech-loading Remington rifles Nelson Story had bought at Fort Leavenworth," continued Miles. "They couldn't figure out how we could shoot and reload so fast—they only knew about the muzzle-loading rifles still used by the Army. They got a few nasty surprises." He would not mention the two herders who had been cut off and found later where they had fallen, pincushioned with arrows, scalped and mutilated, with their genitals stuffed into their tongueless mouths. "We got to Fort Phil Kearny without too much trouble. It was virtually under siege. They had all they could do to protect themselves, much less supply escort for two mad Yankees and a passel of sunburned Texans, ex-rebels to a man, talking like they actually *meant* to drive three thousand longhorns to the Gallatin."

"And they did!" said Lorena proudly.

"Led by a Yankee," said Miles dryly. He couldn't help it. "We actually had to sneak away from Fort Kearny because the commanding officer had forbidden us to go on. We knew that if we stayed there it would only be a matter of time before the Sioux had run off all our horses and cattle. They had already picked off one night herder."

"What happened to him, Miles?"

He looked away. "They killed him." There was no use in itemizing what they had done to him *before he had died.* Even now the memory made Miles a little queasy. "We moved north every night, for the Sioux do not fight at night. We left the Powder River country for the Tongue River. It was late in the season. October was almost gone. The Sioux had closed in behind us. There was no going back. Six weeks later the Sioux wiped out eighty troopers under Captain Fetterman almost within sight of Fort Kearny. We herded during the day, holding off the Sioux raids, then drove at night. We turned west toward the Big Horn and crossed it just about where the Army later built Fort C. F. Smith, which the Sioux burned a few years later after it was abandoned. We headed for the Yellowstone, with the Remingtons hardly ever cooling off. They made one last attack and got beaten. After that there was nothing to it. We forded the Yellowstone, passed through Emigrant Gulch, reached the town of Bozeman, and turned the cattle loose in the valley of the Gallatin. That's all there was to it."

"Just like thet," she said.

"It does sound heroic," he admitted.

"Wasn't it, Miles?"

He shifted in his saddle. "It was a job," he said. "Someone else would have done it if we hadn't."

"I wonder," she said. She looked at him. "Miles, what do they do to white women if they capture them?"

He could not lie to her, nor could he tell her the truth. To be "passed on the prairie" was worse, far worse than sudden death. Stripped naked, spread-eagled on the harsh earth, seeing with horror-stricken eyes the long line of bucks waiting their turn until constant and savage rape brought death the long, slow, agonizing way. Miles had helped bury the pitiful, bloody, broken remnants of such atrocities and had been haunted for months afterward by the memories of them. One girl had been but twelve years old and still alive when they had found her, screaming and staring at them with eyes that held no sense in them.

"Miles?" she said.

He shifted in his saddle. "Ask your husband," he said almost brutally. And why not? It was Jonas Carlisle who was taking her, along with rest of his possessions, up the bloody, dangerous Bozeman Trail. Let *him* answer.

She did not ask again. All that morning, until they saw the wind-blown thread of smoke from the noon campfire, they spoke of many things, but never of what was in each of their minds. Miles thought it must seem obvious to her how he felt.

A cup of steaming Arbuckle's and a good cigar from the store of Jonas Carlisle were enough for Miles at noon. He went on ahead long before the herd moved out. One of the herders had said he had seen antelope on a ridge far ahead, moving away from the oncoming herd.

Lorena Carlisle watched the broad, buckskinned back of the hunter as he rode north from the camp. Thin dust arose from his bay's hoofs and hung about Miles, lending an almost unreal quality to the scene. She looked away for a moment and he was gone, as though cleanly wiped from the landscape by the turpentined rag of an artist impatient with his mistake. There was something disquieting about Miles Flint. He had appeared out of nowhere, almost as though his buffalo hunting had been nothing but a device to while away the time until the trail herd reached the Smoky Hill country. But why had he come? What did he really want? What would he take with him? For she knew, as surely as she stood there, watching the dust of his passage drift away, that Miles Flint would not leave without taking *something* with him.

The late-afternoon sun slanted down on the yellowed grasses. A vagrant wind rippled the grass until it looked like waves washing toward some far and unseen shore. A low line of hills shimmering in the heat marked the line of a distant creek, stippled by cottonwoods and willows. To the south rose a thin wraith of dust that marked the steady approach of the trail herd toward the night camp on the creek. Already, somewhere between Miles and the trail herd, the trail boss or one of his best men would be scouting the trail toward the water.

Miles rested his chin on his crossed wrists, studying the antelope upwind of him. The antelope had moved all that afternoon ahead of the herd, putting plenty of distance between themselves and the cattle. They were not too concerned about the herd. Their incredible eyesight and keen scent were enough to alert them in plenty of time if danger approached. What they did *not* see or sense was the bareheaded man lying at the lip of a buffalo wallow, his head concealed in a clump of scant soapweed, who had been watching them for some time through a pair of binoculars shaded with his dusty hat so that the bright sunlight would not reflect from the polished lenses.

Miles eased up his Sharps and rested it on the lip of the wallow. The wind was constantly fishtailing, and the heat waves shimmered up from the dry earth and made the pronghorns look at times as though they were actually grazing several feet from the ground. Miles fullcocked the rifle's heavy outside hammer and nestled a shoulder against its brass buttplate. The nearest buck was a good two hundred and seventy-five yards away, half hidden in another wallow, his head moving up and down as he grazed. Miles looked back over his shoulder. He didn't want to startle the tired herd with the heavy report of the rifle, and yet he couldn't get any closer to the pronghorns without being seen.

Miles drew in a deep breath and let half of it out. He closed his right hand around the small of the stock and touched the trigger with the first joint of his trigger finger. He took up the slack as the 'scope crosshairs settled on the pronghorn. The antelope seemed to swim into view. For a moment he stood there seemingly looking directly at Miles; then he moved, contracting the muscles on his smooth rump. A white patch appeared on the rump, almost as though someone had thrown a switch. The patch alerted the herd, but before the antelope sprang off the Sharps flashed and roared, and the buck was flung lifelessly into the hollow with half of its head missing. The booming echo of the shot fled across the rolling ground and echoed faintly from the distant line of hills.

"Excellent shooting," said a voice behind Miles.

Miles turned quickly to see Jonas Carlisle sitting on his blocky gray horse beside that of Beck Sterret.

Sterret spat sideways. "A man oughta use open sights," he said. "Ain't hardly fair to a beast to get killed through a sightin' pipe like thet."

Miles stood up and snapped the 'scope loose. He placed it on the ground and reloaded the Sharps. He looked toward the pronghorns. Most of them were out of sight, bounding across the yellowed grasses like blown leaves before the autumn wind, but a smaller group had broken loose from the herd to streak south instead of west. Miles flipped up the rear sight of the Sharps and raised the rifle. He adjusted the rear-sight slide and sighted through the V notch, centering the brass-blade front sight. He fired almost the instant the sights settled on a young buck. The buck rolled rump over head, and where the white patch had been on his rump there was a spreading stain of red. The echo of the shot died away, and the powder-smoke drifted on the wind.

Miles picked up the 'scope and placed it in its case. He ejected the brass hull and reloaded the rifle. He carried the Sharps to the bay and placed the rifle in its slings. He picked up his hat and placed it on his head, then cased his binoculars.

"I'll pick up the meat, Mister Carlisle," he said. He swung up on the bay and rode toward the dead antelopes.

Jonas Carlisle relighted his cigar and looked at Beck Sterret. "What have you to say now?" he said.

Beck began to fashion a smoke. "Luck," he said.

"Not hardly," said Jonas.

Beck passed his tongue along the cigarette paper. "I wonder how good he is with a six-shooter?"

Jonas looked back toward the approaching herd. "Why trouble to find out?" he said quietly. "Get this straight, Beck. I want no trouble between you and that man. I need him. He knows the Bozeman Trail and the ways of the Sioux. With that rifle in his hands he could hold off fifty of them and never raise a sweat. We *need* him. I repeat . . . we *need* him. Remember that!"

Beck snapped a lucifer on his thumbnail and lighted the quirly. He looked after Miles and idly fanned out the match. "How *long* we goin' to need him, Mistah Carlisle?" he said.

"Until we reach the Gallatin, Beck."

Beck nodded. "I'll wait until then."

Jonas turned. His face was set. "One more thing, Beck, as long as we're on the subject. I've heard talk amongst your Texas boys about this man. Cotton, as usual, is shooting off his big mouth, and Cass Starr has been doing a lot of talking, too. You've got a score of Texans thinking the same way you do."

Beck blew a smoke ring. "I can't tell them how to think, Boss."

Jonas reached out a heavy hand and pointed a thick finger at Beck. "No, you can't, but you *can* keep control of their actions. It means their jobs if they go out of their way to rile this man."

Beck grinned. "Yore talkin' like a man protectin' a child, Mistah Carlisle."

Jonas lowered his hand. "Then I'll give it to you straight. I hired you as trail boss and paid you extra wages, with an assured bonus if we get through to the Gallatin, because you're the best in the business. So far you have proven that. Your job is to handle this herd and handle the men who are working for me. It is also your job to prevent trouble *and* bloodshed. Do you follow me?"

Beck nodded sourly. "I follow you, Mistah Carlisle. I can personally wait until we reach the Gallatin."

Jonas kneed his horse away and rode toward the approaching herd. He looked back at Beck. "Don't underestimate that man, Beck. Have you ever seen rifle shooting like that?"

Beck blew another smoke ring. He looked back at Miles,

now dismounted near one of the dead pronghorns. "Yeh," he said thoughtfully. "But thet was a long ways from heah, Mistah Carlisle. Place named Gettysburg."

Miles had both antelope skinned, gutted, and hung up to cool before the first longhorns topped a nearby ridge and smelled the water of the creek. They bellowed and lowed as they streamed down toward the creek, guided by the cursing point riders who headed them downstream from the willows and cottonwoods where Miles had picked the campsite. The chuckwagon topped the ridge and swayed down the slope toward Miles, skillfully driven by Ernie Masland, the cocinero.

While Miles rubbed down the bay Masland set up his office. In no time at all he had a fire going, started from the stock of chips he carried in the "cooney" or "possum belly," a hide slung beneath the wagon body. By the time Miles had finished with the bay and had picketed him upstream in a grassy swale he could smell the mingled odors of the burning buffalo chips and coffee brewing. He carried his rifle to the chuckwagon and was honored with a mug of coffee.

Pomp was setting up Carlisle's camp aided by the drivers of the other Studebakers. Lorena was seated in the shade of one of the wagons, and now and then Miles caught her looking toward the chuckwagon.

Ernie filled a cup for himself and squatted beside the fire. "Thanks again for the meat," he said.

"Por nada," said Miles.

Ernie looked sideways at Miles. "I think I better warn yuh, Miles. Some of these Lone Star boys ain't forgot there was a war a few years back. They don't cater much to Yankees. Beck Sterret fit with Hood's Texans all through the war. Yuh can't get 'em much tougher and meaner than them."

Miles nodded. "I met a few of them."

"You was in the war yourself?"

Miles nodded. "Four years."

"But you was a bluebelly?"

"Yes."

Ernie grinned. "Ain't a one of 'em in the camp outside of me. I fit with the Eighth Kansas. First Brigade, Third Division, Fourth Corps, Army of the Cumberland."

"You've got a good memory," said Miles. "You were telling about these Texas boys."

Ernie drained his cup. "Well, they don't bother me none and they better not. Mister Carlisle hired me because I'm the best cocinero in the business. These boys want to eat right and on time, they don't fool with good ol' Ern, I tell yuh."

"You're an artist," admitted Miles.

Ernie waved a hand in casual acceptance of the God's honest truth. "Oh, I allow as how yuh can handle yoreself with most of these boys. Some of these Texicans is all belt buckle and mouth, but not all of 'em. Cotton is a killer, for all his big mouth. Cass Starr is as rough as a cob. Both are fast men with a gun. The one yuh should watch is the quietest of the lot."

"Who?" said Miles.

Ernie looked toward where the herd was being watered. The strident voice of Beck Sterret rose above the clamor. "Him," he said.

"He's fast?" said Miles.

Ernie nodded. "I've seen him. Faster than thunder and eleven claps of lightnin'. Don't let them gray hairs fool yuh, Miles. He's good. And he don't like you one damned little bit."

Miles stood up. "The feeling is more than mutual."

"Whatever the hell that means." Ernie stood up. "Got to get grub started. The first shift will be along soon. You ridin' to the Gallatin with us?"

"Quien sabe?"

"Well, if I was you, I'd keep away from Beck Sterret. He ramrods this corrida, and I mean *ramrods.* Keep away from him and he won't likely bother yuh. I'd like to see yuh make the whole drive, but for yore own good I'd rather see you leave."

Miles looked toward the herd. "Thanks," he said quietly. "But if I do ride to the Gallatin, maybe you'd better worry a little about Beck Sterret, too, along with worrying about me. I can wait until we reach the Gallatin to finish my business."

Ernie had a puzzled look on his homely face. "Meanin' what?"

Miles walked a few paces and then looked back. "I mean four dead men on the fork of the Smoky Hill." He walked on and did not look back.

Ernie felt a cold shiver of fear work through him. "Jesus God," he said. "I never figgered it thataway."

CHAPTER FOUR

There was a faint touch of moonlight in the eastern sky when Miles finished cleaning his Sharps. He carried the heavy rifle with him to the chuckwagon and leaned it against a front wheel. Ernie Masland ladled food onto a tin plate and filled a cup of coffee. A dozen or so of the trail drivers lay on their sides, propped on an elbow or squatted on their feet beside the fire, the light striking the hard planes of their brown faces. They were talking in low voices, and now and then a ripple of laughter broke out. Ernie placed Miles's plate and cup on the folded-down shelf at the rear of the chuckwagon, a high honor indeed for any member of a trail drive.

Someone came up quietly behind Miles. He turned to see the shining black face of Pomp.

"Mistuh Carlisle says you is to eat with him tonight, suh," said the little Negro.

"My apologies to Mister Carlisle," said Miles. "I have already been served here."

Brown faces turned to watch Miles and the Negro. They were absolutely expressionless.

Pomp looked puzzled. "Mistuh Carlisle might not like that, suh. Beggin' your pardon, suh."

Miles smiled. "I'll talk to him later, Pomp."

"Yessuh," said Pomp. He trotted back to the Studebakers. Miles saw the glow of the firelight on the silverware and the snow-white napery. This drive was a *little* different from that of Nelson Story, for that he-coon of a man had quite often eaten his beans and bacon with his fingers, with the rain running from the brim of his hat into the tin plate, joking with his drivers.

"Don't yuh like hobnobbin' with society, Flint?" drawled one of the drivers.

"Hell's fire, Flint ain't one of *us* boys," said another. "Flint is a *hunter*. Them's big apples out heah."

Ernie shot a warning glance at Miles. "Mebbe yuh shoulda gone," he said out of the side of his mouth. "The boys is lookin' for a little fun."

Miles speared a bit of steak and popped it into his mouth.

"Prime," he said with a sideways tilt of his head. "I'm no social light, Ernie. I agreed to ride with the drive for a time. I'm under no obligation to wield silverware and make with polite conversation. I did my job today. That's all that's required of me."

A rider came pounding through the darkness and flung off near the fire. His spurs rang sharply as he walked to the fire. "Beck wants yuh out theah, Ben," he said. "Pronto!"

"Goin', Cotton," said the lean driver. He placed cup and plate in the big tin basin, belched politely, and fashioned a smoke as he walked toward his horse.

Cotton glanced toward Miles. "Got a plate, Ern?" he said. "Beck is comin' in."

"Do tell," said Ern. "I thought he was goin' to sleep out there with them cows all night."

Cotton rolled a smoke, watching Miles all the while. His gaze drifted toward the big Sharps rifle. He lighted the quirly and sauntered over toward the rifle. Quickly he picked it up and hefted it.

"What yuh aim to do with thet smokepole, Cotton?" said a driver.

Cotton looked at him. "Ain't made up my mind, Vance," he said. He did not look at Miles. None of them did.

Cotton pulled off the fitted leather eyepies of the 'scope and peered curiously through them. The muzzle swung directly on Miles. "Heavy sonofabitch," said Cotton. "Wouldn't be much of a saddle gun, Like to bust a hosse's back."

Ernie looked at Cotton. "It ain't used in the saddle, Cotton," he said. "Most buffler hunters work afoot."

Cotton hefted the rifle. "Figgers," he said thoughtfully. "But the Yankees was nevah any great shakes durin' the wah on hossback anyways."

Miles placed his empty cup on the shelf. "How would you know, Cotton?" he said quietly.

The shot went home. The lean Texan went pale beneath his tan. His knuckles whitened as he gripped the rifle.

One of the men at the fire laughed softly and looked up at Cotton. "He's got yuh theah, Cotton," he said.

Cotton turned sharply. "You keep yore mouth shut, Jonce," he said harshly.

Jonce flushed. He was a good ten years older than Cotton. "I don't take ordehs from you, Cotton," he said.

Cotton stared at him, and it was then that Miles saw something in the young Texan's eyes—a wild, killing look. The barrel of the rifle rang against the tire iron as Cotton slammed the rifle butt on the ground.

"Careful!" snapped Miles.

Cotton tore his wild look from Jonce and looked at Miles, and now his tanned face was forcibly composed, his eyes cold, his lean hands hanging by his sides. "Yuh talkin' to me?" he said.

"I am," said Miles levelly.

The cold blue eyes stared unblinkingly at Miles. "I won't hurt yore gawddam' shootin' iron," he said. His glance flicked down to Miles's holstered Remington.

The challenge was there, ready to be tripped by the trigger sear of Miles's temper. "Let the rifle alone, Cotton," said Miles quietly. "You've had your fun."

Spurs jingled and leather creaked as man after man at the fire stood up and walked from behind Miles. It was suddenly very quiet around the chuckwagon. The distant sound of the restless herd drifted to them, mingled with the murmur of the creek and the soft sigh of the dry wind. The firelight reflected from the eyes of the men and the brass trim of their pistol butts.

Cotton extended his left hand and rested it on the barrel of the Sharps.

"Let the rifle alone," said Miles.

Cotton smiled quickly. "Shore, shore," he said. He gave an almost imperceptible push to the rifle. It fell heavily, clanging against the ironbound hub of the heavy wheel.

"Damn you!" snapped Miles. He walked toward Cotton.

Hoofbeats sounded behind Miles, but he did not turn. A man's boots struck the hard ground, and spurs chimed softly.

"Yuh talkin' to me thet way, Yankee?" drawled Cotton softly.

The die was set. A fraction of a second would tell the tale.

"Pick up thet rifle, Cotton," the quiet voice said from behind Miles.

Cotton stared past Miles with that unblinking look. "I don't take no ordehs from a gawddam' Yankee, Beck!" he snapped.

"You'll take ordehs from *me*, Cotton," said the trail boss.

It was quieter than it had been before, or so it seemed to Miles. There was a scuffling sound and the ringing of spurs as the drivers moved once again. This was a different matter. One Texan against another. An old hand against a comer maybe as fast as John Wesley Hardin, or so some said. But Beck Sterret had once faced down Ben Thompson in Fort Worth.

Cotton shifted on his feet, but his right hand was still hovering over his pistol butt, while he divided his attention between Miles and Beck.

"Pick up thet rifle," repeated Beck. "I won't tell yuh again, Cotton."

Cotton hesitated. God how he hated to back down in front

of this Yankee upstart! He glanced swiftly at Beck, and although Miles could not see Beck's face, he knew what was written on it. Cotton could put up or shut up. It was as simple as that. The fight was out of Miles's hands now. It no longer dealt with the rifle and the hazing of a Yankee by a troublemaking Texan.

Spurs chimed softly as Beck shifted.

Cotton took his lower lip between his even white teeth. He knelt slowly and picked up the Sharps. He placed it as he had found it. His eyes flicked toward Miles, and there was pure hell in them.

"Yuh wasn't told to come heah and hang around, Cotton," said Beck. "I sent yuh for Ben."

"I got him," said Cotton sullenly.

"Yore still on first night shift," said Beck.

Cotton took a deep breath. "All right, Beck," he said. He stalked to his horse and swung up into the saddle with a smashing of leather, wheeled the horse, set the cruel Mex spurs he favored into the quivering flanks of the horse, and shot out of the camp, missing some of the men near the fire by inches.

"Loco bastahd," said Jonce. "He'll kill thet hoss one of these days."

Cass Starr lounged into the glow of the firelight and glanced casually toward Miles. "He'll shore as hell kill somethin'," he drawled.

Miles looked at Beck Sterret. *"Gracias,"* he said.

Beck's eyes were as cold as Cotton's had been, but there was no killing look in them, just utter dislike. "Yuh rile him into thet exhibition?" he asked.

"No, he didn't, Beck," said Ernie Masland.

"I didn't ask you," said Beck coldly.

Miles shook his head.

Beck nodded. "Yuh got to remember these boys is Texans for the most part," he said. "They ain't forgot the wah."

"Cotton evidently wasn't in it," said Miles.

"His pappy was killed at Sharpsburg. His oldest brothah died of fever at Manassas. The next brothah died alongside of me at Gettysburg." He narrowed his eyes. "Near Little Round Top."

"Interesting," said Miles.

Beck shifted a little. "I got a job to do heah, Flint. I aim to do it. One way or anothah. I'd give you what I gave him, if you was to get out of hand on this drive."

"So? I'm not working for *you,* Sterret."

Beck looked beyond Miles, toward the unseen herd, and it seemed as though he was looking far beyond the herd, toward the Saline, the Solomon, the Prairie Dog, and Sappa Greek to the forks of the Republican and beyond, to the North Platte, Rush Creek and Pumpkin Creek, and the Laramie, thence north to the Powder and the Crazy Woman, the Big Horn and the Yellowstone, to the far-distant Gallatin.

Beck Sterret seemed to tear his gaze away from the known, but unseen. He looked at Miles, almost like a sleepwalker. "As long as yuh ride with us, Flint," he said quietly, "yore part of this drive, and don't yuh ever forget it. Yuh come up to measurement or yuh go. *One way or anothah, Flint, yuh go* . . ." Beck turned on a heel, walked to his horse, swung up into the saddle, and rode off toward the herd.

Miles refilled his coffee cup. "Nice fella," he observed to Ernie Masland.

"He didn't interfere there for love of you, that's for certain," said Ernie. He looked off into the darkness. "But, by God, man for man, Texan for Texan, he's the best trail boss in the business."

"Amen," said Miles. He drained his cup and walked to his rifle, inspecting it carefully, running a sleeve over the dusty barrel, under the amused eyes of the drivers who were back in squatting position about the dying fire. None of them said anything . . . maybe not just out of respect for Beck Sterret's orders, but because the tall, gray-eyed Yankee hadn't backed down before Cotton—or Beck Sterret, for that matter. That was a thoughtful cud for a man to chew.

Miles walked to his hotroll, flung on the ground beside the willows not far from the creek edge. He leaned his rifle against a tree and lighted a cigar. He dropped atop his hotroll, locked his hands at the nape of his neck, and studied the winking stars. It had been a nigh thing between him and Cotton. Miles was no leather-slapper, although he was no slouch on the draw. He knew well enough these Texans were teethed on six-shooters, and the worst of them was usually better than other men, non-Texans, with the exception of the Yankee gunfighters, marshals of such peaceful places as Wichita, Dodge City, and Abilene, called by the Texas trail drivers, half with sarcasm and half with respect, "The Fighting Pimps," because they seemed to spend most of their time, when not enforcing the law, with the painted ladies and calico cats of the bordellos.

Jonas Carlisle rode past in the semidarkness beyond the willows. He spent almost as much time with the herd as Beck Sterret did. Miles rolled over on his side. Lorena Carlisle was seated by the fire, its glow reflecting from her lovely face. Even as Miles looked toward her, she looked directly at him, although she could not see him beyond the pool of flickering firelight; he had the uncanny feeling that she was bridging the gap between them and that she *knew* he was looking at her.

Miles looked the other way. It was disquieting to have her so near and yet the property of another man, a man whom Miles respected and liked. He must have dozed off, for suddenly he was alerted, rolling over on his other side, hand gripping pistol butt, the unlighted cigar dropping from his mouth. He drew and cocked the Remington in one fluid motion.

"Land o' Goshen, Mistuh Flint!" quavered Pomp. "It's only me! Pomp! Y'all move like a cat. Mistuh Flint! Please put down that gun! It's only Pomp, I tell you!"

Miles grinned. He let down the pistol hammer. "Don't ever walk up on a man like that in this country, Pomp," he said.

"I on'y come to tell you that Mis' Carlisle wants you to have coffee with her."

Miles sat up and sheathed the Remington. He glanced toward the fire. She was still sitting there. There was no sign of her husband. Miles hesitated. He had avoided having dinner with them. He did not want to expose himself to Lorena Carlisle any more than he had to, and yet he knew he'd have to go. "Tell her I'll be right along, Pomp," he said.

He washed up at the creek's edge. The moon cast a cool glow down the center of the dark waters. The wind had died down a little, rustling the leaves and sighing through the trees. Miles walked toward the campfire. She looked up as she heard him, and the look on her face drove into his heart like a Comanche lance. He knew he should not have come, and yet he knew he could not have stayed away.

"I hoped you would come, Miles," she said.

He took off his hat. "Hunting is a lonely life," he said, "and most of these drivers are not exactly sociable with me."

"Perhaps they have not forgotten the wah," she said.

He sat down and looked at her. "They were not the only ones who suffered," he said. "My brother died in Andersonville. Seventeen years old. My best friend died at Fredericksburg. I have done my best to forget the war."

"The No'th won," she said dryly.

He looked over his shoulder. "Montana is neither North nor South, and by that I do not mean geographically. Many of these men may stay there and become Montanans. They will not be able to carry the chip of the Civil War on their shoulders for the rest of their lives."

She leaned back in her chair and studied him as Pomp served coffee. "And you," she said. "What will you do?"

"I am not going to Montana," he said.

"No?" she said softly.

He did not look at her for a moment. When he did, he knew what she meant, and yet she was not drawing him on, not using her sex as the bait. "I have made no promises," said Miles.

"Why did you join us?" she asked.

He studied her as she had studied him. "I lost four fine friends back there," he said.

"Is it because of Beck Sterret?"

"Perhaps."

"Revenge is bitter fruit, Miles. Besides, just a moment ago you said the Texans who wanted to stay in Montana could not carry the chip of the Civil Wah on their shoulders for the rest of their lives. Are you not doing the same thing?"

He did not answer. The bawling of the cattle mingled with the howling of the coyotes somehow brought home the solitude of life on the Plains.

Lorena raised her head to listen to the coyotes. "How lonely," she said.

Miles smiled. "One gets used to them. I think I'd miss them if they were not around. I have experienced their loneliness."

"A woman?" she said.

He turned quickly to look at her.

She smiled. "I thought so," she said. "Wheah is she, Miles?"

He shifted in his seat and felt for a cigar, then looked at her.

"Please do," she said. "I have grown accustomed to the weed."

He lighted up and blew a satisfying cloud of smoke.

"You did not answer me, Miles," she said.

He looked at her. "She is in Illinois."

"A long way from Kansas and a longer way from Montana."

He bent his head and looked into the flickering fire. "She died right after the war," he said.

"I'm sorry, Miles."

He waved a hand. "You did not know."

"There have been no others?"

He shrugged. "I thought so a few times. It ended up as ashes."

"You are still a young man, Miles."

"I have not yet found a replacement, Lorena. I am not sure I want one."

She was quiet after that. They sat together, wordlessly, looking into the dying fire, listening to the night sounds, and there was a silent companionship between them. She seemed to know him as no other woman, even Ruth, had known him, and yet he knew there could never be anything between them. It would have been far better had he returned to Dodge City, rather than joining the trail herd with a half-mad desire to take vengeance on Beck Sterret. But he knew there would be a reckoning some day, perhaps when least expected, but it would come, perhaps on the Republican, or the Crazy Woman, perhaps even on the Gallatin, if they ever got that far.

"Is Montana a fair land?" she said at last.

He nodded. "The land is wide and open, with freedom and danger. It is a land for the strong, the ambitious, the far-seeking. The breakers of trails."

She glanced sideways at him, for it seemed as though Jonas, instead of Miles, was speaking. They had much in common, these two strong men, and yet they were quite different in other ways.

Miles leaned back in his chair and looked at the fire, instead of at her, almost as though she wasn't there; as though he saw pictures form in the embers of the fire. "Broad expanses of brown prairie, topped here and there by isolated buttes or a range of tree-fringed hills against the blue sky. There are rough breaks along the fresh, swift-flowing streams. Mountains dark-mantled with pine break sharply from the plain. Deeply etched into the vast expanses of prairie are the valleys of the rivers. The Missouri, the Gallatin, the Yellowstone, and all their tributaries. There are badlands, rugged and forbidding, but still with an eerie beauty of their own, with softly blended hues from the hand of the master painter of them all. Blues, grays, and yellowish-browns. The winters can be bitter cold and the summers scorching hot. It is the wind I think of most of all. Restless, everblowing, carrying the scent of the land to you." His voice died away.

Hooves thudded on the hard ground. Jonas Carlisle swung down heavily, and Pomp came to take the gray away.

Lorena looked at Miles. "There is a touch of the poet in you, Miles."

He laughed. "God forbid!" he said.

Jonas came toward the fire. "God forbid what, Miles?" he said.

Miles could have lied, but to this man he could not. "Mrs. Carlisle said I had a touch of the poet in me," he said.

Jonas nodded. "She may have heard that from me," he said.

Miles looked quickly at him. Jonas had taken off his hat and was wiping his brow. "The beeves are restless tonight. Perhaps they know what is ahead of them. I must admit it makes me restless, too. Miles, do you think I am making a mistake?"

Miles took his eyes and thoughts away from the depths of those brown, searching eyes. "I mean to get through," he said from memory. "There is a great future in Montana. I have land there. A great deal of land in the best cattle country in the world. Story broke the way, and the Sioux have closed it. They cannot stand in the way of our progress. They cannot stand in *my* way, Mister Flint! They have closed the way, but someone must reopen it. *I* am that man! It is my destiny!"

It was very quiet around the dying campfire. Lorena Carlisle looked at her husband. Miles Flint looked into the message of the embers and saw things in there that he did not like. Jonas Carlisle slapped his gauntlets against his thick thigh. "By Godfrey," he said softly. "I've heard an echo of myself there."

Miles stood up. "Those were your words not too long ago, Mister Carlisle."

Jonas nodded. He looked at Miles. "I am a man of action, Miles. You know that. Perhaps you know it too well. I offered you the chance to ride with us to the Gallatin. I can use you. Frankly, I need you. Name your price. You can be invaluable to me. Name your price, man!"

Miles tossed his cigar into the fire. "I will ride with you for a time, but as for my price, that no man knows, and I am not even sure I know it myself. Good night, Mrs. Carlisle. Good night, Jonas." He walked off into the shimmering moonlight and in a moment disappeared in the sharply edged shadows of the willows.

Jonas stood there for a long time looking after Miles. He turned slowly. "A strange man, and yet I feel an affinity for him. Can you explain it, Lorena?"

She stood up. "Get rid of him, Jonas, for your own good."

Jonas looked at her uncomprehendingly. "I don't understand. You're talking strangely, Lorena."

She walked out of the dim circle of dying firelight. "For your own good, Jonas, get rid of him." She walked to the Studebaker where her bed was.

Jonas rubbed his heavy jaw. He looked toward the willows and then toward the Studebaker. "I'll be damned," he said.

From across the moonlit prairie came the soft singing of the night herders.

"The years creep slowly by, Lorena;
  The snow is on the grass again;
The sun's low down the sky, Lorena;
  The frost gleams where the flowers have been.
But the heart throbs as warmly now
  As when the summer days were nigh;
Oh! the sun can never dip so low
  Adown affection's cloudless sky."

"A hundred months have passed, Lorena,
  Since last I held that hand in mine,
And felt the pulse beat fast, Lorena,
  Though mine beat faster than thine.
A hundred months—'twas flowery May,
  When up the hilly slope we climbed,
To watch the dying of the day
  And hear the distant churchbells chime."

CHAPTER FIVE

North from the Smoky Hill, the Saline, the Solomon, Prairie Dog Creek, and Sappa Creek to the forks of the Republican rose the slow trail dust. The herd had long ago gained a personality, the cattle losing their original wildness that had stayed with them almost into southern Kansas. It was a mixed herd, steers and cows, harder to handle than a herd of beeves alone, because of the difference in the strides of cow and steer, but a more tractable herd than that of beeves alone, which were much more susceptible to stampeding. There was something else that tended to slow a mixed herd; the birth of calves almost every time the herd was bedded down, the drivers finding the newly born on the bedding grounds in the pale light of the false dawn. A man could tell at a distance how many calves had entered the world during the night, so soon to leave it, by the flat cracking of the six-shooters before the sleepy herd was formed for the trail. The calves could not keep up with the herd, and the mothers would try to return to them if they were left behind. In more settled country the calves had been given to homesteaders or traded for produce, but now they were in country where the settlers were few and far between, and there would be no settlers at all in Wyoming, north of Fort Laramie, for that was Sioux country. Besides, summer was moving swiftly along and winter would follow autumn, and the herd was barely keeping up to the schedule planned for it by Jonas Carlisle, despite the skilled efforts of Beck Sterret and his drivers.

Miles Flint was usually up before the dawn, with a cup or two of Arbuckle's beneath his belt, keeping an eye out for stray Indians, although these would be more sneak thieves than hard-hitting raiders, nor would they be in enough strength to arrogantly demand as tribute a "wo-haw" or two. None of the drivers, including Sterret himself, had been this far north in Kansas, and Sterret had come to depend on Miles's information as to the trail and the distances to the next watering place, as well as to good bedding ground for the herd. He never spoke to Miles unless it was absolutely necessary, and Miles in his turn avoided the trail boss. Jonas Carlisle was the mediator between them; he needed both of these tough, efficient men, each without a peer in his particular line.

Despite Miles's dislike of Beck Sterret, he had grown to have a grudging respect for the trail boss. Most of the success of a trail drive depended on the trail boss. Most of them were paid a hundred dollars a month as compared to thirty for the trail hands, but Beck Sterret rated more than that. Jonas had likely promised him a bonus of some sort for handling a trail herd in hostile country. Men like Beck Sterret came high. He had to know each man's capabilities and faults. He had to know more than his tough, independent drivers knew. It was his job to make sure there were enough provisions. He assigned men to their positions and saw that they carried out their duties. He was first up in the darkness before dawn and was the last into his hotroll each night, long after most of the men were asleep. He was responsible for knowing what lay ahead of the herd, the type of trail and the location and quantity of water, and for selecting the sites for the noon rest and the night halt. He had to keep check on the number of cattle in the herd and make sure there were no losses. Further, he had to settle all differences between his men, and amongst the hardbitten Texans of the corrida this meant that Sterret must lead as well as drive, and must be as good, or better, than his men in the use of pistol, fists, or boots. There was little trouble of this sort in the Carlisle corrida. Beck Sterret had carefully selected his men back in Texas. There was no room for the careless, the inefficient, the weak, or the troublemaking sort.

There was another leader for the trail herd. The huge ten-year-old brute named Old Brimstone who was the "lead steer." Old Brimstone knew the trail from Texas to Dodge City, Wichita, and Abilene better than most of the trail drivers. Beck Sterret had worked with Old Brimstone for over five years, and the huge steer had worked the trails with other trail bosses before he had teamed with Beck. It had been Sterret who had talked Jonas Carlisle into buying Old Brimstone. From the time he was a mature beef he had become a leader, taking his place at the head of the herd to point the way north, working with the point men, guiding the herd during the long dusty days, not only by example but from the steady ling-ling-ling of the brass bell Beck Sterret had bought out of his own pocket. And even though Old Brimstone had never been north of the Kansas or the Smoky Hill, all Beck Sterret had to do was point him north each morning. The big steer seemed to have a compass in his head or a knowledge unknown to man, and all day long he'd lead the herd, the tinkling of the bell heard by the front steers of the herd, who'd follow Old Brimstone, with the rest of the cows and beeves strung out far behind.

The herd was on the move with the first pale light of dawn when Old Brimstone's clapper was freed from his bell. The trick was never to let the herd know they were under restraint. Each step of the way had to be taken voluntarily but guided in the direction best suited for the drive. This apparent freedom made the cattle more tractable and less likely to be troublesome. Then, too, the longhorns' endurance and hardiness fitted them for the longer drives. They usually lost little weight and could be handled with little expense. In stampedes they'd hold together better than most cattle, were easier to encircle at a run, and rarely split off when the front was turned. Above all, they could shift for themselves, could go farther with less water, and could endure more suffering than other types of cattle.

The Carlisle herd was well "road broke" by the time they had reached central Kansas, kept well strung out, perhaps fifty or sixty feet across, with the point, swing, flank, and drag riders occasionally riding out to drive back a one-eyed steer or a muley. Beck Sterret didn't follow the custom of letting the older, more experienced riders have the honor and comparatively dust-free positions of point. Sterret had his men change position for each day's drive, rotating around the herd, taking the miserable drag in turn, eating dust, keeping the back corners of the herd from spreading out too far, while the sound of their buckskin poppers rose time and time again from the wreathing dust as the stragglers and weaklings were driven back into the herd.

Beck Sterret set his daily mileage at ten to twelve miles, but there were times when the longhorns covered as much as twenty miles a day to reach water; a dry camp was to be avoided because of the danger of stampedes. The nearest way on a trail, according to the axiom, was the shortest distance between waterholes.

The one task Beck Sterret had relinquished without question was that of scouting ahead for the easiest trail and the shortest distance to the next watering place. Miles Flint had replaced him in this duty. Beck Sterret seemed to hate the thought of being out of eyeshot of the herd. More than once

Miles, on his way to or from his duties, had seen Beck riding at the head of the herd, between the point riders, sometimes with his left hand resting on the wicked-looking tip of Old Brimstone's right horn, while the steer walked in rhythm with Beck's horse. The lead steer and the trail boss seemed to have something in common; none of the trail drivers or anyone else with the corrida seemed to have Beck Sterret's friendship or confidence. They seemed to suit each other, Miles thought more than once, for both of them were leaders, and like the captain of a ship or the leader of an army they must keep to themselves to avoid familiarity with their subordinates.

There was another thought that ate at Miles Flint's mind, and it had a direct correlation to the fact that Beck Sterret had let Miles take over his duties of riding ahead of the herd. *If Beck Sterret had been riding ahead, as he should have been, his herd would never have stampeded the buffalo herd that had wiped out Miles's skinning camp on the fork of the Smoky Hill. If Beck Sterret was waiting until the herd reached the Gallatin to settle any smoldering differences, he should surely know by now that Miles Flint too had a score to settle in the valley of Gallatin . . . if he stayed with the herd that far.*

The Platte was the next major goal of the trail herd, and from there the trail would trend northwesterly, following the Oregon Trail as far as Ogallala, thence branching off, following the North Platte to Fort Laramie. Miles had first thought of leaving the herd at the Republican, then had changed it to the North Platte, and now thought increasingly of Fort Laramie. It might be fitting to leave the trail herd there, where he had joined Nelson Story for his epic trail-breaking drive to Montana. Yet something held Miles Flint with the herd, although he constantly tried to drive the thought from his mind. It was Lorena Carlisle, and yet nothing had passed between them to hold them together other than the deep-seated feeling Miles had recognized within himself. He did not really know how she felt about him, but he felt her presence, particularly during the nights when he lay on his bed looking up at the stars, knowing she was sleeping within a few minutes' walk of him, or perhaps staring up at the white tilt of the Studebaker over her, sleepless as Miles was sleepless. He wanted to leave the trail herd because of her, and yet he had to stay because of her, and now he knew the meaning of a curse upon one's self.

The long, sun-soaked days passed as the herd moved toward the Platte. Now and then a solitary Indian would be seen sitting his paint pony, watching the dust-shrouded herd, thinking he was well out of rifle range of the strange white men who drove the stinking spotted buffalo through country that had known little but the hoofprints of buffalo and horses. None of these solitary Indians knew that the Texans carried the fast-loading, long-range, accurate Remingtons, or that the white scout who rode far ahead of the herd carried a rifle that could kill easily at half a mile. This was not truly hostile Indian country as yet, but thievery was rampant. Already the herds of buffalo were diminishing, and the fringe tribes of the plains were trying to accustom themselves to the taste of the stinking spotted buffalo. Nor were they averse to snapping up a lone rider, a stray horse, or perhaps a wagon that had fallen too far behind the rest of the wagons and out of protection of the rifles of the trail drivers.

The herd camped and bedded on the North Platte, just north of Big Springs, near the confluence of the North Platte with Blue Creek, for the weeding out of the herd weaklings, the reshoing of the horses and mules, and adding some trail meat to the frames of the cattle. Jonas Carlisle took three wagons and rode into Ogallala for supplies to feed his drivers as far as Fort Laramie.

Times had changed along the North Platte even in the few years that had passed since Miles had last seen it before his ride with Nelson Story to Montana. In those days there had been emigrant trains along the valley of the North Platte, following the Oregon Trail. Now the Union Pacific had extended from Kearny all the way to Cheyenne. There had been warlike groups of Indians along the North Platte, but now there were a few scattered groups—roached-hair Pawnees and slim, slovenly Arikaras, many of them dressed like white men, with a few Poncas and Otoes and perhaps a handful of Arapahoes, still untamed. They came to beg, to steal, and to get drunk and challenge all comers to wild horse races. Many of them were outcasts from their tribes, with little or none of the fierce pride and independence of the warriors who rode with Red Cloud. But there were those who passed on the word about the huge trail herd feeding along the North Platte, not being loaded aboard the cattle cars to be taken east as other herds had been, and the talk was that the herd would move west, along the North Platte, and even farther, but none of the informants were sure just where the herd was bound, nor would any of the people with the herd say where it was bound.

One evening, as Miles Flint rode toward the bedded herd, the campfire smoke hung low over the camp, mingling with a faint mist that arose from the bottoms and partly concealing about half of the great herd. Farther upstream was the wagon camp, upwind of the herd to avoid the smell and heat of the cattle. The blinking red eyes of the campfires were like rubies cast on dark velvet, and some of the wagon tilts were showing faintly yellow from the light of the lanterns that hung within them. One of them would be the Studebaker occupied by Lorena Carlisle, for Jonas Carlisle was seldom in it, sleeping many times with the men or tumbling exhausted into bed only late at night. She was so young and beautiful. The thought was in Miles's mind as he passed the herd, hearing the soft singing of the night herders riding along the flanks of the herd. The herd was quiet. The weather had been exceptionally fine, but there would be thunder and lightning storms and lashing rains farther west and north as the summer died and the fall came on. Now and then a steer or cow would arise, graze a little, then bed down again.

Miles swung down near the chuckwagon, avoiding the huddled forms of the sleeping drivers. He ground-reined the tired bay. He had passed the day before and the night farther along the North Platte, asking questions, talking to anyone who had information about the Bozeman Trail and the activities of the Sioux. A cavalry platoon had been escorting a small supply train from the railroad toward Fort Laramie, but the only information their commander could give Miles was that Regulars were being moved west to take over garrison duty and patrol duty from some of the militia and volunteer outfits that had held those duties during the war and for some time after it. Further, many of the Regulars were recruits, new to the frontier, and their officers, many of whom were war veterans, were inexperienced in fighting Indians. In short, the Army west of Kansas and Nebraska was small in numbers, poorly equipped, and lacking in Indian-fighting experience. The Bozeman Trail was still closed by the Sioux, although they had been quiet all that summer, but then there had been no travelers on the Bozeman. Further, although the Army might advise travelers to stay away from the Bozeman, they had no authority to prevent them from leaving Fort Laramie, nor did they have the strength to turn back all travelers. There was one other thing. Neither did they have the strength to challenge Red Cloud in his own country.

Miles walked to the banked fire and withdrew the smoke-blackened coffeepot. He filled a cup and lighted a cigar leaning against the side of the chuckwagon. Ernie Masland was fast asleep in the front of the wagon, now that all the hot-rolls usually loaded in the chuckwagon were being used. Besides, Ernie was usually up even before Beck Sterret. Miles eyed the sleeping drivers. Nothing short of a cannon shot or the strident voice of Beck Sterret would rouse them from their well-earned rest.

Something moved in the darkness beyond the wagon. Miles

lowered the cup from his lips. He narrowed his eyes as a large form took shape, and then he grinned. It was Old Brimstone. The lead steer considered himself an individual apart from the masses. He often walked right into the camp and made himself known to the cocinero for a handout of bread, meat, dried apples, or anything else he could cadge. Miles felt about the back of the wagon and found a hard loaf of bread. He walked to the steer and held it out to him. The end of the steer's picket line trailed off into the darkness beyond the wagon. It was likely he had pulled the pin free from the ground or away from the scrub tree to which it had been tied, but then he wouldn't wander far from his bedding place except perhaps to graze with the remuda, as he accepted them as workers, as he was, rather than his inferiors, the cattle of the herd.

Miles got the bay and led him toward the place where he would make his own bed. Old Brimstone wandered after him, and Miles grinned in the darkness. The lead steer was at least more friendly than his boss, Beck Sterret, and was quite a pet with the trail drivers, except when Sterret was around and then he was Sterret's personal pet.

Miles passed beyond the chuckwagon and the group of sleeping drivers, then through a motte of willows and cottonwoods. He could see the faint lightness of the Studebaker wagon tilts in the darkness. He picketed the bay near the creek and unsaddled him. He dropped the saddle near his bedroll and glanced toward the Studebakers. This was one night he was glad that there was no light on in Lorena Carlisle's wagon, or that she was not seated alone beside the fire, while Jonas was with the herd or talking with Beck Sterret.

Old Brimstone had stopped twenty feet from Miles. He raised his head into the wind, blowing fresher from upstream past the Studebakers. He was poised almost like a pointer hound. Miles looked at him curiously. A low, almost imperceptible sound came from the big steer. Miles looked toward the wagons. There wasn't a sign of life there. Pomp was probably fast asleep, but Jonas usually had a man assigned as guard near the wagons. Miles dropped his cigar and rubbed it out on the ground. Old Brimstone lowered his head and swung it from side to side. Something was bothering him.

Miles walked toward the wagons. He could just make out the lighter coloring of the faded tilts. The fire was long out, probably thick with ashes. The faint odor of it came to Miles on the wind. He looked back at the steer. Something came back to him, something Ernie Masland had told him one evening. Old Brimstone had once been separated in a storm from a trail herd and had been cut off by hungry Kiowas; when returned to the herd, there was blood on his horntips and an arrow stuck in his flank. From then on, Ernie had said, Old Brimstone had recognized the smell of Indians.

Miles wet his lips and padded toward the wagons. The guard should be close to the wagons, and Miles didn't want a Remington slug in his guts, at least before breakfast. He whistled softly. There was no reply. He shoved back his hat and peered closely at the wagons. If Old Brimstone had a nose for Indians, Miles Flint had one for unseen danger. It had kept him alive through four years of war and while scouting for the Army and later hunting buffalo.

He stopped at the front of the first wagon. It was used to carry the camping gear and other stores. He placed his hand on the butt of his Remington. The wind shifted, whirling the top layer of ashes from the fire, revealing faint red eyes in the thick embers. Then it came to him, the feeling of danger, stronger than ever, and with it a faintly rancid smell as of sour grease. He whirled, freeing the Remington, and a dark form struck at him. Something drove into his right bicep and the shock of it made him drop the Remington. He bent low, driving a shoulder into the gut of his attacker, lifting him on his shoulders and throwing his body backward so that the man fell heavily. Miles smashed a foot down on the man's knife wrist, but the man did not move.

Another dark form rounded the wagon. A woman screamed. It was Lorena. Miles saw her white form against the darkness of the man who held her. He closed in, fending off another knife, hurling Lorena to one side to get her out of the way. He gripped the knife wrist of the man and twisted hard, catching the knife as it fell. As he arose he drove the knife in deep, just below the ribs, twisting the blade and ripping sideways in a figure-seven stroke. He kicked the man in the belly, driving him back so that he fell half across the fire.

Miles staggered sideways, the sweat streaming down his face and the hot blood running down his arm. It was only then that he saw her nakedness. He gripped his arm and swayed a little until he could hold his balance. Somewhere in the darkness a man yelled. Miles rounded the back of the wagon.

The tall form stood in front of Miles and the hammer of the pistol double-clicked back. "Yuh Yankee sonofabitch," said the voice of Beck Sterret. "What did yuh do to thet woman?"

Miles was closer to death now than he had been fighting the two prowlers. "Go look, you Texas bastard," he grated through pain-clenched teeth.

"Mis' Carlisle?" called out Sterret.

"Yes, Beckwith," she said from the darkness of the wagon. "It wasn't Mister Flint. He saved me."

Suddenly the fire flared up and the odor of burning cloth and flesh came to them. Beck Sterret rounded the back of the wagon with softly chiming spurs. The flickering firelight showed the first man Miles had fought lying with his neck twisted at an unnatural angle, his sightless eyes reflecting the firelight. The other man lay face down in the revived fire, supplying the fuel for it. Beck Sterret hooked a boot toe under him and rolled him free of the fire. The smoke rose from the burning clothing and revealed the great killing wound Miles had made in the man's gut.

Boots pounded on the hard ground. Ernie Masland rounded the first wagon, rifle in hand. "That you, Miles?" he called.

"Yes, Ernie," said Miles. "I'm cut bad."

"Who were they?" said Chip Macklin, one of the wagon drivers, as he came into the pool of firelight.

"They might be Rees," said Miles. "They're Indians, all right. Maybe breeds. Sneak thieves. Killers if they can get away with it."

Beck Sterret nodded. "Are yuh all right, Mis' Carlisle?" he said.

"Yes, Beck. Thanks to Miles Flint."

Sterret made no recognition of Miles. "Who was supposed to be on guard heah, Chip?" he said.

"Frank Jeffers," said Chip.

Beck nodded again. "Tell him to pack up and git out. Tonight! Now! I don't want to catch sight of him evah again."

Chip vanished into the darkness.

Miles bent down and picked up the wadded night dress that had been ripped from Lorena's body. He handed it to her, then walked with Ernie toward the chuckwagon. He looked back at Beck Sterret. "You'd better get a spade detail, Sterret," he said. "Those boys might have friends around here. Bury 'em and hide any traces of it."

"I know my business," said the trail boss.

"Is that right?" said Miles. His meaning was clear enough. Those wagons should have never been left unguarded. He walked on toward the chuckwagon, never looking back, but he could almost feel those cold gray eyes boring into his back. Beck Sterret allowed no man in his corrida to make a mistake, but Beck Sterret had made one himself that night.

Ernie doused the wound with whiskey and swabbed it, leaving the rest of the whiskey for internal application by Miles. As he finished binding the deep wound, hoofbeats sounded in the darkness and drummed on the hard ground until they faded away. Ernie looked up. "That'll be Frank Jeffers," he said.

"Beck Sterret allows no mistakes," said Chip Macklin.

Miles lowered the whiskey bottle and handed it to Ernie. "Who takes Beck Sterret to account for his mistakes? God?" he said dryly. He saw the look on Chip's face. Miles turned. The trail boss stood by the fire looking at Miles, and this time Miles caught the full impact of those eyes and he knew that never on God's green earth would he and this man ever be anything but enemies.

CHAPTER SIX

The grass along the North Platte was good, and the longhorns put on some tallow despite the fact that they were being driven harder, doing better than twenty miles a day for the most part, for the water was always there for the noon rest and the night camp. But the summer was beginning to fade. Now and then a spit of rain fell, and the nights grew cooler. In the mornings dew spangled the grass, the wagon covers, and the bedrolls with crystal droplets. The days became smoky with haze, but the nights were bright and clear and the moon was large and luminous.

Past Rush Creek and Pumpkin Creek toward Scotts Bluff they trailed, passing the slowly moving emigrant trains and being passed in turn by the Abbott-Downing "swiftwagons" of the stagecoach lines, with wondering drivers and passengers eyeing the great herd of dusty cattle and the expressionless sunbrowned, longhaired men who drove them ever westward. There was no need for anyone who learned about their ultimate destination to comment too much about such folly, but it went something as follows. "They won't get to the Gallatin. They won't even get past the Powder. They'll likely lose that hull durned herd and their own scalps as well. Ain't nobody more loco than a Texican. This proves it. Jonas Carlisle is supplyin' beef on the hoof to the Sioux and the Cheyennes for the comin' winter. He's leavin' that woman at Fort Laramie, ain't he? *He ain't?* There'll be a half-breed in a Sioux lodge 'bout this time next year." So on and so on, and it never stopped, past Scotts Bluff and into Wyoming on the well-worn trail, the great highway of emigrant travel to the Far West.

They crossed the Laramie River at the end of August to graze the herd northwest of the fort, making camp on a creek that flowed into the Laramie five miles from the fort. It was a time for some rest and to let the longhorns gain a little more tallow for the long trail north to the Gallatin. It was time too for the trail drivers to sport in the disreputable "hog ranches" situated just off the fort reservation. These were stocked with the worst rotgut booze and worked by aging, bedraggled and usually diseased painted ladies and calico cats, perhaps their last port of call before they were through with their trade, for they could not work anywhere else because of the competition except near some lonely Army post far away from any sort of town.

Colonel Denton Long paced back and forth in his headquarters office, with a government map of the country north of Fort Laramie forming a background for the words he was speaking to the three men who sat beyond his desk. Miles Flint was studying the map, recalling geographical features from the symbols on the flat paper. Straight up the center of the map ran a red line, the Bozeman Trail, with red crosses indicating the sites of the forts built after the war, occupied for a short time, then abandoned by the Army and burned by the Sioux.

"Two hundred and fifty miles of unguarded territory," said the colonel. "Not a post, a house, a road other than the Bozeman; not a soldier between here and Montana! Even beyond the Wyoming line you won't be safe from the Sioux—not that you'd ever get there."

"Nelson Story made it," said Carlisle stubbornly.

Jonas blew a smoke ring from his cigar. "Nelson Story made it without the help of the Army, Colonel," he said. "No offense to the Army, of course."

"The Army had all it could do in those days, as it does even now, to defend itself," said Long.

"Miles here was with Story," said Carlisle.

Miles smiled wryly. "I was younger then," he said. "Fortune favors the brave, or so they say."

Long sat down and fiddled with a letter opener fashioned like a miniature saber. "Do you intend to ride with Mister Carlisle, Miles?" he said.

Carlisle smiled. Sterret rubbed his lean jaw and felt for the makings.

Miles looked at the map. How well he knew that trail. Every mile and every topographical feature was etched on his memory. From Fort Fetterman on the Platte north to Willow Creek and Sand Creek, Antelope Creek and Pumpkin Buttes east of the Dry Fork of the Powder, past old Fort Reno and the Crazy Woman Battlefield of 1866, to the crossing of the Crazy Woman.

"Miles?" said the officer.

Miles started a little. It was as though he was bringing his mind back from those dangerous, lonely miles of Wyoming.

"Of course he is," said Jonas Carlisle. "Miles has placed his destiny with mine, Colonel Long."

"I didn't think Miles was that big a fool," said Long. "I've known him since the war. I was surprised when he went with Nelson Story. I was sure he had learned his lesson then. How about it, Miles?"

Miles looked away from the map. "Yes," he said quickly. "I did learn my lesson. Perhaps Mister Carlisle can get through. I hope he can."

Carlisle stared incredulously at Miles. "But you *are* riding with us!"

Miles shook his head. "I never agreed to ride to the Gallatin," he said.

Carlisle slowly took the cigar from his mouth. "But I have been depending on you."

"What did you expect from *him?*" said Beck Sterret.

Miles stood up. "I agreed to ride north with you, first as far as the Republican and then as far as the North Platte. Then I decided to stay with you as far as Fort Laramie. This I have done. I made no promises beyond riding with you to Fort Laramie."

Carlisle relighted his cigar. He looked up at Miles and fanned out the match. "Are you holding me up, Miles?"

"I wouldn't put it past him," growled Sterret.

Miles narrowed his eyes. "I don't follow you, Jonas," he said quietly.

"Name your price," said the trail driver. "A part of the herd? A piece of my land in Montana? A sum of money? Name it, Miles."

Miles shook his head. "You couldn't pay me with the whole herd, Jonas. It isn't that."

"Then dammit, what is it?"

It was then that Beck Sterret's cold gray eyes flicked up at Miles, and Miles knew that the Texan knew why Miles would go no further. By God, he knew!

Miles walked to the door. "I am returning to Kansas," he said. "Buffalo running is my trade. I've been away from it long enough as it is."

"There's a job here for you, Miles," said Colonel Long quickly. "Chief of Scouts."

Miles shook his head.

"Think about it, Miles," said the officer.

Miles closed the door behind him and lighted a cigar. He stood on the porch for a few minutes, looking across the wide, dark parade ground. Yellow rectangles of light showed from the windows of the post buildings. The halyards rattled insistently against the tall flagpole. It would be a rough fall and an early winter from the feeling in the night air. He looked to his left, to the north, into the star-spangled darkness of the prairie night. Beck Sterret had sensed or had figured out why Miles would not accompany the trail herd any further than Fort Laramie. He wanted to go, and could not go, for the very same reason. It was simple enough. It could be answered in two lovely words. *Lorena Carlisle.*

The feeling had come upon him with increasing intensity each day and each week of the long trail north to the Platte River country, particularly since that bloody night beside Blue Creek when he had killed the two Indians, full-bloods or breeds, who had attacked him after their failure to rape or abduct Lorena. His memories of that night were strong because of the wound he had suffered, but there was more than that. Since seeing her in her nakedness he had not been able to drive the thought from his mind. Perhaps he loved her, he really didn't know, although the emotion he felt for her was close enough to be labeled love. But night after night he would lie awake, staring up into the darkness, seeing her as he had seen her in that vivid moment, and he could *not* drive the picture of her from his mind.

He could not let her ride up that dangerous trail to the north, for the odds against the trail herd getting through were very high. He had hoped Carlisle would change his mind and take the western trail, thence through the mountain passes north to Montana, but it was getting late in the season, with the promise of an early winter. There was one other hope. Perhaps Jonas could be persuaded to leave his wife at Fort Laramie until he could send for her in the spring via the western route. But it was not up to Miles Flint to try to persuade Jonas Carlisle, inasmuch as Miles himself was not going to Montana with the trail herd. Not with Beck Sterret already suspecting, if he did not already know, how Miles felt about Lorena.

The truth was that he could not trust himself with her; he thought too much of her and of Jonas as well. It was better this way, and yet . . .

Tattoo blew softly across the post and echoed faintly from the dark hills. Miles could hear the voices of the three men in the colonel's office and then the popping of a cork, followed by the clinking of glass. It looked like a long session, for Jonas Carlisle was a stubborn man; so, too, was Denton Long.

Miles breathed the clear night air. A faint longing came to him for the brass and the blue, the regularity of garrison life, spiced by the occasional Indian fighting and the lonely, dangerous scouting. He shook his head. He had been on his own too long; too long a buffalo runner. Miles walked to the end of the long porch and stepped down upon the gravel path that led past the colonel's quarters. Beyond the quarters was a smaller building, once used by the second-in-command of the post but no longer occupied. Miles walked toward the building. Colonel Long had found him a room at Old Bedlam, the junior officers' quarters, which was more than half empty of occupants.

He paused in front of the empty building and relighted the cigar, the flare of the match in the night wind lighting his lean face. He fanned out the match and drew in a deep breath of the satisfying smoke. There was a bottle in his war sack in his quarters.

He raised his head suddenly. An alertness honed by years of warfare, danger, and hunting had warned him. He took the cigar from his mouth and looked at the empty building. Faintly, ever so faintly, the odor of lilac scent came to him. He shook his head. There was no one there. A cold feeling came over him. Ruth had worn such scent. There were many ghosts at Fort Laramie and beyond, but it wasn't likely the ghost of Ruth Flint would be there. He took one step and paused. He turned and looked at the darkened porch of the quarters. There *was* someone there!

"Miles?" she said out of the darkness.

"Ruth?" he blurted out.

The wind shifted. A door slammed from somewhere in the barracks across the dark parade ground. The flagpole halyards beat the pole in a sudden frenzy. The odor of the lilac scent came strongly to Miles.

She came to the edge of the porch and looked down at him. "Ruth?" she said softly. "Where you expecting a *Ruth,* Miles?"

He pulled off his hat and took the cigar from his mouth. His face flushed in the darkness. "Mrs. Carlisle," he said.

"Lorena, Miles."

"I did not know you were here."

"Colonel Long was kind enough to allow my husband to use these quarters."

"I thought you were camped with the trail herd."

"It's very lonely out theah, Miles. Some of the boys were

riding into the fort and escorted me heah. Jonas doesn't know I am heah. Is he still in conference?"

Miles nodded. "Very much so."

"Come heah, Miles."

He walked toward her and stood at the foot of the steps.

"Is the colonel going to allow Jonas to take the Bozeman Trail?"

Miles shrugged. "He can hardly stop him. He *can* advise him not to."

"And you are against it?"

"Yes."

"And yet you are going, too. Why, Miles?"

He looked up into that shadowy, lovely face, and he could not speak.

"Miles?" she said. "What's wrong?"

"I'm not going to the Gallatin with the trail herd," he said.

It was her turn to be speechless. She stared uncomprehendingly at him and shook her head a little. "I don't understand," she said uncertainly.

"I made no promises. No deals," he said.

"But it was understood. Jonas said . . ." Her voice trailed off.

He knew now what he had wondered about before. There had always been a kind of understanding between them so that neither really had to speak to let his or her thoughts be known. He thanked God he had been able to keep away from her so much on the trail along the Platte to Fort Laramie. If she had been able to read some of his thoughts then . . .

"Jonas planned to repay you for your troubles," she said.

"It isn't that, Lorena. You *know* it isn't that."

She nodded and looked away, toward the north, toward the unseen Bozeman, as he had done a few minutes before she had spoken his name from the clinging darkness of the porch. She knew well enough that payment was the furthest thing from his mind. What payment would he want? She thought uncertainly that she might know what that could be, then thrust it quickly from her mind, for she herself had thought much, far too much about this lean hunter of buffaloes and swift killer of men.

"You must not go with them," said Miles desperately.

She looked down at him. "My place is with my husband," she said softly.

"There is a madness in him," said Miles. "Nelson Story had it; at times I have had it myself. But it *is* madness, Lorena. You can't go with him."

She tilted her lovely head to one side. "What is it you want me to do, Miles?"

"You can stay here until the spring and then travel to Montana via the west, then through the passes. He can send for you then, or you can travel with one of the strong parties that will travel west when the trails dry out."

"But you do not believe he will evah send for me. You believe he will die on the Bozeman."

Softly across the post came the sweet, melancholy sound of taps, floating over the parade ground, bringing with it many memories to the fighting men who had heard it at other. less peaceful times. It echoed softly, almost imperceptibly from the hills. Lights flicked out one after the other, and the darkness, purring softly with the voice of the dry night wind, crept closer and ever closer to the man and woman who faced each other.

"Miles?" she said.

He nodded. "I can't bear to see you go," he said, "and I can't bear to go with you."

"And if I stay heah, what will you do? Will you leave, Miles? Will you forget about me? Will you *try* to forget about me?"

"That is unfair," he said quickly.

She reached out a hand, and the tips of her cool fingers touched his face. "Yes," she said wisely and softly. "I know and you know, Miles. We can't drive it from our minds."

He stepped up to her. She backed away a little but then stopped and came close to him, into his arms, her face tilted up to his. He bent to kiss her, and she turned her soft, full lips away. Her fragrance and softness made him a little savage. He cupped her chin in his left hand, turning her face to meet his lips. Her body was tense for a moment, then she pressed close to him and her lips sought his as eagerly, perhaps more eagerly than his had sought hers, and their bodies were as closely molded together in the darkness as could be possible, with one exception.

She bent back her head. "Come with us, Miles," she said fiercely. *"Come with me."*

"Stay here," he replied. "Stay here with me."

A door rattled somewhere in the darkness. Porch boards creaked. Lorena stepped back from Miles. "Oh God," she said. "I didn't mean to. I still love my husband, Miles!"

He placed a big hand alongside her face and looked into her eyes. Dark as it was, he seemed to be able to see deeply into them. "Yes," he said softly, and he knew she didn't mean it at all.

Spurs chimed softly on the gravel.

Miles touched her lips with his, then walked softly to the end of the porch. He heard the door close as she entered the building. Miles stepped around the corner feeling as guilty as a thief, which perhaps he was in a sense. A thief of love belonging to another man, a man he admired, respected, and called friend.

Miles faded back into the darkness as the spurs chimed again. The chiming stopped. Miles stepped behind an outthrust part of the frame building. The chiming started again, so soft as to be almost indistinct. Miles pressed back against the wall behind him.

There was a quick spurt of yellow, flickering light beyond the building that showed the lean, hard face of Beck Sterret as he cupped the flame about the tip of a cigarette. He fanned out the match. Alternately the glowing and dying away of the tip of the cigarette lighted his face and then let it fade into the darkness beneath the low-pulled hatbrim. Beck Sterret seemed to be looking directly at Miles. Beck turned and looked across the dark parade ground, and as he did so the window alongside Miles glowed with the light of a lamp. Miles cursed under his breath, then slipped along the wall and rounded the corner just as Sterret turned again. Miles was around the corner perhaps a fraction of a second ahead of Beck's piercing gaze —or perhaps a fraction of a second too late.

Still, Beck Sterret would need the eyes of a cat to identify any shadowy figure he might have seen. At that, Miles wouldn't put it past the Texan to be able to see in the dark.

Miles walked toward the dim shape of the icehouse, to keep the commanding officer's quarters between him and Beck Sterret. He walked along the edge of the bluff that skirted the old channel of the Laramie River. He could see the dim, pewter-colored water of the river just beyond the old channel. He looked back over his shoulder. There was no sign of Beck Sterret or anyone else.

He was just passing the provost marshal's office when a thought struck him like the blow of a Sioux pipe-axe. He turned on his heel and looked toward the commanding officer's quarters. The lights were still on in Long's office, and there was a lone light in the quarters that had been loaned to Carlisle. That would be Lorena. No wonder Beck Sterret had been suspicious! Miles had dropped his freshlly lit cigar on the gravel directly in front of the porch steps of the quarters occupied by Jonas and Lorena. Miles shoved back his hat. He had left Long's office only a few minutes before Beck. Trust Beck Sterret to have heard Lorena's door close and, perhaps, their low voices. He could hardly have missed seeing or smelling that cigar. What if he had seen a shadowy figure moving about behind the building? He knew who was in that building alone, and he had certainly seen that light go on in the otherwise unlighted quarters.

Miles hadn't looked for a meeting with Lorena. Had she looked for a meeting with him? *Had she been waiting for him?* There was guilt within him, more for his thoughts than for any of his actions. He had wanted to avoid her because he had realized that seeing her would lead to no good for both of them. Neither of them could willingly deceive Jonas.

He stepped up on the porch of Old Bedlam and looked toward Lorena's quarters. Even as he did so the light winked out. She was likely in bed, thinking of him, and the thought of it was almost too much for him to bear. He opened the door and walked quietly down the hall to his room. There was only one other officer quartered on the first floor that night, and he was on guard duty. There were a number of junior officers quartered on the second floor, but most of them were either on patrol or escort details, shorthanded as the post was of officers.

Miles opened the door, and the light from within struck his tense face. He had not left the lamp on. The lampshade had been tilted up toward the door, casting a pool of light on the tabletop and the floor around it as well as on the doorway, but keeping the rest of the room in darkness.

"I've been waitin' for yuh, Flint," said Beck Sterret from the darkness beyond the lamp.

There was no chance for Miles to draw or run. He raised his head. "What's the game, Sterret?" he said evenly.

Spurs chimed. Miles still could not see the man.

"I'm ridin' back to the herd tonight," said the trail boss.

"Can't bear to stay away from those longhorns?" said Miles.

"Very funny," said the Texan. "But then yuh got a great sense of humor, for a Yankee."

"Gracias," said Miles.

"Por nada," said Beck.

The lamplight was full on Miles's face. What could Beck Sterret see in it? Why was he stalling?

A match snapped in the darkness, and the flare of it revealed Beck's face as he lighted a quirly. Miles could have drawn and shot fast enough to kill the Texan before he could draw, fast as he was reputed to be.

The cigarette glowed as Sterret drew in the smoke. His cold gray eyes studied Miles. "Yuh shouldn't ought to have let Jonas down," he said.

"That was between him and me, Sterret."

The Texan nodded. "I agree. But thet herd is goin' to Montana come hell or high watah, Flint! We can't stand the sight of each othah, but I got to admit we need yuh. God knows I wish it was othawise, but it ain't."

"Gracias," said Miles dryly.

Sterret took the cigarette from his mouth and studied the tip of it. "Thet herd means a lot to me, Flint."

"And nothing else does."

The head snapped up. "Damn yuh! Stop boring into me, Flint! Yuh know so damned much! Mebbe yuh don't know what Jonas Carlisle means to me! He's treated me fair and square and give me a future to look forward to outside of bein' a trail boss. Yuh know what thet means to a man like me? No kin to speak of. No home to go back to. Not a centavo put aside. I'm gettin' along. I don't aim to trail boss all my life, not thet I couldn't make most of 'em look like second raters for yeahs to come!"

"I'll buy that," said Miles. Give the devil his due, he thought. "How about a drink?"

"No," said Sterret.

"Mind if I have one?" Miles wanted to get out of that revealing pool of light.

"Go ahead," said the Texan.

Miles walked to his bag and dug out a bottle.

"Yuh won't reconsider?" said Sterret.

God how it must have eaten into his Texas pride to have to ask a Yankee, and Miles Flint of all Yankees, for help. "No," said Miles.

Sterret paused. Miles glanced at him. The cigarette lighted his face. Miles looked down at his drink.

"Then theah's Mis' Carlisle to consider," said Beck.

Miles left hand closed about the full shot glass. Here it comes! Maybe he could throw the liquor into Sterret's face and close with him before he could draw. "What about Mrs. Carlisle?" said Miles quietly.

"She ain't goin' to stay heah," said Beck.

"So?" said Miles. He turned to look at Sterret.

The Texan seemed at a loss for words. "She means a lot to me, to all of us, mebbe even to you, Flint." There was no obvious guile in his words. "Yuh saw what happened back theah on the Platte. If it hadn't been for yuh, Flint, she'da been raped or killed. Mebbe worse. Mebbe drug off to a filthy Indian camp somewheahs. Yuh follow me?"

"So far," said Miles politely.

Sterret moved, and the spurs chimed. He came closer to Miles. Miles tensed for swift and deadly action. "Jonas ain't right in lettin' her go along, but he will if she insists, and she *does* insist. We might get through and we might not, but I don't aim to see anything happen to her. Understand?"

Miles nodded. He sipped at the rye.

Sterret came closer. "It ain't for me I'm askin' yuh to come along, but for Jonas and his wife. He said once thet he needed yuh. Thet yuh know the Bozeman Trail and the ways of the Sioux. With thet Sharps of yourn yuh could hold off fifty Sioux and never raise a sweat. He said he needed yuh. We need every advantage we can get, Flint."

For a long, long moment Miles stood there. "Indians," he said. "All they ever do is beg for sugar, tobacco, whiskey, and a wo-haw or two. A taste of powdersmoke will drive them off like gnats before a smudge fire. Those were your words, Sterret, the first time I met you. Maybe you've changed your mind."

"Don't be cute, Flint."

Miles turned. "If you and Carlisle are fools enough to go up the Bozeman, you'll have to take the guilt of anything that happens to Mrs. Carlisle. For me, I want no part of it."

"Is thet final?"

"It is."

Sterret nodded. He walked to the door, gripped the handle, then turned so that the light from under the uptilted lampshade revealed his lean face and glacial eyes. "I mighta knowed," he said. "I left yuh alone because of Jonas. I kept the boys away from yuh because of Jonas. I stood for yore lip because of Jonas. But that's all ovah now, Flint."

"So?" said Miles.

A faint smile drifted across the lean face, but there was no trace of it in the set eyes of the Texan. "Maybe it's best this way," he said softly. "If we evah reached the Gallatin, one of us woulda had to kill yuh, Flint. It's in the cards."

Miles bent his head. *"Gracias,"* he said.

"Por nada," said Sterret politely. He opened the door. "One more thing: Stay away from the Gallatin valley, Flint. Don't evah show yore face up theah. *Evah* . . ."

Miles poured another drink. The door closed behind the Texan. Miles downed the liquor. He heard the spurs chime down the hall and then fade away. A few moments later he heard the soft tattoo of hooves on the hard ground, and then they too faded away.

Miles sat down on the bed and slowly wiped the icy sweat from his face. He still didn't know whether or not Beck Sterret suspected or knew Miles had been with Lorena. Maybe he had concealed it because he had wanted Miles to rejoin the trail herd. Maybe, just maybe . . .

CHAPTER SEVEN

The breed rode out of the Laramie River bottoms below Fort Laramie, leaving the filthy skin lodges of the Indians who hung about the fort looking for handouts, doing occasional scouting of dubious value, and selling the services of their women to the drunken troopers. It was the night before Jonas Carlisle's trail herd was to leave for the Bozeman Trail.

The breed's given name was François Gaspard Bertillot. He himself hardly remembered that name. White men, breeds, and full-bloods who knew him simply called him Guts. He had no friends and no relatives. His mother had been a dull-witted girl of the Sans Arcs, while his father, whom he had never known, had been half white, half Negro, and all bad.

Guts rode toward the headwaters of Rawhide Creek with his news. It was how he lived. He picked up information and sold it, to white man or to red—it mattered not as long as he was given food or anything he required. In more civilized areas he would be called "informer." Here his name served the same as such a title. "Ask Guts," one would say if he was asked anything he did not know about the country, the Indians, or the soldiers. Somehow Guts would know, or he would find out. It was how he lived, for all men's hands were against him, although their ears were not, as they sought and bought his information. He lived as a pariah and liked it. That way he was safe, for although he had no friends and no relatives, he had no true enemies either, and he could do what no hostile Indian or white man could do—ride with impunity in either country and go unchallenged.

The trail herd groaned its way along the North Platte road in the cold light of a misty dawn the morning after Guts had gone north to the Rawhide. They would be heading for Fort Fetterman, west of La Prele Creek. From there they would go northwesterly to the Bozeman Trail and the country of the Sioux.

Miles Flint had left Fort Laramie the morning after his talk with Beck Sterret. He had not seen Jonas and Lorena leave the fort and ride out to the trail camp. Miles had not been there, but part of him had gone along with them, and he knew it would never come back to him. A man cannot lose his heart too many times, perhaps only once. He knew he had loved his wife, but the mists of time had closed in, and he was still a young man. His heart had gone with Lorena Carlisle. It would be better if he did not follow it. Miles stayed with an old friend of his, Pete Lingle, who had served with him as a scout at Fort Laramie. Pete had taken over the site of old Fort Bernard, across the Platte from Fort Laramie some miles downstream. Good talk and good liquor, along with the fine cooking of Lingle's Ute squaw, had made the days drift past for Miles, on the long road in time he would have to cover before the face of Lorena faded from his memory.

A faint, misty rain was falling in the valley of the Platte when Miles rode toward the yellow lights of the fort. It was dusk, but it seemed later to Miles. Some of the fumes of Pete Lingle's brandy still hung in his head. He still had the use of quarters in Old Bedlam, for Colonel Long still wanted him as Chief of Scouts. In some ways it wasn't a bad idea, except for the fact that Miles still liked the more solitary life of a buffalo runner. But then the buffalo were doomed. Already the great herds were shrinking at an incredible rate as hunters infested the plains from Texas clear up into Indian country in the Dakotas.

He stabled the bay and unsaddled him, then walked toward his quarters, ready for a hot meal, a few soothing drinks, and a good night's sleep. Maybe the liquor would help him forget Lorena Carlisle, at least for a while. Nothing else seemed able to do it, and then in the morning she was always there again in his waking thoughts.

A young officer came out of the quarters as Miles walked along the path. "Mister Flint, sir," he said. "Colonel Long asked to see you as soon as you returned. He's in his quarters now."

"Thanks," said Miles. "I'll see him tomorrow."

The officer hesitated. "He seemed to think it was important, Mister Flint. I'll take your gear into your room."

Miles nodded. He handed the gear and his Sharps rifle to the shavetail and walked across the corner of the wet parade ground toward the misty lights of the colonel's quarters, glancing toward the quarters that had been occupied by Jonas and Lorena. The place was dark. He had half hoped she might still be there, but he knew without asking that she was not. He rapped on the colonel's door and entered without waiting for a reply.

Long looked up from his desk. He pushed aside a letter he had been writing. "By God," he said. "You took your time about it, Miles! I expected you back no later than yesterday."

Miles smiled wearily. "Am I under your orders, Colonel? Maybe I've been conscripted and don't know it."

Long shook his head. "Help yourself to the spirits," he said. He shoved a cigar box across the table and waited until Miles had his glass and his smoke. Miles sagged back in the chair and rested his head on the back of it, blowing a languorous cloud of smoke toward the ceiling.

Long leaned forward. "Before he left for the Bozeman, Carlisle hired himself another scout."

"Tell me who," said Miles politely.

"Bat Batteau," said the officer.

"Jesus Christ!" exploded Miles.

"I wholeheartedly agree," said Long dryly.

Miles looked at the officer in complete disbelief. "Didn't you tell him about Bat?"

"No. Bat was camped just off the post. I've barred him from the post proper. Bat must have gone out to the trail herd camp and sold Carlisle a real bill of goods."

"Amen to that," said Miles.

"Bat hates your guts. Maybe he did it just to make you look bad."

Miles shook his head. "There's more to it than that. When would Bat Batteau get up the guts to scout in Sioux territory? Carlisle would be better off with no scout at all."

Long sat down and rested his elbows on the desk. "The last time Bat was hanging around here he was telling the story of how he killed the famous Sioux war-chief Bull-over-the-Hill in ferocious hand-to-hand combat."

"It was bull over the hill all right," said Miles.

Long sipped his liquor as his calm eyes studied Miles. "Bat has his famous Ree scouts with him, too—Horns-in-Front, Goose, Stabbed, and Bear's Eyes, to name a few."

Miles drained his glass and went to get a refill. "Jesus God," he said fervently, rolling his eyes upward. "Now I've heard everything. *Everything!*"

Long nodded. "That is why I wanted to see you. Carlisle needs all the help he can get. A man like Batteau can lead him into trouble instead of keeping him out of it. At the sight of one Sioux scout Batteau is likely to pull foot and stand not on the order of his going, and Carlisle cannot possibly get by without a top-grade scout. Such as you, Miles."

"Such as me," said Miles. "You know how I stand on the matter."

Long nodded again. "You really wanted to go, Miles," he said.

"What makes you say that?"

"It's the woman, isn't it?"

The wind had shifted, driving the rain across the post. It pattered against the windows, and the wind moaned softly down the chimney.

"You don't have to answer that," said the colonel.

"I don't intend to," said Miles.

"Perhaps you left the trail herd because of her. No matter. Carlisle needs you now. She needs you now."

"You might be talking me into my own death, Dent," said Miles quietly.

Denton Long smiled. "Who ever talked you into *anything*, Miles?" He leaned forward again. "God knows I can use you here. God knows I don't want you to ride to your own death. But God also knows your mind as no one else does. The decision is yours." The officer got up and walked to the window, looking out across the rainswept parade ground. "An early storm," he said. "Coming from the north. Carlisle's bunch will be feeling this tonight."

"What would you do, Dent, if you were in my position?" said Miles.

"I am *not* in your position, Miles."

"Don't fence with me, Dent."

The officer turned. "If I loved that woman, as I think you do, no matter what the circumstances or what the eventual consequences, I would be riding toward the Bozeman Trail with her."

There was a long silence from Miles. He drained the glass. "Can I borrow a horse? My bay is tired."

"He'll be all right tomorrow."

Miles looked at him. "I'm leaving tonight. Now. I'll lead the bay. I can leave your issue mount at the stagecoach swing station at Muddy Creek. It can be brought back behind the next coach coming east."

Long shook his head. "I'll give you one of my own horses, Miles. Keep it. I owe it to you many times over. Anything else?"

Miles shook his head.

"Carlisle stocked up on a case or two more of split-breech Remingtons, an extra Colt or Remington six-shooter for each man. He hired more men. Men anxious to get to the goldfields but afraid to try it alone or in small parties. He's got a good outfit, Miles. There's a long, long outside chance he might make it."

Miles stood up and relighted his cigar. "The man of destiny," he said. He spat into the garboon.

It wasn't until he hit the ruts of the Bozeman not far from the crossing of Brown's Creek that Miles saw the telltale streamer of dust against the sky to the south. Beck Sterret had been pushing the herd hard as long as there was plenty of grazing, water, and a good road.

Miles unsaddled the bay and picketed both horses in the bottoms. He started a fire and brewed coffee. Ernie Masland would appreciate having a fire when he reached the creek, provided Beck Sterret would agree to stop there.

Miles stayed in the cover of the brush, watching the rutted trail winding up over the southern ridge. Suddenly a horseman appeared, sitting a fine white horse, holding a hand across his eyes in approved scout fashion, studying the creek bottoms. The wind made sport with the thrums of his white buckskin jacket. Miles lazily rolled over and took his binoculars from his saddlebag. He adjusted them and studied the man on the ridge. He grinned as he saw the intricate beadwork of the scout's buckskin jacket and the scalp hair along the sides of the leggings. Oversized thrums hung from the sleeves of the jacket and fringed the yoke of the garment. There was enough beadwork on the jacket to turn a bullet. The wind whipped the scout's long black hair from beneath the brim of his white hat. Once again the scout peered beneath his hand, rising in his stirrups as he did go.

"Gawdamighty," said Miles in awe. "Bat Batteau! The Scout of the Great Plains! The slayer of Bull-over-the-Hill! In person tonight! One performance only!"

Bat rode down the ridge followed by half a dozen riders. They were Arikaras—small, wiry, dirty, and careless in their dress, which was half Indian and half white. They wore their thick black hair combed fully to one side or the other as was their custom.

The dust was rising thickly from behind the ridge. Bat was too damned close to the herd to do effective scouting, and in addition there likely wasn't a hostile Indian within fifty miles. Further, if Bat was scouting, his Rees should have been no less than half a day's ride ahead of the herd. Jonas Carlisle had been gulled by one of the worst hypocrites west of the Mississippi.

A heavy-set horseman topped the ridge and rode down after the "scouts." It was Jonas Carlisle. A moment later Beck Sterret appeared, riding in the deceptively loose fashion of a Texan.

Bat turned in his saddle fifty yards from the creek. "All clear, Mister Carlisle!" he yelled. "Ain't hide nor ha'r of any hostiles. Seen a little smoke awhile back, but we scouted it. A handful of hostiles, but they run when they seen me and the Rees." He laughed uproariously. "They wanted no part of *us!*"

Miles shook his head. Likely a grass fire. Miles had seen

one several miles back, staining the clear air. Bat was playing his role to the hilt.

The Rees crowded toward the creek, jabbering amongst themselves. Miles could have killed every one of them before he was even seen. The Rees stopped short when they saw the picketed horses. The wind fanned the fire, and the smoke drifted toward Bat, Jonas, and Beck. Jonas turned quickly in his saddle. Bat jerked his carbine free from its fancy beaded sheath.

Miles stood up leisurely. "It's all right, Bat," he said dryly. "Like you said: Ain't hide nor ha'r of any hostiles."

Bat's bearded face seemed to go out of focus, changing from a massive grin into a look of pure hate. "Flint," he said. "What the hell are yuh doin' here?"

Miles felt for a cigar. "Colonel Long said Mister Carlisle needed a scout."

"I'm scoutin' for Mister Carlisle!" snapped Bat.

Miles nodded. "That's what the colonel told me."

Beck Sterret shifted in his saddle. His look was cold as compared to the hot hatred on Batteau's face.

The first of the cattle had topped the ridge, bawling as they picked up the odor of the water. Ernie Masland's chuckwagon lurched into sight and rolled down toward the campsite.

Batteau flushed darkly. "Long said you was goin' to scout for him."

Miles lighted the cigar and looked over the flame at Bat. "He must have come out from the post to you to tell you that. It's a cinch *you* never came onto the post to tell him."

"What does that mean?" said Jonas.

Miles fanned out the match. "That's between Bat and me," he said.

"Bat knows this country better than any scout in the business," said Jonas.

"Did he tell you that?" said Miles.

Jonas narrowed his eyes. "Come to think of it, he did."

Beck Sterret leaned forward in his saddle. "Bat says we can get through all right."

"When were you last up that way, Bat?" said Miles.

Bat's green eyes shifted uncertainly. He wiped his mouth with the back of a dirty hand. "The hostiles been quiet all summer. The Bozeman is like a country lane. Maybe quieter."

"The time to look for trouble is when they are quiet," said Miles.

"I got good scouts," said Bat. "Ain't no hostiles goin' to fool them."

"Rees," said Miles contemptuously. "Corn Indians."

Jonas lighted a cigar. "Bat says the Rees are the best scouts and fighters on the Plains," he said.

"And you believed him," said Miles. "My God!"

Bat shifted angrily in his saddle. "By God, Flint," he said, "yuh ain't the only judge of Indians in this country."

"Those Rees won't get within ten miles of a Sioux or Cheyenne, and you know it, Bat. Stop kidding and be honest for once in your life."

"Why, yuh dirty . . ."

Miles took the cigar from his mouth. "Now, Bat," he said quietly.

Bat shut up. He looked angrily at the two other men. "As long as he ain't part of this outfit, we got to listen to *him?*"

Beck Sterret spat. "Not far's I'm concerned," he drawled. "Like I said befoah: All them Indians want is sugah, tobaccy, whiskey, and wo-haw. A taste of powdersmoke will drive 'em off."

The mass of the herd was pouring down the slope toward the creek. Beck began to fashion a smoke. "With scouts out ahead, the herd bunched, every man riding the flanks, and the drag armed with them britchloader rifles, we can drive this herd plumb to Hudson's Bay."

Bat slapped a dirty hand on his buckskin-clad thigh. "Well spoken, Sterret! We'll work well together, you and me!"

There was a moment's pause. The glacial gray eyes studied Bat Batteau. "You do *yore* job, Mistah Batteau," said Beck softly, "and I'll do *mine.* One difference is thet I'll damned well see to it thet you do yores."

"Beck," said Jonas. "That's no way to talk to Bat."

Beck kneed his gray away from the others. "Far's I'm concerned," he said flatly, "we can do without these buckskin boys and theah fightin' talk. But if yuh want to pay them wages, Mistah Carlisle, and have them eat up food the trail drivers can use, it's all right with me. Just keep them out of my way and the way of the herd." He spurred his horse and rode swiftly toward the herd.

Bat whistled softly. "What's in his craw?" he said.

One of the Studebakers topped the ridge and rolled downslope. The wind fluttered a dress. Miles raised his eyes. It was Lorena, and suddenly the world seemed all right again, at least for a little while. Miles looked at Ernie Masland. "Here's your fire, Ernie!" he called out. "Ready to cook coffee and grub."

"*Gracias,* Miles!" yelled the grinning cocinero. "Welcome home!"

"I'm not home yet," said Miles.

Jonas bit off part of the end of his cigar and spat it out. "What does that mean?" he said.

The Studebaker, followed by the others, was moving toward Jonas, Bat, and Miles. Lorena placed a hand across her eyes to shade them. She had seen Miles.

"You mean you'll ride with us, Miles?" said Jonas.

Miles looked up at him. "I'd like to," he said. "If you don't mind."

Jonas rubbed his thick beard. "I can certainly use you."

The Studebaker rolled up and stopped beside Jonas. Lorena smiled a little uncertainly at Miles.

"Yuh got scouts, Mister Carlisle," said Bat. He glanced at Lorena.

Jonas nodded. "But no meat hunter. Miles, will you take that job at least?"

Miles did not dare look at Lorena. "Glad to, Jonas," he said.

That night the wind laughed deep in its throat as it swept across the hills, coming from the north, from the Big Horn and Powder River country. The wind knew a great deal not vouchsafed to puny mortals. Perhaps it was better that they did not know.

CHAPTER EIGHT

Bat Batteau continued leading after Miles Flint rejoined the trail herd, throwing out a screen of his Rees. Bat put on a great show as long as Miles Flint went on his solitary way hunting for the trail drivers. Bat was quite sure that there wasn't a strong hostile party within miles, at least not strong enough to attack the trail drivers and their "britchloader" rifles. The Rees would leave camp at dawn, riding like the wind, to put a few miles between them and the slowly moving herd, and then they'd find a shady draw or a clump of willows along a stream course to rest and play at knucklebones until it was time to move on again ahead of the herd. Naturally they didn't get *too* far ahead, for they liked the thought of the tough, alert Texans and their "britchloader" rifles being fairly close at hand in case there *were* any hostiles within shooting distance. Bat managed to sleep off many a hangover during the day while his Rees kept an eye on the herd rather than on the surrounding country. If nothing else, Bat had thoroughly sold himself and his Rees to Jonas Carlisle.

The country ahead of the herd seemed empty, indeed, except for an occasional hawk drifting against the clear sky with motionless wings in the dry wind, or the sudden movement of pronghorn antelope, or clumsily running buffalo, moving with deceptive speed away from the approaching herd.

Miles Flint did his job, at times being a full day or more ahead of the herd, waiting for them at some watering place with a load of meat, or at times hanging the meat to be picked up later and then moving on by himself. The country seemed empty, and maybe it was, but there was an uneasy feeling within him, particularly when he approached the Pumpkin Buttes country, where the Bozeman trended northwest to follow the Dry Fork of the Powder. The country was closing in on the Bozeman, and what was behind those hills only God, and the Teton Sioux, knew.

The passage had been too easy thus far, too quiet. Miles could use some of Bat's Rees now, to poke into those draws and mottes, to scale the bluffs and look for any sign. Several times in his lone ride far ahead of the herd he had found telltale dark patches along the Bozeman—blackened earth, still coated with ashes beaten down by the rains, and pieces of rust-scaled wagon iron lying amongst them. Lorena Carlisle could hardly miss seeing them. Several times he passed crude crosses, with the names and dates almost illegible, placed close to the trail. Likely few, or perhaps none of them had died natural deaths.

He saw the buffalo one afternoon when he was perhaps half a day's ride ahead of the herd. They had moved out of a deep draw, moving into the freshening north wind, drifting slowly toward the shallow creek some miles ahead. The creek was marked by a scraggly dark line of willows, beyond which there was a low line of rounded hills. Fresh buffalo hump would go good that night with some of Jonas Carlisle's choice liquor. Miles led the bay into a shallow draw and picketed him, taking his rifle and other gear with him as, hatless, he worked his way up a slope stippled with soapweed. He fitted the 'scope to the rifle and thrust it between two clumps, resting it on the crotch of his shooting sticks. The nearest buffalo were about two hundred and fifty yards away, with the wind blowing almost directly toward Miles. He tossed out his lighted cigar butt and watched the smoke rise, then waver with the wind.

Miles selected a big cow at the downwind edge of the herd. The Sharps roared, and when the smoke cleared Miles saw that the cow was still on her feet, walking unsteadily away from the herd. Suddenly she jerked spasmodically and went down on her foreknees, the blood gushing from her nose and mouth. A bull raised his head and sniffed the air. The sun glinted from his horns. Miles reloaded. He needed only a few carcasses, enough to pick the select cuts of meat. He drove his second slug into a young cow. She crumpled instantly. His third shot missed because of a sudden gust of wind.

Miles reloaded and rested his chin on the butt of the rifle, idly waiting to see what the herd would do. He had enough meat. The herd was restless now, sniffing the air, raising their heads. Some of them wandered over to the dead animals, sniffing at them, hooking at them with their horns. Dust rose and drifted with the wind as some of the bulls pawed the ground and snorted. They were not quite ready to panic, but they were getting more restless. Miles suddenly narrowed his eyes. There was a whitish blob in the center of the small herd, as though a beef cow had somehow gotten mixed up with them. The buffalo moved about, shifting in front of the whitish blob, so that Miles couldn't get a clear sight of what it was.

Miles reached for his binoculars and sighted them on the herd, focusing to bring them in more sharply. In the shimmering heat the buffalo looked as if they were suspended above the dry ground. Miles focused on the whitish blob, and his heart skipped a beat, thudding erratically against his ribs. He hurriedly wiped the sweat from his forehead and wiped the misted eyepieces on his shirt. He focused again. The whitish mass stood out clearly. A young bull with a shaggy, dirty pelt of creamy coloration. "By God," said Miles under his breath. "A sure enough snow-back!"

He lowered the glasses and closed his eyes. Maybe he was seeing things. Few hunters, or any men, white or Indian, had likely ever seen a white, or albino, buffalo. Maybe the odds were one in a million, or perhaps less. Miles carefully cleaned the lens and the eyepieces, then adjusted the glasses again. His heart leaped again. He was right! The sun shone clearly on the dirty, matted hide. *Begod, it was a snow-back!*

The wind shifted again, then died away. The cigar smoke wafted straight up into the air. Miles placed the glasses to one side and took up the Sharps. His right hand closed about the small of the stock. He didn't want to hole that precious hide in the wrong place. The young bull turned and looked directly at Miles, as though feeling those keen gray eyes upon him. The Sharps pushed back hard against Miles as smoke and flame spat from the big muzzle. The thunder of the heavy gun report rolled along the face of the low hills and died away.

Miles raised his head from the 'scope and lowered the smoking rifle. The snow-back was down, flat on its side, with blood masking the whitish face. Miles snatched up the glasses and focused them on the bull. "Begod," he said incredulously. "Right in the eye."

The herd was moving swiftly in their jerky up-and-down gallop, the cows and calves in the center, the bulls flanking, slamming into the rising wind, the ground shaking beneath their hooves, leaving their dead behind them on the blood-stained grass. In a few minutes they had topped a swale and were gone from sight, but the ground still trembled faintly beneath the pounding of their hooves and the dust wreathed back on the wind.

Miles reloaded the hot Sharps. He removed the 'scope and slid it into its leather case. He slung rifle and 'scope to the saddle and led the bay toward the dead buffalo. There was enough meat, counting the albino, to keep the drivers happy for a few days. They never seemed to get tired of fresh buffalo hump and steak.

He led the bay near the white bull and then stood studying the dead buffalo. It was a bull about two years old. The hide was far whiter then he had expected it to be, even though it was matted with filth and burrs, stuck with grass and dried dung. It was a much better hide than old Jules Beque had once gotten on the Cimarron. That had been more of a silver gray in color, whited tips on the end of black hair. This one was almost pure white with a creamy tinge to it, not as dark as a claybank.

Miles honed his skinning knife and crescent knife on his belt steel and then carefully set to work, his loaded rifle close to hand and his eyes flicking up regularly, scanning the country on all sides. The reports of the rifle could have been heard for miles, and the trail herd was still a long way off, too far for the drivers to be of any help to Miles should he be attacked. There wasn't much chance that Bat Batteau and his Rees would be close to Miles, as they should have been.

He had no pritchell stick with which to prop the bull on his back, so he fastened his reata to the right legs and fastened the other end to the saddlehorn, leading the bay back until the bull rose flat on its back. "Stand," he said to the bay. The bay would not move.

He slit the thick hide from beneath the lower jaw, working along the neck, constantly renewing the edge on his skinning knife so as not to tear the hide, until he had worked down the belly to the tail. He thrust the skinning knife into the belly meat and drew out the crescent knife, scanning the terrain as he did so. High in the sky there appeared what looked to be scraps of charred paper being driven by the wind; the ravens were already gathering. He worked steadily and surely with the keen-edged crescent knife, cutting around the thick neck, taking the ears but leaving the skin of the head. Then he began the dirty, greasy work of loosening the hide from the carcass.

Flies arrived, crawling and swarming, and time and time again he had to stop to brush them away from his sweating face while they crawled irritatingly over his greasy, bloody hands and naked forearms. He kicked the hide as far as he could under one side of the carcass, then whistled to the bay. The bay moved toward Miles, letting the reata slacken until the carcass rolled sluggishly and fell over. Miles worked under the heavy back until the hide was free from the backbone. Ordinarily he would have fastened the reata to the neck and peeled off the hide by having the bay pull on the reata, but he might have torn the precious albino hide, and this above all he did not want to do.

He heaved the hide over and worked it free from the hot, bloody carcass. The green hide weighed all of eighty or ninety pounds. It was a beauty, free of bare spots and blemishes. Miles lighted a cigar to get the stink of the carcass out of his nostrils and to drive away some of the persistent flies. He began to cut loose the select meat he wanted, cutting free the *depouille* or back fat, and placing it on a square of canvas he took from his cantle roll. He slashed out the tough gristly skin between the prongs of the tightly closed jaws, then pulled the thick tongue through the opening and cut it off. He worked on the hump, cutting down each side of the shoulders and then chopping through the hump ribs with his heavy, brass-backed bowie knife. He cut loose the larger bones for the delicious marrow in them, better than any butter to a veteran plainsman.

He slit open the belly and felt about in the hot, steaming interior until he located the saddlebag-sized liver, which he cut loose and pulled out. He opened the gallbladder, then cut loose a sliver of the hot liver and sprinkled it with gall. He hadn't eaten all day long. He munched Indian-fashion on the tidbit with relish while he removed the heart, kidneys, and intestines, pulling the slippery, greasy intestines through his strong fingers to clean out the body wastes, then knitting the long slippery tubes into a loopy chain.

Miles stood up to ease his back and get his nose away from the stench. He wiped the sweat from his face and reached for the cigar, which he had placed on one upthrust hoof. His hand stopped in midair. Not thirty feet from him a young Sioux buck sat his paint pony on a low knoll. There was no expression on the buck's painted face. His trade musket, studded with brass tacks, was lying in the crook of his left arm, the muzzle pointing directly at Miles.

Miles was too far from the Sharps to make a break for it. He had shoved his holstered Remington pistol around to the middle of his back to keep it out of the way, and the flap was buttoned down. At that short distance the soft ball of the big-bored musket could tear off half his head or gut him as he had gutted the buffalo bull. Damn his carelessness! He should have known better. Why hadn't the bay warned him of the buck's approach? He turned to look for the bay, half expecting to hear the raucous bellow of the trade musket. His guts seemed to turn over. The bay had drifted not far from where another buck sat, his blanket hanging over his naked thighs, the sun shining on his white pipe-bone breast-piece, his long-barreled flintlock rifle casually aimed toward Miles.

Something warned Miles, an insistent needle in the back of his mind. He glanced to the right. Another buck stood on the ground near one of the dead cows, his eyes on Miles, and the black eye of a Jenks carbine studying Miles as well.

Miles looked at the first buck. *"How kola,"* he said stupidly. He raised his bloody hands, palms outward toward the buck in the sign of peace. There was no movement, no change of expression on the buck's face. Miles felt the cold sweat run down his body. Indians hated buffalo runners with a vengeance for killing far, far more of the shaggies than they needed for meat, leaving the good meat to rot on the prairie while they took away only the green hides. The whole economy, indeed the very life of these people depended on *Pte*, the good buffalo. They did not waste a scrap of *Pte*. Everything was used. Meat, sinews, hide, horns, hooves, bones, guts, and blood. Everything but the snort.

I am going to die, thought Miles incredulously. I am going to die, perhaps suddenly, perhaps slowly, but I am going to die. This can't happen to me, Miles Flint. This must be someone else standing here, smeared with buffalo blood and fat, someone else who is going to die.

The buck on the knoll kneed his horse closer to Miles. Young as he was, he wore an erect eagle feather in his hair indicating that he had killed an enemy after striking coup on him. The feather was notched twice, indicating that he had been twice wounded in the fight.

They were playing with Miles now, as a cat plays with a mouse, knowing full well he was powerless. He looked out of the corners of his eyes at the folded hide of the snow-back. Only the inner, flesh-coated side of the hide showed. Miles took in a deep breath and walked casually as he could toward the hide. He heard the sharp snick-snick of a rifle hammer being full-cocked behind him. He reached down and suddenly jerked at the greasy edge of the hide, twisting it so that it unrolled outer side upward, with the sun slanting fully down on it, revealing the dirty cream white of the pelt.

There were three startled cries. Three brown hands covered open mouths in sheer awe. The bucks stared at the hide with wide eyes. This was medicine! This was big medicine indeed!

Miles raised his head and looked directly at each of them in turn, trying to keep fear from showing on his face.

Slowly, foot by foot, the two closest bucks retreated. They suddenly flung themselves on their ponies. The three Sioux savagely quirted their ponies and raced from the wide hollow, and in a few minutes they plunged out of sight into a brushy draw.

Miles dropped to one knee, then sat down suddenly. He felt his guts roil and the sour taste of bile in the back of his throat. His legs were as weak as water. He crawled to his rifle and used it as a prop to get up onto his feet. He looked to the south. The sun glinted on the great spreading horns of the cattle as they streamed down a ridge in a long, sinuous line. Seven riders were flung out ahead of the herd in a fast-riding crescent heading toward Miles and his kill. It was Bat Batteau and his Rees, hard at work, scouting so close to the herd that the smell and sound of it would be sure to stampede any small parties of hostiles.

The six Rees seemed to scent the buffalo meat like coyotes. They drove their lathered ponies full tilt across the rolling ground, lashing them with their quirts, yipping tremulously in their excitement, while Bat Batteau, *the* Scout of the Plains, rode along behind them laughing uproariously. He could afford to laugh, for the day had been a safe and easy one and now good buffalo hump was in the offing.

Miles wiped the grease and blood from his arms and hands. He swept the flies from his face and wiped the skinning knives on the carcass, sheathing them in their oiled leather cases. Swiftly he rolled up the hide, the white pelt inside, securing it with thrums from his saddlebag. He covered the hide with a blanket and slung it from his saddle. These damned Rees and Bat Batteau would surely know the value of a snow-back pelt if none of the others did. Men had been murdered for the possession of such hides.

The Rees leaped from their ponies, screaming, ripping out their knives to slash wildly at the nearest cow, careless of cutting buffalo or the flesh of their mates as they sliced into the big belly, hunting with bloody hands for the huge liver, the steam from the guts streaming up about their painted faces and making them look like demons straight from hell.

Miles picked up his rifle and led the bay away from the carcasses. Jonas Carlisle and Lorena were riding toward the group.

Bat Batteau dismounted, exaggerated thrums fluttering in the wind. The sun glistened on the crusted beadwork of his buckskins. "Good huntin', eh, pardner!" he yelled at Miles, a wide grin creasing his bearded face. "Guess the hostiles won't bother you with me and the Rees scoutin' ahead, hey?"

Miles lighted a fresh cigar and fanned out the match, watching Lorena as she rode her mare sidesaddle with expert skill, riding habit shirt pulled up enough to reveal the tiniest of riding boots.

Bat eyed the carcasses. "Where's the hide from that one?" he asked Miles, pointing to the skinned bull.

Miles shrugged. "Figured I might need a good buffalo coat before we reached the Gallatin."

"I thought you knew your business," said Bat. "That bull can't be mor'n two years old. A four- or five-year-old bull woulda been better. Thicker and hairier."

Miles could smell the stench rising from his sweating body, and he didn't want Lorena to get scent of it. He swung up on the bay.

"Good hunting, eh, Miles?" said Jonas. "I fancy some hump this night."

"Have Bat send one of his Rees for one of the wagons," said Miles. "I'll ride on to the creek and get a fire started for Ernie. The Rees can earn their keep by cutting out the meat."

"Good thinking," agreed Jonas.

Miles's eyes met those of Lorena. There was a faint hurt look in them. She looked away. They rarely saw each other now except at a distance.

Bat placed a moccasined foot on the biggest cow and watched three of the Rees expertly skinning a smaller cow. It was one thing they were good at. "I was tellin' Flint here it was good that me and the Rees was out here watchin' for hostiles so's he could hunt in peace, Mister Carlisle," he said.

Miles blew out a smoke ring. "*Heyoka,*" he said in guttural Sioux. He tipped his dusty hat to Lorena and touched the bay with his heels, riding swiftly toward the distant creek bottoms several miles away.

"What did he mean, Bat?" said Lorena.

Bat's green eyes seemed to be boring a smoking hole in the middle of Miles's broad, buckskin-clad back.

"Bat?" said Lorena.

He turned slowly, the look of hate still on his face, although he tried to bury it with a quick smile. "It's a little joke amongst us plainsmen, Mis' Carlisle. It ain't exactly fittin' for a lady's ears."

Bat Batteau wasn't exactly right. *Heyoka* in the Sioux tongue means "joker."

CHAPTER NINE

It was dry and hot in the dark valley of the Dry Fork, and an uneasiness hung low in the atmosphere. The wind had died away hours back after another exceptionally hot day. Perhaps it was too be a mild fall after all. Miles Flint rode the tired sorrel through the clinging darkness toward the camp of the trail herd somewhere southeast of him. The sky had been clear and starlit when he had left the crossing of the Powder River just before dusk. A three-day scout north of the slow-moving herd had been fruitless. He had not seen a sign of a hostile, although once there had been a faint wraith of smoke rising through the haze of late autumn somewhere far up the valley of the Powder. It could have been a grass fire. There hadn't been enough of it to indicate a large camp of Sioux.

The overcast seemed thicker. There was a faint, insistent flickering along the western horizon etching the fanged hills. The sheet lightning grew in intensity as he rode, and the quiet air grew more oppressive. Faintly, ever so faintly, the Thunder People rolled their drums. The humidity seemed to rise.

Miles stood up in his stirrups. He should have seen or heard the longhorns by now. If the lightning and thunder increased, the cattle might stampede. There had been no stampeding after that fateful afternoon on a fork of the Smoky Hill, and that had been only part of the herd. It was a day Miles would remember bitterly for the rest of his life.

The night grew blacker as the eerie lightning became brighter, etching itself in staghorn fashion across the sky. The thunder pealed louder and louder through the valleys and along the line of hills. Suddenly, far ahead of him down a long slope, Miles saw a creek bed marked by a line of willows and by the dark shapes of thousands of cattle. In the instant of bluish, uncanny light Miles saw that many of the beeves were on their feet; others getting up in the quick, almost catlike movement of a longhorn, from lying down to upright on their legs, without the double movement of other cattle or of buffalo.

Suddenly there was an intense electrical discharge spanning the width of the valley, splitting the charged air right over the herd. The herd began to move slowly at a walk and as darkness plunged down again Miles saw an eerie sight. Almost instantaneously on every horntip of the three thousand or so steers appeared a ball of dull, phosphorescent light. It was foxfire, or St. Elmo's fire, sometimes called will-o-the-wisp. Suddenly it appeared on the ears of the tired, nervous sorrel. The dull balls of fire on the thousands of horntips could be plainly seen in the thick darkness. They were moving slowly toward Miles. There was a faint suggestion of wind moving the heavy air in the valley, and the smell and sound of the herd came to Miles.

As quick as the crack of doom a tremendous flash of staghorn lightning forked across the herd of longhorns, and the flaming tongues seemed almost to touch the backs of the cattle. A crashing of what seemed like heavy artillery followed on the flailing heels of the lightning, and then the herd broke in the direction of the lone horseman. Pounding hooves made the ground tremble, and the clacking of horn against horn was a terrifying sound. Then the sluice gates of the sky opened on the valley of the Dry Fork, and the rain came down in almost impenetrable sheets. The lightning split a fiery path through the deluge to reveal the herd pounding madly up the valley, eyes wide and staring, horns wet and slick.

Miles reined in the sorrel and turned him, driving the steel into his flanks. He knew the rules in a stampede. He had learned them well enough riding with Nelson Story. Hang with the cattle. Trust your horse. But the sorrel was almost dead beat. The ground was already turning slick, and the way was up the slope, with the fresh cattle, running almost as fast as a slow horse, whiplashed by the lightning, thunder, and fear itself.

Miles did not look back. He lay low alongside the sorrel's neck, trusting to God the sorrel had some reserve left. The sound of the pounding hooves and clacking horns came clearly to him in the intervals between the crackling lightning and roaring thunder. His hat flew off and hung at the back of his neck. There was nothing to do but run.

The sorrel was slowing down. Miles shot a look back over his shoulder and his heart skipped a beat. Already a crescent horn of the herd was creeping up on his right flank, gaining ground inch by inch. There was something else. Two horsemen were riding with incredible daring and skill against the leaders of the crescent horn to turn them in on the herd, to mill it, to force it to turn itself into a great revolving mass until it could be quieted down. Only the best could do it.

The horn began to turn a little. One of the horseman jerked his six-shooter free and fired it, driving his horse almost directly into the streaming-wet flanks of the leaders. Miles thought he could clear the crescent. He laid the steel to the sorrel. The sorrel jerked spasmodically and then went down. Miles just managed to kick free from the stirrups and land running on his feet, knowing all the time he had only seconds to live.

The lead horseman swung toward Miles, kicking out a stirrup. Miles braced himself, trying to keep his eyes away from the nearest cattle. He trust a foot into the dangling stirrup and gripped the rider's broad gunbelt, letting the momentum of the horse carry him up and behind the rider.

The second rider smashed against the head of the herd, slowly turning them. Miles's savior rode up a rise and drew rein. "Off!" he said flatly. It was then Miles knew that it was Beck Sterret. Sterret reloaded his pistol as Miles swung down.

"Gracias," said Miles.

"Por nada," said the Texan.

Miles wiped the rain from his face. He looked up at the hard face of the trail boss. "One thing," he said. "Did you know it was me?"

Sterret kneed his horse away from Miles. "You figger it out, Yank," he said. "I got my job to do." He was gone, racing down the slope, seemingly part of the horse itself, to drive into the leaders of the herd. Blackness fell and with it a smashing downpour of icy rain. When lightning flicked across the valley Miles could see the herd slowly turning, but many longhorns had broken free from the herd and were pounding toward the distant hills. It would be hours, perhaps days before the trail herd could be formed again for the drive north.

Miles turned up his jacket collar. There was no use looking for the sorrel. His smashed body would be part and parcel of the trampled, muddy path of the stampeded herd. Miles walked up the slope, away from the stragglers of the herd and toward the creek. Every man would be out that wild night to save the herd.

The day dawned clear and cold along the valley of the Dry Fork. Most of the herd had been penned against the distant hills, but far up and down the valley were the dotted shapes of stragglers. A wisp of smoke rose from the campfire, fired by the dry buffalo chips Ernie Masland carried in the "cooney" slung beneath the chuckwagon. Now and then a herder rode his worn-out horse toward the creek, grabbed a mug of Arbuckle's, roped a fresh horse, and was on his way again in a matter of minutes. A trail herder could always catch up on his sleep in the winter.

Jonas Carlisle returned to the camp in the gathering dusk. "Did you see Bat and his Rees, Miles?" was his first question as he swung down stiffly from his gray.

Miles shook his head. He had finished cleaning his Sharps, which he had left behind in the charge of Ernie Masland when he had gone ahead on his lonely scout. "All I saw was buffalo crap and a little smoke up the valley of the Powder," he said dryly.

Jonas eased his crotch and helped himself to a cup of coffee. "Bat said he'd join you up north. I told him not to stay away more then a day, Miles."

Miles leaned the Sharps against a tree. An odd thought had come to him. Miles had carried the green albino hide with him on his three-day scout. It had been one of the reasons why he had asked Carlisle's permission to scout ahead on his own. In a hidden clearing in the timber crowning a hill not far from the Powder he had firmly staked out the green hide, hair side down, and had covered it with arsenic to kill insects. The days had been hot and sunny. Miles had figured that by the time he returned to the hide it would be fully dry, a flint hide, weighing about half the weight of a green hide and ready for transport. That hide was almost worth its weight in silver. Bat Batteau would have known that, if he had known or suspected that Miles had killed a snow-back.

"But you never saw him, eh, Miles?" said Jonas.

"It's a big country," said Miles.

"Maybe he ran into the Sioux."

Miles grinned as he helped himself to coffee. "Not likely," he said.

"I know you have no use for him," said Jonas testily. "But I had to take what I could get when you backed out on me."

Miles placed the cup on a rock and looked up at the trail driver. "You would have been better off without him," he said. "And I did not back out on you."

Jonas's face worked. He was tired, not used to riding all night and the next day rounding up stray cattle like the hard-butted Texas corrida. "Damn it all, man," he said. "Do you have to have that damned chip on your shoulder all the time?"

Miles stood up. "Only when I'm crowded," he said coldly.

"By God! If you work for me, you'll *learn* to be crowded!"

Cattle bawled along the creek, and the sound of singing came to the two men who faced each other, as the herders kept the longhorns calm. Ernie Masland looked at Jonas and Miles. He had never seen the two of them like this before, but nerves were taut. Jonas wasn't quite so sure of himself now that he was approaching the heart of Sioux country, and the stampede could have been disastrous.

"I don't work under those conditions," said Miles quietly.

"Are you God Almighty or something?" snapped Carlisle.

Miles picked up his rifle. "No," he said. "But I've had a bellyful of this bunch."

Beck Sterret was with the herd. He rode slowly toward the camp through the gathering dusk. Sterret had an uncanny knack of sensing trouble before it started or while it was in the process of getting started.

"You can leave, then," said Carlisle to Miles. "You're through."

Miles nodded. He carried the rifle to his gear and went to get the bay. His temper was hot and he wanted no further words with Jonas or, for that matter, with Beck Sterret. When he had roped and saddled the bay he saw Jonas and Beck riding back toward the herd.

He cursed himself for his hotheadedness. The trail driver needed him even more than he thought, for Bat Batteau and his Rees were more of a liability than an asset. He led the bay to his gear and fashioned cantle and pommel packs. Now and then he caught the eyes of Ernie Masland on him. He did not see Ernie walk to the Studebaker, nor did he see Lorena Carlisle mount her mare and ride into the darkness toward the gathering herd.

There was a faint trace of the new moon in the clear, cloudless sky when Miles swung up on the bay. He kneed him toward the creek. A horseman sat on the far side, smoking a cigar. The flare of the tip revealed the tired, bearded face of Jonas Carlisle. "Miles," he said. "I was a damned fool. On edge. We need you. Even Beck Sterret admits that."

Miles waded the bay through the shallow waters. "That should clinch it then," he said.

Jonas took the cigar from his mouth. "It will take us another day to get set to point them north, Miles. I don't know where Bat and his Rees are. See if you can find them. If not, I'll have to depend completely on you." His voice died away, and from the tone of it Miles knew how much Jonas Carlisle did depend on him.

"I owe you something," said Miles quietly. "I agreed to go along this time. I won't let you down. Come to think of it, I owe something to Beck Sterret as well."

"Such as?"

"My life," said Miles. "Say hello to Mrs. Carlisle for me. See you at the crossing of the Powder." He touched the bay with his spurs and rode off into the darkness.

"I'll be damned," said Jonas. He shoved back his hat. He rode to his wagon and dismounted stiffly.

Lorena looked up from her chair. "Well, Jonas?" she said.

He nodded. "You were right," he said. "A proud man, but a good man."

"You're tired. Beck is tired. Miles is tired. We're all tired."

He looked down at her and passed a hand across her dark hair. "We are not going back," he said.

She looked up at him. "I didn't mean that, Jonas. We're all in this to the end now."

Somewhere near the hills a coyote greeted the rising moon.

The rising moon was a pale wash in the eastern sky. The wind which had died away after sunset, rose again in the velvety darkness, moaning softly down the great valley of the Powder River, keening over the blackened ruins of Fort Reno, built by the Army in 1866 to protect the Bozeman Trail and burned by the Sioux in 1868, along with Forts Phil Kearny and C. F. Smith, further north on the Bozeman, leaving the route entirely without Army protection.

Miles Flint lay on his lean belly overlooking the river crossing. He had traveled at night, hiding by day, watching for Sioux sign without any luck until he had reached the crossing. Shortly before dusk he had seen a party of warriors cross the ford and disappear into the broken country to the north. There had been about a score of them, hardly enough to stop the trail herd. Later in the clinging darkness he had seen faint lights north of the Pumpkin Buttes, but they had soon vanished. There were no whites settled in that dangerous country, and a party of whites would hardly be stupid enough to show lights at night in the Powder River country. There could only be one source for those lights. This was the territory of Plenty Kills's powerful band of Oglalas.

The Sioux would not fight at night, but that didn't mean they would not scout at night. The crossing would be a dangerous one for the traveling herd. Stippled with scattered hemlock and yellow pine timber, thick with eroded draws and sharp ridges angling every whichway, it offered excellent concealment for large war parties. Miles led the bay down to the river, sniffing the air for the scent of burning buffalo chips or lathered ponies. The smell of the river came to him instead.

Miles crossed the river before the moon cast its lights upon the shallow, rippling waters. He rode through the dark timber and tethered the bay, climbing up the steep slope to pass into a clearing just being lighted by the moon. The pegged-out hide was still there. He knelt and examined it. It had cured well under the hot suns and was firm and dry. The rain that had deluged the Dry Fork country had evidently passed south of the Powder River crossing. Miles crimped it down the middle, lashed it together, and carried it to the bay. He folded a square of canvas about it and bound it tightly so that it could not be seen.

He led the bay back toward the crossing. He would have felt much better if he had seen the yellow lights of Fort Reno reflected across the rippling waters to meet the silvery path of the moonlight down the river center.

The moon was well up when he caught the sound of the herd. Beck Sterret must have been pushing them, riding through dusk and darkness to reach the Powder, after his loss of time with the stampede. The far side of the river was bathed in silvery light when Bat Batteau and his Rees appeared, clumped together. As fine a target as a group of Dog Soldiers would have wished for. Miles speculated idly that he could probably get all seven of them within three minutes.

Bat set his white horse at the river and splashed noisily across. Miles had seen neither hide nor hair of Bat and his Rees on his second scout to the Powder. Miles did not move from the log where he sat, watching Bat leave the river.

"Flint!" said Bat cheerfully. "All clear here?"

"You can see for yourself," said Miles dryly.

"Yeh. Well, how far you aimin' to go with Jonas?"

Miles felt for a cigar. "Maybe to the Gallatin."

Bat slid from his horse. "I heard talk around the camp last night that Jonas might cut you in on the herd if you was to go all the way."

"That's news to me," said Miles.

Bat shoved back his hat. "I'd like to get in on that," he said.

Miles lighted the cigar. "So?"

Bat squatted in front of Miles. "If you was to pull out in the next few days, say, or maybe go on just to the Buffalo, I could maybe make a deal like that myself with Jonas."

Miles studied the bearded scout. "Go on," he said mildly.

Bat took out a plug and bit off a chew. "Say you was gone, and me and the Rees was all he had to scout for him. Well, supposin' you had left, and we was in hostile country, and I told Jonas me and the Rees was pullin' out, like." He paused to work the chew into pliability. "Mebbe Jonas might, just *might,* mind you, cut *me* in on the herd like he might have thought of doin' for you. By Jesus, up on the Gallatin, with some of them cows, a man could make himself some *dinero.* A man can't go on forever livin' dangerously like this, and I ain't gettin' any younger, Flint, and sometimes I think my hair is goin' to get a lot looser if I keep foolin' around the Sioux. Not from old age, you understand. You see what I mean?"

Miles blew a smoke ring. "The way you're going about it,

Bat, you're safe enough. You're hardly ever out of range of those Remington rolling-blocks anymore."

Bat spat juicily and wiped his mouth on a sleeve. "Hell, them Sioux ain't likely to bother us this side of the Crazy Woman."

"How do you know that?" said Miles.

Bat shifted his green eyes. "Just guessin'," he said quickly.

"Where the hell have you been laying low these past days?"

Bat stood up. "What's that to you?" he said.

"All right to cross, Bat?" called out Jonas Carlisle from the other side of the river.

Bat shifted into character, striding to the edge of the river, his thrums fluttering in the night breeze. "Come on with them longhorns!" he yelled. "Water is shallow and bottom is hard. Ain't hide nor ha'r of a hostile for miles."

Miles walked to the edge of the river. Bat was shrewd enough to know that Miles wouldn't have been sitting there smoking if there were hostiles around. The herd was lowing and bellowing as it streamed toward the crossing. The moonlight was almost as bright as day now, and the crossing was safe enough. It might have been dangerous if it had rained as hard here as it had farther south. He saw the white tilts of the wagons moving toward the river and wondered how Lorena was. Rather than see her he walked to the bay and rode along the riverbank downstream from the noisy herd. Where had Bat been those few days? Probably holed up in the hills.

A mile from the crossing Miles drew rein and slid from the bay. He picked up his rifle and padded forward, keeping in the cover of the brush and trees, which were thinning out. He stayed behind cover and watched the broken hills. Something moved a little on one of them. Miles took out his field-glasses and focused on the hill. A wolf sat up there, watching the moonlight glittering on the water. Miles studied the face of the beast, and an instant before it moved out of sight he recognized it as a human face painted to resemble a wolf's. The pointed ears and long snout belonged to the wolf pelt that covered the scout. To the Sioux the words "scout" and "wolf" are interchangeable. Even as he scanned the moonlit hill he heard the howling of a wolf drifting down toward him. A moment later the haunting cry seemed to echo from the far side of the river and then again from the bottom timber further downstream.

Miles led the bay back toward the herd. He glanced over his shoulder and saw that the wolf had returned to the hillside. From its movements, in absolute mimicry of a wolf, it was hard to tell that it was indeed a man within that furry pelt.

Miles dropped a hand to his Sharps but thought better of it. There was no percentage in killing one scout.

The words of Bat Batteau came back to him as he neared the camp. "Hell, them Sioux ain't likely to bother us this side of the Crazy Woman." Had Bat been guessing *or did he know something?* Why had he been so anxious to get rid of Miles?

The herd was bedded down on the north side of the river. The smoke of the dying fires hung low in the bottoms. Now and then the mournful howling of wolves drifted down to the camp, and the Texans who rode night herd tightened their grips on the long-barreled Remingtons across their thighs. A wolf might slip in to rip at a young cow.

"Wolves is yella," said Bat Batteau as he emptied his whiskey glass and looked sideways at the half-full bottle on the folding table. "They won't bother them cows tonight."

Lorena Carlisle glanced at the lean man who sat just beyond the fire, his face alternately in darkness and in dim light as he drew on his cigar. Miles had hardly said a word since dinner.

Jonas Carlisle sipped at his whiskey. "Just the same," he said. "They don't seem much afraid of us. Actually it isn't really the wolves I'm thinking about. It's those human wolves somewhere beyond those hills that are bothering me."

Bat waved a careless hand. "Trust me and the Rees," he said. "You'll know when the Sioux are about. We done all right so far, ain't we? You ain't seen a one of 'em, have you?"

"No," admitted Jonas. "What's your opinion, Miles?"

Miles took the cigar from his mouth. "You should have your scouts at least half a day ahead of you from now on."

Bat shot Miles a killing glance. "That's my work, Flint," he said. "*I'm* doing the scouting for this drive."

Miles shrugged. "Then why don't you tell him those aren't wolves up in those hills?"

Bat flushed. He reached for the whiskey bottle.

Jonas stared at Miles. "If those aren't wolves, what are they?"

"Ask Bat," said Miles. "Like he said, *he's* doing the scouting."

Bat drained half the glass and wiped his mouth. "All right! All right!" he snapped. "Them are Sioux scouts up in them hills. I say the same thing about them I said about the wolves. They're yella, and besides, they won't bother us at night."

Lorena looked nervously toward the hills. "Will they watch us all night?"

"Don't worry none, ma'am," said Bat. "Me and the Rees will watch over yuh all right."

"Right from the camp." said Miles dryly. He stood up. "The day I killed those three buffalo there were Sioux scouts practically within sight of the herd, but Bat and his Rees didn't see them. A party of them crossed the Powder right here shortly before dusk. I saw lights north of the buttes after dusk, and there are no white men living there or even traveling there. Jonas, *we're riding right through the middle of them.* So far, perhaps out of pure luck but probably for some perverse reason of their own, they haven't hit you, *but they will when you least expect it!* Perhaps not a full-scale attack at first, but more of a whittling process until they've weakened you enough to stop you. Keep the herd bunched from now on. Don't let one driver get beyond rifle range of the next two drivers. Above all, if you must rely on Bat and his Rees, *make them get out where they belong!* They can't see, smell, or hear Sioux riding within sight of the herd. Right now they're absolutely useless and it's downright foolhardy to depend upon them."

Bat dropped his empty whiskey glass and stood up to face Miles. "What was that you said, Flint?" he said in a low tone.

"You heard me, Bat. By God, try to do your job! These people are depending on you, or doesn't that make any difference to you?" said Miles.

Jonas got to his feet. "Bat does his best, Miles," he said. "I want no trouble here."

Miles looked at Jonas. "You're paying this man for a job he isn't doing and never intended doing. At the first sign of real trouble he and his Rees will stampede worse than your longhorns did."

Bat shot a sideways glance at Jonas. "He's been drinkin' too much," he said.

"He's letting me do his work," said Miles. "He knows as long as I am out ahead of the herd I'm not going to allow you to run into the Sioux, but I can't cover all of the country between here and the Gallatin. Sometime, sooner or later, they'll get in at you unless Bat and his Rees do their job."

"No man talks about me that way and gets away with it!" snarled Bat.

"I am," said Miles quietly. "Keep your hand away from that pistol. You're risking the lives of these people playing at being scout."

Bat spat at Miles's feet. "He's jealous of me. I know plenty about him, Mister Carlisle. They say he's made deals with the hostiles before. Deny *that,* Flint!"

It was very quiet around the dying fire. Lorena stood up

and looked at Miles. Jonas placed his whiskey glass on the table. "What does he mean, Miles?" he said.

"I've done some trading in the past with some tribal groups for the right to hunt buffalo in their country. The Sioux and Cheyenne and the Arapahoes. They were small groups, not the whole tribe."

"You see what I mean?" crowed Bat. "He speaks their tongue. He knows their ways. He rides right through their country alone and is never bothered. How do yuh know he ain't already made a deal with them for the cattle, rifles, horses, and the *woman?*"

Miles stepped close to the scout, gripped him by the front of his fancy beaded jacket, and hit him with a short right jab that sent him staggering back against the table, scattering glasses, bottle, plates, and cutlery across the ground. Bat cursed and clawed for his pistol, but Miles closed the gap, hit him in the gut with a left hook, and followed with a right hook to the jaw that sent him smashing back against a wagon wheel. Bat rushed Miles, both arms flailing. Miles sidestepped and jumped back, tripping over a fallen chair. He went down on one knee.

Bat ripped his knife loose from its fringed beaded sheath. The dying firelight glistened from the shiny blade. Miles fell backward, driving both feet up into Bat's lean gut, raising him into the air as the blade swiped an inch away from Miles's sweating face. Miles dumped Bat on his head, then leaped to his feet to stamp a foot down on the scout's knife wrist.

Something hit Miles alongside the head. He reeled sideways and went down on one knee again. His senses reeled. Vaguely he heard Lorena screaming and the silvery chiming of spurs before he was hit again. He went down flat on his face, blood running into his dazed eyes, and rolled over to look up into the gray, expressionless face of Beck Sterret. The Texan's pistol was in his hand.

Bat had rolled up onto his feet like a cat to charge at his helpless opponent. The Colt in Beck's hand barked flatly, and the knife spun out of Bat's hand. He grunted in savage pain as he gripped his tingling hand. The echo of the shot fled through the bottoms and died away in the hills.

Miles pressed his hands to the ground to get up on his feet. His head was spinning.

"Keep yore hands away from thet sixgun," said Beck coldly.

Miles looked up at him. "When I reach for it, Sterret," he said quietly, "you'll likely damned soon know about it."

"Any time," said Sterret politely. "But not heah and now."

Jonas helped Miles to his feet. "Are you all right?" he said anxiously.

Miles nodded. He gingerly felt his lacerated scalp. "Mister Sterret buffaloes like an expert," he said dryly. "Some day I hope to pay him back with interest."

Miles picked up the whiskey bottle and drank deeply. "Thanks for the drink, Mister Carlisle," said he.

"Lorena," said Jonas. "Get bandages and medicines."

Miles shook his head. "Don't bother," he said. "Ernie can give me a hand." He did not look at Lorena. He wiped the blood from the side of his head and walked unsteadily toward the chuckwagon. Bat stood there, his eyes filled with hate, as he watched Miles walk away.

Beck Sterret looked at Jonas. "I had a feelin' somethin' like this would happen. Those two Yankees been primin' for a hassle for days. I wouldn't have the two of them together in my camp."

Jonas shrugged. "I haven't much choice, Beck."

"I ain't sayin' Flint is wrong about Batteau."

"If I leave," said Bat sullenly, "the Rees leave with me."

Neither of the two men spoke. It was as if they hadn't heard the scout speak at all.

Bat picked up his knife and inspected the blade. The slug had struck the heavy brass backing of the blade and nicked it deeply. He slid the weapon into its beaded sheath. "That was a lucky shot for Flint," he said.

Beck Sterret holstered his Colt. "That wasn't a lucky shot, Batteau," he said. "I *meant* it for the knife. But then again, it might have been a lucky shot for *you*."

Bat knew what the trail boss meant. He swaggered away from the pool of firelight.

The crying of the wolves came through the windy darkness. They seemed much closer now to the camp and to the herd.

CHAPTER TEN

The herd moved out at dawn the next day to begin the drive to Crazy Woman Creek. Beck Sterret had roused his men an hour before dawn, but there had been no sign of the Sioux and the hills had been empty and quiet except for the twittering of the birds. Beck had Old Brimstone's bell clapper loosed, and the big lead steer had started out along the ruts of the Bozeman Trail, his bell echoing from the hills until the noise of the herd's passage drowned it out.

The eyes of the drivers studied those quiet and ominous hills as the sun arose, but nothing happened. As the sun climbed higher the spirits of the Texans returned. They had two features they depended on to beat off any Sioux attack—the rolling-block rifles and the fact that most of the drivers were Texans. What more could one want? As far as the Texans were concerned, they could have eliminated the rolling-block rifles and come up with the same answer, Texans being what they say they are, and *usually* are.

Northwest, toward the distant and unseen Crazy Woman, under the clear morning sky and then under the cloud-dotted sky of early afternoon, with the bitter dust wreathing up and the ground shaking under thousands of hooves, moved the great herd of longhorns. Now and then the keenest sighted drivers thought they saw a lone horseman on the distant hills, but he would disappear before they were quite sure they had seen anything at all. The herd flowed smoothly up, over, and down the spurs of the hills, making good time toward the Crazy Woman after the noon halt. The cattle had been well watered at the Powder, and Beck Sterret had determined to drive on through the darkness to reach the Crazy Woman, a hard and waterless day's drive but well worth the effort—if the Sioux did not interfere. Maybe Beck had been right. Maybe the Sioux would not challenge the herd. They had had enough opportunities.

Late in the afternoon one of Bat's Rees, farther ahead of the herd then usual, stopped his pony between the faint ruts of the Bozeman and swung his dirty blanket back and forth over his head. Bat and the rest of the Rees, in a fan-shaped scouting front but still close enough to the herd drivers for support in case of an attack, galloped to the lone Ree. The scouts sat their horses in the middle of the road. Jonas Carlisle and Beck Sterret joined the group. Miles Flint, working along the east side of the valley, turned the bay to join them. There seemed to be something uneasy about them, something ominous.

Miles's aching head was pounding beneath the bandage when he neared the group. There was something in the middle of the road. Miles drew rein and looked at it. In the center of the road was a heap of stones from which protruded a red painted pole. To one side of the stones was a buffalo cow skull and on the other was a buffalo bull skull, both of them freshly daubed with red paint. The pole slanted toward the cow skull.

"What does it mean, Bat?" said Jonas.

Bat glanced at Miles.

"I'm asking *you,* Bat!" snapped Jonas.

Miles hooked a leg around his pommel and felt for a cigar. "War trail," he said. He lighted the cigar. "Red arrow, or buffalo skull sometimes, marks a war trail."

Beck Sterret looked up at Miles. "For us or them?"

Miles blew a smoke ring. "What difference does that make? It's a warning for us. Go no further, it means."

Beck spat tobacco at the bull's skull, splashing it liberally. "In a pig's eye," he said.

"They're just being polite. Formal," said Miles. "They didn't have to put this here."

"What does it mean?" said Jonas.

Miles leaned forward in his saddle. "It simply means that if you pass it, the Sioux will fight like buffalo bulls and we'll fight like women."

"Bullshit!" said Beck.

Miles looked at the Rees. "You'd better hogtie that bunch, Sterret, or you won't see them at dawn," he said.

"I'll take care of them Rees!" said Bat angrily.

"Best scouts and fighters on the Plains, Bat," said Miles.

Jonas looked at Miles. "What do you suggest, Miles?"

Miles looked at the empty hills and the ridge ahead of the oncoming herd. "It's your decision. There's an old saying that applies to this, and the Sioux have put the choice squarely in your trail."

"Such as?" said Beck Sterret.

"Crap or get off the pot. Put up or shut up," said Miles. "It's as simple as that."

"How far is the Crazy Woman?" said Jonas.

"Fifteen miles maybe," said Miles. "You won't make it today."

"There's no watah out heah," said the trail boss.

"You can make a dry camp or push on with thirsty, tired cattle," said Miles. "You know how easy they can be stampeded when they're like that. The Sioux can move in after dark and stampede them if you're on the trail. It wouldn't be so easy if you bunched them under guard and pushed on before dawn."

"The Sioux won't fight at night," said Bat.

"They won't have to," said Miles. "They can stampede the herd tonight without even being seen. They can do it half a dozen ways. They can set fire to the grass upwind, for one thing."

Jonas took out a cigar and bit off the end. "Maybe we should have stayed at the Powder awhile."

Beck kicked the bull skull, his spur ringing clearly. "Yuh sayin' I made a mistake, Jonas?"

"Hell no, Beck! I was all for it this morning. I was just thinking out loud."

Miles shifted in his saddle. "Have those Rees take a look-see over that ridge, Jonas," he said.

"I'm chief of scouts here!" said Bat angrily.

Miles looked at him. "Then you tell them," he said quietly.

Beck shoved back his hat and eyed the ridge. "I wonder if they'd jump us if we stayed on this side of the skulls tonight?"

Miles shrugged. "You can't ever tell," he said. Beck was beginning to get the idea. The Sioux meant exactly what they said. They never indulged in useless talk.

"All right, Bat," said Jonas. "Go on."

Bat wiped his mouth both ways. "Is that an order?" he said nervously.

"It will be full daylight for at least an hour," said Miles. "That is, if you're afraid of the dark, Bat."

Bat looked down at the skulls lying in the middle of the road. He knew as well as Miles did what it meant to pass them. *Crap or get off the pot,* Flint had said. It was a simple as that.

There was a sudden flash of crisp metal action. Bat found himself looking into the cold metal eye of the converted Navy Colt Beck Sterret carried and used so uncommonly well. "*Git,* you, and earn yore keep!" said Beck Sterret.

Bat got. He quirted his horse and set off at a gallop, followed by his Rees, like a small flock of ragged, half-starved crows, their filthy blankets hanging about their lean hips and floating behind them in the wind of their passage.

"Useless sonofabitch," said Beck. He let down the hammer of his Colt, sheathed it, then walked with softly chiming steps to his gray. "Well, Jonas, do we stay or move?"

"We stay here tonight," said Jonas.

Beck spurred toward the oncoming herd, waving his dusty hat in a circle over his head. Immediately the point drivers turned in the lead, led by Old Brimstone, so that the longhorns began a slow mill. The dust churned up and drifted off on the wind, shot through with the slanting rays of the sinking sun.

Jonas watched Bat and his Rees riding toward the ridge. "I wish I had taken your advice on them long ago, Miles," he said. "I could almost smell their green fear, amongst other things. God forgive me for making such a mistake."

"Bat puts on a prime act," said Miles. "He can fool some of the best of them."

They rode toward the dust-shrouded herd. The wind had

shifted, and the heat of the massed cattle seemed to strike at their faces.

"A dry camp," said Jonas reflectively. "I don't like this."

One of the Texans suddenly stood up in his stirrups and pointed with his rifle toward the ridge. A shot flatted off down the wind, and the echo died away in the hills.

Miles and Jonas turned in their saddles. The Rees were riding like furies down the slope, lashing their ponies at each stride. A hundred yards ahead of them was Bat Batteau, his exaggerated thrums whipping in the wind. Bat had won many a horse race on Saturday afternoons at Fort Laramie. He could have cleaned up any field of racers this day. His hat blew off and floated behind him, held by the barbequejo strap. His right arm was like a piston as it wielded the quirt on the flanks of his horse.

"Jesus God," said Jonas in an awed voice. "Look at that!"

The ridge had suddenly bloomed as the desert blooms after a spring flash storm, but there was no greenery or flowers on the ridge. It had bloomed hundreds of horsemen sitting mounts of every conceivable coloring, piebalds and paints, duns, bays, sorrels, claybanks, whites and off-whites, grays and appaloosas. War bonnets, worn only by the bravest of the brave, rippled in the dry wind. Coup sticks fluttered with colored feathers. Scalps fluttered from poles or from the fringing of leggings, while a few of the greatest warriors, the war-chiefs, had them at their horse's bits. The sun flashed from white pipe-bone breastplates, rifle barrels, pipe-axes, and other weapons.

Even the tough, battlewise Texans were hushed. They had never seen anything like this.

It was beneath the dignity of the Sioux to chase Bat Batteau and his corn Indians. These were *fighting* men, these Tetons. They sat their horses in the dying sunlight looking down impassively on the vast herd of cattle that filled the center of the valley.

"Will they attack?" said Jonas.

Miles uncased his glasses and focused them on the Sioux, scanning the long line of fierce, high-cheekboned, noble-nosed, painted faces. His glasses settled on a chief in the center of the line. His great war bonnet trailed almost to the heels of his appaloosa, and the fluffy breath feathers that trimmed the bonnet itself moved fitfully in the dry wind. Miles narrowed his eyes. He had seen that fierce visage once before, when he had ridden with Nelson Story. A touch of fear came into his mind.

"Miles?" said Jonas.

Miles lowered the glasses. "Not now. The war shields are

still in their covers. I think it's only a show to put the fear of God into us."

Beck Sterret had ridden up beside Jonas. "Scare who?" he said. He spat tobacco. "Let me have twenty men, Jonas. *Texans*. I'll drive them from thet ridge befoah dusk."

Miles looked at him. "By God, Sterret," he said quietly, "they might not scare you but they sure as hell scare me."

Beck spat again. He wiped his mouth. "Indians," he said. with vast contempt.

Miles cased his glasses. "That happens to be the band of Ota Kte of the Oglalas. His name means Plenty Kills, and you'd better, by God, believe it means just that."

"Will they attack tonight?" said Jonas.

Miles shook his head. "But the wolves will be in close, Jonas. None of them want to die at night, but if they think their medicine is good, they'll take a chance at a guard or in snapping up a horse. Best to get the whole corrida up an hour before dawn. It will be a lonely night for some of these younger Texas boys." Miles turned the bay and rode toward the herd.

Some of the herd had already begun to graze, and others had dropped to rest. The wagons had been corraled. The remuda was kept between the herd and the wagons. It would be hard for the young Sioux scouts not to take a crack at those horses. It was in their blood. The drivers went about their business, but they were quieter than usual, and none of them could help but steal sideways glances up at that ridge, feeling those hundreds of fierce eyes that seemed to leap the gap between ridge and herd and to strike into a man's innermost soul.

Suddenly, just as they had appeared, and almost as one, as though lifted from the ridge as a clerk would lift boxes of painted lead Indians from a toy-shop window, the warriors were gone. There was nothing to mark their passage except a lone feather blowing down the ridge toward the camp. Then the sun was gone, and the warm and windy darkness flowed into the great valley between the rolling hills and the distant Big Horns.

Miles walked through the darkness carrying the valuable snow-back pelt, still wrapped and concealed from view. He would stand guard that night as the others would, and he had stripped cantle and pommel packs from the bay. He could not carry the heavy pelt with him into action. The smell of burning buffalo chips hung over the camp mingled with the strong odor of the herd. It was quiet except for the occasional bawling of a thirsty steer, but the ominous darkness seemed to have quieted even them. Still, it wouldn't take much to get them going.

The fire within the wagon corral had been banked with earth. The drivers paced around the corral, long rifles held in the crooks of their arms, peering into the darkness. Each man had a horse saddled and tethered inside the corral. There was the faintest suggestion of moonlight in the eastern sky, but it only seemed to accentuate the thick, velvety darkness in the great valley.

A wolf howled from the ridge. A moment later another howled east of the herd. One after another the sound came until it had traveled completely around the great herd. God alone knew how many of them were out there, creeping closer and closer in the concealing darkness. The moonlight might drive them off. Bat and his frightened Rees had been sent out beyond the perimeter of the camp after each Ree had been daubed with clay moistened by the spit of Horns-in-Front, their leader. Miles placed no reliance on them. Fear might have already winged their dirty moccasins and sent them flying through the darkness toward the Powder. Still, they might be afraid to leave the protection of the trail herders.

Miles padded toward Jonas, who leaned on a rifle near the fire, an unlighted cigar in his mouth. "Indian Summer," said Miles dryly.

"It sure as hell is," said the trail herder.

Miles held out the bundled pelt. "Can you keep this in one of your wagons?"

"Sure, Miles. What is it?"

"A buffalo pelt, Jonas."

Jonas shrugged. "What's so valuable about that?"

Miles looked about. "It's an albino. On the market it's worth its weight in silver. Big medicine to an Indian, too."

"I wondered why you were so damned secretive about it. Let me have it. I'll keep it in the supply wagon." Jonas took the pelt and walked to the wagon in front of the one where he and Lorena bunked. He stowed it inside and drew the cover tightly together. "I don't want to disturb Lorena tonight so I'll sleep in this wagon." He laughed dryly. "Not that I expect much sleep tonight."

Miles walked over toward the outer line of wagons.

"Who goes dere?" came a frightened challenge.

"Miles Flint," said Miles. "How do you like standing guard, Pomp?"

"Not much. Sho' is a lot of Indians 'round heah, Mistah Flint."

Miles grinned. "Don't worry, Pomp. They will not attack tonight."

"Oh, Lawd!" said Pomp. "I hope not!"

Miles padded through the darkness. Someone was standing between two wagons. Miles reached out a hand and touched the softness of a breast. "Sorry, Lorena," he said quickly.

"You didn't know it was me," she said. She eyed him. Or did he know?

"You shouldn't be here alone," he said.

She leaned back against the wagon. "I have a gun," she said.

"Do you know how to use it?"

"Yes. Beck said to use only five of the six rounds if I had to." She looked at him again. "The sixth round is for me, if it comes to that."

"God forbid!"

She looked out in the darkness again. "I asked you long ago what they did to white women. You never told me," she said.

He looked down at her. The memory of what he had seen years ago came back to him. The torn and ravaged bodies of white women who had been "passed on the prairie," by every buck in a large war party.

"Miles?" she said. She placed a hand on his forearm.

The moonlight had touched the eastern hills. Something moved atop one of them—a wolf, or the next thing to it. It moved its head a little, and the whitish face peered back and forth exactly like that of a wolf. It raised its head. The opened mouth poured forth the melancholy, haunting cry.

"Lorena!" called Jonas. "Where are you?"

She touched Miles's face with a soft, cool hand and then was gone. Miles studied the scout atop the hill. A long shot in the bad light. Another wolf howled. Miles could see him on the next hill, squatted on a hump, his head to one side. Miles could almost see in his mind's eye the grinning face and lolling tongue of a real wolf.

The great moon swung up slowly, flooding the valley with light. It was so bright that Miles could read the lettering stamped into the metal of his Sharps barrel. The wolves had vanished from sight, but they were still up there, as their howling indicated. They likely knew they were working on the nerves of the men who stood behind the wagons, or circled the herd, softly singing. There would be no attack in that moonlight.

The herd was restless with its gigantic thirst, and now and then a sleepwalker would rise and start out from the mass of longhorns, to be turned back by a driver. There would be no sleep that night. Ernie Masland had his banked fire between the chuckwagon and the bunched remuda, and the coffeepot was played heavily as the night wore on and the moon drifted slowly overhead, peering down blankly into the valley.

The moon was almost gone when Jonas came to find Miles. "Any sign of Bat and his Rees?" he said. "Cass Starr said he had seen two of them hanging around the remuda. No sign of Bat and the others, though. Maybe they pulled foot."

Miles shrugged. "Either that or they're lying plenty low," he said.

"We'll need them in close in this darkness," said Jonas.

Miles nodded. He handed his Sharps to Jonas. "I'll take a look-see," he said.

Miles stepped over a wagon tongue and walked softly along the line of wagons. He was more concerned about the guards then he was about skulking Sioux. He stopped now and then to listen. The ground was rolling, pitted here and there with great, shallow buffalo wallows. Miles shoved back his hat and rubbed his jaw. Wherever Bat was he was certainly lying low.

Miles stepped into a deeper than usual buffalo wallow. Something made him turn his head. A man stood at the lip of the wallow, looking down at Miles. If he hadn't been wearing a hat, he might have gotten a bowie blade slammed into his gut. "Thet you, Flint?" said Beck Sterret softly.

"Jesus God," said Miles in a strained tone. "You want to get yourself gutted with a Sioux knife. Get off that skyline!"

For once Beck Sterret had not heralded his coming with the chiming of his spurs. He came down the slope and faced Miles. "What are yuh doin' out heah?" he said softly.

"Looking for daisies," said Miles.

Beck raised a hand. "Damn yuh!" he snapped. "I asked yuh a question!"

"Jonas wanted me to look for Bat and his Rees."

Beck raised his head. "Out heah? They been back at the waggins for five minutes."

"Good," said Miles. "By God, I don't mind going back."

Beck did not move. "Somethin' mighty peculiar about yuh, Flint. Mebbe Bat was right at thet."

Miles stared at him. "What are you talking about?"

"I heard Bat say mor'n once he knew yuh had dealin's with Indians."

"You believe that lyin' sonofabitch?"

"No, but he made me think about it, Flint."

"This isn't the time or place for such talk, Sterret."

"Yuh make yoreself mighty big in yore boots, Flint. Comin' and goin' like yuh please. By God, yuh even acted like yuh *knowed* them Sioux was goin' to stop us today."

Miles tried to hold his temper. Sweat worked down his

sides and wet his shirt. "Get out of the way," he said thinly. "I've had enough of you this drive, Sterret."

"I thought once yuh was a squawman. I ain't so sure you ain't dealin' with these dirty redskins."

Beck Sterret was a fast man with fists, boots, or pistols, but he never saw the fist that smashed against his mouth, pasting his lips bloodily to his teeth. Before he could recover, a left smashed into his lean gut just above the big belt buckle, and as his head came down involuntarily his chin met a smashing right uppercut that snapped his head back. His breath sobbed bloodily in his throat as he went back and down under those terribly punishing blows.

Miles stepped back blowing on his skinned right knuckles. "That was for that buffaloing, you Texas sonofabitch," he said. "Get up. I've got a few more scores to settle with you, Sterret."

Beck Sterret lay there on his back, blood leaking darkly from his mouth, his eyes fixed on Miles. He could have drawn and killed Miles from where he lay but instead he got slowly to his feet. "Yuh Yankee sonofabitch," he said slowly through his smashed mouth, "I been waitin' for a chance like this." He rushed Miles, driving out a long left that Miles blocked but connecting with a right that smashed over Miles's heart, driving him back. Miles stopped Beck with a straight left jab, and the Texan closed, smashing down with booted feet on Miles's insteps as he slammed vicious and unscientific punches to Miles's face and belly. A knee drove up into Miles's crotch, and as he bent over he was hit on the jaw with a stinging right hook that sent him sprawling. He rolled over to escape the boot, grabbed the outthrust leg, and rammed himself up to his feet, upending the softly cursing trail boss so that his head hit the hard ground with stunning force. Beck rolled away from Miles's smashing feet and doubled himself on the ground until he seemed to uncoil like a tightly wound spring. His head drove up through Miles's guard and struck him on the chin, smashing his teeth together. He spat out blood and bits of powdered teeth as he drove a left against the Texan's nose, drawing blood, and then followed through with a right to the jaw that drove Beck back across the trampled grass.

They circled in the moonlight, as though the natural confines of the wallow were a fighting ring, all thought of guns and knives out of their minds as they reverted to the atavistic blood lust of savage fighting men to clash with fists, feet, and teeth.

They closed and shook each other with jolting savage punches that hurt each of them, but pain and fear were gone now. All that was left was the desire to make the other hurt and hurt again. Beck at last went down flat on his back from a slugging that would have knocked out a lesser man. He lay there looking up at Miles, then got up slowly and rushed Miles almost as though nothing had happened.

Three times Miles stopped the mad rush of the Texan. Blows sounded soggily as they struck sweat-wet, bloody flesh. Then a blow hit Miles. He had not seen it coming and it lifted his feet off the ground. He smashed down on his back looking up into the bruised and bloody face of Beck Sterret. He wasn't sure he could get up again but he *had* to.

Miles opened his mouth. He slapped his hand down to his side for his Remington. Beck jumped to one side and drew just as Miles fired. Miles rolled over and over on the ground as Beck slammed a shot inches from Miles's head. "Goddammit, Beck!" yelled Miles. "Behind you! Behind you!" He fired twice from the ground.

Beck whirled, and a pipe-axe slashed the air where his head had been. He instinctively fired from the hip. The soft slug hit the Sioux buck just below the breastbone. Another buck launched himself from the rim of the wallow toward Beck, and his knife reached out like a great fang for the throat of the Texan. Miles got to his knees and fired twice. The heavy slugs drove the buck to one side.

Beck dropped to one knee and fired upward toward the skylighted warrior who stood at the lip of the wallow. He fell heavily, thrashing about in silent agony, his nerveless legs flopping about. Miles's last shot mercifully killed him.

Moccasins slapped the hard ground beyond the wallow. The powdersmoke hung heavily, being slowly rifted by the dry wind. The echo of the last shot rolled along the hills and then died away. Men yelled from the herd camp.

Miles wiped the blood from his mouth as he got up. Dazedly he flipped open the loading gate of the Remington and filled the hot cylinder with fresh cartridges while Beck swiftly reloaded his Colt. It was typical of both men.

Rifles cracked from beyond the wallow. "Got the sonofabitch!" yelled Cotton.

The bearded face of Jonas Carlisle showed over the edge of the wallow. "For the love of God," he said. "How can they come this close without being seen?"

Cass Starr and Cotton appeared beside Jonas to look down at the two battered men standing there in the wreathing powdersmoke. "Chihuahua!" said Cass. "What happened to yore face, Beck?"

Beck wiped the blood from his face. "Run into a couple of 'em at close range is all," he said.

Three pairs of eyes flicked to Miles. "Me too," said Miles.

They walked together up the wallow slope and stood beside

the three men. Three pairs of knowing eyes flicked down to abraded knuckles and then up to swollen faces, bloody noses, and puffed lips. "It musta been one helluva fracas," said Cass dryly.

"Reload that gawddam' rifle!" snapped Beck. He walked beside Miles toward the dim tilts of the wagons.

"What the hell!" said Cotton. "What was they doin' out heah anyways?"

Jonas shouldered his rifle. "The ways of the Lord are sometimes inscrutable," he said quietly.

"What the hell does thet mean?" said Cotton.

Cass spat. "Sometimes yuh ought to read a book, Cotton," he said. "Thet is, if you *can* read."

Beck stopped beside the wagons. *"Gracias,"* he said.

Miles looked at him. *"Por nada,"* he said.

Beck nodded. He walked off into the darkness, and although his back was ramrod straight as usual, he swayed a little in his stride. Miles gripped a wagon wheel. He wasn't feeling so steady himself.

It was quiet in the camp; the herd had settled down despite their thirst. The hilltop wolves would be gone now. In the camp of the Sioux the squaws would soon be gashing their legs with skinning knives. They would wipe the blood on the faces of the "soldiers" of the warrior societies, pleading with them to avenge the dead. Their pleas would not go unfulfilled.

CHAPTER ELEVEN

The trail camp was quietly astir in the blackness of the predawn, each man walking and working as softly as possible, although they knew they could hardly fool the Sioux. Ernie Masland had kept his fire banked all night, and the coffee was bitter as gall. But no one complained. Each driver roped his horse, stuffed hardtack into his pockets, checked his supply of cartridges, filled his big canteen from the water barrel, and went about his business.

Miles Flint finished his second cup of coffee. He touched his bruised and swollen face. Ernie Masland had studiously avoided mentioning anything about it, but everyone had a damned good idea of what had happened out there in that buffalo wallow. Fact is, both men had been on their feet, with three dead bucks lying in their own blood in the wallow. Hell's fire, it must have been a classic fight between the big Yankee and the hard-bitten Texan, and, begod, not a man to see it except a few dirty Sioux who hadn't lived long enough to talk about it.

Miles fashioned his cantle roll and swung it over the bay. He fastened it, then filled his canteen.

Chip Macklin came toward the chuckwagon. "Mistuh Carlisle heah?" he said.

"Ain't seen him, Chip," said Ernie.

"Likely out with the herd," said Miles.

Cass Starr led his claybank past the chuckwagon. "I just come back from theah," he said. "He ain't out theah, Chip."

Pomp came through the darkness. "I come for coffee for Mistuh and Mis' Carlisle, Mistuh Masland," he said.

"Help yourself, Pomp," said the cocinero. "Mister Carlisle is over there then?"

Pomp shook his head. "He didn' sleep in his Studebaker," he said.

Miles checked his Sharps and slung it. "He said he was going to sleep in one of the supply wagons," he said.

"I been callin' for him, suh," said Pomp.

Beck Sterret chimed into the group. "Wheah's them damned scouts?" he demanded.

Cass Starr shrugged. "Ain't seen them since around moonset," he said.

"Mistuh Carlisle with you, suh?" asked Pomp.

Beck shook his head. As he helped himself to a cup of coffee the faint light of the shielded lantern struck his battered face. "I ain't seen him since last night," he said.

Pomp stood there bewildered.

Miles placed a hand on the Negro's shoulder. "Take the coffee and some biscuits over there, Pomp," he said. "I'll find Mister Carlisle."

Miles walked with Chip Macklin toward the wagons. "Ain't like him," said Chip. "Mis' Carlisle been askin' for him."

Miles saw Lorena standing beside her wagon, dressed in her Confederate gray riding habit, her mare tethered to the wheel beside her. Miles walked to the supply wagon where Jonas had stowed the buffalo pelt. Chip Macklin had already harnessed the mules to it.

"Jonas?" said Miles.

There was no answer. Miles parted the wagon cover. "Jonas?" he said. He waited a moment and then thrust in a hand. Something sliced into the side of it. He snatched back his hand and thrust it into his mouth. "Damn it! He stuck me with a knife!" he said.

"Mister Carlisle?" said Chip. "That ain't likely, Miles."

Chip pulled aside the cover and snapped a match on his thumbnail. "Jesus God!" he said. He quickly dropped the cover and looked back at Lorena Carlisle.

"What is it, man?" said Miles.

"Look for yourself," said the wagon driver. "But don't let her see!"

Miles pulled back the cover and lighted a match. In the wavering light he saw Jonas Carlisle lying face downward on a pile of sacks. Something alien protruded from the trail driver's back. It was a yellowish-white, bone-handled knife, and it was buried almost to the hilt in Jonas Carlisle's body. It was that which had cut Miles. He dropped the cover and looked quickly toward Lorena.

Somewhere in the darkness a driver had loosed Old Brimstone's bell clapper. It sounded clearly through the darkness. The herd was grunting to its feet.

Lorena walked toward Miles and Chip. Spurs chimed behind her, and Beck Sterret, with that uncanny sixth sense of his, showed up where the trouble was. "What is it, Miles?" said Lorena.

Miles looked away. He gripped the side of the wagon

"Miles?" she said.

"Yuh got to tell her, Miles," said Chip out of the side of his mouth.

"Don't look in the wagon," said Miles to Lorena.

She looked uncertainly at him. "He's in theah, isn't he?"

Miles nodded.

"He's hurt?" she said quietly.

Miles looked at Beck Sterret. The Texan nodded. Miles took the young woman by the shoulders. "Jonas is dead," he said softly.

She buried her head against his chest, and her body shook. Miles looked over her head at Beck. "God knows how they got in this close."

Beck looked at the woman, and his meaning was clear. *Thank God they hadn't gotten to her.*

Lorena raised her head. She fought to compose herself. "What shall we do now?" she said.

Beck took off his hat. "It's yore herd now, ma'am," he said simply. "I got to take yore orders, ma'am."

She raised her head again and looked at the tough trail boss, at homely Chip Macklin, at little Pomp, and then at Miles Flint. "The way to the Gallatin is north," she said.

Beck smiled swiftly, then turned on his heel. He chimed

off into the darkness to get the herd moving toward the crossing of the Crazy Woman.

Lorena stepped back from Miles. "There's no time to bury him properly heah," she said. A tear rolled down her cheek. "We'll take my husband's body to the Crazy Woman and bury him theah, gentlemen." She turned and walked to her mare.

Miles nodded to Chip. The driver tied the cover shut and walked to the front of the wagon. As the first faint touch of false dawn made itself known in the eastern sky the wagons rolled on behind the slowly moving herd.

Miles looked at Lorena. She touched her mare lightly with her quirt and rode on after the wagons. This day would be one of pure hell for her.

Miles walked to his bay and untethered it. He swung up into the saddle and rode toward the front of the herd. Beck Sterret turned in his saddle. "God help her," he said.

Miles nodded. "Where are Bat and his Rees?"

"Pulled foot," said the trail boss.

"I thought so," said Miles.

"We'll have to go on without them, Flint."

Miles shoved back his hat and felt for a cigar. He lighted it. "I'll try to keep one ridge ahead of you, Sterret," he said. "About all I can do is warn you. You'll likely have no more than a few minutes to get ready, but it might mean the difference between life and death." He touched the bay with his heels and galloped off into the lonely darkness ahead of the herd.

Cass Starr shifted his chew and spat. "Theah goes a man, Beck," he said.

Beck Sterret did not answer. He touched his gray with his spurs and rode down the side of the herd, his hard gray eyes, one of them well puffed, taking in everything.

The wind shifted with the coming of the false dawn. Each shadow on the rolling ground seemed to hold hidden menace to the drivers, and they gripped their Remingtons just a little tighter.

Miles Flint felt the cool wind against his bruised face. The ridge was a dim line against the northern horizon like a barrier between the herd and the Sioux. To Miles it was more of a psychological barrier than the red-daubed buffalo skulls had been. An uneasy feeling came to rest on his shoulders. He passed beyond the sound of the herd and seemed to move into a little world of his own as he rode up the slope of the ridge. Far behind him the herd moved north. Old Brimstone was squarely in the middle of the road, as was his custom. His hooves struck the pile of stones, snapped the red-painted pole, and scattered the red-painted skulls. The grinding hooves of the herd smashed the skulls into powder. It was too late to go back now.

Miles loosed the Spencer carbine in its sheath. Jonas had issued him one from his supply of extra weapons. Miles preferred the stubby carbine to the longer-ranged single-shot Remingtons. The repeater carried seven rounds of bottle-necked .56/50 caliber cartridges in the magazine and one more in the chamber, and he had three brass reloading tubes containing seven cartridges each with which he could refill the butt magazine in jig time. With the repeating carbine and his Remington pistol he could give a good account of himself at short range, but it would hardly be adequate to stop a concerted charge of Cheyenne Dog Soldiers or Sioux Kit Foxes. The Sharps could hold off an attack at the longer ranges. If he was wounded or unhorsed at the outset of a fight, he wouldn't stand a chance.

He breasted the crest of the ridge. There was no time to scout by sight, sound, or smell. He'd have to look right now and keep pushing on if there was no sign of the hostiles. The northern slope was empty of life as far as he could see. The grass was moving dimly in the faint light as the wind swept it. There was no odor of pony droppings or of burning buffalo chips.

As the light grew brighter he could see much farther, and by the time he reached the next ridge he could see that the country, so far at least, was empty of the Sioux. He eased the bay. He might need all of his reserve strength before too long. An eerie loneliness came over him. The old gnawing fear of the plainsman came to roost in his mind. What was beyond those empty-looking hills?

He looked back to see Old Brimstone top the last ridge, followed by the other lead steers and guided by the two point riders. Suddenly the rising sun flashed from the many horns of the cattle. Miles lighted a cigar. The Sioux were experts in hitting you where and when you least expected it. There were no finer light cavalry in the world, and it was a gigantic error to think that they wouldn't or couldn't fight under their own type of discipline.

Hour after hour passed slowly by, with the trail dust rising into the bright sunlight. Beck Sterret would allow no noon halt. There would be no water before the Crazy Woman. The trail drivers changed mounts practically on the move and raced back to their posts. But there was still no sign of the Sioux—not even a pile of droppings from one of their ponies.

Miles found it hard to believe when at last he reined in the bay and looked far down the long grassy slope toward the crossing of the Crazy Woman. The willows and cottonwoods bordering the stream swayed in the dry wind. Heat waves shimmered up from the ground, and the late-afternoon sun sparkled from the rippling waters. Miles lighted a cigar. "Beats the hell outta me," he said thoughtfully.

Maybe the Oglalas thought their medicine had failed because of the deaths of their scouts the night before. Those who had died could not cross the Great Shadow Waters because they had been killed at night. It wouldn't be fear of the white men, but rather fear of their medicine that might be holding them back.

Miles heard, faintly at first, the bawling of the cattle and the braying of the mules as the shifting wind brought the tantalizing scent of the fresh water to them. He turned to look back at them. Old Brimstone rose over a ridge and strode steadily down the center of the faint track of the Bozeman. Beck Sterret rode close beside him, his right hand resting lightly on Old Brimstone's left horn tip. Two of a kind, thought Miles; set them to a job and they'll do it, come hell or high water.

The herd came closer and closer. The wagons jounced and bounced over the rougher ground. Lashes popped over the long, dusty ears of the mules. Dust swirled thickly down the slopes. The way was clear to the Crazy Woman at least; Miles had done the job that should have been done by Bat Batteau and his Rees. He stood up in his stirrups. He had been lucky at that, for one man could hardly cover all the approaches to the Crazy Woman. He sat down and kneed the bay toward the closest hills. From the top of one of them he could see the country northeasterly along the valley of the Crazy Woman. He urged the tired bay up the slope.

Somewhere behind him, beyond the Bozeman Trail, in the cut-up ground thickly strewn with trees, a sound arose like grease popping in a gigantic skillet. Miles snapped his head around. A sickle of feathered horsemen seemed to rise out of the ground itself, to the west of the herd *and almost behind it*. They screamed and fired, while some of them flapped blankets to stampede the tired, thirsty longhorns. Miles hurled his cigar aside and launched the bay down the slope. He had done his part by seeing that the way *ahead* of the herd was clear. But the Sioux, knowing there was only one scout ahead of the herd, had played it smart by *tailing* the herd, because Bat Batteau and his Rees had not been there as they should have been to cut for Sioux sign and warn the trail drivers.

Damn Beck Sterret! The thought raged through Miles's mind as he raced toward the herd. The Texan should have flung out some of his men to watch the vulnerable flanks of the herd and to take up some of the shock of that swiftly approaching charge. Even a Texan should have known enough to do that! Where the hell had *he* gone to war!

The remuda stampeded, smashing into the line of fast-moving wagons. Rifles began to flash and crack from the wagons and from the flanks of the herd. Here and there in the swirling dust blossomed orange-red bursts of gunfire.

Three horses, driven by two shrieking bucks, broke from the remuda and raced along the slope. Another buck rode right into the center of the remuda and transferred himself from his paint pony to the back of a rearing sorrel, clinging like a monkey on a stick, guiding the sorrel through the press, followed by the paint pony. Only a leg and an arm showed as target for the cursing Texans.

A knot of pounding steers struck the side of the chuckwagon just as it hit the ruts and bounced up on two wheels. The weight of the steers dumped it over, wheels spinning, and the mules began to kick each other to death in the tangle of harness. A supply wagon smashed into the dumped chuckwagon, and the driver flew from the seat, arms outspread, just as a buck drove in close and fired a double-barreled shotgun full into his face. He was dead before he hit the ground.

Miles reined in the bay and fired swiftly, three times, slamming the lever down and up and firing the instant the breech was closed. A warrior's horse went down. A buck died with a slug in his screaming mouth. A third buck badly wounded bounced on the hard ground, dragged by his frightened pony.

Beck Sterret and Cass Starr drove into a knot of Sioux, firing six-shooters from both hands, and left half a dozen Sioux dead or writhing on the dusty ground.

A dozen horses had been driven off along with at least fifty longhorns, but the herd was on its way to the waters of the Crazy Woman and nothing could stop them, and to hell with the Texans, the Sioux, and everything else.

Miles emptied the smoking Spencer, flipped open the loading gate in the butt plate, and poured in seven fresh rounds in a matter of seconds. He kneed the lathered bay toward the herd, slamming shot after shot into the speeding feathered horsemen who appeared and disappeared in the thick swirling cloud of dust.

The Sioux were breaking for the ridge, driving the captured longhorns and horses ahead of them. Here and there other warriors held onto the flanks of the herd and snapped shots at the dusty Texans. Beck Sterret led a quartet of drivers toward the captured animals. Miles raced toward them. He drove his bay close beside the trail boss. "For God's sake, don't follow them over that ridge. Sterret! They're waiting for you! They'll cut you to pieces! Let them have those longhorns!"

Beck stared at Miles through a mask of dust. For a moment there was no recognition, but then sanity came to him. "All right, boys," he said. "Back to the herd!"

"Dammit, Beck!" yelled George Livesey. "We can git 'em back!"

"No!" yelled the trail boss. "Flint is right! We'd nevah git back! Back to the herd! That's yore job now!"

Already Old Brimstone had reached the Crazy Woman and the bellowing cattle were flowing into the creek after him, filling the shallow waters of the crossing from bank to bank, spreading up and down stream. No one, not Old Brimstone or Beck Sterret or even a passel of shrieking Sioux, could make them move from that water.

Miles reloaded the hot, smoking Spencer. Above the uproar of the bawling steers and ripple of gunfire he heard a scream that somehow sounded different from the voices of the Sioux. The whole herd now filled the Crazy Woman, bank to bank up and down the stream as far as the eye could see. The Texans were bunched together, firing steadily at the last few bucks who were racing uphill to where the longhorns and captured horses had vanished, leaving a pall of bitter dust to mark their passing.

Miles stopped beside the dumped chuckwagon. Ernie Masland was nursing a broken arm. Cass Starr and several drivers threw loops over the wagon wheels and pulled the wagon back upright. Pots and pans flew as the wagon smashed down. The Texans untangled the harness, shot two of the broken-legged mules, then one of them drove the wagon down to the creek.

Miles shoved back his hat and wiped the sweat from his face. It had been cheap enough at half the price. Here and there in the settling dust lay dead warriors. Two Texans lay dead, as well as one of the drivers of a supply wagon.

All of the wagons were moved to the shelter of the willows and cottonwoods of the creek bottom. Beck Sterret placed a line of mounted drivers between the herd and the open ground. Others gathered near the wagons. Miles rode slowly down the slope toward them. There would be more than one burial beside the Crazy Woman that evening.

Beck Sterret looked up at Miles. "Wheah's Mis' Carlisle, Flint?" he said in a strained voice.

Miles stared at him. He looked at other taut, dusty faces. He looked back toward the scattered bodies on the open ground.

"She ain't out theah, Flint," said Cotton.

"She ain't around heah either," said Chip Macklin.

Then something came back to Miles. That scream he had heard. He turned in his saddle and looked up the ridge to the hill where the captured horses and longhorns had been driven, still marked by a drifting wraith of thin dust shot through with the last rays of the sinking sun.

"My God! No!" said Cass Starr.

Miles touched the bay with his heels and rode up the slope alongside the ruts of the Bozeman. Half a mile from the creek he saw the sun glinting from something. It was a silver-mounted six-shooter, chased and engraved. He slid from his saddle and picked it up. The initials L.A.C. had been engraved on each side of the butt frame. "Lorena Alice Carlisle," he said aloud. He opened the loading gate. Five cartridges had been expended. The last one was still in the chamber. *"Beck said to use only five of the six rounds if I had to,"* she had said. *"The sixth round is for me, if it comes to that."*

Miles swung up onto the bay and rode toward the creek. The wind had shifted, driving the yellowish dust across the Crazy Woman and over the backs of the longhorns. *"I asked you long ago what they did to white women,"* she had also said. *"You never told me."*

CHAPTER TWELVE

They forted up in the bottoms, corraling the wagons, keeping the longhorns close herded, doubling the number of night herders. Now and then a shot cracked out as something moved in the brush beyond the herd. It wouldn't be easy to stampede the longhorns from the water and the thick grass of the bottoms, and the Sioux had learned respect for the rolling-block Remingtons and the accuracy of the men who used them.

Spades rang against the ground as a common grave was dug for the dead. A shielded bull's-eye lantern showed just enough light to place the blanket-wrapped forms into the grave. Ernie Masland brought the worn Bible from the chuckwagon. Those drivers who could be spared gathered in the little clearing. The service was solemn but swift. There was little time now for the dead. It was the living that mattered.

Beck Sterret walked beside Miles Flint back to the chuckwagon. "We owe it to Jonas and ouahselves to git Mis' Carlisle back, Flint," he said.

Miles shook his head. "Impossible," he said firmly.

"We can leave a few men with the herd. Them Sioux won't

likely be able to stampede the herd from heah. Yuh say they won't fight at night. *Bueno!* We kin fight at night."

"You wouldn't get two miles from here, Sterret, and they'd have you cut off. You know that as well as I do."

The trail boss smashed a fist into his other palm. "Jesus, oh, Jesus," he said. "It was my fault! I was so damn' busy watchin' them beeves I forgot about her."

"We were all busy," said Miles. Thoughts about rescuing Lorena raced through his mind, but none of them made any sense. She was young and pretty. Some honored buck might want her for a squaw, and in that case she might be unharmed by the others, but if she was not wanted. . . . Miles knew one thing for sure; no white man could leave the valley of the Crazy Woman and come back alive. A regiment of cavalry couldn't do it. Five miles from Fort Phil Kearny, shortly after the war, three officers and seventy-nine men had chased a small party of Sioux into the hills, and not a man of them had come back. They had hardly been a match for the estimated two thousand Sioux and Cheyenne who had trapped them. That had been thirty miles north of the crossing of the Crazy Woman.

"Gawd's sake!" burst out the trail boss. "We can't stand here doin' nothin'!"

Miles fashioned a cigarette. He lighted it. "There's one long chance," he said.

"Name it!"

Miles walked to the supply wagon where Jonas Carlisle had died. He rooted around in it feeling for the wrapped albino pelt. He couldn't find it. He lighted match after match and looked thoroughly. The pelt just wasn't in there. He dropped from the tailgate, and as he did so something rang on the ground. Miles picked up the bone-handled knife that had killed Jonas.

"He'p, yuh?" said Chip Macklin.

"There was a wrapped buffalo pelt in here, Chip," said Miles, hefting the knife. "You take it out?"

"Haven't touched a thing, Miles. Mebbe it fell out."

Miles nodded. "Maybe."

Pomp came slowly through the darkness. "You goin' after Mis' Carlisle, Mistuh Flint?" he said miserably.

"We'll do the best we can, Pomp."

"I'll go along too, suh," said the little Negro.

Miles knew he was scared to death of the Sioux, but he knew Pomp meant it.

The light from the shielded lantern touched the knife Miles had in his hand. Pomp eyed it. "Mistuh Batteau done forgot his knife when he left," he said. "Mistuh Batteau set a heap of store by that knife. He tole me he made it outta the arm bones of the Indian he kill hand-to-hand. Bull-ovah-the-Mount'in, somethin' lak that."

"Bull-over-the-Hill," said Miles. He looked down at the knife and then up at Chip Macklin. "Jesus Christ!" he said.

Chip nodded. "Yeh. No wonder the killer got past the guards," he said quietly. "He was in camp all the time."

Things fitted together in Miles's mind. The disappearance of Bat and his Rees the same night Jonas had been murdered. The disappearance of the valuable snow-back buffalo pelt.

A rifle cracked amongst the willows. "Kill the sonofabitch!" yelled a Texan.

There was a thrashing noise, and a dark figure splashed into the stream. "God's sake, don't shoot ol' Guts!" screamed the odd-sounding voice.

"Lemme git a shot at him, Cotton!" yelled Ben Horton.

Miles ran to the stream edge. "Don't shoot that man!" he yelled. "Hold your fire!"

The dark figure crawled out of the stream, shaking with fright. Miles wrinkled his nose at the stench of the man and dragged him toward the shielded bull's-eye lantern. A fantastic sight met the eyes of the onlookers. A battered, greasy stovepipe hat, topped by a bedraggled feather sat crookedly atop the dark, braided hair of the man. The dirty, grayish braids were wrapped with raccoon skin. He wore a ragged military vest over his bare upper body. A threadbare blanket hung like a kilt about his bowed legs. On his feet were moccasins from which depended a rusty pair of huge Mexican spurs. Miles plucked a knife from its sheath and dropped it on the ground. He removed a huge double-barreled, percussion-lock pistol from the man's belt.

The captive looked about wildly at the hard faces of the men who surrounded him. He was like a frightened captive animal, more animal than human.

"Hello, Guts," said Miles. "You're out late tonight."

"Befo' God, Misser Flint," he blurted. A sob broke his voice. "I done nothin'! I was just lookin' for dried meat and gravy biscuit! I ain't with them Oglalas! I just Guts! Good ol' Guts, thass all!"

"Yeh," said Miles dryly. "Good ol' Guts, thass all!" He pulled the breed to his feet, wincing at the sour stench of the man. "What the hell are you doing around here?"

"They leave ol' Guts alone?" said the breed. He looked fearfully over his shoulder. "They kill ol' Guts' mule."

Miles gripped him by the vest front. "Tell me the truth, you breed bastard," he said thinly. "What are you doing here?"

"I come to see Batteau."

"Why Batteau?" said Miles.

"Batteau owe me money."

"For what?" said Miles.

The loose dirty face of the breed seemed to shift in and out of focus. "He tells Guts when is best time for attack," he said. He grinned widely. "Guts tell Lakota."

Spurs chimed. "Let me at him," said Beck Sterret.

"Wait," said Miles. "This poor bastard doesn't know the difference between right and wrong. He'll help you as well as hinder you for a price. We need information right now. He might just have it."

Guts smiled. He was on familiar ground now. "Sure, sure," he said quickly. "Guts tell. Guts know everything. Guts get money, horse, gun, food, maybe wo-haw?"

"Guts will get his filthy guts torn out," said Beck.

Miles pushed Guts back against a wagon. "You mean Batteau sent you on ahead to tell the Lakotas about this trail drive?"

"Thass Guts' business," said the breed.

Miles pushed a little, and the breed's head struck the side of the wagon. His plug hat hung rakishly over one bloodshot eye. He knew better than to try to force information out of the breed, for Guts had ethics of his own; he simply had to be paid, one way or another, for what he knew.

"Tell me about Batteau, Guts," said Miles. He shook the breed a little.

"Guts get paid?"

"Guts get paid," said Miles.

Guts grinned. "Bat say he take away Rees at right time. Rees no good. Rees dirty. Rees Corn Indians. Not like ol' Guts. Ol' Guts Sans Arc. Guts talk to Lakota. Lakota know when Rees leave. Come in behind. Ha! Ha! Ol' Miles Flint, he in front with gun that shoot today, kill tomorrow. Ha! Ha!"

Miles shoved Guts's head back against the wagon. "Ha! Ha!" he mimicked. "Where's Batteau now?"

"Ol' Bat, he not here?" said the breed in surprise.

"You dumb bastard," said Miles thinly. "You think he'd come back here after he pulled foot and let us walk into the Lakotas?"

Guts waggled his head. "He say he *might* be here. If not, he say *you* pay me off. He make deal with ol' Miles Flint. Miles Flint, he pay off Guts."

Beck Sterret moved. "So?" he said.

Miles looked back at him. "Don't be a damned fool, Sterret," he said. "Don't you get Bat's game? He sends this fool here to get paid off. Sure, Guts would have been paid off—with a slug in his head!"

Guts waggled his head. "Bat say trail boss owe him money for scouting. Ol' Guts collect and keep. Good deal, hey?"

Miles released the breed. "You're lucky you're not dead now," he said.

"You not pay ol' Guts?" said the breed incredulously.

There was no use in explaining it to the breed. "Where is Batteau?" said Miles.

The bloodshot eyes shifted. Guts picked at his broken nose and feigned indifference. He scuffed his moccasins in the dirt and cleared his throat.

"A good horse to replace your mules," said Miles.

Guts twisted a braid, looked up at the sky, examined a button on his vest.

"What more do you want?" said Miles.

Guts grinned. "Gun that loads today, shoots all week," he said in a wild rush of words. His eyes gleamed.

"It's yours," said Miles. "With two boxes of cartridges."

Guts bobbed his head delightedly.

"Why did Bat pull foot so suddenly?" said Miles.

Guts looked about. "Bat got big medicine," he said in an awed voice.

Miles gripped him by his greasy vest. "Such as a snow-back buffalo pelt?"

Guts nodded. "Big medicine! Big! Big! Bat want to trade pelt to Lakota. Afraid to go near camp. Bat tell Guts to go to Lakotas. Guts no afraid of Lakotas. Bat want Guts to go to camp of Lakotas and make deal for Bat. Then Guts to come here for pay. Bat smart. Guts smarter. Guts come here to get paid first, *then* go to camp of Ota Kte. Guts no fool, hey?"

"Were you in the camp of the Lakotas?"

"Long time ago. Guts watch fight today. See Lakotas run off spotted buffalo and horses."

"Did you see a white woman with them?"

Every eye was on the breed. Again the feigned indifference; the detached, pensive air.

"A good hunting knife," said Miles.

Guts rubbed his greasy face.

"What is it you want?" said Miles.

Guts went into an act as though winding something, then holding it up to his ear in great delight.

"A watch?" said Miles. "It's yours."

"Woman with Lakotas. White woman. Clothes torn. Guts see bare white tits. Ha! Ha! Woman's face wet. Cry allatime."

"She's safe?"

Guts rolled eyes upward. "Mebbe, Mebbe not. Not know. Lakotas sometimes crazy with white squaws. Sometimes kill. Sometimes screw. Sometimes marry."

"You can find Batteau?"

"Mebbe."

Miles shook his head. "Sack of flour. Sack of beans. Bag of coffee."

"Guts show you."

"Is it far?"

"Not far."

Miles walked to Beck Sterret. Half a dozen drivers stood with the big trail boss. "With that snow-back pelt I might be able to dicker with the Sioux," said Miles in a low voice.

"You've got to git it away from Bat and his Rees first," said Beck Sterret. "How many men do you want?"

Miles held up two fingers.

Beck turned. "Cotton?"

"Yuh know it, Boss," said the young Texan.

"Who else?" said Miles.

Beck turned. "Are you joshin'?" he said. "I want to see Bat and his Rees once more. Thet should be enough."

The valley was shrouded in premoon darkness when the four horsemen rode on hoof-muffled horses into the dark, forbidding hills bordering the Crazy Woman.

It was Guts who picked up the faint odor of burning buffalo chips as the moon hung low atop the Big Horns. Guts stopped his horse at the mouth of a tree-filled ravine. He bobbed his head up and down. His meaning was plain enough.

Miles leaned close to the breed. "How many?" he whispered.

"Batteau and four Rees," said Guts.

Miles swung down and tethered his bay to a tree. "No shooting," he said quietly.

"We got knives, ain't we?" said Beck.

Miles nodded. "Bat is mine," he said.

"We owe yuh thet," said Cotton.

"Watch the horses," said Miles to Guts.

Beck Sterret fingered his knife. "Mebbe he'll pull out," he said.

Miles shook his head. "Looney as he is, once he makes a deal he keeps it. That's more than you can say for a helluva lot of white men."

Miles let his hat drop to the back of his neck. The two Texans did the same, then removed their spurs. Miles led the way down into the darkness of the ravine. He went bellyflat as he neared a clearing, faintly lighted by the dying moon. The smell of burning chips was stronger, mingled with the acrid odor of horse droppings. The wind blew a little stronger, lifting the ashes from atop the fire and revealing the winking red eyes of low flame. There were four blanketed forms lying with their feet toward the fire. Beyond them, seated against a tree, was another blanket-wrapped form with a rifle lying across his lap. Miles watched him for a time. He did not move. Likely the guard was asleep or at least dozing.

Miles tested the honed edge of his heavy bowie knife. He looked at the two hardfaced Texans, pointed to the guard, then to himself. They nodded. Miles worked his way bellyflat through the tangle of brush and rustling fallen leaves. A horse whinnied softly upwind. Miles worked his way behind the guard. Beyond the fire and the sleepers he saw two shadowy forms. Miles slid an arm around the tree and the guard's throat and pinned the guard back against the tree. He struggled a little. Miles put on more pressure. The moccasined heels of the Ree beat a soft tattoo on the leaf-covered ground and then stopped. Miles eased the dead Ree to the ground and stood up. He motioned toward the sleeping forms.

The two Texans came in on catfeet. A knife rose and fell. A Ree gasped once. Another thrust of a knife and a Ree grunted, raised his head, then let it fall back again with a thud. The third Ree sat up and opened his mouth to yell. Beck hit him from the back at the same time Cotton caught him gut low.

The last sleeper awoke. He stared at Beck and Cotton, blood-dripping knives in their hands. It was Bat Batteau. He leaped to his feet from the tangle of blankets and bolted for the horses. Miles hurdled a log and ran lightly on moccasined feet after Bat. Bat turned once and saw that grim hawk's face behind him. He opened his mouth to scream in terror just as the bowie left Miles's hand in an overhand whip. The heavy brass-backed blade sank deeply in between Bat's shoulderblades. He was still running when death claimed him and brought him crashing to earth.

Miles walked on catfeet to the scout. He withdrew the bowie and kicked the scout over on his back. He wiped the blade clean on the exaggerated thrums.

"Yuh throw a *cuchillo* like a greaser," said Cotton.

"Make sure of them." said Miles, jerking his head toward the Rees.

"We know ouah business," said Beck.

Miles kicked aside Bat's blankets. The wrapped snow-back pelt had been Bat's last pillow on earth. Miles cut the thrums to make sure it was the pelt. He tied it together and stood up.

"What now, Flint?" said Beck.

Miles shrugged. "I'll try to make a dicker with Ota Kte," he said.

"With thet hide?" said Cotton. "Yore loco."

Miles looked at him. "You got any better ideas?"

There was no answer. Miles whistled softly three times.

Guts led up the four horses. Miles tied the pelt to his cantle roll and mounted the bay. "Take the other horses back with you, Sterret. The remuda could use a few replacements. If I'm not back with Mrs. Carlisle in forty-eight hours, you can use your own judgment with the herd. Go back to the Platte or on to the Gallatin. You can let Ernie Masland have my Sharps."

Cotton looked at the dead men. "What about this carrion heah?" he said.

"Let the ravens gather," said Miles. "Come on, Guts." The two of them rode from the darkening ravine.

Beck spat tobacco juice. "I think I know now wheah I seen him befo'," he said quietly as he wiped the juice from his mouth.

Cotton rolled a cigarette. "Yeh? Wheah, Beck?"

"Durin' the wah. At Gettysburg. He was lookin' ovah the sights of one of them damned hairsplittin' Sharps at us boys of the Fifth Texas. Yeh. It was him, all right."

Cotton snapped a match on his thumbnail and lighted the cigarette. "Yuh think he'll come back, Beck?"

Beck swung up onto his gray. He rested his hands on the pommel and looked down at his companion. "I ain't bettin' on it," he said.

"Me neither."

They rode from the ravine leading the extra horses. The wind flared up the fire. The yellow light reflected from the staring eyes of the dead. Somewhere in the hills a wolf howled.

CHAPTER THIRTEEN

The late afternoon sun hung over the Big Horns, the rays slanting down into the timbered valley through which a clear stream wandered in serpentine fashion. Guts drew rein and turned in his saddle. He pointed up the valley. There was a faint wraith of smoke drifting upward in the almost windless air.

"How far?" said Miles.

"T'ree miles mebbe, mebbe little more." Guts grinned. "If Lakota let you get that far."

"Never mind about that," said Miles. He turned in his saddle and looked back the way they had come. The sun's rays slanted through the timber. There wasn't a sign of life. For all Miles knew they might have been seen long ago.

"This back way," said Guts. "Main way farther north. Lakota there. Many. Many. Guts take long way around. Guts no want to see Lakota now."

Miles dismounted. He unbuckled the carbine sheath and handed it and the Spencer to Guts. He unbuckled his gunbelt, heavy with sheathed Remington and bowie knife, and draped it over the withers of Guts's horse. "These are yours. The horse you ride is yours. Go back to the camp and get the rest of the things we agreed upon. Fair enough?"

Guts looked up the valley with feigned indifference.

"Damn you!" said Miles. He removed his gold repeater watch from inside his jacket and handed it to Guts. "My father gave me that watch when I went to war."

Guts grinned. "Nice father," he said. "Never knew mine."

"You dirty bastard," said Miles under his breath as he mounted the bay.

Guts nodded. "Guts dirty bastard. Guts too smart to go into Lakota camp." He watched Miles ride down the slope toward the stream. *"H'gun, h'gun,"* said Guts. It was the Sioux courage word.

Miles splashed across the shallow stream and looked back. Guts had vanished. Miles pressed a hand down on the rolled snow-back pelt and kneed the bay to ride upstream. It was quiet except for the twittering of the birds, and even that sound died away as he advanced. The wind arose a little and brought with it the faint odor of horse droppings. He cleared the timber and rode into a meadowland area. His heart failed a little as he looked to the far side of the meadow and saw the mass of the horse herd. It was one big helluva herd, much bigger than he had expected. "This is a good day to die," he said. "Have courage."

A young horse guard saw him first. He rode a little closer, peered at Miles, then raised a long-barreled rifle. Miles dropped the reins and guided the bay with his knees. He raised both hands, palms outward, and rode slowly toward the guard. The guard raised his voice in a shrill, penetrating cry that echoed back from the valley sides.

Miles reined in the bay and waited. There would be no going back if he waited just a few minutes longer. The hair prickled on the back of his neck. He heard the raucous cries of the blackbirds as they fluttered over the ponies, snapping up the grasshoppers stirred up by the grazing herd. The wind shifted a little and swayed the trees. Leaves fell in a pale-yellow shower, some of them swirling along on the surface of the stream.

He seemed to feel something behind him. He turned slowly in his saddle. Four bucks sat their horses fifty yards from him, rifles or carbines across their thighs, the wind swaying the feathers they were wearing. Miles took out a cigar and lighted it, trying to keep his hands from shaking. The way of retreat was closed now. He could do nothing but go forward, and God have mercy on Miles Flint, sinner.

The young horse guard came trotting toward Miles, followed by an older warrior. The two of them halted their horses and looked at Miles. He again made the sign of peace. No expression crossed their faces. They could see that he was alone and unarmed. They had nothing to lose. Their curiosity was probably getting the better of them.

The day was late. Herders appeared around the flanks of the herd and began to drive them toward the unseen village for the night. Miles blew a smoke ring and thrust a finger through it. Still no movement from the two watching bucks. Then something touched Miles in the small of the back. He didn't have to look to know that it was a rifle muzzle. The older buck jerked his head toward the upper part of the valley. Miles touched the bay with his heels and rode in that direction, not looking back into the four grim faces behind him.

He could see the smoke rising from the village before he saw it, and then the harsh barking of many dogs came to him. His two guides rode up and over a slope. As he reached the crest he saw the village spread out before him in concentric rings, with the opening facing the east as it always did. In the center of the village he could see the big council tepee and a smaller red-painted medicine tepee just beyond it. It was a big village, a very big village. This was no temporary hunting camp or the village of a small band. This was a semi-permanent camp.

They knew he was coming. Squaws stood in front of their lodges looking toward the strange *Wasicun* who rode toward them. The warriors had grouped themselves nearer the center of the village, on the bare, pounded ground before the council lodge and the medicine tepee. They almost filled the cleared area. Miles reached the first ring of lodges, passing many racks upon which hung blackened strips of drying buffalo meat, hundreds and hundreds of pounds of it. It would be a good winter for the village of Ota Kte.

Although the village looked as though each lodge had been set up at whim, Miles knew that each lodge always had a certain place in the order and that this order was never broken. It was the ancient custom. Thus each village circle had a place for each band within it, and each band had a certain place for each lodge of that particular band so that every member of the village had a specific "address." Beside each lodge was tethered the night horse of the owner so that he need never be caught by surprise without a mount. Before each lodge was a tripod from which hung the owner's personal medicine bundle, a case containing a war bonnet, if he rated one, and often some of his weapons and his cased war shield. On some of the lodges pictographs depicted the deeds of the owner, although some warriors preferred these on a robe rather than on the lodge skins.

He saw the impassive faces of the squaws and their strong brown hands. If he was killed at once, it would be the work of a brave. It he was saved for the work of the squaws, he might live for a long time before they let him die. An icy feeling came into his guts. One of their favorite tricks was to saw off a living man's genitals with a dull-edged knife. He could almost read their thoughts as he rode past them. Would he be so brave pegged out like a drying hide while the squaws worked on him? *Hoh?*

He neared the massed warriors. Many of them had their faces painted red for luck, but here and there a black-painted face stood out, indicating that the warrior had recently killed an enemy . . . perhaps some of the men who had ridden with the trail herd. He looked beyond the massed warriors to see a tall, broad-shouldered warrior standing in front of the council lodge. He was over six feet in height, and Miles had no difficulty in recognizing him. It was Ota Kte, the Oglala war-chief with at least fifty coups, and entitled to wear on his war bonnet the bison horns that signified his position as one of the bravest of the brave.

The warriors parted to leave a narrow path for Miles to approach the chief, but he knew better than to do this mounted. He swung down from the bay, inches away from the nearest warriors, trying to keep his eyes away from their hands gripping sheathed scalping knives. He casually ground out the cigar. He had never felt so utterly alone in his entire life.

Miles led the bay forward through the mass of warriors. He stood twenty feet from the chief and again made the sign of peace with his outstretched hands. There was no expression on Ota Kte's red-painted face.

The wind shifted and swirled the smoke layer over the village, rifting it and driving it down the valley. The sun was touching the tips of the Big Horns, and deep purple shadows were filling the valleys and draws.

Miles wet his dry lips. He could feel those murderous eyes on his back. It wasn't easy to talk with a dry throat and a pounding heart. "I have come to the village of Ota Kte to trade," he said loudly in his passable Oglala.

There was no answer. A medicine man had appeared at the door of the medicine lodge, his head fully covered by a bison bull head, horns and all. Miles had an uncanny feeling he was being watched by the actual living bull itself rather than by the medicine man.

Ota Kte folded his muscular arms over the pipebone breastplate he wore. "You speak our tongue," he said. "That is good. Then you will understand me. You have not come to the village of Ota Kte to trade, but to die, white man."

Miles wet his lips again and swallowed hard. "I have no war with Ota Kte and his Oglalas," he said.

"He lies," said a scar-faced warrior. "He is with those *Wasicun* who drive the spotted buffalo through our hunting grounds."

"That is true," said Miles. "But we did not attack you. It was you who attacked us."

Ota Kte scowled. "You talk in twisted words. Is this not *our* land? Did your people not come here unbidden? That trail was not to be used. They will die. You will die."

Miles tried not to appear excited or frightened, but it took all the control he had. "I am ready to die when it is my time to die," he said calmly. "Does Ota Kte know when he will die?"

"No man knows that," said the Oglala.

"There is a way to find out," said Miles.

It was very quiet after he spoke. Those who could hear him knew what he meant. Miles looked beyond the council lodge and the medicine lodge. A young boy stood with a rope tied about the squat, powerful body of a young badger. Miles dropped the reins of the bay and walked slowly and calmly toward the boy and his pet. Miles held out his empty hands and smiled reassuringly. He pointed to the badger and then to himself. "I want the badger," he said slowly. "Will you trade?"

The boy had no expression on his face as he stood looking up at the tall *Wasicun* who was so soon to die.

Miles took a small brass compass from his pocket and removed the small file sheathed beside his belt stone. He passed the file back and forth so that the needle followed it. The boy quickly covered his mouth in awe. Miles handed him the compass and the file. The boy handed him the rope and promptly vanished amongst the many tepees.

Miles half led and half dragged the badger to the bare area before Ota Kte. The chief had been joined by some older men, likely the members of the council. The sun was fully gone now, and the only light came from the flickering fires.

Miles stood there, the firelight playing on his bronzed, seemingly fearless face. "I came here in peace, Ota Kte, and unarmed. I will need a knife. Do not be afraid." He smiled.

There was a look of scorn upon the chief's face. He walked forward, took his knife from its sheath, and handed it, handle first, to Miles. Miles could have killed him in an instant, but there was no fear upon the face of the Oglala.

Miles tested the edge of the knife as Ota Kte turned his broad back, hesitated a moment, then walked slowly to his place.

The crowd moved in closer. Miles could feel the massed heat of their bodies and smell the odor of their sweat and paint. His breath came erratically in his dry throat. He wanted to scream, to yell, to run from that place of sudden death. He raised his head. "No man knows his future," he said slowly and clearly. "There is but one way to learn how long he will live. Will Ota Kte take that way?"

There was a long silence. Ota Kte raised a hand. He looked at the badger and then at Miles. "I have no wish to know my future now," he said. "My medicine is not prepared for such a test."

It was as good a way as any of getting out of a situation, thought Miles. Miles drew the badger close, twisted the rope about his left hand, and thrust hard and true for the heart. The badger jerked and then stiffened. His claws scraped the ground, and then he was still. Miles looked up at the chief. The firelight flickered on the painted face and reflected from the pipebone breastplate. For a long moment the two men looked at each other. Then Miles knelt down, ripped the belly of the badger from one end to the other, and forced the gaping wound wide apart with his bloody hands, so that the belly formed a container for the gushing blood.

Miles stood up and calmly lighted a cigar with his blood-smeared hands. He blew a puff of smoke to the four points of the compass, to the earth and to the sky. He folded his arms and waited. It was pure unadulterated hell to stand there waiting for the badger's blood to congeal, but there was nothing he *could* do but wait.

It was fully dark now. The odor of cooking food drifted across the village. Not a warrior moved from his position as they watched this mad *Wasicun* who had ridden so boldly into their village to face Ota Kte.

The cigar was almost gone when Miles at last removed it from his lips. Perhaps the badger's blood was not congealed enough as yet, but he couldn't wait any longer. His legs felt weak, his body was soaked with sweat. Cool as the evening was, he could feel the sweat soaking through his buckskin jacket. Miles looked up at the sky as though praying, which he certainly was, although not to the spirits of the Lakotas. He knelt beside the stiffening badger. He held the sides of the great wound with his bloody hands and looked into the cavity. Gasps of awe came from all sides, hands covered open mouths, and eyes turned quickly away. The *Wasicun* had dared all! The *Wasicun* was still alive!

Miles looked into the dark blood. He wasn't sure if he saw it then, and he would never be sure for the rest of his life, but it seemed to him that he saw a face in the jelling blood. It was the face of Miles Flint, all right, but the face of a Miles Flint who had seen many, many winters.

Miles stood up and wiped his hands on his trousers. Only the bravest of the brave amongst the Lakotas would have done such a thing. If a young face was seen reflected in the blood, they would soon die; if the face was older, they would experience many more years of life.

Ota Kte studied Miles. "You are a brave man. I will not ask you what you saw, for that is your medicine. What is it you want from the Oglalas?"

"There is a woman here," said Miles. "A squaw captured from the white men who drive the spotted buffalo north to the land of the Great White Giant. I wish to trade for her."

"You have horses? Guns? Blankets? What will you trade?"

Miles waited a moment. "I have big medicine for the Oglalas," he said. "For this big medicine, I want two things."

"You talk much," said Ota Kte. "How can a *Wasicun* have medicine for the Oglalas? Speak, and speak well, white man, for your every word will be weighed. If your words are not well, the squaws will have you this night. We will then see how brave you really are."

"I looked into the belly of the badger," said Miles. "Even if Ota Kte condemns me to death, he will let me die like a man, not like a screaming animal. This much he owes me."

A faint flicker of admiration crossed the red-painted face. "You white men are full of promises for which you give nothing," said the chief.

Miles turned, and his heart damned near stopped as he saw the massed faces behind him. It was like looking through a smoky portal into hell itself. The warriors had crowded in around the bay, and the sweetish, greasy smell of them almost sickened Miles. He rested a hand on the rolled-up buffalo pelt and motioned the nearest warriors back. He untied the bundle and carried it to the bare firelit space in front of Ota Kte, the medicine man, and the older members of the council.

The buffalo bull mask turned toward Ota Kte, the firelight glistening on the horns, and the medicine man spoke swiftly. They were too far away for Miles to catch the words, which were muffled by the mask. The medicine man stepped back, and Ota Kte looked at Miles. "This medicine you have," he said quietly. "How did you get it?"

Miles took a long chance. "*Wakan Tanka,*" he said loudly.

"The white man does not have *Wakan Tanka,*" said a pock-marked elder. "No white man has *Wakan Tanka!*"

Miles wet his dry lips. The ice was thin, so very thin. *Wakan Tanka* was an exalted and sacred power, an all-pervading vital force. It had no existence of its own but was a kind of quality in something already existing.

"Speak, white man," said Ota Kte.

Miles raised his hand and pointed to the east. "The sun is first amongst deities for the Lakotas, and beside it the sky, the earth, and the solid rock. Then there are the spirits of the moon, the winds, and the bison. The thunderbirds, whose beating wings make the air tremble, are gods of war and gave the Lakotas the spear and the tomahawk. These all have *Wakan Tanka.*" Miles spoke loudly and earnestly, filling in his sometimes inadequate knowledge of the tongue with the gestures of the sign language, so that all might understand.

"Tell us of the *Wakan Tanka* of the *Wasicun,*" said a hawk-faced warrior who stood with the elders.

"Does not the *Wasicun* have the horse and the rifle? Is this not *Wakan Tanka?* Did not the Lakotas get the horse and the rifle from the *Wasicun?*" said Miles, almost in scorn. "Any Lakota should know that!"

It was a telling blow, for Miles had spoken the truth.

Once again the bison head moved, and the medicine man spoke to Ota Kte. As the bison head turned to look at Miles he again had the uncanny feeling that an actual, living buffalo bull was looking at him.

Ota Kte eyed Miles. "You have spoken well," he said. "But you have not shown us any big medicine. Speak now. Tell us of this medicine." He pointed to the dark eastern sky. "If the moon arises before you finish, you will not leave this camp alive. Perhaps the dawn will look upon your face, if you are still alive. You are strong and brave. You will live a long time under the knives of the squaws."

Miles's throat went dry. He had no idea of how much time had passed, but the moon would rise early. Perhaps even now it was almost touching the eastern sky beyond the valley of the Powder River. He could feel the tension amongst the silent Lakotas. Whatever he said or did from now on would have to impress them, or he would die, and Lorena Carlisle would face her fate alone in one of the many lodges of the village.

Miles drew in a deep breath. He raised his hands to the dark sky. "Long winters ago, during a time of great hunger, two hunters of the Sans Arc had gone out to hunt for game, which was very scarce," he said. "They were returning empty-handed when they encountered a beautiful maiden, garbed in flowing white buckskin, carrying a bundle of the holy sage." He paused. He knew the story as well as they did, but he wasn't sure whether or not he was impressing them with his knowledge. "One of the hunters had evil ideas about this beautiful maiden, but the other was of pure mind. A cloud had enveloped both of them, and when it cleared the pure-minded hunter saw his companion at his feet, a bare skeleton from which bloated, flesh-eating snakes sluggishly crawled. 'Behold!' the maiden said. 'I am coming to your people, and will bring them something of importance. Tell them to prepare for my coming.' "

The fires had died down and shadows filled in between the tepees while the smoke drifted in the now windless air, rifting about the tops of the many tepees. It was very quiet. Not a dog barked. Not a moccasin husked on the hard bare ground.

"The maiden came to the village of the Sans Arcs," continued Miles, "and to Standing Hollow Horn, who was then chief of the tribe. She gave solemn instructions, and from the bundle of holy sage she took a pipe. 'With this sacred pipe,' she said, 'you will walk the earth, which is your Mother, as the Great Mystery is your Father. The bowl of the pipe is red stone. It is the earth. Every step you take upon the earth should be as a prayer. The stem of the pipe is wood and represents all that grows upon the earth. These twelve eagle feathers that hang upon the stem are from the Spotted Eagle and represent all the winged things of the air. All the things of the universe are joined to you who smoke this pipe. All send their voices to the Great Mystery, for when you pray with this pipe you pray *for* and *with* everything!' "

Miles did not dare turn to look at the eastern sky, but it seemed to him as though the sky overhead and to the west was a little lighter, as though receiving some of the light of the rising moon.

"She gave the pipe to Standing Hollow Horn and said, 'Behold this pipe! Always remember that it is sacred and treat it as such, for it will take you to the end of time. I am leaving you now, but I shall always watch over your people. At the end I shall return to you again,'" spoke Miles in a slow, earnest tone. He was sure now the moon was touching the eastern sky beyond the valley of the Powder.

Miles still had the knife given to him by Ota Kte. He did not look at the impassive faces ringing him on each side. "The maiden then walked away to a hill, where she sat down. She arose as a white buffalo and trotted over the hill out of sight of the Sans Arcs." Miles bent swiftly, before he could be stopped, and slashed through the thrums that bound together the snow-back buffalo pelt. He gripped the cured hide and flipped it, unrolling it on the bare earth, so that it fell outer side upward almost at the moccasined feet of Ota Kte. The firelight shone on the albino hair.

There were awestruck gasps from the massed Lakotas. Hands covered opened mouths. The sacred Buffalo Calf Pipe was still in possession of the same band of Sans Arcs to whom the maiden had appeared, handed down from generation to generation always within the same blood. *It was the most sacred object of the Sioux Nation,* wrapped always in the purifying sage and treated with the utmost awe and respect.

The die was cast. If Ota Kte accepted the albino hide, no harm would come to Miles, for did he not possess *Wakan Tanka* to have found such a sacred object? To harm him might spoil the medicine of the hide.

Ota Kte looked at Miles and then at his people. Three bucks came from the crowd, and the oldest of them spoke to the chief. Miles knew them. They were the three who had moved in on him unseen the day he had killed the snow-back. They knew he had killed the snow-back.

Ota Kte held up a hand. "You are free, *Wasicun,*" he said. "You may leave in peace from the village of Ota Kte."

"And the woman?" said Miles.

Ota Kte spoke to a brave, who trotted off behind the council lodge. The chief folded his arms and studied Miles. There was a faint trace of admiration on his strong face. "The way is open to the north," he said. "Drive the spotted buffalo away from our hunting grounds. No harm will come to them and to the *Wasicun* who drive them. *But do not come back, Wasicun.* If you do, your medicine will not protect you."

Miles held out the chief's hunting knife, but Ota Kte shook

his head. "It is yours," he said. His meaning was plain enough. As one brave man to another, the knife was the parting gift of Ota Kte.

Miles turned on his heel just as the moon revealed itself, softly filling the eastern sky. He led the bay through the Lakotas, who parted respectfully to let him make his way.

He saw her beyond the crowd, standing by herself, dressed in the softest of white buckskin, beaded moccasins on her tiny feet, her hair braided in the style of the women of the Lakotas. He led the bay to her, picked her up and easily lifted her to the cantle of the bay. He mounted, feeling her arms creep about his waist. "Miles, Miles," she said softly. She pressed her tear-stained face against his broad back.

He guided the bay through the empty streets of the village. He rode through the dark timber into the grassy valley, now filling with the light of the rising moon. Miles rode toward the distant valley of the Crazy Woman. He did not look back. There was nothing to fear now.

CHAPTER FOURTEEN

The first snowfall of the year drifted through the gray skies over the great valley of the Gallatin as almost three thousand head of longhorns who had been driven almost three thousand miles from Texas, starting in April—the Moon of the Red Grass Appearing, in the language of the Lakotas—and now it was November—the Moon of Falling Leaves—and almost the time of December—the Moon of Popping Trees—walked the last mile of their journey.

Since leaving the crossing of the Crazy Woman, the longhorns, still led by Old Brimstone and his clear-sounding bell, had moved north, always north, leaving the Powder River for the Tongue River, turning westerly toward the Little Big Horn and then the Big Horn itself, then northwest to the fording of the Yellowstone. They passed through Emigrant Gap to reach Bozeman and the valley of the Gallatin.

Chip Macklin had been sent many days ahead to the Carlisle land grant to hire men to build the ranch buildings, according to the plan Jonas Carlisle had carried with him from Texas.

They would be ready by the time the heavy snows fell. Ghost Face would be early that year, but Lorena Carlisle and the Carlisle corrida as well as the thousands of longhorns would be ready for it.

The ringing of axes and the whining of saws drifted through the swirling snow as the last of the longhorns came to a halt in a sheltered area where grass could still be found. The clapper of Old Brimstone's bell was tied down permanently after the thousands of miles it had rung to guide the trail herd to its new home in Montana territory.

The chuckwagon, the Studebakers, and the supply wagons, creaking and groaning, rolling on thin iron tires, were driven to the ranchsite, close to the new buildings, and the teams were unhitched. The remuda was driven to the fenced pasture and turned loose.

Miles Flint rode through the swirling snow to where Lorena Carlisle stood beside Beck Sterret, looking at the rapidly rising buildings. Miles swung down from the bay and took off his hat. "I'll be riding on to Virginia City," he said.

Lorena Carlisle nodded. She had been expecting this.

Beck Sterret looked up the great valley. "I doubt if Texas could beat this for cattle country," he said, almost as though to himself.

"Beck and all the drivers are staying on," said Lorena.

Miles raised his eyebrows. "I thought the Texans could hardly wait to return to the Lone Star State," he said in mock surprise.

Beck shrugged. "We intend to become Montanans," he said. "Somebody has to people this coming state. Yuh can hardly get better blood to do it then Texans, can yuh?"

"*Ex*-Texans," said Miles. "I'll have to agree with that."

"Yuh won't stay on then?" said the trail boss.

"No," said Miles. "I'm not a cattleman."

"The buffalo won't last forever," said Lorena. She looked at Miles. "Beck is staying with me to foreman the ranch."

"You won't find a better man," said Miles.

"Gracias," said the Texan.

"Por nada," said Miles.

Miles took her hand in his. "Good-bye," he said.

She looked at him for a long moment. "Good-bye, Miles." She turned and walked to the front of her Studebaker.

Miles thrust out a hand to Beck. "Good-bye," he said.

The hard hand of the Texan gripped that of Miles. "Good-bye, Miles," he said quietly.

Miles swung up on the bay. It was the first time in the long months since he had known Beck Sterret that the trail boss had called him by his first name. He touched the bay with his heels and rode toward the road that led to the Madison and then to Virginia City.

Beck's spurs chimed softly as he walked to Lorena. "He'll be back, Mis' Carlisle," he said. "He'll be back when the grass first shows itself in the spring."

She did not answer or indicate that she agreed. She knew why Miles Flint had not stayed on in the valley of the Gallatin. Jonas Carlisle was not long dead. Miles had given her time, but he would be back in May, in the Moon When the Ponies Shed. Her medicine told her that.

Barranca

BARRANCA

Chapter One

The sun was almost gone beyond the softly rounded mountains. Long shadows moved down the leaden-hued slopes toward the smooth flow of rifted earth that buried the base of the range. The harsh light of the day had long been softened, but the sodden heat still hung heavily over mesa and mountain. It was too early for the desert to cool after the living hell of the summer day. The mountains and mesas seemed like islands rising from a dry sea-bed, waterless for countless ages. In all that burning land, still vague and indefinite from the heat haze of the day, there was no sign of man except for the faint wagon ruts that slanted across the desert and the thin thread of smoke that rose high in the windless air.

There was nothing friendly about that smoke. The thought haunted the heat-hazed mind of Sheldon Burnett. He raised his pounding head from his crossed forearms and stared stupidly at the smoke. His swollen tongue cautiously explored his cracked lips. His thirst had long passed from mouth and throat into his overheated blood and now seemed to be penetrating his bones. He closed his burning eyes. The idle thought drifted through his mind that in other places and at other times he had looked eagerly for signs of smoke —the cheering symbol of hospitality in an otherwise barren land. He passed a dirty hand through his dusty, reddish beard, scrabbling in the stiff hair. He itched all over. It had been so long ago that he had stripped and bathed that he could not quite recall the incident.

He slowly opened his eyes again. The smoke was still there. The thread of it was a little thinner but it was still rising in the air as it had been doing for seemingly endless hours.

There was only one source for smoke in that country. No white man would dare betray his presence by kindling a fire. Neither would an Apache, unless he had left it *behind* him, and that fire had never been lighted to cook food. There was something evil about that smoke, something that haunted one's mind.

Matthew Dustin moved sluggishly in the shadows beyond Sheldon. "By God, Shell," he husked. "How much longer?"

Shell pressed a hand against his burning eyes. "Until we're sure, Dusty," he said patiently. For God's sake, he thought, I hope he keeps quiet this time.

"They won't be down there now," rasped Dusty.

The sear slipped on Shell's temper. He turned his head and looked at the dusty, bearded face of his companion. "Damn you!" he snapped. "Go on down and look then! Go on, you ornery sonofabitch! I'll bury what's left of you! *Go on down!*"

Dusty sat up and rubbed his right forearm across his eyes. "By Christ," he said, "it's either die up here or down there! I ain't about to sit here and wait for it! That ain't *my* way!"

Shell sat up too. "Haven't you got the guts to stick it out?" he said in a low voice.

Dusty lowered his arm, and his cold blue eyes flicked at Shell. Shell knew that look well enough. It had prophesied the quick and violent death of a number of men. In the hot thickness of the gathering shadows their minds seemed to reach out for each other for an opening hold in the death grapple. Flames of hate seemed to be fanned by the enervating heat and the destroying thirst. For a fraction of time, perhaps a few heartbeats, the hostility hung between them and then Dusty laughed. *"Compañero,"* he said, "I'll match you to see who goes down alone to the waterhole."

Shell turned away from Dusty. The sun was gone but there was still a great wash of rose and gold in the western sky stained with darker streamers. "We go down together, *compañero,*" he said quietly.

That was enough. Words like those, or the thought behind them, had held them together for more than five years. Through the blood and smoke of the war, from Wilson's Creek to the bitter end. It had held them together the night they had crossed the Rio Grande, riding with General Jo Shelby, the Confederate who had refused to accept Appomattox. Before the dripping horses had reached the Mexican shore, the stained and shot-riddled Stars and Bars had been reverently dropped into the dark waters, well weighted so that the battle flag should not rise again. To the south Maximilian had needed fighting men and was willing to pay in gold for veteran cavalrymen to help him win his fight against Juarez and his Republican forces. There had been no argument from Dusty and Shell.

"There'll be a new moon tonight," said Dusty.

Shell nodded. He tore his mind from the past.

"We ought'a move down to the lower ground before then," said Dusty.

Shell nodded again. "While the Apaches are moving up," he said sarcastically.

"Yuh always have to be so damned knowing?" snapped Dusty.

Shell had the obvious answer but he was too dead beat to care.

"How much longer do we wait?" persisted Dusty.

The sun was fully gone and the western sky had changed from rose and gold to fainter hues banded with streamers of light gray to a mottled grayness streaked with darker lines. The air was completely motionless. A foreboding silence hung over the dark desert between the eastern mesas of naked lava to the rounded mountains west of the great valley. Shell felt as though he and Dusty had strayed somehow from the Earth of the living into limbo, or perhaps to some unknown planet whirling through space, where the two of them were the only living creatures. It was eerie and uncanny, and despite the clinging heat a chill crept through him and raised his flesh.

"I asked a question," said Dusty.

He was like a canker worm gnawing at one's mind. It was his way. It was *always* his way. Dusty aimed directly for his immediate goal and went for it hell for leather and to the devil with the hindmost. It was his way and he was good at it. When he came unwound, *something* had to give.

Shell moved a little to ease his lean frame against the warm rock. The sour, acrid odor of his sweat-soaked clothing hung about him. The heat brought out an aura of odors. Sour sweat and sweat-damp leather, unwashed hair and flesh, and even the brassy odor of the cartridges in his gunbelt. Shell reached out and placed a big hand on his Spencer repeating carbine. The wood and metal were almost hot to the touch.

Shell suddenly raised his head. Something had come to him from the darkness of the steep slopes below them. "Listen!" he said tersely.

It was deathly quiet. Somewhere in the darkness behind

them something rustled. A sharp, pitiful squeaking arose and then died as suddenly as it had come. It was the death cry of some small creature caught by a nocturnal predator. Something else had alerted Shell. He wasn't even sure he had *heard* anything. Years of war and of traveling in hostile Indian country had honed some sixth sense within him. One either developed such a sense under such circumstances or died . . . *fast.*

Shell sniffed the warm air. He slowly swung his shaggy head from side to side. He couldn't see anything but the darkness of the lower slopes and the thicker darkness of the thorned brush clumps, *yet there was something down there.*

Dusty moved softly. Shell mentally cursed him.

The two horses were well hidden in a deep draw a quarter of a mile away. No sensible man kept his animals near him when he stopped for the night in that country. One soft whinny could be picked up at almost unbelievable distances by the sharp ears of an Apache.

Shell hooked a thumb over the big hammer of the Spencer. It was already half-cocked. He touched his cracked lips with his tongue and almost stopped breathing to hear better, but his heart thudded so he was sure it could be heard twenty feet away. Shell put a curb rein on his emotions. *Apaches!* Despite his years of experience in Indian country and in war he had never quite been able to govern the reaction that one word set off in his mind. He fought the faint, cloying sickness that rose in his lean gut and then hovered at the pit of his throat. The thought of dying wasn't so bad. One gets fatalistic after four years of war. It wasn't the thought of dying that unnerved him. *It was the thought of being caught alive by them.*

The darkness was full and thick by now, pressing down upon them, alive with the unseen. Dusty hissed softly. He had eyes like a cat.

Vaguely, as though seen through a misty waterfall, or a drifting, tenuous fog, there was a movement in the darkness. There were twin metallic clicks as Spencer hammers came back to full cock. Trigger fingers gently took up the slack. The clicking sound seem inordinately magnified.

A rounded object moved into view, faintly silhouetted against the skyline. There was no mistaking it. It wasn't a hat. It was a head, thickly maned. Only white men wore hats in that country. Higher and higher rose the head until the shoulders were seen and the tossing head of a horse appeared. The warrior came higher along the dim trail as though manipulated by the strings of a master of marionettes. The Apache turned his head and looked directly toward the two breathless men lying bellyflat on the rocks. The white bottom clay with which he had banded upper cheeks and the bridge of his nose could now be seen. There was a ghostliness about the appearance of this mounted buck. The soft thudding of the horse's hoofs came to them. The mount must be wearing rawhide boots.

The Apache was silhouetted fully now, an easy shot for the two expert marksmen who watched him. It looked so easy. The buck looked back down the unseen trail and then passed from view behind an upthrust boulder that seemed to raise an admonishing finger toward the sky. For a moment he was heard and seen and then he was gone. It seemed as though he had been unreal, a phantom conjured up in the thirst-ridden minds of the two white men.

It was quiet again, but something unseen still haunted the velvety darkness. Something that still pinned the two white men to the rock. Their thirst became aggravated to such an extent that both of them wanted to curse and to shout, to charge stiff-legged down the slope, slamming lead from side to side like a fireman playing a hose. It was a madness and it had to be fought down. Shell heard a sharp intake of breath and was about to curse Dusty when he realized it was his own unconscious action.

Dusty hissed again.

Sweat ran down Shell's face, cutting tiny furrows in the dust, crawling into his beard, setting up an intolerable itching. His sweat greased the stock of his repeater. It worked through his beard and mercilessly stung his cracked lips with a kiss of salt.

Another thickly maned head arose out of the darkness, followed by another and another, and still another, with the soft thudding of the hoofs beating steadily. A horse suddenly snorted.

Oh God, thought Shell, *he's scented our damned stink!*

One after another until fully a score of them were moving toward the upthrust pinnacle of rock. Lance shafts rose above their heads like single antennae. The heads of the warriors moved constantly, from side to side, then back, then ahead again, then from side to side again, in ceaseless vigilance, for an Apache hates surprise worse than anything.

The last warrior vanished behind the pinnacle. A thin cloud of bitter-smelling dust hung in the quiet air and drifted slowly down on the two white men, coating them, working into their eyes and nostrils, touching their cracked and burning lips.

"Now?" husked Dusty.

Shell fiercely shook his aching head.

Minutes ticked past, each tick feeling like a hammer blow to the gut.

Dusty moved restlessly. He winced in savage pain, but did not cry out as Shell drove a boot toe into his side.

A horse blew in the darkness. Shell raised his carbine. The head of the buck and the head of his mount appeared as though rising from a pool of ink.

Dusty moved a little. His metal-shod carbine butt faintly tapped a rock. The Apache halted his horse. He sat his mount, looking directly at the two men. He couldn't possibly see them! It was physically impossible, and yet it seemed as though he *did* see them.

Shell pressed trigger finger against trigger. They'd have a few minutes' grace before the rest of them came back. A damned few minutes!

The buck touched his horse with his moccasined heels and rode on. The greasy loops of a swollen horse intestine hung across the withers of his horse. Just before he passed the rock pinnacle he glanced quickly back toward the two white men. It seemed to each of them that he was looking directly into their eyes with a prophecy of death. Then he was gone, as the others had gone, into the darkness of the upper slopes.

Shell released the trigger slack. His breath poured from his aching lungs. He rested his shaking head on his crossed forearms. He was too weak to move, to talk, to think. Too weak almost to get down to the life-giving water in the desert below the mesa.

Half an hour passed.

"Now?" said Dusty in a cracked voice.

Shell raised his head a little. He nodded. "Now," he said.

They got stiffly to their feet and swayed a little like drunken men. They pushed their way through the brush, heedless of the catclaw and wait-a-bit thorns. Far to the east, beyond the ragged line of mountains, there was a faint, ever so faint, promise of the coming moonlight.

Chapter Two

The lower slopes of the towering mesa were badly cut up, riven with crumbling draws filled with thorny brush. It was still dark on the western slopes, although the faint light of the rising moon had already touched the rounded tops of the mountains beyond the deep well of the lower land between mesa and mountains. Sweat trickled down the sun-ravaged faces of the two men as they led the stumbling horses toward the unseen lower ground. It seemed as though the clashing hoofs and the clattering of loose rock could be heard for miles. Time and time again they would halt to listen, impatient with the harsh breathing and blowing of the horses.

The eastern upper areas of the mountains were bathed in the light of the moon when at last Shell and Dusty reached the smoother land that flowed from the base of the mesa out onto the desert floor. They stopped for a breather, dying for a smoke, but knowing better than to show a pinpoint of light. Their red-rimmed eyes constantly scanned the heights above them, half expecting to see those bushy-headed devils in human form closing in on them, but there was no sign of life up there.

A faint breath of wind whispered softly through the still motionless masses of heated air that filled the great trough of the valley. It rustled the dry brush and dried the sweat on the men's taut faces. Slowly, almost imperceptibly, the moonlight crept down the eastern slopes of the mountains and touched the edge of the desert, but there was still a thick pool of darkness in the lower ground where the waterhole was located.

The smoke was still drifting upward, slanted a little by the wind. It either marked the site of the waterhole or was close to it. Shell tried to reconstruct the lay of the land in his tired mind. It had been a full seven years since he had passed that way.

"Supposin' there ain't any water?" said Dusty.

"The Apaches had water," said Shell.

"That ain't to say they got it here," said Dusty.

Shell turned his head. "You saw that horse-gut canteen that last buck had," he said slowly. "We've got to copper our bet that they got their water here. Because if they didn't. . . ." His voice trailed off. It was better left unsaid.

Their worn boot soles husked on the warm sand as they slogged on. Shell sketched a picture of the place in his mind. A roughly oval area of upthrust rocks tip-tilted toward the south, with their bases buried deep in the ocher-colored sands. One who did not know that country would never suspect that there was water within that natural palisade of bone-dry rocks except possibly for the fact that the faint ruts of the long disused wagon road drove straight toward them from the western mountains and then slanted toward the northern end of the looming mesa to slant northeasterly toward Soldier Springs, thirty-five miles away. Soldier Springs had been almost bone-dry when Dusty and Shell had stopped there two days past.

"Yuh sure there's water out here?" said Dusty. "Don't look like it to me."

"Horno Tanks," said Shell.

Dusty glanced sideways. *"Horno? Oven* Tanks? They picked the right name for this damned suburb of hell!"

Shell touched his raw lips. "There's water all right. Holes worn in the rock inside the formation. A spring fills the holes. Tanks, the Mexes call them."

"Likely dry," said Dusty.

Shell shrugged. "What's the use?" he said to the sky. "They've never been dry in the history of this country. Not in the memory of the Indians, the Spaniards, the Mexicans and the Americans—and *he* doubts it."

Dusty wiped his face with his forearm and looked at Shell over the arm. "Jesus," he said softly. He winced as another crack split his raw lips. "Here we go with that gawddamned history again. I told you once, if not fifty times, that damned history don't mean a thing!"

"Then you'd better, by God, *hope* it's right! Don't you believe in anything except those guns of yours?"

Dusty grinned wickedly. "No," he said. "Do *you?"*

There was no answer from Shell. Dusty was right. Their lives and hopes were dependent on each other and their guns. It had been that way all during the war and later in Mexico. It had been that way since Maximilian had been executed at Querétaro and since Dusty and Shell had ridden and hidden through seven hundred miles of a hostile Mexico hunted by the Republican forces who had no use for gringo mercenaries. They had crossed the Rio Grande near Ojinago in the State of Chihuahua with Mexican slugs dimpling the moonlit waters of the river. The moonlight had glinted on something else too, on the Texas side of the river. The brass buttons of a patrol of Yankee cavalry. They hadn't been waiting for "unreconstructed" Rebels, but any game was fair game to them. Shell and Dusty had no intention of taking the oath of allegiance. Dusty had killed two troopers and Shell had wounded one before they broke loose into the Sierra Vieja heading northwesterly along the Rio Grande for the El Paso del Norte area.

"There are the Tanks," said Dusty suddenly.

They halted. Dimly seen, for the full moonlight had not yet touched the area, were the upthrust rocks just as Shell had remembered them from years past. They hadn't changed. It was very quiet except for the breathing of the thirsty horses. Now and then the dry brush rustled. The Tanks looked peaceful enough except for one thing. The smoke was very thin, raveling out in the fitful wind, but it was still rising from beyond the Tanks.

Dusty grounded his carbine. "That damned smoke," he said quietly.

Shell nodded. That smoke stuck in his mind like a cholla needle, a nagging thrust of fear that he could not eliminate. Horno Tanks had been a swing station on the old Southern Overland Stage Line before the war. A branch line had been run through this area to service the mines. The war had swept everything away. Stagelines, mining camps, *placitas*, and forts had been abandoned or destroyed when the Federal troops had been pulled out to let Arizona survive by itself if it could. The Apaches had been barely kept in check up until that time. Without the soldiers there was nothing to stop them.

"Stay here," said Shell. He handed the reins to Dusty. Shell drew out his converted Navy Colt and checked the cylinder. The metallic whirring of the spinning cylinder sounded crisply in the quiet. Shell half-cocked the Spencer, pulled his faded military hat lower over his eyes and walked toward the dim outline of the Tanks. He glanced back as he reached the halfway mark. Dusty had already vanished into the thicker brush to cover Shell if need be.

The rocks seemed to rise higher and higher from the drifted sand as Shell approached the Tanks. Then he remembered how high they really were, rising thirty-five to forty-five feet from the desert floor like some ancient ruin. The entrance to the interior of the palisade of rocks was on the southern side. It was out of his view but the swing station structure and corrals should be there if they too had not been swept away by the Apaches. That mysterious smoke certainly could not be rising from the chimney of the station.

A faint, sweetish odor reached him on the invisible hands of the shifting wind. He stopped short. That smell was familiar enough to him. In some unnamed engagement in the war he remembered all too well that same odor drifting through the rifted battle smoke of the piney woods which had been set ablaze by shellfire. He halted as he rounded the corner of the rock formation. The skeletal ruins of the station were now lighted by the first rays of the rising moon. The roof had partially collapsed and the wall nearest him had collapsed within the structure in a diagonal fault from top to bottom corners of the eastern side. The heavy, bolt-studded door had fallen on the bare ground in front of the station. The smoke drifted thinly upward from beyond the building. The sickening, cloying odor was stronger now.

Shell wiped the cold sweat from his dirty face. He wondered where it came from, for it seemed that long ago all the juices had been drained from his lean body, leaving it like a piece of beef jerky. He glanced up at the ragged-looking top of the rock formation, half expecting to see white-banded faces peering down at him over rifle sights. There was no one there.

He touched his cracked lips with the tip of his tongue. He could not smell the water. The cloying odor overpowered everything else except the sour-sweat aura that hung about Shell like an old familiar cloak. He forced himself to go on, carbine muzzle swinging back and forth in an arc at hip level while his trigger finger took up the slack, ready to touch off seven rounds of bottle-necked .56.50. Tired and thirsty as he was, Shell was always the professional, ready to shake out instant death at the drop of a hat, or faster if need be. Shell suddenly realized he could see much better. The moonlight was beginning to fill the great desert valley. He saw a pile of horse droppings and bent down on one knee to rake his right hand through the manure, although he never took his eyes from the surroundings. The crust of the manure was stiff, but the interior was still slightly moist. Likely left by an Apache mount.

Shell stood up and saw the rounded, humped shape of a dead mule. His throat had been slashed wide open. The upper flank had been ravaged by keen-bladed knives, and fragments of the dusty hide littered the ground, while the dripping blood had stained the light soil in a black patch. The Apaches had been there, all right. There is nothing an Apache likes better than sweet mule meat.

Shell paused at the gaping doorway of the ruin. A foul

stench drifted out to meet him. He stepped inside and flattened his back against the wall. The moonlight penetrated the half-collapsed wall and came into the room through the gaping roof hole. The stench sickened him, but it was not the same as the sweetish, cloying odor that haunted the outside air. This place had been recently used as a latrine. Shell took a lucifer from his shirt pocket and snapped it on a thumbnail as he walked about the darker area. The wavering light revealed a filthy shambles. Piles of excrement were mingled with shattered crockery, scattered book leaves, rags of clothing and other nondescript articles impossible to identify. The acrid odor of urine hung in the corners.

Shell blew an explosive breath to kill the match flame and to drive the foul aura from his lungs. He stepped outside and walked toward the corrals to the west of the station partially set within an arc of the rock formation and fenced across the front with peeled poles hauled from the mountains miles away. The fence had been destroyed. The poles had been shattered or chopped into short lengths, littering the ground within and without the corral. The corral was empty. Shell turned to look back the way he had come and realized the smoke was rising from the center of the corral, and the sickening odor hung more heavily there than elsewhere. He turned slowly. The corral was *not* empty.

Shell walked slowly toward the center of the corral. Something lay in the middle of it. Something from which the smoke still arose. The moonlight gave enough illumination for him to identify the object when he was within ten feet of it. He stared, whirled, gripped his mouth with his right hand and took half a dozen stiff-legged strides before his outraged guts revolted and spewed out their contents. There wasn't much to spew, but Shell did a thorough job of it. His lips split with the strain and added blood to the greenish, dripping bile.

"Jesus God," slobbered Shell. Tears flooded his eyes and rolled down his dirty face. He shook his throbbing head to clear it. Now he knew why the corral poles had been chopped or broken into convenient lengths. There wasn't much else in the way of firewood around Horno Tanks.

Shell wiped his mouth and forced himself to walk back to what lay smoking in the center of the corral. The earth was gouged and trampled, and the object lay in the middle of it. He didn't quite know what to call it now. It had been human . . . *once*. The moonlight clearly revealed what it was. The naked body had been exquisitely mutilated. It was curiously mottled with a combination of dried blood, the soft yellowish-white of exposed bones and muscles, the charred areas of softer parts. The arms and legs were but blackened stubs with short pieces of charred wood radiating out from them, and from these arose the thin smoke. No surgeon could have operated with the deftness and delicacy of the Apaches who had worked on their helpless, screaming victim. They had kept him alive as long as possible before submitting his extremities to the slowly burning wood. They had kept the last flickering spark of life in him so that he might still feel the torture of the flames. The eyes and nose were gone, leaving thick black blood scabs to mark their former position on the caricature of a face. The white teeth, a fine and perfect set, were fully revealed in a wide lipless grin as though the dead man was laughing up at Shell for having played a ghastly prank on him.

Shell cinched his courage and kicked away the smoldering wood. God himself would have a hard time recognizing this victim of Apache torture. Shell walked away from the corpse. He reached the station and whistled sharply three times. The faint response sounded almost like an echo. There would be no fear of Apaches now. They would not return to that place of death. The restless soul of their murdered victim would haunt the darkness, disguising his voice to imitate Bú, the Owl, to lure his murderers into a trap.

Shell waited by the ruin. Hoofs thudded on the hard earth. Dusty appeared, leading the horses. "All clear?" he asked in a strained voice.

"All clear," said Shell.

"What about the water?"

"Inside," said Shell with a jerk of his head toward the rocks.

"Didn't you look?"

"It'll be there," said Shell laconically.

"What's that stink?"

Shell pointed toward the corral. "Go look," he invited.

Dusty dropped the reins, and Shell walked over to pick them up. Dusty walked into the corral toward the still-smoking object in the center of it. "What the hell!" he said. He walked a little closer to it. "Jesus God!" he spat out. He whirled, just as Shell had done, and ran a few awkward steps before he too spilled his guts.

Shell grinned evilly. Dusty wasn't quite as hardened as he always tried to appear. Shell led the horses into the entrance to the Tanks. He looked back at Dusty.

Dusty dashed away the strings of bile from his dripping mouth. "Yuh dirty bastard!" he spluttered.

Shell grinned again. He led the horses into the natural tunnel that gave entry to the tanks. His heart leaped as he smelled the water. The horses whinnied and pushed against him. The moonlight glinted from the shallow waters trapped in the natural rock tanks from a spring that welled from beneath a rock overhang.

The enclosed area was fully sixty yards across, roughly oval in shape, with the tanks close to the entrance and the remainder of the area covered with littered rock and drifted sand stippled with low scrub brush. The enclosure was shut off from the movement of the rising night wind, and the lifeless, heavy air still retained the heat of the day, bringing a fresh outpouring of sweat from Shell although he still wondered where it came from.

He watered the horses and dropped bellyflat beside them to drink a little himself. It was warm and a little gamey to the taste, but he had to force himself to stop drinking it as he felt his guts tighten again preparatory to retching.

Dusty dropped on the far side of the horses and drank as Shell had done. He raised his head and looked hard at Shell. "Yuh got a great sense of humor, *hombre,*" he said thinly.

Shell sat up and felt for the makings. He withdrew the sweat-damp sack of tobacco and fashioned a cigarette from them and the thin corn husks. He snapped a lucifer on a thumbnail and lighted up. He tossed the makings to Dusty. "You once asked me if the Apaches were worse than the Comanches," he said dryly. "Now you know."

Dusty deftly caught the makings. He formed a tube of the husks and tobacco and lighted it. He drew the sweet smoke gratefully into his lungs. "They won't be back then?"

Shell shook his head. "Not likely. Not for twenty-four hours at least. By that time we'll be water-soaked and on our way again."

Dusty blew a smoke ring. "To where?" he said quietly.

Shell led the horses away from the water and tethered them. "To Sonora," he said over his shoulder. "You knew that."

"We got run out of Coahuila a little more than two months past," Dusty said.

Shell walked toward him. "And Texas," he said. "Because we fought those Yankees. And New Mexico because the Bluebellies were hunting us. If they know we're here in Arizona they'll track us down. We could have taken the oath of allegiance and avoided all this."

"Not likely," said Dusty. He spat to one side.

Shell squatted at the edge of the tank. He flipped a pebble into the water. "That leaves Sonora," he said quietly.

"What about California?"

"Same as Texas, New Mexico, and Arizona. There's no place for 'unreconstructed' Rebels in the United States, *compañero*. We take the oath or we get out. It's as simple as that."

Dusty lay flat on his back and studied the moonlit sky. "Maybe the word got down to Sonora from Juarez' boys that we might come this way," he said thoughtfully. "Them Mexicans won't take kindly to two men who fought for Maximilian."

"Sonora is a long way from Mexico City," said Shell.

"They got telegraphs in Mexico too," said Dusty. "And couriers. Word gets around fast and we've been on the way well over two months."

Shell had no ready answer. A cold feeling came over him. His temples tightened. A strange sort of fear settled in his gut. There really wasn't *any* place they could go. Four years of fighting a war that was doomed from the start. Six months of fighting for Maximilian, whose cause was also doomed when the French troops pulled out of Mexico. Two and a half months of running and hiding, first from the Mexican Republicans, then the Yankee soldiers in Texas and New Mexico. Too, they had had to avoid Comanches and Lipans, Mescalero Apaches and now the Chiricahua Apaches. If they went into Sonora the Mexicans would perhaps be waiting for them.

Dusty blew a smoke ring and idly watched it float up into the quiet air. "Maybe Colonel De Tassigny ain't even down in Sonora now," he said. "What then?"

"We've got to take a chance on that," said Shell.

Dusty turned his head and looked at him. "Yeh, but the colonel fought *for* Benito Juarez, not *against* him, like we done. Sure, Juarez granted him and his men the right to land in Sonora to start a *colonia,* but that was for ex-Rebels that fought on the Republican side. Yuh think De Tassigny's got enough pull with ol' Benito to keep us out'a the hands of the Republicans? They got plenty of ammunition, *compañero,* and plenty of rifles, and all kinds of walls to stand a couple of *hombres* like us up against. You know what kind of trial we might get, Shell. *Ley del fuego!*"

Shell sipped a little water. *Ley del fuego* . . . the law of fire. Free a man and let him run for his freedom. If he outran the bullets he was free. It saved the time and bother of a trial and, besides, God would sort out the just and the unjust.

"You hear me?" said Dusty.

Shell nodded. "Maybe the colonel might be able to hide us out for a time. Maybe the heat will cool off. Maybe the Republicans will forget us."

"Maybe . . . maybe . . . maybe . . . ," mimicked Dusty. "Yuh better, by all that's holy, hope so!" He rolled over on his belly and looked at Shell. His blue eyes narrowed. He took the cigarette butt from his lips. "What the hell is that?" he added in a low voice.

Shell turned his head. Sand had drifted in a slope from halfway up the full height of the rock wall at the northern end of the enclosure. The moonlight fell upon a cleared area in the center of the slope. It was clear and sharp. Something protruded from the sand, like some alien growth, for it was like nothing Shell had ever seen. It was rather oval in shape, but was not smoothly contoured like a rock shaped by wind and sand. It wasn't a rock. Of that he was sure.

Dusty stood up slowly, his leather creaking softly. "Shell?" he said in a low voice.

Shell stood up. He dropped the cigarette butt to the ground and pressed a worn boot sole on it, slowly grinding it into the rock. He narrowed his eyes. The moonlight was bright enough now to read print with ease. He studied the object and then he knew what it was. *By God, he knew what it was!* He walked past the tanks and stopped for a fraction of a minute at the base of the slope. His boots grated as he walked on. They husked through the sand as he went up the slope. He knew without looking back that Dusty was not far behind him, drawn as irresistibly as Shell had been drawn.

Shell stopped twenty feet from the object. An eerie feeling came over him. The object had human features. The eyes were staring fixedly at him.

Dusty stopped beside Shell. He cleared his throat. "It's a head," he said huskily. "*A human head. . . .*"

Chapter Three

Shell moved forward as though in a dream, gazing at the head. The eyes were looking directly at him in a fixed, unwinking stare. It was the head of a dead man buried up to his neck in the hot sand. The Apaches had been at work, or rather at *play,* inside the rock enclosure as well as on the outside. They must have really *hated* this one. The long dirty gray hair had been gathered together and tied to a stake which had been driven deep into the sand thus drawing the head back so that it would stare upward a little toward the southern sky. The face was set and taut. How long had he been helpless there, staring at the burning sun until his mind had cracked and he had died a gibbering idiot?

"Jesus God," said Dusty. He passed a hand across his eyes.

One of the horses whinnied and the sound of it echoed around the rock enclosure and died quickly away. The wind whispered through the crevices and stirred the heavy air within Horno Tanks.

"There's an old shovel back there," said Shell. "Go get it so we can cover this thing."

Dusty turned on a heel and took three paces.

"Wait!" snapped Shell.

The head had moved a little. It had hardly been perceptible. Shell dropped to one knee. The head moved again and the swollen tongue was thrust between the cracked lips. The mouth worked. The man was trying to speak.

"Get that shovel!" yelled Shell. He began to dig at the warm sand with his bare hands as Dusty ran back up the slope. Shell cut loose the gray hair. Dusty shoved him aside and drew his Navy Colt in one fluid motion, hooking his thumb over the hammer spur to cock it. He leveled it at the head.

Shell jumped to his feet. "You loco!" he shouted. "You'll arouse every Apache within five miles of here!"

Dusty turned slowly, his eyes wide in his head. He let down the hammer of the Colt and sheathed the heavy weapon. He drew his thick-bladed bowie knife and stepped forward again. "*This* won't arouse them," he said quietly.

"He's still alive," said Shell.

Dusty looked at Shell. "For how long?" he said. "He can't live after that."

It wasn't mercy in the mind of Matt Dustin. They had no time to waste trying to bring this pitiful relic of humanity back to life. The man should have died hours ago. It was a miracle that he was still alive. Dusty was the practical one, the materialist.

"No," said Shell a fraction of a second before the razor-honed blade would leap toward that taut-corded throat. Dusty's eyes held Shell's for a fleeting moment. Dusty knew what he saw in those red-rimmed gray eyes. He looked away. "Christ!" he said disgustedly. That and nothing more. He sheathed the heavy knife and turned to plunge down the slope. Shell watched him for a moment and then resumed his digging. In a few moments Dusty was back with the old shovel. The moon was fully up by the time they were able to free the man from his sandy prison. He was partly clothed but his boots were gone. They carried him to the nearest tank and placed him gently atop a pair of blankets Dusty got from his cantle roll. Dusty plucked the makings from Shell's shirt pocket and teetered on his heels as he squatted beside the tank watching Shell with amused eyes as Shell worked on the limp body.

Shell washed the face and upper body. He bathed the swollen lips and allowed a little water to trickle into the dry mouth by inserting a wet rag between the lips.

"The Good Samaritan," said Dusty dryly as he lighted up.

The eyes puzzled Shell. They stared fixedly at the sky. The lids never lowered or raised. He placed his face close to that of the dying man. He touched the lids and turned away with a sickness in his soul. "Get my razor case," he said thickly.

"Yuh aimin' to shave him?" said Dusty sarcastically.

Shell looked at his partner. "They sewed his eyelids up with fine gut," he said quietly, "so that he'd be sure to get the full benefit of the sun tomorrow until he died."

Dusty got to his feet, casting a horrified glance at the fixed stare of the man. He hurried to Shell's horse and got the razor case.

"Make a small fire. Boil some water. Clean my best razor," said Shell.

"What about the smoke?" said Dusty.

"I said the Apaches wouldn't be back," said Shell patiently.

"They can wait on the trail," said Dusty.

Shell looked up at him. "God's blood!" he snapped. "Can't you make a fire *without* smoke?"

Shell looked down at the set face of the man. He was likely dying anyway. Dusty was right. The face moved a little. The lips worked. It was difficult to tell what he really looked like, but he was a man of spare build, perhaps in his middle or late fifties. "From the looks of him," he said thoughtfully, "he couldn't have been out in the sun very long. An hour or so. If it had been longer than that he'd likely have been dead by now. The devils wanted him to stay alive all night with the water right near him and then face the sun all day tomorrow."

"Beats me how he stayed alive at all," said Dusty as he lighted the fire he had built from scraps of dry brush. He scooped up some water in his old camp kettle and placed it near the fire. They sat and smoked until the water boiled. Dusty cleaned the razor and handed it to Shell. The light wasn't the best but there wasn't much Shell could do about it. He wet his cracked lips. "Hold his head firm," he said.

Carefully, delicately, he severed the fine gut that held back the lids. Blood flowed a little, but at last the lids could be lowered. Shell covered them with salve and bandaged the eyes. The moonlight was slanting from the west when he finished. He covered the spare body against the rising chill of the desert night.

Dusty had boiled some coffee. He handed a battered tin cup to Shell. "Bet you even-up he don't last until dawn," he said.

Shell did not answer. Dusty was probably right. He had seen enough men die in his time. Weariness swept through his body. He seemed to be more tired than he had been in many days.

"What about us?" said Dusty. "We can't stay here too long."

"We can stay until he dies," said Shell. "We owe him that much at least."

Dusty sipped at his coffee. "After Corinth I saw you walk away with half the company lying dead or dying on the battlefield. You never even looked back."

Shell did not answer. He placed his empty cup on the ground and studied the dying man. Somehow this was different. No soldier can remain efficient while breaking his heart over the many dead comrades and agonized wounded he has seen, for then his use as a soldier is gone.

The moon died. Darkness once again crept across the desert. It seemed to move in a little, crouch and listen, then advance a little further. The rocks began to crack and whisper as they cooled and contracted. Dusty took his carbine and patrolled outside of the rock enclosure. It was still difficult for him to accept the fact that the Apaches would not return.

Shell looked at the dying fire. The bed of ashes flared fitfully now and then, showing a glowing red eye like a ruby on velvet. He should have put it out but somehow he felt that if he did, the lingering soul of the dying man would drift off into the windy darkness of the desert. Now and then he would raise his head and listen. In a sense, Dusty was right. There was nothing to prevent the Apaches from waiting along the trail if they learned that two white men had reached Horno Tanks after they had left. It was just the immediate vicinity of the Tanks that would be haunted by the soul of the dead man, or men, for they would certainly believe the man they had buried to the neck could hardly survive. Nothing went on in that country they did not know about. They could move faster than white men. They could find water and food where a white man would die of starvation or thirst. They would never be seen but they would see everything. No man moved there without them knowing about it. Dusty and Shell had been the exception but that had been because Shell had out-Indianed them. It had likely been more luck than skill. A white man was a fool to think he could survive in that country in such times.

The wind began to die away as the hours passed. It became much quieter, but there was no peace in the quiet. The loneliness of the place moved in to settle over the Tanks. Shell could not sleep. He fashioned smoke after smoke and thanked God he had brought along a plentiful supply of the weed. Increasingly, in the past months, the intense feeling of loneliness seemed to move in on him out of the dark emptiness beyond the dying campfire. He had never mentioned it to Dusty. That rawhide-souled *hombre* would have laughed at Shell. There was no better man to stand beside one in a hard fight, or back to back if the odds got too great, but unless one talked in generalities Dusty was hardly the type for deep, soul-searching talk late at night about a bed of glowing coals when a man strives to reach his soul and learn the significance of his life.

"*Barranca,*" the voice husked out of the darkness.

The flickering lucifer stopped an inch short of the cigarette tip. Shell narrowed his eyes. It was the wind. But the wind had almost died away. Shell shook his head. He was hearing things. He cupped the match about the tip of the cigarette.

"Barranca," said the low voice again.

Shell looked up. Dusty was moving through the darkness toward him. "What about barranca?" said Shell.

Dusty stopped and grounded his carbine. "What the hell are yuh talkin' about?" he said.

"You spoke, didn't you?"

Dusty shook his head. "Yuh been hearin' things. Quiet as the grave out there." He laughed shortly at the suggestive simile. "Toss me the makin's, *compañero.*"

"Haven't you any of your own?"

Dusty grinned crookedly. "Not as long as I can use yours." He caught the tossed makings out of the air. "Barranca? What's that?"

"A deep canyon. A river gorge."

Dusty digested that while he shaped a smoke. He lighted it and looked curiously at Shell over the flare of the lucifer.

"Barranca," repeated the voice.

They both turned and looked at the dim shape of the dying man. Shell got up and went to him. The ravaged lips moved and a faint sound came from them. *"Barranca. . . ."*

"What does he mean?" said Dusty.

Shell shook his head. He drew the blanket about the stranger's shoulders. "Get some water," he said.

Dusty handed Shell a tin cup. Shell tenderly raised the gray head and dribbled a little water over the cracked lips. The tongue greedily licked at the moisture. The head sagged.

"Is he gone?" said Dusty.

"Not yet. Beats the hell out of me how he's still alive. How long can he live?"

Dusty blew a smoke ring. "Even-odds he don't make the dawn," he said.

"Barranca," said the faraway-sounding voice. *"La Barranca Escondida."*

Shell wet the lips again. Something touched his memory with a light finger and then was gone. "What is it, old-timer?" he said.

The lips moved but no sound came from them.

"He's delirious," said Shell.

The two of them sat smoking beside the tank. It was like a death watch. "Get some sleep," said Dusty at last.

Shell shook his head. "No use. Go ahead yourself."

Dusty yawned widely. He picked up a blanket. "Wake me when yuh want to sleep," he said. He looked about. "I believe yuh when yuh say *they* won't be back, but just the same I'll feel a helluva lot better with someone on watch." He walked to the sand slope and hollowed a place for hips and shoulders. He placed his Spencer at one side and his Colt at the other. He dropped to the sand, pulled the blanket over him, and was asleep almost the moment he lay still.

Time drifted on. The fire died. The ashes cooled. A faint puff of wind came through the entrance to the Tanks and scattered a fine film of ashes over the nearest tank. The darkness was now intense, like a living thing, filling the night with only the winking ice-chip stars as contrast.

"La Barranca Escondida," said Shell suddenly. He mulled the phrase over in his tired mind. Sometime, someplace he had heard it.

Shell started and his head snapped up. He shivered a little in the night chill. The wind had come again and was whispering over the rock palisade and rippling the water in the tanks. Shell had dropped off to sleep. He realized with a start that he could almost make out the ancient Indian pictographs that had been scratched in the rock wall on the far side of the tanks. It was the false dawn.

Shell stood up stiffly. He walked to the stranger and knelt beside him. Dusty's words came back to him. *"Even-odds he don't make the dawn."* Shell passed a hand beneath the blanket to feel for the heart. He waited a moment and then grinned. He should have taken up Dusty's bet.

Dusty moved. He sat up, threw back the blanket, and instinctively reached for his pistol.

Shell looked at Dusty. "You lose, *compañero,*" he said with a tired smile. "He's still alive."

Chapter Four

The pungent odor of the cooking mule meat hung heavily in the rock enclosure. Already the heat of the day was beginning to be felt. Dusty had cut thin strips of mule meat and had broken up the tough tissues with his knife. He watched with an amused expression as Shell carried the spare-framed stranger into one of the shallow caves eroded in the rock wall beyond the Tanks.

Shell eased the stranger onto the bed he had prepared for him. "Barranca," whispered the man.

"Yes, yes," said Shell. "We know. Barranca."

Dusty grinned. "Probably the name of his horse. Maybe a woman."

Shell picked up his carbine and walked through the echoing tunnel to the bright light of the desert. The sun was already topping the mountains beyond the eastern mesa pouring a flood of light and heat across the great valley. There was no sign of life. No movement. No dust. Nothing except the windless desert and the stark, looming mountains. It was almost like being on the moon.

"La Barranca Escondida," said Shell aloud. "The hidden canyon. The hidden gorge." He rubbed his shaggy beard. What did it mean? The stranger might die that day. His secret might very well die with him.

Shell walked into the stinking corral and fought back the green sickness. He found a rusted spade and dug a hole close to the edge of the rocks in the soft sandy earth that had drifted there. He cut loose the thongs that had not been burned through by the fire and dragged the pitiful relic of a man to the hole. He quickly filled it in, fighting back the sickness in his gut, but even so he had just mounded the grave when he whirled and ran, heaving out his gut. He stood there a long time, then returned to the grave and spoke a few words, then bowed his head and prayed. There was no way of telling who the man was. God would know. He picked up two pieces of wood, tied them into a cross shape, and thrust the cross into the head of the mound.

Shell walked back to the station and looked south across the bright desert. Already the heat waves were shimmering upward from the harsh surface. Far to the south, still distinguishable before the thicker heat haze arose, were two small ranges that formed a great V-shape pointing south. Somewhere roughly midway between Horno Tanks and the northern flanks of those ranges was the unmarked border between Arizona and Sonora. The country was waterless as far as he knew, until one reached the area beyond the tip of the V, and beyond that, at the northern end of the Sierra Madre Occidental, was the Mesa del Campanero—the Mesa of the Bellmaker. It was there that Colonel Marcus De Tassigny, who had commanded Shell's battalion of South Kansas-Texas Mounted Rifles until he had lost his left arm at Champion's Hill, had been given a huge grant of land to form a *colonia* composed of men whom he had led in battle during the war and also on the side of the Republican forces of Mexico in the fight against Maximilian. De Tassigny and his men were "unreconstructed" Rebels as were Dusty and Shell, but they had fought *for*, not *against* Benito Juarez. It would make no difference, of course, to De Tassigny that Shell and Dusty had fought on the opposite side in Mexico, for he'd likely welcome two fighting men. His *colonia* was on the frontier of Mexico, in Yaqui country, and two more guns would be more than welcome.

"Fighting men," said Shell. He slanted his faded campaign hat lower over his eyes against the glare of the desert. Two wars and sundry other fighting had etched one lesson into his mind. The wind was always blowing in his face; the battlegrounds were usually ill-chosen; the odds were always too great; the cause perhaps too insufficient to justify his death. "Above all," he said aloud, "no one seems to care whether I win or lose, live or die."

"Grub pile!" yelled Dusty from the mouth of the passageway.

Shell looked at him. Dusty likely had never considered the facts that had just been in Shell's mind. To Dusty a fight was a fight; a drink was a drink; one woman was the same as another. Likely he would have fought just as cheerfully on one side of the war in Mexico as he would have fought on the other. Maximilian had just paid more. Shell walked to the entrance of the tunnel. Once more he looked to the south. A bitter hopelessness descended upon him. It was something he could not eliminate, something he could not cope with in his mind. Guns, knives, fists, or boots had no effect on the unseen.

They ate silently, gnawing at the tough meat, the grease running down into their ragged beards. Now and then Shell would look at the still form of the stranger.

"We move today?" said Dusty.

Shell picked a stringy piece of meat from between his teeth with a dirty broken fingernail. "He's still alive, isn't he?"

Dusty picked up another piece of meat. "He won't last out the day."

"We can't move out of here during daylight."

The hard blue eyes looked at Shell over the dripping piece of meat. "We could have left last night."

Shell emptied the dregs of coffee from his cup. It was the last in the cup and about the last in their supplies. Supplies? They had nothing much left except tobacco and cartridges.

Dusty tore at the meat with his strong white teeth. "Now we've got to sit here for hours," he said thickly. "How long do they stay away from the dead?"

"Forty-eight hours."

"You said twenty-four before."

Shell leveled his gaze at Dusty. "You calling me a liar?" he said in a low voice.

"Don't get ringy," said Dusty. He wiped the grease from his mouth. He looked thoughtfully at the stranger. "What is this Barranca Escondida thing?"

"Beats the hell out of me," said Shell.

Dusty looked at Shell. "Does it mean anything to you?"

Shell shrugged. "Seems to me I've heard it somewhere before."

"Is it around here?"

"Not likely. Sounds Mex to me."

"Yeh. Yeh. But that don't mean a damned thing. It could be on this side of the border."

"Not likely. They call a gorge a gorge and a canyon a canyon on this side."

"What does it mean?"

"A hidden gorge. What else?"

Dusty emptied his coffee cup. "It must have more meaning than that. It's important to him, ain't it?"

"Ask *him* then." Shell stood up and rolled a cigarette. He dropped the makings into Dusty's greasy outstretched hand.

"How far to the border?" said Dusty.

"Twenty or thirty miles."

"Water?"

Shell nodded. He retrieved the makings after Dusty built his smoke. "Place called Papago Springs."

"That's Indian, ain't it?"

"Yeh. They're usually harmless. The Sand Papagos can get mean at times."

"What's beyond Papago Springs?"

"Sonora."

"And more Apaches," said Dusty dryly.

Shell blew a smoke ring. "Some," he said. "There are also Opatas, Tarahumares, and Yaquis."

Dusty looked up. "You sound like the Yaquis are something big, *compañero*."

"They are. Cousins to the Apaches. Some say they're *rougher* than the Apaches. The Mexes call them *La raza de bronce que sabe morir*."

Dusty inspected the glowing end of his cigarette. "The bronze race that knows how to die," he said thoughtfully. He looked up at Shell. "Great! From the frying pan into the fire. Salt, pepper, and gravel in the grease."

Shell spat. "You have any other ideas?"

Dusty slowly shook his head. "Man," he said reflectively, "we've got to go, whether we like it or not. But when?"

Shell sucked in lungfuls of smoke and blew it out. "We can take turns watching the desert today. We can't move during the day. If they do come back we can't make a break for it. We'll have to hold them off here. At least *we'll* have the water. The horses are not fully rested yet. By tonight they should be all right."

"How long can we hold them off if they do come back?"

Shell ran a hand along the bright brass cartridges in his gunbelt. His meaning was clear enough. "Save one for yourself, *compañero*. You saw what they did to the two men they caught here."

The heat came slowly, with insensate fury, pouring down inside the rock enclosure until it seemed the water in the tanks would rise in steam and the rock itself would melt and fuse with the burning sands. There was no escape from it. It weighted the body and burned into the lungs with every labored breath. There was nothing that could be done but to lie in the hot shade and try to live through it.

The motionless figure in the cave should have given up the ghost. It was impossible for him to live in the condition he was in, coupled with the hellish heat, *but he lived on and on.* All through that day of living hell, the very core of the summer's blasting heat, the man held on to life. It was hard to believe when at last the shadows grew on the western side of the enclosure and crept slowly across the burning rock and sand to touch the edge of the Tanks and then cover them as well. Minute after minute passed until at last the sun was gone behind the western range, painting the sky in rose and gold.

Dusty came through the passageway, his Mexican spurs chiming softly. Now that there was no fear of the Apaches he had put his silver spurs on again. They had been as much a part of him as his guns when he had fought with Maximilian. He had taken them from the corpse of an officer of the Republican cavalry after killing him. It was something Shell could not have done, but then Dusty was a materialist. He needed spurs. The man he had killed wore fine silver spurs. Therefore the spurs were now Dusty's. It was as simple as that. They were indeed fine spurs.

The moon touched the tips of the eastern mountains as Dusty and Shell ate the last of the mule meat. There would be no more. The bloated carcass had given off foul gas all during that day until Dusty, in disgust, had gutted the putrefying flesh to let the gas escape. Even so, the stench of it still drifted about Horno Tanks.

The moon touched the Tanks. If they planned to move that night they would have to wait until darkness came again. Both of them sat smoking, their backs against the warm rocks, their thoughts their own.

"La Barranca Escondida," said the voice clearly.

Dusty snapped his head around. "By God! I don't believe it!" he said. "He's still alive!"

Shell started a small fire and heated a container of broth he had made earlier that evening. He took it to the stranger and slowly fed him. By the time the moon slanted down toward the western range the man seemed to have regained some of his strength. He mumbled at intervals and then spoke clearly, and it was always the same. "La Barranca Escondida."

Shell went to get some water. He knelt beside the tank.

"Look!" said Dusty in an incredulous tone.

Shell turned. The stranger was sitting up. He pointed a gaunt hand at Shell, almost as though he could see him through the thick bandage he wore across his eyes. "La Barranca Escondida," he said clearly. *"Departamento de Camino a Las Minas de La Barranca Escondida y El Naranjal."*

"By Jesus!" yelled Shell. "That's it! That's it!"

"You gone loco?" cried Dusty.

Shell ran to Dusty and grabbed him by the arm. "He's talking about some of the biggest, richest, damndest silver mines that ever existed! Some say they were richer than Tayopa!"

Dusty gripped Shell by the arm. "Are you in your right mind? What the hell *are* yuh talking about?"

Shell looked at the stranger. He had spoken in almost flawless Spanish and the accent was hardly perceptible, but Shell was almost sure he wasn't Mexican. "Those mines have been lost for over a hundred years," said Shell in a low voice so that the stranger might not hear. "I heard about them when I was out here before the war. I didn't pay much attention to the stories. Like all lost-mine legends they grow mightily with the telling."

"You still think he's out of his mind?"

"Can you blame him?"

They walked quietly over to the stranger. He had fallen back on his blankets again and was breathing harshly. Shell placed a hand on his forehead. He wasn't too feverish. "Who are you?" asked Shell.

The man moved a little. "We didn't know they were

here," he said. "My horse died in the mountains. Ignacio's horse died twenty miles from here. We took turns riding the mule. *We didn't know they were here!*" His voice rose almost to a scream and then broke.

Shell felt the cold sweat break out on his body.

"Jesus," said Dusty in a shaken voice. "Can you imagine what it must'a felt like to get here ready for a long drink and then see *them?*"

"They made me watch," said the stranger.

That was all he had to say. He didn't have to elaborate on it. They could imagine well enough.

"Your name?" said Shell.

The man moved. "Harley," he said. "Frank Harley."

"Where were you going?"

Harley threw an arm over his bandaged eyes. "La Barranca Escondida!" he said. "They shod the mules with silver. They didn't have enough iron for shoes. They had *metal* though. Silver! Silver in great chunks! They shod the mules with silver because the mine was so rich."

"Jesus God," breathed Dusty. He looked at Shell with wide eyes.

There was still enough moonlight to see Harley's bandaged face. Shell let him sip a little water, but not too much. He was afraid the man's stomach might revolt.

Harley lay still for a long time. "Tayopa?" he said, cocking his head as though someone had mentioned the name. "Tayopa?" He laughed. "Tayopa was great! But La Barranca Escondida and El Naranjal! They were the greatest. The records lie! The Jesuits were too clever to report how much they actually took out of La Barranca Escondida and El Naranjal. The Crown got one-fifth, *or so they thought.* But the Jesuits owed no allegiance to the King of Spain. Lip service perhaps, but not loyalty. They owed their loyalty to their order and to the Black Pope who was the head of their order!"

"What the hell is he jabberin' about?" demanded Dusty.

Harley was quiet now, breathing erratically. Shell felt his pulse. Harley was hanging on to life. Something had kept him alive; *something* was still keeping him alive.

"Is there any truth in what he says?" said Dusty.

Shell squatted on his heels and rolled a cigarette. He nodded his head. "The Jesuits owned a great deal of land in Mexico. Ranches and mines. The Indians worked for them. There wasn't much control over the mine operators. The Indians were actually slaves and could be worked to death. I've heard reports that back in those days you could smell the mine workings a long distance off by the stench of rotting human flesh given off by the bodies of the Indians who had died working the mines and who had been dumped aside like offal. What puzzles me, though, is that Tayopa was always considered the greatest. I've heard vaguely of El Naranjal and the legend that it was greater than Tayopa. La Barranca Escondida is, or was, just a fairy tale, as far as I know." Shell lighted his cigarette and handed the makings to Dusty. "Don't get excited, *compañero*. These desert rats have more stories to tell than Shakespeare did. They weave 'em by the mile and cut 'em off by the yard."

Dusty fashioned his smoke. "But supposin' he *does* know something about those mines?"

Shell blew a leisurely smoke ring. "Sure, sure," he said soothingly. "Supposing he does? Hundreds of miles south of here through Apache and Yaqui country. Country that is trackless. Country that hasn't had a mine worked in a hundred years!"

Dusty wet his lips. "But the Indians would know about them mines, wouldn't they? Hell! Butter them up with a few beads on a string or a looking glass or something like that. They'd talk all right. Them tales are all handed down to them from father to son. They'd know where they were all right."

Shell took his cigarette from his mouth. "So? Supposing *your* great-grandfather had worked in those mines? Supposing he had seen his brother, his friends, and maybe even his own father die in them for silver that meant absolutely nothing to him. For wealth that poured out of Mexico in a silver flood to Spain. Was there profit of any kind in it for him and his people? You bet your life there wasn't! They couldn't even live the simple life of their forefathers. Every day in those damned mines away from the blessed air and sun until you dropped dead! So one day the Jesuits have to leave Mexico. They can't even go back to Spain! Would they leave those mines for anyone else? The hell they would! So they had the Indians conceal them and you know damned well when an Indian hides something no one else can ever find it."

"Then they *would* know where the mines were!" said Dusty triumphantly.

Shell shook his head in disgust. "Sure they would! But they wouldn't tell any white man where they were for fear the old ways would come back. Furthermore, my simple friend, *they aren't about to let any white man come poking around in that country looking for the mines himself.*"

Harley stirred. "They called them The Masters of Secrecy," he said.

"Who?" asked Shell quickly.

Harley looked directly at Shell although he could not see him. "Why, the Jesuits of course! They hoarded the silver, and when they left forever they could not take it with them. It is still there."

"Where?" said Shell.

Harley hesitated. He passed a hand over his bandage. "I . . . I. . . ." His voice faltered and died.

"At La Barranca Escondida?" said Shell.

"Yes! Yes! That is it! The mines were of such wonderful richness, it is said, that blocks hewed from the veins had to be cut into pieces so that mules might carry them to the coast for shipment to Spain."

Dusty's cigarette dropped from his gaping mouth.

Harley moved restlessly. Shell wet his cracked lips and bathed his sweating face with a wet rag. "They were in bonanza since sixteen thirty-two," said Harley.

Dusty stared. He looked quickly at Shell. "When did these Jesuits leave Mexico?" he said.

Shell half closed his eyes. "About a hundred years ago. I think they were expelled in seventeen sixty-seven."

Harley nodded eagerly. "That is correct! A hundred years ago!"

"No one has been there since?" said Dusty incredulously.

Shell touched a finger to his lips. They sat there like two dusty ravens on a fence watching the tortured face of the older man. Shell bathed the face and allowed Harley more water. He thrashed about a bit in his fever. "The Jesuits had a control over the Indians that no other representatives of the Christian faith have ever been able to gain," Harley said quietly. "Therefore, when they left Mexico they charged the Indians, under penalty of a terrible curse, never to reveal the hidden treasures except to those of the Jesuit Order. They have kept their word."

Dusty stared at Shell's dim face. "By God," he said, "then that stuff must still be there!"

Shell quickly shook his head to silence Dusty. Shell leaned toward Harley. "You know where this place is?"

There was a long silence. For a moment or two Shell thought the older man had passed on, but then Harley spoke in a low voice, so very low that Shell had to place his ear directly over Harley's mouth. "Cerro de Huesos is the first key. Cerro de Huesos. For there, on a quiet night, one might hear the dogs of La Barranca Escondida barking." Harley shifted a little. "When the wind comes from the south, a bell may be heard at. . . ." Shell did not catch the name. Harley gripped Shell by the arm. "That bell hangs in the bell tower of the church at El Naranjal." His voice died away.

Shell bathed Harley's face. He patted it. He felt Harley's heart and pulse. The man was still alive but he was in a deep sleep or a coma. There would be no more from him for a long time. Perhaps he would die before that time. Shell covered Harley with a blanket. Shell and Dusty walked back to the tank and sat by the edge. It was cooler there.

Dusty sat quietly for a long time. "What do you think, *compañero?*" he said.

Shell shrugged. "He knows a lot, Dusty," he said quietly.

"Yuh think it's the truth?"

Shell blew a smoke ring and stabbed a dirty finger through it. He looked directly at Dusty. "Let's put it this way: he knows *something*. More than any other man I have heard talk about those lost mines."

Dusty looked back over his shoulder. "By God," he breathed. "Mules shod with silver! Mines in bonanza for a hundred years! Pieces of silver chopped into smaller pieces for easier transportation to the coast!"

"Maybe it's just delirium," said Shell.

Dusty wet his cracked lips. "Mebbe," he said in a low, hard voice. "But if it ain't. . . ." He looked at Shell and the two of them agreed mentally. They knew each other well enough. There was no hope for them in the United States and Mexico, but with silver to pay the way . . . silver enough for Croesus . . . *silver enough to buy anything they wanted.*

Chapter Five

They should have pulled foot during the long night. They could have abandoned Harley or taken him along. They did neither. All night long, between dozing, they felt their minds teeming with the thoughts Harley had planted in them. Supposing he was completely mad? Supposing it had been sheer delirium? Supposing it was the senseless wanderings of a sick mind? *Supposing it was true?*

They had almost forgotten the Apache menace. A glittering sheen of silver stood between them and the bushy-headed devils. It almost completely blinded them except for the fact they still took turns standing guard. If the Apaches did come back that would be the end. If they did not, and Harley lived, it might be the beginning. The beginning of a life such as Dusty and Shell had never, in their wildest imaginings, dreamed about.

The dawn came again. The sun arose. The heat returned. Midday came. There was no sign of dust on the desert. There was no sign of life out there. Harley was still alive, but he did not speak. Late in the afternoon he stirred, and as the shadows crept down the slopes and into the rock enclosure, Shell kept a close watch on the older man. Shell's gut ached. He was a little faint from hunger and the enervating heat.

Harley moved. "Is there anyone here?" he said.

"Yes," said Shell. He beckoned quickly to Dusty. Spurs softly chimed as Dusty strode over to them.

"You have saved my life," said the older man.

"Por nada," said Shell carelessly.

"You speak Spanish?"

"Enough," said Shell. "But not as well as you."

Harley was quiet for a moment or two. "There are two of you," he said. "Who are you?"

"Call me Shell," said Shell. "My *compañero* is named Dusty."

"You have no other names?"

Dusty grinned. "Somewhere, someplace, oldtimer," he said.

Harley smiled. "I understand."

"How do you feel?" said Shell.

"Weak, but lucid. I was in fever?"

"Very much so."

"I smell water," said Harley. "Are we at the Tanks?"

"Yes," said Shell.

"My eyes," said Harley. He pressed thin hands against the bandage.

"You'll be all right," said Shell.

"How did you get past the Apaches?" said Harley.

Dusty spat. "Shell knows their ways. I must admit I didn't like the way we had to do it, but ol' Shell was right. He says they won't be back because of the dead man out there."

"That would be Ignacio," said Harley quietly. He looked at Shell, although he could not see him. *"They made me watch."*

"We know," said Shell.

"They didn't kill me because I must have gone out of my mind."

"Mind-gone-far," said Shell.

"You know them very well," said the older man. "They would not kill me then, but they made sure I would die. The sun would kill me, not them. You know them well, Shell."

"Well enough to stay as far away as possible from them," said Shell.

"So?" said Harley. "Then why are you here?"

A look sped between Dusty and Shell. "That doesn't matter," said Shell quickly.

"Let me have some water," said Harley.

Dusty rubbed his shaggy beard. "Is that all yuh got to tell us?" he said.

Harley touched his cracked lips. "A few hours of that sun," he said. He shivered.

"Yuh didn't answer me," said Dusty.

It was very quiet except for the whisper of the rising wind. Harley stopped exploring his ravaged lips. He could not see the two men, but he looked from one to the other of them.

"Well?" prompted Dusty.

Harley tilted his head to one side. "Can I please have some water?" he asked politely.

Shell reached for the water container but Dusty fiercely gripped Shell's wrist so that the water splashed over the side. Dusty shook his head. Dusty moved closer to Harley. "Yuh said something about La Barranca Escondida," he said.

"I did?" said Harley in surprise.

"You did," said Dusty.

It was quiet for a moment or two. The wind rippled the shallow water. It lapped against the side of the tank. "How about that water?" asked Harley.

"How about it?" repeated Dusty.

Shell placed the container to one side. It clinked faintly against the rock. "La Barranca Escondida," prompted Shell. Greed crawled in his mind like a canker worm. *"Departamento de Camino a Las Minas de La Barranca Escondida y El Naranjal."*

"What has that to do with me?" said Harley.

"You tell *us,"* said Shell.

A cold fear seemed to settle in the older man. He could not, of course, see those two fierce, bearded faces watching him, but he could *feel* them. Their greed seemed to reach overpoweringly out to him.

Shell tapped Harley's bony knee. "I'll refresh your memory, oldtimer. Road to the Mines of the Hidden Gorge and Orange Grove. Come on, Harley! You know what we're talking about! You speak excellent Spanish but you're no Mexican. I don't know anything about Hidden Gorge, but I've heard of the Orange Grove and the Lost Tayopa as well."

"Who hasn't?" said Harley dryly.

Dusty gripped Harley by the shoulder. "Don't get cute!" he growled.

"You were heading south when the Apaches caught you and your friend," prompted Shell.

Harley shook his head. "East to the Santa Cruz."

"There's nothing along the Santa Cruz except the ruins of Tubac and Tumacacori," said Shell. "Nothing south of Tucson for white men but death with a painted face. You know the jingle . . . Tucson, Tubac, Tumacacori To-Hell! You were heading *south,* oldtimer."

"What do you know about it? How do you know *where* we were going?"

Shell spread out a big left hand with the tips of fingers pointing south. "My left hand is before you," he said. "Tips of the fingers pointing south." He tapped the hand with a right forefinger. "The right edge of the palm are the mountains through which you came. The palm is the desert where we are now, with Horno Tanks in the center. The thumb is the great mesa east of here. My fingers are the parallel ranges of the Sierra Madre south of the border. If you have been heading for the Santa Cruz, as you claim, you would not have come from the west by way of the Tanks. You would have avoided them for two obvious reasons. The Apaches and the fact that you could find water north of here at Dripping Springs. But, to go south, to Papago Springs, you would *have* to come to Horno Tanks. You aren't ignorant of the Apaches, but you took a hell of a risk coming here to Horno Tanks. Something made you take that deadly risk, Harley. *Something big!*"

"Like lost silver mines," said Dusty.

"Water," said Harley.

Dusty picked up the container and refilled it. He sloshed the water around within the container but did not offer it to the thirsty man. Harley held out a trembling hand. Dusty drank noisily and then poured out the rest of the water.

Shell rolled a smoke and lighted it. He passed the makings to Dusty. They sat there blowing smoke toward the bandaged face. Harley sniffed eagerly. He too was addicted to the weed. "Give me a cigarette at least," he pleaded.

Dusty grinned at Shell. Lack of tobacco might break Harley faster than the lack of water. "When did you say the Apaches would be back, Shell?" he asked.

"They won't come near the dead," said Harley.

"Not for a time," said Shell. "That time is running out."

"Especially if they know two white men are here with horses and guns," added Dusty.

"We can be out of here by then," said Harley.

"We can?" said Dusty politely.

Harley knew well enough what Dusty meant. A tremor ran through him.

"Can you imagine how surprised they'll be to find him still alive?" said Shell.

Dusty nodded. "It'll be quiet as the grave after we leave. So quiet he won't even hear them come in here. Then, all of a sudden he'll *know* they're here, standing watching him."

"I'd kill myself first!" said Harley.

"You wouldn't have a chance," said Shell. He eyed the older man speculatively. "Besides, you aren't the type to give up. You'll stick to the last cartridge, the last drop of water, the last drop of blood. Even if they don't come back there's no food here. All the water you want, but no food. Weak as you are, how long do you think you'd last? Three days? A week? That's hardly likely."

"You won't leave me here," said Harley. "You saved my life. You wouldn't throw it away again."

"Wouldn't we?" murmured Dusty.

Harley touched his lips with the tip of his tongue. "Look," he said desperately. "I'll pay you well to take me along. Anywhere!"

Dusty spat. "Yuh ain't got a centavo in your jeans," he said.

Shell glanced at Dusty. Shell hadn't gone through Harley's pockets when he had been helpless. He remembered now how in more than one scrap in the war Dusty had prowled out into the night after the shooting was over, armed with a rusted bayonet. It was handy to pry open jaws for gold fillings. His bowie had served to chop off swollen fingers that resisted having their rings pulled off. He should have known Dusty would have searched Harley when Shell wasn't around.

"Yuh can't dicker with us," said Dusty. "Not *that* way."

Shell almost felt sorry for the older man. He could smell the green fear emanating in Harley's cold sweat.

"La Barranca Escondida," said Dusty.

"They shod the mules with silver," said Shell.

"Tayopa was great," said Dusty, "but La Barranca and El Naranjal were the greatest. The records lie!"

"They hoarded the silver and when they left forever they could not take it with them," said Shell. *"It is still there."*

"Cerro de Huesos, the Hill of Bones, is the first key," murmured Dusty.

"When the wind comes from the south a bell may be heard at Cerro de Huesos," said Shell. "That bell hangs in the bell tower of the church at El Naranjal."

Harley sat still for a long time. "You win," he said. "May I have some water?"

Dusty looked at Shell. Shell nodded. Harley greedily sucked in the fluid. "A cigarette?" he said. Shell rolled one and thrust it between the cracked lips. He snapped a lucifer on his thumb and lighted the tip of the cigarette. Harley gratefully drew in the smoke. He smiled. "You have a persuasive way about you," he said quietly.

Shell grinned. Dusty laughed. "When do we leave?" said Dusty.

Shell blew out a puff of smoke. "As soon as possible," he said. "You feel well enough to ride, Harley?"

Harley raised his head. "God, yes!" he said. "I'd crawl on my hands and knees to get away from here before the Apaches return."

"Where's the treasure map?" said Dusty.

Harley tapped his head. "In here," he said.

Dusty narrowed his eyes. "What do you mean?"

"I memorized it."

Dusty looked at Shell. "Mebbe he's kidding us?"

"How could we know?" said Shell.

Harley inhaled the tobacco smoke. "You don't," he said quietly. "You put up your money and you take your chance."

Shell burst out laughing. "By God!" he said. "You've got us there, haven't you! Now we *have* to take you!"

Harley laughed with Shell, but Dusty's face tightened beneath the dust that masked it. "One thing, oldtimer," he said. "This is a great joke. I'm splitting my sides. But you pull a fast one on us and you'd wish to God we *had* left you to the Apaches!"

Harley's laughter died away. A coldness seemed to settle about him. He ground out the cigarette. "Fair enough," he said.

Shell stood up. "Let's get moving," he said. "We've time before the moon rises."

"We'd better wait until the dark after the moon," said Harley.

"No," said Shell. He looked about. He had had enough of Horno Tanks. "If we move fast enough we can be at Papago Springs tomorrow morning."

They moved fast. Fear and greed were the spurs. They hid or wiped out all traces of their presence as best they could. Likely it wouldn't deceive the Apaches, but they'd have to chance that. The canteens were filled. Each of them drank as much water as he could hold. They mounted Harley on the rump of Dusty's rangy bay. Shell led the way with Dusty riding close behind. They did not look back as they rode south. The Apaches weren't there, but they had left something behind them, a brooding, malevolent feeling that would haunt Horno Tanks forever.

They rode steadily until the moon began to rise, making good time, reeling off the miles, until by the time the first light flowed into the valley, they were riding in a low, wide swale that cut off the view from either side. It wasn't Shell's desire to ride in the swale, for if the Apaches couldn't see them, neither could they see the Apaches, but there was little choice. Movement, or a thread of dust on that moonlit desert, would bring them down.

They halted ten minutes on the hour. Once Shell took his battered German fieldglasses, the only thing he had ever picked up from the enemy dead, and climbed to the lip of the swale to look back along the trail. It was almost as bright as day. Something hung in the quiet air between the mesa and the Tanks. Dust rose thinly. The dust of many horses. His guts contracted. They had just cleared the Tanks in time.

He did not mention the fact to Dusty or Harley, but Dusty knew. He had served too long with Shell not to know.

Hour after hour they kept on. Sometimes riding, sometimes walking, leading Dusty's bay, with Harley swaying weakly in the saddle, but he never complained. He knew what would happen if he could not keep on. *Ride or die!*

The moon waned and died. There was no sound in the blackness of the night except the steady thudding of the hoofs. No one spoke. It wasn't a time for speaking. It wasn't a time for doing anything except to keep moving south, putting as many miles as possible between themselves and Horno Tanks. The danger was relative. They knew what was behind them, but they didn't know what was ahead of them except the promise of uncounted riches. Such a promise blotted out the fear of the unknown to the south.

Shell suddenly realized there were low mountain ranges on either hand. The ground was harder now and the worn hoofs rang like cracked bells as they struck rock. He could see the dim ranges more clearly now and knew the false dawn would soon be there. He didn't know if they had crossed the border or not. He really didn't care. One side of the line was as dangerous as the other, and the Apaches knew no such boundaries. It was all their country whether it be Arizona, Sonora, Chihuahua, and even as far south as Durango.

Dusty looked at the faintly graying sky and then up at Harley. "Papago Springs next," he said, like a train conductor. "Where to from there?"

"Cerro del Piloncillo," he said. "It can be seen when one is twenty miles south of Papago Springs."

Dusty looked at Shell. Shell shrugged as though to say: What else can we do?

The sun was slowly brightening the gray tones of the eastern sky when Shell called a halt. They led the tired horses into a draw and then climbed higher on a rugged slope to where a natural bastion was shaped amongst the tumbled rocks. They could hold off any number of Apaches here, providing their water held out, and they had no food at all.

Dusty made himself comfortable. It would be a long, hellish day amongst those rocks. Shell unbandaged Harley's eyes and examined them. "How do you feel?" he asked.

Harley smiled and nodded his head. He kept his eyes closed while Shell bathed them, removing the sticky salve.

Dusty shifted, blowing up a puff of smoke. "Where to beyond Cerro del Piloncillo?" he asked.

Harley hesitated. He rubbed his sunbeaten face.

"Well?" said Dusty shortly.

"Mesa del Campanero," said the older man.

Shell looked quickly at Harley and then at Dusty. They did not speak, but they knew Mesa del Campanero—the Mesa of the Bellmaker—was where Colonel De Tassigny had his *colonia.*

"Then where?" said Dusty.

Harley smiled secretively. "I'll tell you when the time comes, Dusty."

"You'll tell us now!" snapped Dusty.

Harley did not answer. The sun had tipped the eastern mountains and now shone down into the valley. Shell eased off his gunbelt and draped it over a rock. He checked both guns and placed them close at hand. He was dead tired and hungry. Maybe sleep would temporarily cancel out the hunger. The sun was warm on his bent back.

"It is a great country," said Harley. "Mountains a mile high and barrancas a mile deep. Sun-blasted mesas. The mountains are high, so very high. Gigantic and windswept, crossed only by the eagles. There are deer, bears, and jaguars in the lower country. On the heights there is no life except specks in the sky, like bits of charred paper, betraying the presence of the eagles."

The sun was hot on Shell's back. He eased off a boot to inspect a blistered heel.

"For miles there is no sign of the white man, and the Indian is seen only when he wants to be seen," said Harley. There was almost a dreamlike quality to his soft voice.

Shell eased off the other boot, wrinkling his nose at the stench. "Jesus," he said softly.

"You know that country well, eh, oldtimer?" said Dusty as he rolled a cigarette.

"Yes," said Harley. "I've been there many times."

"But never found the silver."

"It takes time. This time I *know* where it is."

"You'd better," said Dusty as he lighted up.

"I do," said Harley. "I'll lead you there."

"Keno," said Shell. He straightened up and wiped his mouth with the back of a dirty hand. He reached for the makings and began to fashion a cigarette. He looked at Dusty. His companion sat with the cigarette pasted to his lower lip, his dusty hat slanted low over his blue eyes. He didn't move. He was watching Harley. "You're certain for sure you can lead us there?" said Dusty quietly.

"Positive," said Harley.

Dusty looked up at Shell. Shell turned. The blow of the intensely bright sun against his eyes made him wince. He slanted his hat over his eyes. Dusty jerked his head toward Harley. The older man sat hatless on a rock, thin hands resting on gaunt thighs, looking to the east with wide open eyes, *directly into the glare of the sun.*

Shell took the unlighted cigarette from his lips. He walked softly over to Harley and looked into his sun-ravaged face. The eyes were wide open. Shell passed a hand quickly up and down before those staring eyes and they did not blink. The man who was to lead them to La Barranca Escondida and El Naranjal, richer even than Tayopa, where mules were shod with silver, was completely, totally, absolutely blind!

Chapter Six

The heat was a living thing, beating down from the pitiless sun and blasting the land. The dark rock absorbed the heat, and the lighter colored ground radiated it. Shimmering, dancing heat waves moved upward from everything and everywhere. Nothing could possibly live in that inferno, but three men and two horses did. There was no escape, no alleviation, nothing but to endure the endless blazing hours. The heat haze was like an enveloping fog until it seemed that the dividing line between earth and sky no longer existed. Everything was distorted, hidden, or partially obscured. The shade of the greater rocks meant nothing. The heat was the same, the only difference was that the sun did not burn itself into the skin in the shade. Water seemed sucked from the body, but they could not drink as much as they liked. The only thing to do was to rinse the dry, gummy mouth and squirt the gamey water back into the canteens. Shell allowed each of the suffering horses half a hatful of water, begrudging them every drop. His only solace was the temporary coolness of his battered campaign hat as he put it back on his burning head.

Surprisingly enough it was Frank Harley who stood the heat better than his two younger and stronger companions. He sat in the hot shade, his back against a rock, looking steadily at the rock face opposite him, thinking his own thoughts. Dusty lay flat on his belly, forearms crossed, bearded chin resting on his forearms, watching the peaceful, impassive face of the blind man. Taut lines etched themselves on Dusty's mahogany-hued skin. It was almost as though he was trying to worm the secret of La Barranca Escondida out of Frank Harley's mind.

Shell sat in the shade, knees up, forearms resting on his knees, hat slanted low over his burning eyes. There was no taste in him for the tobacco. At any given moment he would have traded his third share of the lost mines for a quart of ice-cold water. His third share? He grinned weakly to himself. All they had to go on was the delirious mumblings of a man who might be an utter dreamer or whose mind might have slipped from its hinges when the Apaches worked on Ignacio. Shell looked at the older man. "Who was Ignacio?" he asked in a cracked voice.

Dusty's red-rimmed eyes slanted toward Shell and then back at Harley.

Harley did not move. "My friend," he said.

"Sure, sure," said Shell patiently. "But what else was he to you?"

Harley smiled faintly. "What more would one want than true friendship?" he said.

"I'm not interested in your second-rate philosophy," said Shell coldly. "Who was he? What did he know? Why was he with you?"

Harley looked directly at Shell with his sightless eyes. "He was my friend. That was why he was with me."

Dusty shifted a little. "Mebbe it was Ignacio who knew the way to the mines. Mebbe it was *him,* not *you,* Harley."

Frank Harley looked in Dusty's direction. "But you don't know that, do you, Dusty?"

Dusty raised his head. "Mebbe I can find out," he said.

They did not speak for five minutes. The sun was directly overhead and the scant shade had fled. There was nothing to protect them now but their clothing. Shell fashioned a hat for Harley out of an extra shirt, a sort of a turban effect that gave the older man the air of a magi or a Hindu fakir.

Dusty grinned sardonically. "The Three Wise Men," he said. He laughed again. He looked about. "The Three Wise Men missed Bethlehem and ended up in hell!"

The long hours dragged past until it seemed that human flesh and blood could stand no more, and then the sun was gone behind the western ranges, dyeing the sky in an intense agony of rose and gold. The relief was almost instantaneous despite the fact that the motionless air was still thick and oppressive with heat.

Shell stood up. "Let's go," he said. "We can make Papago Springs before moonrise."

They carried the limp figure of Harley to Shell's horse. Despite his light weight the two big men staggered weakly. Dusty panted hard as he stood there in the darkness. "What about food?" he said.

Shell wiped the stinging sweat from his eyes. "Water first," he said. "We'll have to trust in luck for food."

"That's the story of our lives," said Dusty bitterly.

They led the horses down the slope of loose rock, clattering in the darkness. Shell struck out, heading due south. He had never been at Papago Springs but they'd have to chance it. It was somewhere at the southern end of the great V of naked mountains that seemed to move in closer in the darkness. Supposing the Apaches were there? Or maybe the Yaquis? One or the other, the results would be the same.

The moon had not yet arisen when both horses whinnied almost in unison. Shell stopped short. His dun pushed against him with his head. Shell turned. "What do you think?" he asked Dusty.

"We got to go ahead," said Dusty.

"Stay with the horses and Harley," said Shell.

Shell took his Spencer from the saddle scabbard and walked softly through the darkness. Each bush and rock looked as though it was alive, as though it was moving. A faint wind whispered through the valley. The southern slopes of the mountains angled slightly together. Shell was closer to the western side of the great V. He walked toward the humped shape of the lower slopes. He stopped often to look and listen. He moved on through the darkness like a great lean cat. He stopped to listen. There was a faint, fresh odor in the quiet air. He looked behind him. There was no movement and not a sound. He padded on and suddenly his worn boots splashed into shallow water. He had found Papago Springs.

Shell drank quickly. He started back for his two companions. Something moved in the brush near him. He whirled, thumbing back the hammer of the Spencer to full cock, but he didn't want to shoot. The soft thrashing noise continued. Shell peered toward the sound. He could see the brush swaying a little. There was something alive in the midst of the brush. Shell unsheathed his bowie knife. He could just make out a thick-shaped creature lying there. The tail thrashed out toward him and his knife came down with the full strength of his arm. The head fell from the thick body. Shell hoped to God it wasn't a gila monster. He knelt beside the quivering body. He grinned. It was a chuckwalla. The biggest one he had ever seen. He picked it up and walked toward his two companions, whistling softly three times. He halted. In a little while he heard the thudding of the hoofs.

Dusty staggered a little. "Yuh find it?" he gasped.

Shell nodded. He held up the chuckwalla. "Food *and* drink," he said with a grin.

"A damned lizard?" said Dusty.

"By God," said Shell. "The Indians can eat 'em and so can we. Beggars can't be choosers, *compañero!*"

They watered the horses, filled the canteens, then vanished over a rise as the first light of the moon appeared.

Dusty stood watch atop the rim of the great cup of black rock as Shell cooked the chuckwalla meat over a small fire. It had taken guts to make even a small fire, well shielded as it was, in the thick darkness before the rising of the moon, and the smell of the fire and the cooking meat would alert any Apache in the vicinity. Harley lay quietly, breathing erratically.

"Get it over with!" hissed Dusty from atop the rocks.

"Gawddammit!" snapped Shell. "I'm doing the best I can!"

The meat was done at last. Shell covered the fire with sand and carefully portioned out the meat. There wasn't a great deal of it, but there was enough to keep them going and that was all that mattered.

Shell awakened Harley and gave him his food. The three of them sat in a circle gnawing at the tender flesh. It was delicious, but there just wasn't enough of it.

Dusty laughed suddenly. The others stopped eating. "Roasted lizard and dirty water," said Dusty. "Helluva fare for three of the richest men in North America."

Shell grinned. He wiped his mouth. "Our time will come," he said, "eh, Harley?"

The blind man nodded. "You can have anything you want with that silver," he said quietly.

Dusty leaned back. "Wimmen," he said thoughtfully. "Big ones, little ones, redheads, brunettes, and blondes. Champagne by the bucket. Pheasant under glass. A pair of blooded horses to pull you around. Anything you want to eat, drink, or sleep with. What about you, Shell?"

Shell was dying for a smoke but they didn't dare light up. The smell of the tobacco smoke might carry too far on the night wind. He leaned back against the rock and picked the last scrap of meat from the bone he held. "Books," he said. "All the books I ever wanted to read and never got around to. Maybe a trip to Europe. China even."

"No fillies?" said Dusty in shocked surprise. "No champagne?"

"I can have them and the books too," said Shell.

Dusty shook his head in bewilderment.

Shell touched Harley's arm. "How about you, oldtimer?" he asked.

Harley wiped his mouth. He looked at Shell. "I never thought much about that," he said.

"With the richest silver mines in Mexico waiting out there for us?" said Shell.

Dusty glanced at Harley. "It's a cinch *he* wouldn't go for the fillies and the champagne. Maybe he's a secret drinker. How about that, Frank, old boy?"

Harley shook his head. "I need no strong drink," he said.

"Women?" said Shell.

Harley shook his head. "I had one once," he said. "I didn't know what I had. That was long ago." His voice died away with a haunting note of bitterness and regret. An intense loneliness seemed to settle about the three men. Dusty cleared his throat, looked as though he was about to speak, and then remained quiet.

Shell studied the older man. Suddenly he knew what Harley wanted. To find La Barranca Escondida and El Naranjal. How many years had he lived with that dream? A vision that had led him almost to death and into blindness and which was now leading him into Mexico with two hardcase mercenaries as his eyes. It had already cost him Ignacio, whom he must have loved very much. Perhaps it had even cost him the woman of whom he had spoken in such bittersweet tones. Whatever led Frank Harley on was deep within him, so deep that no one, outside of God, could possibly ever know. Suddenly Shell felt uncomfortable as though he was trying to probe into something that did not concern him—and yet it *did* concern him. If it was the lost silver hoard that lured Frank Harley on, the fever had passed from him into Dusty and Shell, enough for them to go with the blind man into the heart of a country virtually unknown to white men for a hundred years.

They took turns sleeping during the hours of moonlight and as soon as the moon was gone behind the western ranges they struck out again. Somewhere south of them was Cerro del Piloncillo. It could be seen when one was twenty miles south of Papago Springs. A sugar-loaf-shaped hill, from the name.

At dawn they were far south of the waterhole. Dusty's bay was in bad shape. Harley rode the dun and Dusty led the bay, but the big horse was not taking it as well as the dun. Shell wondered at the wisdom of traveling at such a steady pace, and yet there was no place they could stop and rest. No water and no food. They must keep on.

Just before the sun came up Dusty spoke. "There it is!" he said.

The sugar-loaf hill stood out boldly from a flat plain with mountains ranges far to each side of it.

"Describe it," said Harley.

"Rounded," said Dusty. "A sharper slope to the east."

"Is there a notch?"

"No," said Shell.

Dusty looked hard at the older man. "What's the notch got to do with it?"

"Cerro del Piloncillo has a notch," said Harley.

Dusty wiped his mouth with a quick dash of the back of his right hand. "It ain't notched!" he snapped. His eyes grew hard.

"Keep on," said Harley.

Two miles passed and as the light grew and the angle of the hill changed, a sharp notch appeared. Shell looked at Dusty. He shrugged and spread out his hands, palms upward. Thus far Harley had been right.

"We will cross the Rio Magdalena seventy-five miles due south of here," said Harley quietly.

They halted. Shell rolled a cigarette for Harley and one for himself, passing the last of the makings to Dusty. They were in a hard way now, without food and tobacco, one horse dying on its feet, and no prospect of getting food or other mounts for many miles.

Harley sucked in the good smoke. "Ten miles from here," he said, "there is a small *placita,* almost fully deserted. The Apaches have driven almost everyone from it, but there is a man there who is my friend. The Apaches do not bother him."

"Why not?" asked Dusty suspiciously.

Harley looked down at Dusty almost as though he could see him. "His wife is full-blooded Chiricahua," he said.

"Great!" said Dusty.

Harley shook his head. "We will not be harmed," he said.

"As long as you're with us, eh, Frank?" said Shell.

Harley nodded.

They moved on. Now and then Shell looked back at the impassive face of the blind man. What secrets did he know? An uneasiness came over Shell. He felt almost as though he was moving in a dream, but the blistered feet, the hungry gut, the gathering heat, and the haunting fear of Apache country were real enough. *Too* real.

The hill grew and changed shape and then Dusty motioned to Shell. On a slope of the western line of mountains could be seen something that looked as though a giant child had carelessly scattered his blocks, but they were too evenly spaced to be a natural feature of the land. Even as they looked, a thin thread of smoke arose from the blocks. It was the *placita* and someone was living there.

"There's the *placita,*" said Shell. He looked up at Harley. "Are you sure it's all right?"

"As long as you are with me," said the older man.

"We haven't any choice," said Shell.

Within two miles of the *placita* the bay went down for good. Dusty impassively stripped him of his gear and loaded it on the dun. He pulled out his pistol, shook his head, and drew out his heavy bowie knife. He pulled back the bay's head, tightening the throat muscles. The blade sliced through the throat as though it was soft soap. The steaming blood gushed out and blackened the ground. They did not look back as they went on.

High, high in the sky was a speck. It grew larger. It was a Sonoran buzzard. A zopilote. By the time the trio reached the outskirts of the *placita* the intense blue sky was dotted with them, leisurely swinging around in great circles, lower and lower, over the still quivering body of the dead bay.

Chapter Seven

The one street of the little *placita* was empty of life except for a mangy-looking dog who eyed the approaching trio and then bared his teeth. He slinked away with his tail between his legs when Dusty scooped up a fist-sized rock from the ground. Most of the adobes and jacales were crumbling from long disuse. Earthen roofs had collapsed into interiors. Weeds and grass sprouted from the roofs of others like scrofulous hair. A sagging *carreta* leaned against an adobe wall. Somewhere behind the largest of the buildings a mule brayed hoarsely and horses whinnied.

Shell carried his Spencer in his right hand, leading the worn-out dun with his left. Dusty walked slowly on the far side of the street, Spencer at the ready, eyes darting here and there, watching for any overt movement. His spurs chimed softly. The smoke had thinned out but still drifted wispily from the chimney of the largest building. The faint odor of chile beans hung in the street. Shell felt his mouth water.

"Hola!" yelled Dusty. "Anybody here?"

There was no response. Down at the end of the street was a sagging *torreón* with a door that hung loose on its hinges. It had been built many years ago to protect the *placita,* but it had not stopped the Apaches. Northern Sonora and Chihuahua, as well as Southern Arizona and New Mexico, had many such *placitas,* each with its own *torreón,* but most of them had one thing in common; they were all abandoned, melting back into the earth from which they had been fashioned.

There was still no sign of life. Dusty looked at Shell. "What do you think, *compañero?*"

"We scared them," said Shell. "Frank is right though. I don't think the Apaches bother this place."

"How so?"

Shell jerked his head. "You hear that mule music? You think the Apaches would allow anyone to keep a mule in this country unless he was a friend of the Apaches?"

Dusty nodded. "If he's a friend of the Apaches, he likely won't be friendly to us."

They stopped in front of the largest building. Dusty tried the door. It was barred from within. He tapped on the thick, bolt-studded door with the metal-shod butt of his Spencer. There was no answer. Shell looked toward the *torreón.* Something had moved just within the open doorway. Shell dropped the reins and raised his carbine. "You there!" he called out. "Show yourself!"

"What is it you want?" asked a man with a deep voice.

"Food first."

"There is none to spare."

"We can take what we want."

The challenge hung in the thin air. There was no movement from the man in the *torreón* but Shell knew he had a gun.

"Anselmo Chacón, my friend!" called out Frank Harley.

Again the hesitation and then the man spoke. "Is it you, Frank, my old friend?"

"That is so and these are my friends. They will not harm you, Anselmo."

The man laughed. "I could kill both of them from here, and they are covered as well from across the street."

Shell looked quickly toward a tumbled ruin. There was someone in there.

A squat man with a thick, grizzled beard stepped out into the street from the *torreón.* The bright sunlight glinted from the heavy coin-silver ornamentation of his sombrero and from the well polished Henry rifle he held in huge hands. He walked slowly toward them. Shell helped Frank down from the saddle. Anselmo looked curiously at Frank as he approached him. He gripped Frank in his arms, looking for all the world like a squat grizzly hugging an opponent.

Shell looked across the street. A figure stood there in the ruins. A woman dressed in Mexican fashion, but her face was that of a pure quill Indian, and Apache at that. But, by God, she was a damned sight younger than Anselmo, and she was actually pretty. Not a flat-faced squaw as so many of them were. Dusty whistled softly. Shell shot him a hard look.

"What is wrong, my friend?" asked Anselmo of Frank.

"I'm blind, Anselmo," said Harley quietly.

Anselmo crossed himself. "Body of God! How did this happen?"

Dusty leaned against the front of the house watching the Apache woman walk gracefully toward them, trailing a single-shot rifle. "Her relatives did it," said Dusty out of the side of his mouth. "Buried him up to the neck in sand at Horno Tanks, just long enough for him to lose his sight."

Anselmo stared at Frank. "And you have lived!"

"Thanks to my two friends here. If they had not come along. . . ." His voice trailed off.

Shell looked at Anselmo. "My name is Shell," he said. "My partner is called Dusty. We need food and a couple of horses. Three, if you're willing to trade."

Anselmo shoved back his hat and looked at the dun. "Yes," he said. "I think I can trade a horse for this one."

"Two," said Shell.

Anselmo shrugged. "I have two horses and one mule for trading."

"A mule is good enough for me," said Frank.

"You ride with them, my old friend?" asked Anselmo. "I thought you would stay with me. It gets lonely at times, although Theresa is good company."

"Odd name for an Indian," said Dusty.

Anselmo looked at him. "Her real name is Pretty Hands, but I call her Theresa after my sainted mother."

"Cute," said Dusty. He shifted a little and looked at the side doorway into which Theresa had vanished. Smoke had thickened from the chimney.

The dark eyes of the Mexican studied Dusty thoughtfully. He took Frank by the arm and led him into the house. Shell led the dun to the watering trough, and as he drank, he stripped the horse of Dusty's gear and Shell's own saddle.

He rubbed the dun's neck. They had come a long way together but the dun could not go on. Maybe, on the way back. . . . It was a long maybe.

"Cute little devil," said Dusty from behind Shell.

Shell turned. "Keep away from her," he said.

Dusty smiled in amusement. "Why? You got an eye on her?"

"No, but Anselmo has."

Dusty spat. "That old bastard?"

Shell looked beyond his companion. The heat haze was rising. Something flashed quickly and brightly across the wide valley. He turned quickly. An answering flash came from a pinnacle of rock thrust up from a gaunt ridge a mile from the *placita*. A cold feeling came over him. They had been followed. The Apaches knew exactly where they were. "You see that?" he said dryly to Dusty.

Dusty had stripped to his worn and dirty undershirt. He thrust his head into the water trough and came up dripping and spluttering. "Sure," he said. "I ain't blind like Harley."

"Harley can see a helluva lot better than you can. He didn't bring us here to hand us over to the Apaches."

Dusty wrung out his beard. "No? How do *we* know? He was never very keen on letting us in on his damned lost mine. Supposing he and ol' Anselmo are in there right now figgerin' on how to let the Apaches know how best to take us?"

Shell had never thought of that. The cold feeling crept over him again as he led the dun to the peeled pole corral and turned him loose with the other horses. He washed up at the trough as Dusty had done, reveling in the unlimited supply of water. He and Dusty walked back to the house. The odor of the rich chile and beans hung in the sunlit street. Shell tapped on the door and was bidden to enter by Anselmo.

The room was low-ceiled and huge, with a corbeled ceiling, with painted willow sticks set herring-bone fashion between the thick beams. The furniture was huge, dark, and ancient. A beehive fireplace was in the corner, and here and there along the walls were niches in which stood stolid-faced *santos,* plainly revealing the part-Indian ancestry of the wood carver. A candle guttered in front of one of the *santos,* and Shell was willing to bet it was that of Saint Theresa. The whitewashed walls were hung with skillfully woven rugs, and the beaten earth floor was also covered with the same style rugs. Dusty whistled softly. Always the materialist, he was impressed with such things, and Anselmo lived in the style of a *don.*

Frank was seated at the huge table beside an ancient bell, green with age. Places had been set for four. Dusty eyed a dark bottle that graced the center of the table.

Anselmo bowed a little. "Sit down, gentlemen," he said in courtly fashion.

Shell eyed the rich furnishings, seemingly so out of place in such a country, and the odd thought came to him that Anselmo must be a rich man. But where did he get his riches from?

The Mexican sat down and smiled at Shell. "Before the war," he said, "I was a *comanchero.*"

Then Shell knew. He was a man who had traded with the Indians, illegally perhaps, depending on the type of goods he had to offer. Most likely Anselmo had offered guns and ammunition, which was strictly against the law, but with the proper greasing of palms, nothing would have been said.

The Apache woman silently served the meal. Crisp tacos and rich chile beans were placed on the table. There was little talking while they ate. Anselmo had an amused look on his face as he watched Dusty and Shell stow away the food. Harley ate very little. Now and then his hand would touch the ancient bell beside him. Anselmo filled glasses with Baconora brandy. Harley shook his head as the glass was placed in front of him. Dusty calmly appropriated Harley's full glass.

The woman cleared the table as silently as she had brought the food, and her liquid eyes never looked at the two companions, although now and then she glanced at Frank Harley. She vanished, leaving the men alone. Shell wondered uncomfortably where she had gone. He listened for the sound of hoofbeats but heard nothing. He glanced at their carbines leaning against the wall near the door and as he looked back at the table he saw the thoughtful eyes of Anselmo on him. Maybe Dusty had been right. The Apaches could come into the *placita* and be waiting outside for Dusty and Shell, for it was a certainty that they would not bother Frank Harley under the protection of Anselmo, even though they had left him to die a horrible death at Horno Tanks.

There wasn't much Dusty and Shell could do about it if Frank had led them into a trap. Dusty made the most of it. His eyes grew a little brighter as the good Baconora caught hold. Frank Harley touched the bell and passed a hand over the molded surface of it.

"Yes," said Anselmo. "It is *the* bell, Frank."

"I thought as much," said the blind man.

Dusty eyed the old bell. "What's it doing in here?" he said.

Frank looked at him. "Let Anselmo tell you," he said.

Anselmo refilled his glass. "It is the Bell of Saint Joseph," he said. "For many years it rang in a mission far south of here. In seventeen sixty-seven that mission was abandoned. My ancestor was the sacristan of the church. There were four bells in the bell tower. One of them fell and was shattered when they attempted to lower it from the tower. Two had already been taken from the tower. The last of the four bells was left hanging in the tower."

"What's the deal?" said Dusty. He refilled his glass.

Anselmo continued as though he had not heard Dusty. "The two bells that had been taken from the tower were hauled from the barranca. One of them has been lost. The other one, the one you see here, was hung in a small church near the Rio Magdalena until Apache raids forced the abandonment of that church as well. My father was the sacristan there and the bell was in his charge as it had been in the charge of his father and his father's father. He brought the bell here. When this *placita* was at last abandoned, the first year of your Civil War, the bell was left behind. It is in my charge now."

Shell looked at him curiously and then at the bell. He leaned closer to it. The date 1750 had been molded above the flare of the bell mouth. He stood up and looked closer. He read the name Saint Joseph. He glanced around the side of the bell and his heart skipped a beat. He could make out the faint lettering. "El Naranjal," he said. He looked at Anselmo. "Then El Naranjal *does* exist?"

"It is not a tale made up by old men," said the Mexican. "It is a legend, but it is true. That is the bell brought from La Barranca Escondida in seventeen sixty-seven."

"When the Jesuits were forced to leave Mexico," said Shell.

"Exactly," said Anselmo. He looked at Frank Harley. "He knows La Barranca Escondida and El Naranjal are real."

Dusty emptied his glass. "He had better," he said.

The dark eyes of the Mexican studied Dusty and then Shell. "No man knows more about La Barranca Escondida than my friend," said Anselmo. "But now that he cannot see, how can he possibly hunt for it?"

Harley leaned forward. "These two men are my eyes."

Anselmo nodded. "So?"

Shell sipped his brandy. "The idea doesn't appeal to you?"

"A blind man is helpless," said Anselmo.

"He still wants to go," said Dusty.

There was a tension in the room. Anselmo leaned back in his chair. "Let us speak plainly," he said. "Who are you two men? Who is to say what will happen to Frank if the treasure is found?"

"That is my risk," said the blind man. "I know the way without sight, Anselmo. They can't possibly find La Barranca Escondida without my guidance."

Anselmo looked quickly at him. "And if you do *not* find it? What then?" His meaning was plain enough. He did not like the looks of the two hardbitten adventurers who had come out of the desert with his old friend.

Shell selected a cigar from the box on the table. He bit off the end and lighted it, eyeing Anselmo over the flare of the match. "Our risk is as great as his," he said. "How do we know he really knows where La Barranca Escondida is? You say he knows more about La Barranca Escondida than any other man, but he doesn't really know where it is. It has been lost for a hundred years, hasn't it? A man can go into that country and never find his way out again. The Indians do not want white men looking for lost mines in their country. He has a risk and we have a risk. We're willing to take a chance. Why shouldn't he?"

Harley nodded. "I am going with them, Anselmo."

Anselmo bowed his head. "It is the will of God," he said quietly. "Come, Señor Shell, let us look at the horses."

They walked outside, leaving Dusty and Harley. Harley was passing a questing hand over the ancient bell while Dusty plied the brandy bottle.

The heat was intense after the coolness of the thick-walled house. Waves of it shimmered up from the lower ground and hazed the mountains on the east side of the valley. Shell saw no mirror flashes but he knew well enough the Apaches were still up there. The only thing that would keep them there would be their friendship with Anselmo. It gave Shell an eerie feeling.

Shell selected a blocky gray and a clean-limbed sorrel for the dun, taking a mule as well, and paying Anselmo fifty dollars besides. He hated to lose the dun, but there was nothing he could do about it. "We'll need supplies," he said.

"There is not much," said the Mexican. "I will see what I can do. When will you leave?"

"In a few days. Frank is not fully recovered. I haven't figured out yet how he survived."

Anselmo relighted his cigar. "A man with such a dream cannot die, my friend. It is what keeps him alive."

"Do you think he will realize that dream, Anselmo?"

Anselmo slanted his sombrero lower over his eyes and looked out across the burning landscape. "All men have dreams, my friend. I had a dream. It is gone now. Once I thought this *placita* would become a great place because of the mines in the hills behind us. I was content to live here as alcalde with my brothers and sisters and their wives and husbands. There would be many children." His voice died away.

Shell looked at him. "And so?"

Anselmo shrugged. He held out his hands palms upward. "I was gone to make money. The mines could not be worked because of the Apaches. There was plague. Those that did not die in the plague were killed by the Apaches. Those that survived the plague and the Apaches fled to the south. They will not come back to this hostile land."

"Then why do you stay?"

Anselmo smiled. "Perhaps it is still my dream, my friend. A man must never give up his dream, his hopes, for if he does, he might as well be dead."

Shell looked curiously at the house. The smoke still drifted from the chimney but there was no sign of the woman.

Anselmo seemed to read his mind. "Her father and younger brother were captured by my people. They were to die. I saved them. In time they let me visit their camp. I was a lonely man. Kayitah, the man I had saved, was her father. Now she is my wife." He looked at Shell. "You do not like the idea of having an Apache woman for a wife?"

"I didn't say that," said Shell.

Anselmo nodded. "Here, in Mexico, perhaps we think differently, but then most of us have Indian blood in our veins." Anselmo studied Shell curiously. "I have my dream, or what is left of it. Frank has his dream of La Barranca Escondida. Your friend Dusty has a dream of great riches with which he thinks he can buy happiness. What is *your* dream, my friend?"

Shell laughed. "The same as Dusty's," he said.

Anselmo shook his head. "I do not think so," he said.

Shell looked angrily at the Mexican. "Why not?"

"There is something within you that tries to get out. If you do find all that silver it will not pay your way to happiness."

Shell hurled the cigar from his mouth. "What else is there?" he said harshly. "After five years of war we have nothing but our lives and our guns. How much longer can we keep on? What future is there for men such as us?"

Anselmo shrugged. He looked sideways at Shell. "I cannot answer those questions," he said quietly. "The answers are in *you*, my friend."

"You talk like a fool!" snapped Shell. He strode away.

Anselmo blew a puff of smoke. "Perhaps," he said softly to himself. "But you know that I am right, my friend."

Far across the valley a small hand mirror caught the bright light of the sun and reflected it like a shard of silver. There was no sign of life. Then another mirror flashed from the sharp pinnacle of rock that stood on the gaunt ridge just north of the *placita*. Then there was nothing but the empty valley, with heat waves shimmering upward. A dust devil arose, whirled swiftly across the baking ground, and disappeared as mysteriously as it had appeared. It was the only movement aside from the shimmering heat waves. A feeling of watchful waiting hung over the empty country. Nothing could move out there without being seen from the hills. Nothing. . . .

Chapter Eight

In the week that had passed, Frank Harley regained his strength. For a time he had hoped his sight, or at least part of it, would return, but at the end of the week he knew there was no hope left for that. For the rest of his life he would move in complete darkness. He knew Anselmo wanted him to stay at the *placita*. They were good friends and spent many hours talking together of many things. It was a strong temptation, but ever and again Frank's hands would touch the smooth metal of the bell and then trace the words molded about the flare of the mouth. 1750 . . . Saint Joseph . . . El Naranjal. He knew El Naranjal was no fantasy. *Cerro de Huesos is the first key. For there, on a quiet night, one might hear the dogs of La Barranca Escondida barking.* The dogs, of course, would no longer be there, but—*when the wind comes from the south, a bell may be heard. That bell hangs in the bell tower of the church at El Naranjal.*

Frank knew he had to go. He didn't trust his two companions, *but he had to go.* He needed their eyes and they needed his knowledge. If they found the silver, there would be more to each share than any of them could spend in a lifetime of prodigious spending. If they didn't find the silver it would not matter. The country would kill them one way or another. The Yaquis, or the lack of water, or the tangled, almost impenetrable country itself would finish them off. They were harsh odds, almost hopeless, but Frank Harley had to go.

Dusty stood at the barred window of the big, low-ceiled bedroom he shared with Shell. He blew a stream of smoke between the rusted bars. "We've got to do it my way," he said.

Shell raised his head from the pillow. "How far do you think we'd get?"

Dusty spoke over his shoulder. "I don't want to rot here. We're safe enough as long as Anselmo keeps his boys in the hills, but supposin' he changes his mind? I don't trust that smiling bastard."

"For that matter, he doesn't trust you either. He's seen you looking at that woman of his."

Dusty spat between the bars. "Maybe she needs a *real* man, not that bearded old goat."

"Like you?" said Shell dryly.

"Like me."

Shell sat up and dropped his feet to the floor, feeling for his boots. "I don't like it here any better than you do, but until Anselmo says we can leave, we stay."

Dusty whirled. "What's to prevent him from letting us go and having his bushy-headed buzzards waitin' out there for us?"

"We'd have Frank with us. He won't let anything happen to Frank, will he?"

"That don't mean they couldn't pick us off and then deliver Frank back to his *amigo* Anselmo. No, *my* plan is right. I know you don't like it, but by God you haven't come up with any other idea!"

Shell pulled on his seam-split boots. He rolled a cigarette and lighted it. Maybe Dusty was right at that. He wanted to force Anselmo and his woman along as hostages. It was risky, but Shell had no other plan. They'd never make it alone. Even if Anselmo believed the Apaches would not harm the trio if he asked them not to, there was nothing to prove that the Apaches would honor his request. Certainly, Anselmo and his beloved Pretty Hands were safe from them.

Pretty Hands was the daughter of a chief and Anselmo was his blood brother.

"The sun will be gone in an hour," said Dusty from the window.

Shell nodded. He swung his gunbelt about his lean hips with practiced ease and buckled it, settling it down. He took the Colt from its holster and checked it. Anselmo had given them supplies enough for two days at least. Flour, beans, coffee, and a few cans of embalmed beef, greasy relic of the war. The three animals were handy. There were other horses in the corral. Enough for all five of them to ride south that night. How far would the Apaches follow them? What lay ahead? Those two questions harried Shell. The country south of Papago Springs was unknown to him and Dusty. Only Frank Harley knew it. Anselmo would never open his mouth.

Shell walked back and forth. They were damned if they stayed and damned if they moved. It was like being in limbo. But he had a feeling the Apaches could not be held off forever. They might not harm Frank, but Dusty and Shell would be another matter.

"Well?" said Dusty.

Shell stopped pacing and looked at him. "All right," he said. "When?"

Dusty came forward. "We eat at dusk. Anselmo doesn't carry a sidearm. His rifle is racked near the door. You sit in between him and the door. We'll have to take over when the woman comes into the room. If she breaks loose we'll never get her, short of killing her, and you know what would happen if we *did* kill her."

Shell nodded. He still didn't like the idea but, as Dusty had bluntly pointed out, Shell hadn't come up with any other solution.

"You cover Anselmo," said Dusty. "I'll take care of the woman."

Shell looked quickly at his companion.

Dusty grinned like a lobo. "I haven't got any loose ideas, if that's what's botherin' yuh."

Shell fashioned a cigarette. "How far will we take them?"

"How about the Rio Magdalena?"

"The Apaches will follow us all the way to Durango if they feel like it, Dusty."

Dusty shook his head. "I'll see to that," he said.

His meaning wasn't clear to Shell, but it didn't matter. They had to get out of the *placita*. They sat and smoked until the long shadows crept down the slopes behind the *placita.* Then the sun was fully gone. They could hear the woman setting the table in the big room. Anselmo had trained her well. Now and then the murmuring of voices drifted in to them. Frank and Anselmo were off on one of their interminable discussions.

Shell took over now. "Go and saddle the horses," he said over his shoulder as he stood by the door that led into the big room. "Keep them in the corral. Make damned sure *she* doesn't see you."

"Yuh think I was born yesterday?"

"Sometimes you act like it. Fill the canteens. The food is packed and ready in the shed near the corral. Make it fast. I'll keep Frank and Anselmo occupied."

Dusty rubbed out his cigarette and spat into the beehive fireplace. "Yes suh, lootenant, suh! Yes suh!"

Shell looked back at him in the gathering darkness of the room. Shell had been commissioned second lieutenant from first sergeant during the Vicksburg Campaign by the old tried-and-true method of the South Kansas-Texas Mounted Rifles. A company election. Their company commander and first lieutenant had been killed in action. Shell's only opponent in the election had been Acting Color Sergeant Matt Dustin. No man fought better than Matt Dustin. The devil would have been hard put to keep up with him when the *Minié* balls played their strident, killing music. But Dusty could never lead other men. He was an individualist in battle. There was nothing inspiring about his fighting. He fought like a butcher slaughters beef. Kill, kill, and kill, like a Highlander who has gone fey and does not feel his own bloody wounds until the fighting is over.

"You'll never forget that, will you?" said Shell quietly.

"It was only a joke."

"The joke is *old,* Dusty. It's worn out. Retire it."

Their eyes held each other's in the darkness. "Keno," said Dusty at last. He quietly opened the side door, removed his spurs, and was gone like a hunting cat.

Shell opened the door into the big common room. Frank and Anselmo were already seated at the table, deep in conversation. Shell lighted a cigarette and walked about, ostensibly interested in the hangings and relics on the whitewashed walls. Anselmo's polished Henry rifle was in its rack near the wide door. The woman also had a rifle, but Shell had never been able to find out where she kept it. It was a cinch she wouldn't bring it into the big room while she served the evening meal. He could hear her working in the kitchen. She was making enough noise to cover anything Dusty was doing.

Shell usually sat near Anselmo, between him and the door, while Dusty sat opposite Shell and close to the kitchen door.

"Where is Dusty?" said Frank. Already he had begun to develop that uncanny sense of the blind wherein they can feel a presence.

"He'll be right along," said Shell.

A few minutes later Dusty opened the bedroom door and came into the big room, yawning a little as though he had just awakened. He winked to Shell over the head of Anselmo.

They sat down and the woman came in silently and began to serve the meal. Dusty looked at Shell and nodded. Shell stood up just as Dusty gripped the woman by her right wrist. Shell drew swiftly and covered the Mexican. "Don't move!" he said. Dusty yelled and cursed. He jerked his hand away from the woman. She had driven her firm white teeth into his forearm. He staggered back, mouthing curses, then lunged for her. The knife came from somewhere, but from where only God and Pretty Hands knew. The hooked blade swept out at Dusty's face, and only his upflung right arm fended the blow, but even so the tip raked his right cheek from cheekbone to the very edge of his mouth. Bright red droplets sprayed from the wound as he gripped her knife wrist and fought her for the bloody blade. There was no outcry from the woman.

Dusty gripped at her dress with his left hand, and the fabric ripped from throat to waist exposing her swinging, dark-nippled breasts. She broke loose and slashed skillfully with the knife, falling halfway over the table as Dusty drew back. Crockery and cutlery clattered on the floor. The brandy bottle smashed against the bell of Saint Joseph and the rich fruity odor of the spirits mingled with that of the spilled food. Dusty stepped in close, his wild fighting blood heated to a killing pitch. He backhanded Pretty Hands, sending her staggering back against the wall. Her bloody knife tinkled on the earthen floor. Once again Dusty struck her. She had no defense for the white man's way of fighting. She sagged sideways and Dusty struck a third time. Her mouth flew open. Blood gushed from her nose and mouth, and she hit the floor in the corner.

Dusty stepped back, clapping a hand to his slashed face. His breathing was harsh. "The bitch!" he said. "The Indian bitch! I ought'a kill her for that!"

Anselmo looked at Shell with cold eyes. He did not move

but his eyes swiveled to Dusty. "I'll kill *you* for that," he said between his teeth.

Dusty dipped a bandanna into the spilled brandy and wiped the streaming wound, wincing as the alcohol bit deeply into it. He bandaged his face and walked to the cabinet in the corner where Anselmo kept his liquor. He ripped open one of the half-doors and gripped the neck of another brandy bottle. He jerked out the cork with his teeth and spat it into the fireplace. He tilted the bottle and gulped deeply.

"Sit still, Anselmo," said Shell. He half-cocked his Colt.

Anselmo looked up. "Is this how you repay my hospitality?" he murmured.

Dusty whirled. "Hospitality *shit!*" he snapped. "You planned all along to turn us over to the Apaches. You were fattening us for the slaughter!"

"That is a lie," said Frank Harley quietly. "Only an hour ago Anselmo told me he'd guide us to the Rio Magdalena."

"Bullshit!" said Dusty.

Shell looked at Frank. "We couldn't take a chance, Frank," he said.

"Get them out to the horses," said Dusty.

Shell stepped behind Anselmo and tapped him on the shoulder. The Mexican stood up, glanced at his wife, then walked to the door. Shell took Harley by the shoulder and guided him to the door. "Lead him to the corral, Anselmo," said Shell. "Don't try anything."

Dusty took a pair of bottles from the cabinet and placed them in a fiber morral. He looked at Shell. "Go on," he said.

Shell jerked his head toward the woman. "What about her?"

Dusty's eyes were enigmatical. "I'll take care of her," he said.

Shell raised his head a little. "By God," he said. "If you touch her I'll kill you myself!"

Dusty laughed. "With her family and friends out there waiting in the darkness? Don't be loco!"

Shell stepped outside, quickly closing the door. It was very dark. He marched Anselmo and Frank toward the corral. The horses whinnied a little. Shell talked quietly to them as he gave Frank a leg up into the saddle of the mule and then had Anselmo mount. He lashed the Mexican to the saddle with a riata. He looked up at Anselmo. "Do I gag you or do you keep your mouth shut?" he asked.

"I will not cry out," said the Mexican.

Dusty had fashioned pommel and cantle packs with the

supplies inside of them. Canteens hung like ripe fruit from the saddles. Shell led the four horses and the mule slowly up the dark street to the big house. He whistled softly.

Dusty came to the door of the house. "She's still unconscious," he said. "I tied her and gagged her. We can leave her here. I left the lamps on in the kitchen and living room."

There was no time to lose. They led the horses from the street, begrudging every hoofbeat on the hard caliche of the street. They mounted when they were a quarter of a mile from the *placita.* Now and then Anselmo looked back at the darker patch that indicated the *placita,* then his dark eyes would rest steadily on the broad back of Dusty.

Cold sweat worked down Shell's sides. He gripped his half-cocked Spencer in his right hand and swung his head from front to each side in turn and then to the rear. There was only one thing that kept hope alive in him. Apaches do not like to fight at night, for fear that if they die, their souls will wander forever in limbo. Still, perhaps if they had the chance, they might possibly attack. But the deadly time was in the cold gray light of the predawn, when a man's morale is at the lowest.

They could see the dark humped shapes of the hills on either hand, closing in on them as they rode further south. An hour passed uneventfully. Shell looked back. He could see the faintest of yellow specks off in the velvety darkness. Dusty had left the lamps on in the house in an attempt to convince the Apaches that the house was occupied. But if they came down to the house and found the woman. . . .

They rode fifty minutes, rested the horses ten minutes, on and on, all through the tension of that night, and when the faintest light appeared in the eastern sky they were almost sure they had fooled the Apaches.

When the sun came up they had taken cover in a shallow arroyo that meandered down from the broken hills. Shell helped Frank from his saddle. The blind man had not spoken all night. There was no telling what he was thinking. Anselmo was his good friend, but, on the other hand, Frank's consuming goal was La Barranca Escondida.

Dusty slowly worked the blood-soaked bandage from his face. The blood had coagulated. Shell examined the wound. "It'll be all right, but you're marked for life, *compañero.*"

Dusty nodded. He uncorked the bottle of brandy and took a deep slug. He had been nipping steadily all through the night. His bloodshot eyes flicked toward Anselmo.

"Take it easy on the brandy," said Shell.

Dusty spat. "It's me that got cut up," he said thinly. "You had the easy part."

"It was your idea to handle the woman," said Shell.

Dusty did not answer. He sat down on a rock with the bottle in his hand. "How far do we take him?" he said, jerking his head toward Anselmo.

Anselmo sat on a rock, with his bound hands resting in his lap. He never took his eyes from Dusty.

"Let him go," said Frank Harley.

"Hell no!" snapped Dusty. "He'd have every Apache between here and the border on our asses by noon!"

Shell shoved back his hat and wiped the sweat from his face. He looked curiously at Dusty. Something was riling Dusty; something deep inside. An uneasy feeling came over Shell. "The woman," he said. "She's still bound and gagged back there."

Dusty nipped at the bottle again. "She can work loose once she regains her senses," he said.

Anselmo moved swiftly. He reached for Shell's Spencer that had been leaned against a rock not far from him. The loosened thongs fell from his swollen wrists. He moved swiftly but he had underestimated Dusty as many another man had done. Anselmo snatched up the heavy weapon and thumbed back the big hammer to full cock. Dusty dropped the bottle, rose into a half crouch, swung back his hand, swept the Colt up and forward, letting the weight of it cock the spur hammer under his thumb. He fired an instant before Anselmo did, and the roar of the Spencer sounded like an echo of the Colt. Anselmo went backward and fell heavily, the Spencer dropping from his nerveless hands. The Spencer slug struck the sorrel in the side of the head and he went down as though poleaxed.

Powder smoke swirled through the arroyo, and the twin echoes died away in the nearby hills. Dusty let down the hammer of the smoking Colt. There was no need for a second shot. A black hole between Anselmo's staring eyes leaked blood and matter.

"Anselmo!" cried Frank Harley.

There was no answer. There would never be an answer.

Shell whirled and ran up the crumbling side of the arroyo with short, digging steps. The sun had flooded the valley. How far had those shots been heard? There was no sign of life, but that didn't mean anything. An Apache is seen only when he *wants* to be seen. Shell slid down into the arroyo. "Let's go!" he snapped.

There was no argument from Dusty. The only thing that

could save them now was speed. They led the three horses and the mule out of the arroyo, and Shell helped Harley up into the saddle of the third horse. There was no time to take care of Anselmo's body or to strip the dead sorrel. They spurred their horses and rode south toward the distant Rio Magdalena. Even Frank Harley had no other thought in his mind at that time despite the killing of his dear friend. His recent memory of his treatment by the Apaches crowded every other thought out of his mind.

They cleared the broken hills and struck open country that sloped gradually down toward the distant river. It would be dry, but there would be springs or waterholes nearby. But, supposing the Apaches had got ahead of them during the night?

Shell looked back. A thought had struck his mind. The woman might still be bound and gagged in that distant house. Supposing the Apaches did *not* come for her? Supposing she had not been able to free herself?

Dusty drained the bottle and hurled it to one side. It shattered on the hard ground. He wiped his mouth with the back of a dusty hand. "Don't worry," he said thickly. "Ain't nothing more can happen to her."

Shell stared unbelievingly at him.

Dusty nodded. "I hit her too damned hard, Shell. I didn't mean to."

Shell was sickened. He looked away from his friend. No, Dusty never *meant* to kill, it just happened. It had been that way in the past and it would be that way again. As Shell rode south, with the lurking fear of painted death in his soul, he could see the bearded face of Anselmo looking fondly at his young Apache wife. "Her name is Pretty Hands," he had said. "But I call her Theresa after my sainted mother."

Chapter Nine

Shell worked his way slowly down the mountain side. He winced as he scraped past a jumping cholla. The needles seemed to leap out at him. Not for nothing had the vicious plant been given its name. The sweat poured down his face although the sun was gone. He wiped it from his face as he reached the talus slope above the waterhole. He worked his way in through the thick brush to where they had made their simple camp.

Dusty looked up from the boot he was roughly cobbling. "Well?" he said coldly.

Shell looked at Frank Harley. The older man sat with his back against a rock, breathing harshly. "I covered the whole area southwest of here trying to see a twin peak with a white area on the north side."

"So?" said Dusty. He pulled on the worn-out boot.

Shell shook his head. "Nothing," he said.

"Are you sure?" said Frank.

"Positive," said Shell.

Dusty scratched in his ragged beard. "Now what?" he said to Harley.

The older man did not answer. He could feel the menace emanating from Dusty although he could not see those icy blue eyes staring at him.

"Five gawddamned days in this hellhole," said Dusty, "and we ain't seen anything like twin peaks with a white area on the north side. Maybe we're lost, eh, Harley?"

Shell put down the field glasses. He rolled a cigarette and thrust it into Harley's mouth. He lighted it. "Maybe you're wrong, Frank," he suggested.

The blind man shook his head. Dusty spat to one side. He caught the makings out of the air as Shell tossed them over to him.

They had been on the way for over a week, and in the last five days Harley had insisted there was such a twin peak, but neither Shell nor Dusty had been able to spot it. They had crossed the dry Rio Magdalena and then the San Miguel and had reached the fork of another dry river, unknown to them. Harley himself had become a little dubious at that time.

"I'm sure it must be there. Ignacio said it would be there," said the blind man patiently.

"I'm sure it *must* be there," mimicked Dusty. He lighted his cigarette and hurled the match to one side. "Damn you! You blind bastard! You've led us on a wild goose chase! I got a damned good mind to leave you here!"

Harley looked toward him. "You won't," he said.

"Why not?"

"Your greed won't let you."

Dusty spat. "The hell it won't!"

Harley sucked in the smoke. He took the cigarette from his dry lips. "Then Shell won't let you."

Shell narrowed his eyes. He looked at Dusty. Dusty was ringy. He had been so ever since they had crossed the San Miguel. "Let's go over it once more, Frank," suggested Shell. "We crossed the Rio Magdalena, and then the San Miguel. We bore southeasterly for two days after crossing the river fork and followed the canyon for about twenty miles."

"To a dry waterhole," said Dusty.

"He didn't dry it up," said Shell.

"Who the hell asked you?" snapped Dusty.

Shell ignored him. "Are you sure this is the way, Frank?" he asked.

Harley nodded. "Ignacio would not lie to me."

"Look at him sitting there!" said Dusty. "Damn him! He doesn't know, I tell you, Shell! It was *Ignacio* who knew the way!"

Shell sat down on a rock. He studied the calm face of Frank Harley. There was no way they could tell whether Harley was lying to them or whether he just didn't know, and nothing seemed able to jolt him out of that complacency. There was a growing suspicion in Shell that Harley might just be playing with them. Perhaps he *did* know the way but was taking revenge for the death of his beloved friend Anselmo.

They ate the last of their food as they sat there in the gathering darkness. There would still be some moonlight that night, but not enough to reflect from the twin peaks' white area, as Harley had once suggested. If there was any such landmark in that part of Sonora, Shell was sure they weren't near it.

The moon arose, shedding a faint light over the tangled, trackless country. A lurking fear hung in Shell's mind. Maybe they were hopelessly lost. They hadn't seen a living person for four days, with the one exception of a Mexican who had fled from them as though they had the plague. There was no desire within Shell to backtrack. Somewhere between them and the border would be the Apaches, led by Kayitah, their chief, hunting for the white men who had killed Anselmo and Pretty Hands. "The Apaches will follow us all the way to Durango if they feel like it," Shell had said to Dusty back at the *placita*. They couldn't go back, and they didn't know what lay ahead.

Shell looked at the placid face of Frank Harley, and a spark of anger, fanned by fear, began to burn brighter within him. He looked at Dusty. The message seemed to leap between them.

Dusty got up and walked slowly to Frank, his spurs chiming softly. He stopped in front of Harley. "Once more," he said thinly. "Are you lost? Or are you bullshitting us?"

Harley did not answer. Dusty swung out a big hand, sweeping the cigarette from Harley's lips. A thin trickle of blood wormed from the blind man's mouth and worked down into his beard.

Dusty placed both hands on his hips. He leaned forward. "Once again," he said. "Are you lost? Maybe you're misleadin' us?"

Harley raised his head. The trickling blood looked black in the moonlight. "I am not lying to you," he said.

The open hand caught him alongside the head and he rocked with the vicious impact. Blood and spittle flew from his mouth. For a moment Shell almost felt compassion for the blind man, and then the lurking fear settled on his shoulders again.

Dusty's next blow drove Harley from the rock. He lay on his side, drawing up his legs. Dusty kicked him lightly. "Talk, you stubborn bastard," he said.

"For the love of God," the hoarse voice said in Spanish from the thick brush, "do not beat that old man, my son."

Two men whirled. Colts leaped from holsters and hammers were swept back. A bareheaded man stood in the brush looking sadly at them. "I am unarmed," he said. He held up his arms. He wore some kind of cowled robe. "I am Father Eusebio," he added.

"A padre?" said Shell.

"That's what *he* says," said Dusty. "Come on out here, you!"

The man pushed his way through the brush. He staggered a little. His brown Franciscan robe was torn and patched, filthy with dust and stippled with burrs and thorns. His feet were shod in sandals that looked paper thin. A cross hung from his roped belt. He touched his lips. "I can hardly speak," he said. "Do you have water to spare?" His brown eyes were as soft as those of a doe.

Shell nodded to Dusty. Dusty picked up a canteen. He looked at Shell. "Do we have enough for ourselves?"

"I can guide you to the next waterhole," said the padre.

"We've just about had enough of guides," said Dusty.

"Give him a drink," said Shell.

Dusty handed the padre the canteen. "Take it easy," he said.

Father Eusebio drank a little and rinsed it back and forth in his mouth. He sipped a little more after he had swallowed the first draught. He stoppered the canteen and handed it back to Dusty. "Bless you, my son," he said.

Frank Harley sat up and pulled himself up on a rock. His face was white and drawn in the pale moonlight. He wiped the dark blood from his face.

The padre looked from one to the other of the two tall Americans. "I can guide you to the next waterhole, as I have said, but where is it you wish to go from there?"

Dusty eyed the padre. "That's our business, ain't it?"

The padre raised a placating hand. "Certainly, my son, but it appears that you *are* lost, from the conversation I heard. I did not mean to eavesdrop."

"Yuh did a good job," said Dusty. "Just what are *you* doin' in this hell's hole?"

The padre sat down and pulled off his sandals. His feet were torn and bleeding. He poked a finger through a hole in one of the thin sandals. He looked so lugubrious that Shell couldn't help but smile. Shell walked to his horse and unbuckled a saddlebag. He withdrew a pair of worn but serviceable moccasins and tossed them to the padre.

"Bless you, bless you," said Father Eusebio. "I am penitent, but not quite penitent enough to walk barefooted in this country."

"Jesus himself would have had a hard time in this country," said Dusty. "Yuh didn't tell us what you were doin' around here."

The padre looked up. "The word of God has not been amongst the poor people of these mountains for many years. There are people living here in sin. The unmarried and the unbaptized, the dead who did not receive final absolution. I have been in these mountains for months and was working my way back to the mission when the Apaches cut me off. I had to flee this way."

"Apaches?" said Shell.

Father Eusebio nodded. "The band of Kayitah," he said. "A creature of Satan."

Dusty glanced at Shell. "How far was that from here, padre?" asked Dusty.

The padre waved a dirty hand. "Ten, perhaps fifteen miles."

"Which way were they headed?" asked Shell.

"This way," said the Mexican.

"When did you last see them?" asked Shell quickly.

The padre rubbed his unshaven face. "Just at dusk," he said.

"Jesus Christ!" said Dusty.

The padre quickly crossed himself.

Shell wearily shook his head. They'd have to move on.

Dusty raised his hand as though to strike Frank. "You and your damned twin peaks," he said.

"Wait!" said Father Eusebio. "Do not strike that man!"

Dusty turned slowly with the wolf look on his lean dirty face. "This is my business," he said.

The padre stood up. "You need water. There is none here. You are lost and do not know the way. I can lead you to water. I think I know of these twin peaks of which you speak."

"So?" said Dusty.

The padre looked at the blind man. "I have a price," he said.

Dusty grinned evilly. "I thought so! Even a man of God has his price. Every man has his price, Shell. Yuh hear that?"

"Hear me out," said the padre. "Do not touch that old man, and I will guide you."

"You'll guide us with a pistol muzzle at your neck," said Dusty angrily.

Father Eusebio shook his head. "My guidance in exchange for the safety of the old man," he said firmly.

For a moment they stood there. The tall, lean American with the icy blue eyes and swift death in his holster. The short, squat padre with the soft brown eyes and the great cross hanging at his belt. Neither one of them moved. Neither one would give an inch.

"It's a deal," said Shell.

They both looked at him. "Get the horses, Dusty," said Shell. "We've got the extra one for the padre."

Dusty hesitated a moment longer. God how he hated to be told what to do!

Shell smiled a little. "Kayitah is on the way, *compañero,*" he said quietly.

That was enough for Dusty. He got the horses.

Father Eusebio led them in an easterly direction, rather than to the south to which they had been heading, according to Harley's directions. They passed through a tangle of thorny brush and riven rock and rounded a great gaunt shoulder of naked rock, and there before them was the dark mouth of a narrow canyon that trended southeasterly. The padre kicked his horse with his moccasined heels and plunged into the dark and uninviting mouth of the canyon without hesitation.

The walls were sheer, hung with masses of rock loosened by rain and frost. The uneven floor of the canyon was littered with detritus and the walls closed in as Father Eusebio pushed ever deeper into the canyon as though determined to enter the very bowels of the earth itself.

Now and then Shell looked up at the higher parts of the canyon walls faintly lighted by the rays of the moon. Dried-out brush and driftwood hung in crevices and littered ledges high overhead. A flash flood would fill that canyon with a savage churning millrace of liquid death that would sweep before it and destroy any living or growing thing. Thank God the weather had been dry for months.

The moon was almost gone when at last Father Eusebio looked back at Shell and smiled. "It is but a little way," he said.

The dust swirled about them in the draft that flowed down the canyon, coating their faces and hands as well as their clothing. It seeped into nostrils and gritted between one's teeth. It burned the eyes and itched beneath the clothing.

Then suddenly it was lighter, and the ground sloped downward toward a thick line of brush and stunted trees denoting the line of a waterway. Father Eusebio slid easily from his sweating horse and led it forward. He pushed his way through the brush and was gone out of sight. They heard him cry out. "Water! Water! Water! Thank the Blessed Lord!"

Shell slid from the saddle and led his horse and Harley's mule into the thick, clinging brush. The horse whinnied and the mule brayed softly as they picked up the scent of the water. There was a clear area along the little stream. Father Eusebio raised a dripping face. *"Gracias a Dios!"* he said fervently. "By the grace of God it has not gone dry as it usually does at this time of the year."

"Lucky for you," said Dusty shortly.

Shell drank and then wiped his mouth. He rolled a cigarette and looked to the southwest. He lowered the cigarette. "Look," he said.

Clearly outlined against the sky were twin peaks, and on the side still lighted by the dying moon could be seen an irregularly shaped patch of white.

"Dos Cabezas," said Father Eusebio.

"That's it! That's it!" cried out Frank Harley.

Dusty raised his head from the water. "Yuh can thank *your* God for that, Harley," he said. "If we *hadn't* found it. . . ."

Harley wiped his wet mouth. "You could learn something from the padre here," he said quietly. "A man has to have faith in something else beside his guns."

"Don't preach to me!" snapped Dusty.

Harley looked toward Shell. "Cigarette, friend?" he said.

Shell handed him the makings. Harley rolled a cigarette. He was still a little clumsy at it but he was learning quickly. He placed the tube of tobacco in his mouth and snapped a lucifer on his thumbnail. The three men watched him raise the flickering match to the end of the cigarette and light it.

"Bueno!" said Shell.

Father Eusebio smiled. "The Good Lord makes allowances for those who are handicapped," he said.

Shell sat down on a rock and washed his face and hands. "You know this country well," he said. "Do you know where the Mesa del Campanero is?"

"I have been there," said the padre. He looked curiously at Shell. "There are other Americans there I have heard. Men who fought for Benito Juarez in his struggles for the freedom of our beloved Mexico. There is a *colonia* there now, although I have never seen it. My superior suggested that I might pass that way when I was through with God's work in these mountains. Perhaps some of these people are Catholics?"

Shell nodded. "Colonel De Tassigny, the leader of the *colonia,* is a Catholic. There may be others."

Father Eusebio nodded. He looked back at the tangled, almost impassable country through which they had come. "I do not wish to go back that way." He smiled wanly. "Nor would Kayitah let me. He has no use for the people of the Church. Why do you ask about the Mesa del Campanero?"

Shell and Dusty looked at each other. The padre looked puzzled for a moment. "But yes! You are Americans and quite likely Rebels, as De Tassigny is. What is it they call you? Unregenerated Rebels?"

Shell smiled. "Hardly, padre. *Unreconstructed* is the word."

The padre laughed heartily.

"You will guide us there, padre?" said Frank Harley.

The padre looked at the lean, scarred face of Dusty. "Yes," he said, "I think so. After all, it is my duty."

Dusty knew well enough what Father Eusebio meant. The padre's price to guide them was that Dusty must leave Frank Harley alone. Fair enough. After that, Frank would be on his own, and God help him if he went wrong again.

They moved away from the water after they and the animals had had their fill. The padre led them for several miles into broken country. Here they picketed the tired horses and slept, Dusty, Shell, and the padre taking turns on guard.

Shell lay awake for a time, staring up into the darkness, watching the winking ice-chip stars. Padre Eusebio had come along just at the right time. Shell had no idea in his mind as to what would have happened if the padre had *not* come along. Dusty had already killed two people in his quest for the lost silver mines. It wasn't likely he would have killed Frank Harley, for that would have scotched the whole deal, but the older man would have suffered. Shell felt a wave of shame creep through him. He had allowed his own greed to take over. He too had been bitter and angry at Frank because the man had become lost. Shell smiled wryly up into the darkness. A blind man becoming lost in a country where few men with sight could find their way. The shame in Shell was that he himself had not stopped Dusty beating the blind man. What had come over him?

He turned his head and looked toward Dusty, asleep a few feet away. They had been together a long time. Shell had forgotten how many times they had owed each other their lives. Shell narrowed his eyes. Was it possible that he was *afraid* of Dusty? He tried to cast the thought from his mind. He had never thought of it much before, but Dusty seemed to have changed for the worse since the sheen of silver riches had struck into his brain. The cold thought crept into Shell's mind and settled down comfortably, eyeing its new surroundings. Was it possible that the silver sheen had also outshone Shell's morals and principles as well as those of Dusty?

Frank Harley shifted in his sleep. "La Barranca Escondida," he said clearly. *"Departamento de Camino a Las Minas de La Barranca Escondida y El Naranjal."*

Father Eusebio moved a little in the darkness. He turned his face toward the supposedly sleeping trio. He padded closer on his moccasined feet and waited a long time as though to hear Frank speak in his sleep again. After a while he walked back to his post.

Shell looked toward the padre. How much had he heard? Surely he would know about the lost silver mines. What Mexican hadn't heard of Tayopa, La Barranca Escondida, and El Naranjal? To them it was the truth of God—not a myth, but a legend with a basis of truth. A wandering padre like Father Eusebio would know that country as well, or perhaps better, than most men. He would have learned a great deal from the simple people of those mountains. If nothing else the good padre would keep Dusty's hands from Frank Harley. It was better that way, for Shell felt as though he'd have to interfere the next time Dusty tried to beat the older man, and the results would be unpredictable. No one could stand in the way of Matt Dustin when he wanted something, at least not for long, and if Matt Dustin had ever really wanted anything in his life it was the lost riches of La Barranca Escondida.

Chapter Ten

The sorrel had gone down thrashing with a snapped leg, hurling Padre Eusebio from the saddle. The padre had landed like a cat to clear the fallen horse. A canteen burst beneath the weight of the struggling animal, and the water darkened the light, powdery soil. It flowed into the hole into which the sorrel had stepped. Shell looked stupidly at the water as it vanished into the thirsty earth. It had been filled three days past somewhere in the unmapped country between the Rio Sonora and some unknown watercourse. It was the last of their water. They had run out of food two days past, existing on a pair of rabbits snared by Padre Eusebio. Now the sorrel was lost to them, and the gray Dusty had been riding limped badly from a punctured hoof that was now infected.

Padre Eusebio looked sorrowfully at the sorrel. *"Muy bravo,"* he said quietly. "A fine *caballo*."

Dusty slid from the saddle. "You'll walk from now on," he said.

Shell dismounted. "We'll take turns riding." He looked up at Frank Harley. "How do you feel, Frank?"

"Muy bravo," said Frank weakly.

"Mesa del Campanero," said Dusty. He glanced toward the blind man and then at the padre.

"We'll get there," said Shell.

Dusty spat. He had become more silent in the past few days. More silent and more gaunt, seemingly burning with an inner fever, and yet he was not sick. That is to say he was not physically sick. His sickness was of the mind.

"The silver will not run away," said Father Eusebio as he picked a cactus needle from his hand. For a moment he studied his hand, and then he looked up because of the sudden silence that had come over the three Americans. A weaker man than Padre Eusebio might have quailed before the hard eyes of the two tall Americans.

"What about silver?" said Dusty quietly.

The padre shrugged. "You are not in here to enjoy the scenery," he said. "There is an unholy haste within you to get to the Mesa del Campanero, and beyond that. . . ."

"Beyond that?" prompted Shell.

The Mexican rubbed his dusty face. "La Barranca Escondida," he said.

Dusty's hand dropped to the butt of his Colt.

Eusebio shook his head. "I have taken the vow of poverty," he said. "Lost treasures mean nothing to me."

"They do to the Church," said Shell, "and to your order."

"I am not a Jesuit," said the padre.

"A fortune in silver can make even a Franciscan padre's head turn," said Dusty.

The padre smiled. "I will go as far as the Mesa del Campanero," he said. "That and no more."

"Yeh," said Dusty. He looked at the sorrel and at the water-soaked earth. His meaning was clear enough. No water, and short one horse.

"Where is the next waterhole?" said Shell.

"Tinajas Altas," said the padre.

"That's in Arizona," said Shell.

"There are many places with the same name," said the padre.

"How far?"

Father Eusebio shrugged. "Perhaps within ten miles. Perhaps closer. These mountains begin to look much alike after a time."

"Christ!" said Dusty. "You too? Harley gets his directions mixed up, that's bad enough, but you made a deal, Eusebio. Yuh mean to tell me yuh don't know where the water is?"

The padre stood up and looked to the south. "There are three canyons south of here," he said thoughtfully. "One them is a box canyon as you Americans call it. One leads deep into the mountains east of here. There is no water there. The third has the Tinajas Altas high on one flank. They are never dry, or so it is said."

"Or so it is said," repeated Dusty. "By God, people in this damned country always manage to cover up, don't they?"

The padre did not answer. He looked at the horse. "We cannot leave him here like this. He will be torn to pieces by tonight." The padre jerked with a startled expression on his face as the heavy bowie knife flashed past him and buried itself to the cross piece in the throat of the sorrel. The head dropped instantly and the dark blood gushed forth over the padre's worn moccasins. He leaped back and looked incredulously at Dusty. There was a faint smile on Dusty's face. A tinge of white showed beneath the brown patina of the padre's face. He hurriedly crossed himself.

Dusty walked over to the dead horse, his spurs softly chiming, and began to strip the saddle from him. He threw the saddle over the rump of Shell's horse, then jerked the bloody blade from the throat of the sorrel. He wiped it on the sorrel's dusty mane. He looked casually at Padre Eusebio, tested the edge of the knife with his thumb, feeling for nicks, then slid the bowie into its sheath. "Padre," he said softly, "you had better, by God, find the *right* canyon."

Padre Eusebio hurriedly set off afoot, glancing back now and then as Shell and Dusty led the animals behind him. He looked up at the sky. Already a speck hung there. The scout for the zopilotes. The padre shivered. These Americans dealt out death as casually as a monte dealer dealt out his cards.

The sun was slanting from the west when the faint sound of shooting echoed along the twisted canyon. The little party stopped in its tracks. There was no sound for a time except the dry wind, and then a shot flatted off to send its echo slamming back and forth between the canyon walls.

"Hunters?" said Father Eusebio.

Shell shook his head. He withdrew his Spencer from its saddle scabbard and levered a round into the chamber. He let the hammer down to half-cock. Dusty led the animals into the brush. He looked at the padre. "Stay here with Frank," he said. He also took his Spencer and followed Shell through the swaying brush. In a moment they were gone, hardly leaving a sign of their passage except a few faint boot marks.

Shell held Dusty back with a hand motion. He dropped to his knees and crawled through the tangled brush and broken rock to a point where he could look up the canyon. A shot cracked out and the echo died away. The right side of the great canyon was talus-sloped, a vast area of broken rock stippled with brush. The canyon wall above the talus slope was riven, with masses of rock looking as though the sound of the shot echoes would cause thousands of tons of rock to fall crashing to the slopes below. There was a place that was level, and here the rock had not fallen as thickly as on the talus slope. There was a rough oval of tumbled rock, head high, set on the level area. Even as Shell watched, a puff of smoke broke from between two of these rocks to be followed by the flat crack of a rifle.

Shell uncased his German-made fieldglasses. He took

off his hat and placed the glasses to his eyes, focusing to bring in the ring of rock. The first thing he saw was a mule, laden with hide *aparejos* on each side. Beyond the mule he saw the rumps of two other animals, likely horses. A horse's head showed in a clump of brush. What interested him more were the shining pools of water held in the natural rock tanks within the oval. There was a lot of water in those tanks. The sight of it set his dry mouth and throat to aching.

A shot flatted off, closely followed by another, and the twin puffs of cottony smoke drifted downwind into the canyon. He could not see the riflemen—there must be at least two of them. What were they shooting at? He scanned the slopes. The powerful lens brought out a moccasined foot thrust out behind a clump of brush seventy-five yards from the waterhole. He slowly scanned the area on his side of the waterhole, then the lower slopes, and finally the rock wall behind the tanks. He counted nine men who showed little more than an arm, a leg, or a quick movement of a head. None of the heads had hats on them. He lowered the glasses. He touched his cracked lips with his tongue.

"Well?" demanded Dusty.

Shell looked back at him. "Waterhole," he said. "Two or three people holed up there. At least nine outside the waterhole."

"Mexicans?"

Shell shook his head. "Indians, *compañero.*"

Dusty hesitated. "Apaches?"

"Quién sabe?"

Shell did not look at Dusty again. He knew what his companion was thinking. If those were Apaches they could very well be the band of Kayitah. It was possible they had got ahead of Shell, Dusty, Frank, and Padre Eusebio.

"Maybe they're Yaquis?" said Dusty.

"What difference does it make?" said Shell.

There was a sudden outburst of gunfire, sending rolling echoes down the canyon. Powdersmoke swirled about the waterhole and drifted up from the rifles of the besiegers.

Dusty bellied up beside Shell and took the glasses. He studied the situation and then the terrain. "Those people at the waterhole have horses, and it looks like they have food aplenty. They've got control of the waterhole, for a time at least. If we let those Apaches or Yaquis, or whatever the hell they are, get that waterhole, it's the end for us, *compañero.*"

Shell nodded. He looked along the canyon wall. There was an area there, like a wide shelf with a natural rampart of rock ledges extending almost to above the waterhole. At the end of it were two of the besiegers, firing almost directly down into the oval of rocks. Whoever held that position had the key to the siege. He eyed the waterhole. Horses, food, and water, and they needed all three.

Dusty shifted. He looked at Shell. "We can take those Indians," he said. "After that we can take care of them Mexes at the waterhole."

Shell cased the glasses. He picked up his Spencer and led the way into the thick brush that covered the gentler slope that lay at the base of the rock shelf. The gunfire was sporadic and the Indians were so intense on their siege they'd hardly notice the approach of Dusty and Shell; at least Shell hoped so.

It took them the better part of an hour to reach the rock ledge and to lie bellyflat there, breathing harshly, their thirst a terrible thing, their sweat stinging the myriad cuts and scratches they had suffered in their stealthy approach. Shell rested his head on his forearms. His heart was thudding erratically and his lungs seemed to be on fire. It took all his discipline to crawl on, taking advantage of every scrap of cover. If they were seen they'd never get off that ledge alive.

Shell stopped fifty yards from the end of the rock shelf. Nothing could been seen of the pair of riflemen at the end of the shelf, but now and then a shot indicated they were still there. Shell placed his carbine between two rocks. He felt for his bowie and withdrew it. Foot by foot he wormed his way along. He stopped. Someone was crawling back from the end of the rock shelf. He quickly rolled into a clump of scraggly brush and behind a flat rock, cursing mentally as the hooked thorns ripped through worn clothing into flesh.

There was no sign of Dusty. Rocks clattered a little as the Indian came closer. Shell held his breath. The bare brown back of the Indian could be seen on the other side of the flat rock. As the Indian passed, Shell rolled over the rock. His bowie sank into the small of the back as Dusty's swiped clean across the throat of the buck. He fell without a sound.

The hot, sweet smell of blood filled the windless air along the rock shelf. Shell sat back resting against a rock. He looked at Dusty. Dusty grinned. He was in his element. Dusty casually wiped his bloody blade on the thick hair of the dead buck. "Apache?" he said to Shell.

"Quién sabe?" said Shell. He wasn't that much of an expert.

Dusty rifled the bloody corpse, cursing softly to himself.

He shoved the thing aside. "Let's get the other one," he said. "I can last about another hour without a drink."

Shell bellied along the ledge until he could see a pair of thick-soled moccasins protruding from the brush that fringed the end of the ledge. A rifle cracked. He heard the tinkle of the smoking brass hull on the rock. He moved swiftly in as the buck reloaded. The warrior was only ten feet from him, settling himself for another shot down into the waterhole area. As he squeezed off, Shell closed in, the noise of his approach covered by the roar of the shot. The buck never knew what hit him. He died even as he opened the breech of his single-shot rifle.

Dusty and Shell lay flat at the end of the ledge. Now and then Dusty would fire a wild shot from the buck's rifle. Shell peered between two rocks. He counted seven places where gunsmoke appeared as the warriors fired at the waterhole. Even as he watched, a buck stood up, pitched forward, and fell heavily, dropping his smoking rifle. A good clean head shot at seventy-five yards, thought Shell. Whoever was handling that long gun was no amateur.

Shell touched Dusty on the shoulder. Silently he pointed out the positions of five of the Indians. None of them were concerned about who was behind them. They thought the shooting from the ledge was being done by their mates. Shell drew up his Spencer and full-cocked it. Dusty did the same. Together they sighted on brown backs not fifty yards below them. The two Spencers crashed together driving flame and smoke from the muzzles. One of the bucks leaped to his feet, whirled about and fell heavily. The other did not move. Shell and Dusty levered round after round into hot, smoking Spencers. The 385-grain slugs smashed into flesh and bone or ricocheted off into space screaming eerily. Startled brown faces, banded with white paint, looked up at the ledge. One face exploded into a mass of red jelly as two soft slugs tore into it.

The hell of the rattling repeater fire slammed back and forth in the canyon like rolling thunder. Shell rammed cartridges into the loading aperture in the repeater's metal-shod butt and dropped over the side of the ledge, plunging stiff-legged down the treacherous slope. From behind him came the piercing, thrilling rebel yell. A startled buck caught a slug in his chest and another in his back as he was spun about by the impact of the first bullet.

The two men plunged through the thorny brush, ripping clothing and flesh, firing from the hip at times until suddenly there was nothing to shoot at. The echoes died away. The smoke drifted thickly, then rifted out and slowly vanished. Then it was very quiet in the canyon except for the thrashing sound of a wounded buck who clawed for his knife, his pain-stricken eyes on the two hated white men. Dusty raised his smoking repeater and fired once, at twenty-foot range. The heavy slug ripped through the wounded buck's gaping mouth. The shot echo died away.

Shell reloaded the Spencer. He shoved back his hat and wiped the sweat and dirt from his face. His breathing was harsh and erratic, and all of a sudden his legs grew weak beneath him and he almost sat down on the rocky ground. He leaned on his Spencer and looked toward the waterhole.

"Who is it?" someone called out in Spanish. The voice was surprisingly high pitched.

"Friends!" yelled Shell hoarsely.

Dusty looked about. "I thought yuh said there was nine of these bastards," he said. "I tally eleven."

"Mark it up to profit," Shell said dryly. "They're all *good* Indians now."

They plodded toward the ring of rocks that held the full tanks within them. A sombrero bobbed about. The barrel of a long rifle showed.

"Christ!" said Dusty. "Smell that water!"

Shell walked between two rocks that stood like a natural entrance way. A bareheaded man stood with a single-shot rifle in his hands. A band of dingy cloth held back his thick black hair. His great eyes studied the two white men.

Dusty dropped a hand to his Colt.

"No," said Shell. "He's likely a *mozo*."

The other man stood with his back to them, bent to the waist, and there was no question about what he was doing. He was swiftly losing his last meal. He staggered a little as he held his hands to his face.

Dusty grinned. "Yuh don't like bloodlettin' even if it saves your life, eh, *amigo?*"

The man turned and withdrew his slim hands from his face. Shell whistled softly. A pair of great pain-wracked eyes looked at him. A slim hand took the heavy, silver-banded sombrero from the head, and a wealth of dark hair fell to the slim shoulders.

"My God," breathed Dusty. His eyes fell from the lovely oval face to the full, firm breasts that pushed out against the thin material of the shirt. The rounded hips beneath the rather tight charro trousers. The dusty figured boots on the small feet.

The Indian *mozo* moved quietly over beside the woman.

The rifle began to rise. Dusty walked forward, his Spencer at hip level. "Put down that rifle, you," he said coldly.

The *mozo* did not move. The woman looked at him. She spoke swiftly. "It is all right, Victor," she said. "These men are our friends. They have saved our lives." Slowly he lowered the rifle. She looked at Shell. "He cannot speak," she said.

Dusty knelt by the nearest tank and scooped water up in his free hand, but he never took his cold blue eyes from the *mozo*. "Tell him to throw down that rifle," he said.

She spoke to the *mozo*. Obediently he threw down the rifle, but he did not move away from the woman.

"I am Rafaela Padilla of Hermosillo," she said. "This is our *mozo* Victor."

"Our?" said Shell. He looked quickly about.

Her lovely face changed. "My brother . . . Rodrigo . . . he. . . ." Her voice died away and a stricken look came over her face. She looked beyond the water tanks. A slim hand crept up to her full-lipped mouth.

Shell scooped up some water to wet his mouth and throat. He skirted the tanks and walked among the scattered rocks to where a man lay face down, tightly clutching a Henry rifle in his slim brown hands. Shell hooked a boot toe under him and rolled him over. The great brown eyes stared unseeingly at Shell. The white shirt and soft leather charro jacket were darkly stained with blood. The resemblance to the young woman was unmistakable. They must have been twins.

Shell took the rifle from the stiffening hands. He walked back to the water tanks. Her eyes held his from across the tanks. He shook his head. She turned away and covered her face with her hands. Sobs racked her body.

Dusty drank again. He walked to the nearest horse, a fine, clean-limbed bay. He swung up into the saddle. "I'll get the others," he said. The dark eyes of the *mozo* followed Dusty as he rode down the slope.

Shell drank again. "We got into a water scrape," he said. "Horse broke a leg. We were on our way here when we heard the firing. My name is Shell."

She nodded. "We were on our way back to Hermosillo from the ranch of my uncle Teodoro who died last month. We had a strong party with us, but they became frightened when we heard that the Yaquis had arisen between the ranch and river. They split away from us during the night and rode further south. Rodrigo insisted that we come here to Tinajas Altas. Thanks to God we reached the water first.

But Rodrigo is dead. It is a terrible price we paid."

Shell sipped a little more water. It seemed to revive him. He glanced at the animals. "What will you do now?" he asked.

She took her full lower lip between perfect white teeth. "I do not know," she said. She glanced at him. "Perhaps you will ride with us toward Hermosillo?"

"Hardly," said Shell.

Hoofs clattered on the slope below the water tanks. Dusty appeared, urging the bay up the slope. There was a grin on his scarred face. "By God!" he said. "What a horse!"

"It was Rodrigo's," said Rafaela.

The woman watched curiously as Shell helped Frank Harley down from the saddle. The worried look fled from her face as she saw Padre Eusebio. She ran to him. The padre took her in his arms and comforted her. "It is the will of God, my child," he said soothingly.

Afterward, when the simple meal, furnished by the supplies of the Padillas, had been finished, they sat about the bed of coals in the gathering darkness. Father Eusebio spoke quietly and reassuringly to Rafaela. "You cannot ride toward Hermosillo with just a *mozo*, my child. It is said that the Yaquis are raiding between here and Hermosillo. This was just a small party of them. There may be many more of them west of here."

"With Kayitah and his Chiricahuas coming down from the north," said Shell.

Dusty had spoken very little. It was plain that he didn't want to burden his little party with a woman, but, on the other hand, his eyes would wander again and again to the body of Rafaela Padilla. He rarely looked at her lovely face. Always the body. To Dusty, one woman was like another. When he had his fill of one he would walk away from her and close her from his mind.

"I can pay you well to escort us to Soyopa, at least," she said.

Dusty's eyes flicked up at the mention of pay.

Rafaela flushed. "I have a little silver with me," she said.

"Where's the rest of it?" said Dusty.

"In Hermosillo," she said.

"We ain't goin' there," he said.

It was very quiet except for the moaning of the wind down the canyon. One of the horses blew.

Shell picked up a stone and tossed it from one hand to the other. He looked at the horses and at the filled *aparejos* lying near the sturdy mule. There was enough food in those packs to supply Shell, Dusty, Frank, and the padre for at least a week, on short rations. They needed that extra horse as well. Still, from what the padre had told him privately, it would take them only a few days to escort the woman and the *mozo* to the Rio Yaqui in the hope that she might be able to work her way safely back to Hermosillo.

"There will be soldiers at Soyopa," she said.

Dusty flicked his eyes at Shell. That was all *they* needed. Soldiers! Soldiers of the Republic of Mexico.

"No go," said Shell. He tossed the stone back and forth.

She bit her lip and looked uncertainly at the two tall Americans and then at the dust brown padre. Eusebio shrugged expressively. "There is our own safety to consider, my child," he said. "Who knows how many Yaquis are between us and Soyopa, or that there *are* soldiers there? We have no supplies and you have more than enough. Come, Rafaela Padilla! Ride south with us. I know this country as far south as Mesa del Campanero to which we are riding. There will be soldiers there, or at least one can stay there in safety until such time as it is safe to travel again."

There was no further argument from the young woman. She nodded. There was no expression on Victor's wooden-looking face.

Shell stood up, tossing the stone into the nearest tank. "We'll move as quickly as we can," he said.

"Tonight?" asked Rafaela in astonishment.

Shell looked at her. "We've wiped out about a dozen of them," he said. "They won't forget that. Ever! We have water and food, and the horses are in fair shape. We'll ride and walk this night."

"My brother," she said.

The padre looked at Shell. "There is time enough for that at least," he said.

"No!" snapped Dusty.

The padre looked steadily at him. "We do not leave," he said quietly, "until that boy is buried."

Dusty opened, then closed his mouth as he saw the look on Shell's face. "I'll saddle the horses. Come on, you!" he said to the *mozo*.

It was fully dark when they covered the slim body of Rodrigo Padilla with earth, then piled rocks atop the grave. Father Eusebio spoke over the grave. Rafaela, between sobs, placed a gaily striated stone atop the lonely grave. She did not look back as Shell took her arm and guided her to her horse.

They rode down the slope past the scattered bodies of the

Yaqui dead. In the coolness of the night the dead spoke restlessly as the expanded gases in their swollen bodies sought to escape, filling the clear night air with a foul and lingering stench. The zopilotes would take care of them in the morning. By dusk of the next day the picked yellowish skeletons would have begun to dry and bleach. In a few days the stench would have vanished as well, and Tinajas Altas would be the same as it had been for hundreds of years—with one exception. In the years to come it would be known as Tinajas de la Muerte—the Tanks of Death.

Chapter Eleven

The mesa was high, with riven sides, thickly covered with brush and scrub trees, but the backdrop of the towering mountains made it seem small in comparison. The approach to Mesa del Campanero was tortuous, crossing steep-sided arroyos and dropping down into shallow, rough-floored valleys. Smoke rose leisurely from the western end of the mesa which overlooked sloping country that carried down to a line of broken hills, and thence, by a week's travel on rough trails, to the Gulf of California.

The sky was bright and cottony puffs of clouds drifted lazily toward the unseen Gulf. The air was clear, with a sharper feeling to it, and the hellish heat of the lower land had become dissipated except during midday and in the middle of the long, sunny afternoons. The wind brought the pungent odor of the warm brush and trees with it.

Shell squatted on his heels looking up at the mesa. Dusty lay in the shade, his hat tilted down over his eyes and nose. Frank Harley sat with his back against a rock, hands lying in his lap, his sightless eyes looking to the south.

Somewhere between the mesa and the place where the trio of Americans were resting were Rafaela, Victor, and Padre Eusebio. The great mesa was Mesa del Campanero. The smoke might be rising from Colonel De Tassigny's *colonia*. There might be soldiers there. They would not bother Rafaela and Victor, and of course the padre could go anywhere he liked. He had guided them well in the past week, and when he had been in doubt it had been Victor who had gone ahead on foot to scout the lay of the land. The *mozo* was a

Tarahumare, Rafaela had told Shell. An outcast from his tribe for some crime he had committed years ago. He had been found by Rafaela's father, close to death in the mountains, and Señor Padilla had taken him to his home in the vicinity of Hermosillo. The *mozo* had served him tirelessly until Señor Padilla's death and then had transferred his loyalty and his services to Rodrigo and Rafaela. He never rode, preferring to trot along at a tireless gait. His people lived in the great canyons to the east, in Las Gran Barrancas de las Tarahumaras. Twenty in number, at least, of formidable gorges, covering an estimated area of ten thousand square miles. These people spoke no Spanish and lived in stone-age style in their almost inaccessible country. The Tarahumares were great runners. Rafaela had told Shell that a pair of them would spend two or three days running down a deer until it fell from exhaustion.

Shell rolled a cigarette. There was something else that was noteworthy about Victor. He was never very far from Rafaela, and he did not seem to fear the two bearded Americanos, particularly the blue-eyed one who always covertly watched Victor's mistress. Shell knew well enough that if Dusty made a pass at Rafaela either Dusty would die himself at the hands of Victor or Dusty would have to kill Victor. It was as simple as that.

It was late afternoon when Rafaela returned, with Victor running tirelessly ahead of her. She slid from her saddle and took off her sombrero. "Padre Eusebio stayed there," she said. "Colonel De Tassigny told me to tell you that you must come up the side trail of the mesa and remain at the top of the trail until he comes. There are soldiers near the *colonia,* camped at the springs. Their officer, Capitán Hernán Galeras, has warned the colonel not to give aid or shelter to men such as you."

"He knows of us then?" said Shell.

"Not by name," she said. She glanced at Dusty. "He described both of you rather well to the colonel. He does not know that the colonel was once your commanding officer."

Dusty sat up. "All we want is supplies and fresh horses," he said. "He owes us that at least."

Shell looked up at the mesa. The riven sides were deepening in shadow. He didn't like the idea of going up there. If Captain Galeras had scouts out, as he should have, the presence of American strangers would have been noted.

Shell fashioned a cigarette and lighted it. He looked at

the young woman over the flare of the match. "You did not have to return," he said. "Why did you?"

She shrugged. "I owed that much to you."

"You will leave for Hermosillo from the Mesa del Campanero?"

She hesitated. "The trails are not safe as yet," she said.

"Yuh can stay with the colonel," said Dusty. He looked slantways at her with his cold blue eyes.

Rafaela slapped the side of her charro trousers with her quirt. She studied Shell for a moment and then turned on a heel. She walked to Frank Harley. "Do you feel well enough for the climb up the mesa, Señor Harley?" she asked.

He looked up at her and smiled. "Yes," he said. "We can't go on without food and fresh horses."

"Must you go on?" she asked.

He nodded.

"It is a terrible country," she said. "Broken by great gorges and towering mountains. It is said that even the birds require a map and compass to pass over it."

"I know," he said. "I have been there."

She sat down beside him. "To La Barranca Escondida?"

Dusty and Shell turned slowly to look at her. None of them, including Frank, had once mentioned their goal to Rafaela. As far as she knew, they were heading for the *colonia* at Mesa del Campanero.

Rafaela looked calmly up at them. "The padre told me," she said simply.

"How did he know?" said Dusty.

Shell waved a hand. "Frank talked in his sleep one night while the padre was on guard. We can't hide it, Dusty. These people can easily guess why we are here."

"There is such a place," said Rafaela. "The stories of La Barranca Escondida and of El Naranjal are true. When I was a child my grandfather told me of them."

Frank Harley sat up straight. He reached out a gaunt hand and held her shoulder. "Go on," he said quietly.

"My grandfather was a man such as you men," she said. "Always he was in the mountains and the barrancas, looking for lost silver or gold mines. Much of his life was spent in treasure hunting. He had many maps and charts. He would listen eagerly to every tale that was told of Tayopa, of El Naranjal, of Scalp Hunter's Ledge, and of the Treasure of Moctezuma. But somehow he always returned to his search for La Barranca Escondida and El Naranjal.

"Some years before I was born he was trapped by Yaquis in the mountains near a broken hill, not too far from

Nayarit. His companions and servants were all killed, but he managed to escape. For two full days he hid from them, and on the third day he was forced south, into unknown country. He fled through waterless, tangled *chaparral*. When night came he was nearly dead of thirst and exhaustion. He slept that night on the brink of a barranca. It was so deep he could not hear dropped stones strike the bottom and he was afraid to move in the dark.

"In the morning he awoke to a deathly silence. There was no sign of life. No, not one! Not a bird, or a rabbit, or anything alive. He lay there until the rising sun warmed his body. The wind rose a little with the coming of the sun, and then he distinctly heard the faint, ever so faint, sound of a bell." Her voice died away as she saw the look on Frank Harley's face.

"Go on! Go on!" said Dusty hoarsely.

"He crawled to the very lip of the barranca and looked down," she continued. "He could see straight down for thousands of feet. The sun was already shining on the western wall of the great gorge. It sparkled on water. A running stream that passed through dark groves of trees. The floor of that great canyon was more than a mile across. As far as he could see, the walls of the huge canyon were sheer. He watched those dark trees as the sun crept to them and he saw what he swore—until the very day he died—were oranges, hanging thickly from those dark-foliaged trees."

Shell whistled softly. Frank gestured impatiently at him.

"Far back in the groves," said Rafaela in a low voice, "he saw patches of white and he was sure there were many buildings there. Something arose above the trees. It looked like a tower of some kind. Perhaps a bell tower. He never was sure about that. He sat there for hours looking down at the unattainable, for he knew he could never get to the bottom of the gorge, at least not in his condition. At noon he heard the bell again, or he *thought* he heard it. He could not remain there any longer. He walked to the west and late that night he found water. A week later he stumbled out onto the road that leads to Los Mochis. It was a month before he had the strength to travel. He was in delirium for days."

Dusty spat. "He *thought* he saw it."

She shrugged. "Perhaps," she said. She looked up at Shell. "He was a man of honor. A simple man. Many people doubted his story, but I never did. I never knew him to lie."

Frank Harley nodded. "It jibes," he said excitedly. "It

jibes! You spoke of the broken hill not far from Nayarit. Do you remember if he had a name for it?"

She bit her lip for a moment and narrowed her eyes. "It had an odd name," she said thoughtfully.

"Go on!" snapped Dusty.

Shell hurled the cigarette from his lips and looked at her.

"Cerro de. . . ." She shook her head.

"Rafaela!" said Shell.

She looked up at him, her lovely face taut with tension. "Cerro de. . . ."

Frank Harley wet his cracked lips. "Cerro de Huesos, Rafaela?" he suggested softly.

She smiled. "Yes! Yes! That is it! The Hill of Bones!"

"Jesus God!" said Dusty. "He was right there! It was right in his dirty greaser hands and *he walked away from it!*"

Rafaela flushed at Dusty's description of her beloved grandfather. "There was nothing he could have done," she said. "There was no water. The Yaquis were hard on his trail. He had no food and no way to go except to walk toward the setting sun. If he had stayed there he would have died, one way or another. You dishonor the dead, *hombre!*"

Dusty grinned. "Take it easy," he said.

"For many years he tried to find that barranca again," she said, "but he never did. Time and time again he would journey for days to Nayarit and thence to the Hill of Bones. There were times when he thought he heard that mysterious bell, but he was never sure about that. He died without ever finding any treasure."

"Poor old bastard," said Dusty.

"No!" she said. "He was happy! It was the dream that made him happy. He always knew in his heart that some day he would find El Naranjal again."

"But he never did," said Dusty.

She stood up. "Perhaps it was best that way," she said. She walked to her horse and mounted it, touching it with her quirt, to ride back toward the mesa. Victor trotted ahead of her into the gathering darkness.

Shell gave Frank a foot up into the saddle. "What do you think, Frank?" he said.

The blind man looked to the south. "She knows a great deal more than she lets on, Shell," he said.

The two tall Americans looked at each other. The same thought had struck both of them.

"She might know more than I do," said Frank. "I have never met anyone who has seen El Naranjal or who has known anyone else who has seen it."

"Maybe she is lying?" said Dusty.

Shell shook his head. "No," he said.

The other two knew he was right. Rafaela might have the key to La Barranca Escondida and El Naranjal locked in her lovely head.

"Supposin' she decides to stay here at Mesa del Campanero?" said Dusty. He swung up into his saddle and looked down at Shell. "Supposin' she decides to return to Hermosillo?"

"She won't," said Frank Harley.

They looked back at him. "Why?" said Shell.

The blind man leaned forward in his saddle. "I think she is falling in love with you, Shell," he said. "So long as she feels that way she'll go with us. It's up to you, Shell."

Dusty's cold eyes studied Shell. A tinge of jealousy swept through him. *He* wanted to sleep with her. On the other hand, she was just a woman. With all that silver he could have one like her each night in the week and perhaps matinees besides.

"What about it, Shell?" said Frank.

Shell mounted. He touched his horse with his spurs. "It's damned dirty," he said. He rode down the trail.

"Well?" said Dusty to Frank.

The blind man nodded. "He'll do it," he said. He touched the mule with his heels and rode forward. "God help her," he added softly.

Chapter Twelve

The wind moaned softly over the top of the great mesa, swaying the brush and the scrub trees. On the wide slopes to the west there was a cluster of faint yellow light where the adobes and jacales of the *colonia* were situated. The faint odor of wood-smoke drifted across the top of the mesa.

Shell Burnett sat on a flat rock, looking down at the warm and friendly lights of the *colonia*. There would be men down there he had known. Men who had fought with him at Wilson's Creek, Pea Ridge, Corinth, and throughout the Vicksburg Campaign as well as the Red River Campaign. The South Kansas-Texas Mounted Rifles had virtually ceased to exist as a unit after the Vicksburg Campaign, but there had been plenty of fighting left for the remnants. There would be men down there who had fought beside Shell and Dusty throughout the war and who later had fought against them on the side of the forces of the Republic of Mexico.

Hoofs clattered on rock. Dusty was on his feet in an instant, Spencer cocked and ready. Shell stepped behind a tree and picked up his Spencer.

"Señor Shell?" came the hesitant voice of Padre Eusebio.

"Here, padre," said Shell.

"It is the colonel," said the Mexican.

A horseman appeared behind the mounted figure of the padre. "Burnett?" he said eagerly. "Is it really you?"

Shell smiled. "Yes, sir! It's good to hear your voice, Colonel De Tassigny."

The tall officer slid from his saddle. "We meet in a strange place, lieutenant. Dustin is with you, is he not?"

"Here, sir," said Dusty. He had always had a respect for De Tassigny, not so much for his gentlemanly manner and his background, but for his ability as a first-class fighting man.

De Tassigny strode to meet them. In the faint light Shell could see the narrow face, trimmed with a small neat beard and the sweeping mustachios the officer affected. The colonel still wore his Confederate gray coat, the brass buttons showing clearly through the dimness. He thrust out his right hand and gripped Shell's hand hard. "By God," he said, "this is wonderful! I heard you both were executed at Querétaro."

Dusty laughed. "We moved a little too fast for you Republicans, sir."

The colonel smiled. "Maybe we didn't try very hard to catch you Royalists, Dustin."

Shell looked down the dark slope of the mesa side to the site of the *colonia* village. "How does it go, sir?" he asked.

De Tassigny felt inside his coat and took out a cigar case. He handed it to Shell. Shell helped himself and Dusty also selected a cigar. They lighted up along with the colonel. Padre Eusebio had vanished up the slope to where Frank Harley sat in the darkness with Rafaela and Victor.

De Tassigny sat down and puffed his cigar into life. His brown eyes looked across the flare of the cigar tip at Shell. "Not too well," he admitted. "Times are hard. Many of the Mexicans do not accept us. We have four times as many men as women. It is a hard country for men, let alone women. The country is alive with animal and human predators. Banditry is rife. The soldiers who have been sent to protect us and the other villagers are little more than bandits themselves, for they haven't been paid and have to live off the country. Only our unity and our skill with arms, coupled with the appreciation of Benito Juarez for what we did in his cause, have thus far saved us from greater trouble than we have already had."

"Do you plan to stay?" said Shell.

The colonel shrugged. "We plan to give it a fair trial," he said. "If it doesn't work out we'll have to leave."

"For where?" said Dusty.

"The United States," said the colonel.

Dusty spat. "To take the oath?"

The officer nodded. He puffed at his cigar. "It is a great country, Dustin. We fought for our cause and we lost. It might have been better that way. The Lord works in mysterious ways," he said quietly.

"I never thought I would hear you talk like that," said Dusty coldly.

The officer looked at him. "You are a single man, Dustin. An adventurer. A mercenary, if you'll pardon the expression, sir. Many of us have wives and children here at the *colonia.* In the short time we have been here our children have begun to speak Spanish more frequently than English. Some of my men have married Mexican women. In time we will cease to exist as a unit and will be absorbed into their culture, sir. In two generations nothing will exist of our *colonia* except for the Anglo-Saxon names and the light-colored eyes."

"That's better than crawling back to the United States to take the oath," said Dusty.

De Tassigny inspected the end of his cigar. "Is it?" he said thoughtfully. "I wonder?"

Shell could see the colonel's point. The planting of the *colonia* had been idealistic; the results were factual. De Tassigny had likely predicted the future with accuracy.

The officer looked at Shell. "I can't give you shelter," he said. "The soldiers are always hanging around the *colonia.* You'd be seen and likely identified. You must return to the States, Burnett."

Shell shook his head. "Even if we wanted to," he said, "it is impossible. The Apaches and Yaquis are behind us, and following us, sir."

De Tassigny looked quickly at him. "Did you have anything to do with the death of Anselmo Chacón and his Indian wife?"

There was no answer from Shell. He had never found it easy to lie to his commanding officer.

"A runner came in a day ago to tell us of a fight at Tinajas Altas. Many Yaquis were slain. It is said the Yaquis have joined forces with the band of Kayitah the Chiricahua, to hunt down the slayers of Anselmo Chacón and his wife, as well as those men who killed the Yaquis at Tinajas Altas. By God! I would not want to be in the boots of those men!"

"Chacón tried to kill me," said Dusty.

"The Yaquis were in between us and the waterhole," said Shell. "It was them or us, colonel."

De Tassigny took the cigar from his mouth. "For the love of God!" he said. He looked quickly at them. "You must not stay here then."

"We need supplies and fresh horses," said Dusty.

The colonel stood up. "Agreed! As much as I want you to stay with me and work at the *colonia,* I can't risk the lives of my people by doing so. Do you understand?"

"Yes, sir," said Shell.

The colonel nodded. "Send the padre and the *mozo* down to the *colonia* for horses and supplies. They can bring the woman with them. I will let her stay with us until such time as she can be helped to Hermosillo."

"No," said the soft voice behind them.

They turned to see Rafaela Padilla. "But you cannot go with these hunted men, young lady," said the colonel.

"I am being hunted as much as they are," she said. "The Yaquis know both myself and my *mozo.* They will track us down. If they find us in your *colonia,* Colonel De Tassigny, there will be no safety for anyone. The soldiers will run away as they usually do."

The officer wiped the sweat from his forehead. "As you will," he said. He gripped Shell's hand and then that of Dusty. "Go with God," he said in Spanish. He swung up into his saddle. "I had hoped you could stay," he said. He shook his head and touched his horse with his spurs, riding down the dark slope toward the distant lights of the *colonia.*

Dusty spat. "Take the oath? He makes me sick."

Shell leaned back against the tree and relighted his cigar. There was nothing to say. He knew, or at least felt, the way De Tassigny must feel. The colonel and his people were Americans, and in time, perhaps in one generation, they would no longer be Americans, and their only impress on this wild and lonely country would be what the colonel had said. Light-colored eyes and Anglo-Saxon names.

"There was nothing else he could do for us," said Rafaela. "Thank God he can give us fresh mounts and food."

In the long dark hours of the night, past midnight and on toward the dawn, the padre and the *mozo* went down to the *colonia* with the worn-out horses and mule. They brought back fresh mounts and a pair of burros laden with supplies. In the few hours until dawn they crossed the great Mesa of the Bellmaker to the southern side, and as they reached the dim trail that led deep down into a wide barranca, the false dawn began to tinge the eastern sky.

Shell looked at Padre Eusebio. "Is it good-by here, padre?" he asked.

The padre shook his head. "There is no need for me at the *colonia,* and the soldiers are all godless men. There is no reason for me to stay here and I cannot go back the way I came. May I ride with you?"

Dusty tilted his head to one side and eyed the padre and Shell. There was a thoughtful look on his scarred face.

"Let him come along," said Frank Harley. "We will have need of someone who can perhaps communicate with God before we are through with this mission."

Shell looked at Rafaela. She nodded.

Dusty shrugged. He swung down from his mount. "Who knows this trail?" he said.

"I do," said the padre.

There was no argument from Dusty. Padre Eusebio slid agilely from his horse, gripped the reins, and led the animal down into the dimness below.

Chapter Thirteen

The bottom of the barranca was still in darkness although the sky was faintly gray from the coming dawn. A cold wind swept up the barranca scattering dried leaves and whirling dust before it. Padre Eusebio led the way to the south, following a trail that was hardly visible, but there seemed to be a confidence in the Franciscan.

Shell rode behind the padre while behind Shell was Frank Harley. Dusty was close behind Frank, and Rafaela rode a little way back from Dusty. Victor brought up the rear, leading the supply-laden burros.

The padre looked back at Shell. "We can make good time

this day," he said. "The trail will be good and the horses are fresh."

His sentence was punctuated by a loud voice. *"Halte!* In the name of the Republic of Mexico! *Halte!"*

"Go on!" yelled Shell at Padre Eusebio.

The padre crouched like a monkey on the back of the horse and lashed it with his quirt. The horse buck-jumped down the trail hurling a big-hatted man aside into the brush.

"Halte! Halt or we shoot!" cried the voice from the darkness.

Shell spurred his horse, crouching low in the saddle. A man jumped back out of his way, raised a rifle, and fired. The slug plucked at the slack in Shell's jacket. He looked back, dragging at the reins of Frank's horse. "Lay low, Frank!" he yelled. The blind man dropped to the horse's neck and gripped his arms about it.

Dusty fired once from the saddle and then broke through the brush, crashing along the dry stream bed. The echo of the shot was followed by other shots. Orange-red flashes sparkled through the darkness, and the acrid smell of powder-smoke swirled along the barranca, borne by the freshening wind.

Shell tore into a clump of willows, digging in his spurs. The claybank took the slope in mighty surging jumps. Shell hoped to God that Frank could hold on. He looked back as the claybank cleared the rise. Gunfire rattled through the dimness. There was no sign of Dusty, Rafaela, or the *mozo* Victor. Shell galloped through the dimness, following the faintly defined trail. Somewhere ahead of him was Padre Eusebio. For a padre, the Franciscan could ride like a Comanche when he had to.

The sky was fully alight when Shell drew in the lathered claybank. "Are you all right, Frank?" he said.

The blind man raised his white face. "Yes," he said faintly. "Who were they?"

"Soldiers," said Padre Eusebio from the brush. He led out his horse. "I saw them plainly. Their leader was Capitán Galeras. It was he who ordered us to halt. I recognized his voice."

Hoofs clattered in the thicket. Shell raised his Spencer. He saw the faded and dusty hat of his *compañero.* Dusty rode out onto the trail. His scarred face was scratched and bloody. He wiped the blood from his face. "Gawddamn them greasers!" he said. "They got the supplies!"

"What about Rafaela and Victor?" asked the padre.

Dusty spat. "What about 'em?" he said. "Good riddance! It's them supplies I'm concerned about."

It was very quiet now in the barranca except for the sighing of the wind. Something Colonel De Tassigny had said came swiftly back to Shell. "Banditry is rife. The soldiers who have been sent to protect us and the other villagers are little more than bandits themselves, for they haven't been paid and have to live off the country."

Father Eusebio wiped the cold sweat from his face. "There were not too many of them," he said. "Perhaps a dozen. It was hard to tell in that light."

Shell looked down at him. "What are you hinting at, padre?"

The padre shrugged. "We need those supplies. Those soldiers are little better than the Yaquis or Apaches. Galeras himself has a foul reputation with drink and with women."

"There were at least a dozen bottles of brandy in the supplies," said Frank Harley.

There was nothing more to be said. Shell had a vivid picture of Rafaela Padilla as he had first seen her. The great eyes, the full red lips, and even white teeth, the firm breasts pushing out against the thin material of her shirt, the rounded fullness of her hips beneath the taut charro trousers. A dozen bottles of potent Baconora and a captive woman in that lonely country. Who would ask questions? What was it Padre Eusebio had said? "Galeras himself has a foul reputation with drink and with women."

"No use sweatin' it out," said Dusty. "We'd best make tracks while we can."

There was no answer from any of the others.

Dusty dismounted and tightened his girth. "Sun'll be up soon enough," he said over his shoulder.

Shell shoved back his hat. "Give them a couple of hours with those brandy bottles," he said, "and a drummer boy could take them."

Dusty straightened up slowly. "What the hell yuh mean?" he said.

"We need those supplies ourselves," said Shell.

The icy blue eyes studied Shell, as though to penetrate into his mind for the *real* reason Shell was willing to go back.

"Shell is right," said the padre.

"Nobody asked you, Eusebio!" snapped Dusty.

"There are no inhabited *placitas* south of here," said Frank. "No place to get more supplies, and we can't go back to the Mesa of the Bellmaker. Not now. They know about us."

Dusty leaned against his horse and rolled a cigarette. "All right," he said, "I'll go. But for the supplies! Not for that woman and that gawddamned *mozo!*"

"They likely won't go back to the springs," said Shell. "Galeras isn't fool enough to do that as yet. Likely he'll find a place to camp out for a few days, giving the impression he was doing his duty in hunting us down. When the brandy is gone he'll go back."

"What about the woman?" said Frank.

Padre Eusebio crossed himself. "She could talk if they took her back," he said. His meaning was plain enough.

The light grew brighter as they talked. Shell knew it would be up to him and Dusty to go back. Father Eusebio was not a fighting man, and of course Frank Harley was of no value because of his blindness. There was no sound from the direction of the ambush. They might be at the bottles and at the woman already. Somehow the supplies seemed of no importance to Shell, but the thought of that lithe, full-breasted body being torn at by greasy, dirty hands made him sick within his soul.

"We can't go on without those supplies," said Dusty. He wiped the blood from his face with the back of a hand. "If we can save the woman *after* we get the supplies, it's all right with me." Maybe Dusty was also thinking of that lovely body, but not in the same sense as Shell thought.

Father Eusebio looked up at Shell. "Twenty miles south of here," he said, "there are springs. One follows the barranca to them. The way is not hard. I will take Señor Harley with me in a roundabout way and wait for you near those springs."

Shell nodded. He was tired. They had had no sleep during the night and little enough in the preceding nights. The thought of going back to tackle at least a dozen Mexican soldiers was pure hell in his mind, but it had to be done. Didn't anything come easy in this damned world?

Dusty swung up into his saddle. "Come on," he said. "No use wasting time."

They rode down the wooded slope and when they neared the dry stream bed Dusty scouted ahead. He came back through the shadows. "Nothing," he said. "Empty brass hulls and foot and hoof marks. Tracks heading *up,* instead of *down* the canyon."

They both knew what that meant. Galeras wasn't returning to the springs at the base of Mesa del Campanero. Not with two burro-loads of supplies and brandy, and with a lush-bodied woman to occupy his time when he should have been chasing Shell and Dusty.

It was almost noon before they caught up with Galeras' party of big-hatted, somewhat undersized *soldados*. Some of them rode horses and others rode mules. In the middle of the party were Rafaela Padilla and the *mozo* Victor. Victor had his wrists lashed with the cords crossing his deep chest. A stick had been thrust through the crooks of his elbows and against his back. A noosed lariat was about his corded neck and he was half dragged, half pulled behind the horse of one of the soldiers. The dust veiled the party as it rode slowly up the canyon.

Dusty wiped the sweat from his face and looked at Shell. "Well, they ain't touched the supplies, *or* the woman, from the looks of things."

Shell rested his chin on his crossed forearms and looked down the steep slope at the soldiers. "They're riding to water," he said. "Likely to the same springs the padre told us about. All set for a real fiesta. Wine, women and song."

"On *our* damned supplies," said Dusty bitterly.

Shell looked up the canyon. "We can't pass them," he said. He looked up at the canyon rim. "If we got up there we could cut across the higher land and maybe get ahead of them."

"Maybe," said Dusty. He rolled a cigarette. "We might get lost too, *compañero*."

"We'll have to take a chance on that. You game?"

Dusty nodded. "Keno," he said as he lighted up.

They led the horses up the crumbling side of the canyon. The soldiers and their captives were almost out of sight by the time Dusty and Shell reached the top of the canyon wall and stopped for a blow. The dust trailed up from the canyon and was dissipated by the dry wind. The mesa top on which they stood was badly broken up, stippled with dry brush and scrub trees. There didn't seem to be any sign of habitation up there, or water either.

Shell led the way. The barranca curved far to their left and then curved back to the south. Shell reasoned that by cutting across the curve, like following the string of a bow, instead of the curved bow itself, they might come out ahead of the soldiers and get to the springs first.

"I hope to God the padre has enough sense to camp away from the springs," said Dusty.

"He will," said Shell. "He's a damned capable man, for a padre."

"Yeh," said Dusty. He fashioned another cigarette. "Almost too damned capable in things a padre shouldn't ought to know."

Shell shrugged. "They are trained to live in this country," he said. "They could hardly survive otherwise. Some of the old padres founded the main trails running through this country and up into the States. They had to be capable beyond most men to do that."

"Jesus," said Dusty dryly. "We're off on the history again."

Shell clammed up. He should have known better. Just keep the subject on horses, weapons, gambling, booze, and women, and Dusty was a good conversationalist—but digress in the least, and Dusty was completely lost.

Shell led the way, orienting himself by landmarks. He checked his battered brass compass again and again. If they missed the canyon, and the springs, it wouldn't make much difference about the supplies *or* the woman.

The sun lanced down upon the mesa top and reflected from the mounds of naked black rock, setting up a shimmering heat haze that bored into the eyes as though trying to reach the brain and destroy the reason within. They ran out of water by the middle of the afternoon. By early dusk they were completely lost.

Dusty looked at Shell with red-rimmed eyes. His tongue explored his cracked lips. "To hell with the supplies," he said. "What about water?"

Shell shoved back his hat and wiped the sweat from his forehead. He looked toward what he thought was the dim line of the barranca far ahead of them. It would be dark soon enough, and if they kept on through the darkness there would be no telling where they would end up. It would be easy enough to keep on until one found the barranca by simply stepping off into it. The bottom would be a long way down.

"Well?" said Dusty.

He was depending on Shell as he always did in such situations—the situations that required reasoning powers.

Shell checked the compass.

"What the hell good is that thing?" demanded Dusty.

Shell checked the landmarks. Far to the south was an irregular line of mountains, like a saw set edge-up. A peak stood out. A peak shaped like a thick-bladed knife. He had been using that as a landmark for hours.

Dusty leaned against his horse and shaped a cigarette. He lighted it and flipped away the match. "Christ," he said in sheer disgust.

"You said you were game," said Shell. "You losing your guts now that the going is getting tough, *hombre?*"

Their eyes locked. The tiny seed of hate that had sprouted in the past weeks was growing every day.

Shell looked beyond the icy eyes of his companion. He narrowed his eyes. "Look!" he said.

Dusty turned. A faint streamer of smoke arose from a darker area, not more than a thousand yards from where they stood. "Come on," he said.

They led the tired horses toward the smoke. They tethered them to scrub trees not far from the edge of the barranca and walked ahead, trailing their carbines. They went down fifty feet from the edge and worked their way forward, with the smell of smoke and cooking food rising to meet them.

The shadows had already filled the barranca. Firelight leaped and postured on the rough canyon walls. Here the canyon had widened out and branched and at the junction of the branch canyon was a cluster of tumbledown buildings, seemingly long abandoned. Some of the roofs had fallen in. Several of the buildings had collapsed completely. Beyond the buildings the firelight reflected from a shallow pool of water. Horses and a pair of burros were in a makeshift corral. The odor of cooking meat drifted up to the two hungry, thirsty Americans who peered like lobo wolves over the canyon rim.

Some of the soldiers sat about the roaring fire. Now and then one of them would raise a bottle to his lips, then pass it on to the man next to him. Already two of them lay in the shadows, perhaps asleep, but more likely dead drunk. There was no sign of an officer. A squat, broad-shouldered man with sergeant's insignia sat on a rock, his shoulders hunched forward, staring into the fire. Now and then he would look toward one of the smaller buildings, then back into the fire.

Shell could only locate seven of the soldiers, and two of them seemed helpless. Maybe Galeras had sent some of his men back. Maybe. . . .

Dusty wet his lips. "We can take 'em," he said.

Shell did not answer. It went against his grain to attack them. Bad enough that they had been hunted by Yankee soldiers for the killings at Ojinago, and by the Apaches and Yaquis for a little more killing. If they killed Mexican soldiers on Mexican soil they would eventually be hunted down. There would be no going back after that.

Dusty was ready for more killing, but, as usual, he was

waiting for orders. Trust him to carry them out to the letter if there was killing to be done.

The sergeant looked back at the building. He drank deeply from a bottle he kept between his feet. He did not pass *his* bottle to the others. Their bottle had been emptied. It crashed in the shadows and another bottle was opened.

"Quite a party," said Dusty dryly. "We wait up here long enough and we can walk in and take 'em *without* shooting."

Shell looked back at the horses. There was no way of getting them down into the canyon. "Come on," he said to Dusty.

They stripped off the saddles and took whatever they needed. Shell cut their tethers almost all the way through. In time they would break loose. They'd have to find water on their own.

Shell led the way across the dark mesa top. He dropped his long legs over the brink of the canyon and felt for a hold. He struck a ledge. Slowly he worked his way along the ledge. He stopped and fashioned a sling for his carbine and slung the heavy weapon over his back. Drunken laughter echoed through the canyon. The firelight flared up and died down sporadically. The smoke drifted along the canyon wall, partially concealing the two men who worked their way down that treacherous, crumbling wall of rock.

Halfway down the wall the fire flared brightly as more wood was thrown on it, and the light leaped up, fully illuminating the two men who clung to the rock face like insect specimens pinned to a board. The Mexicans were tearing into the cooked meat. The sergeant was not eating. He raised his head to drink and his eyes looked directly at the two Americans just as the fire died down, leaving them in partial shadow. For a moment he stared at the rock wall. He shook his head and took another drink, wiping his mouth on the back of a hand, staring at that darker patch on the shadowed wall. If he saw them, all he had to do was have more wood thrown on the fire, and drunk as his men were, they could hardly miss their living targets.

One of the soldiers handed the sergeant a full plate of food. He looked down at it and picked up a dripping piece of meat in his thick hand. He gnawed at it, the grease dripping down his chin.

Shell moved as quickly as he could. He worked along a ledge, passed behind a rock that tilted outward, seemingly held in place by magnetism, and then he lay bellyflat on a rock shelf not twenty feet above the talus slope at the base of the cliff. Dusty inched up behind him, breathing harshly.

It took half an hour to belly down the ledge. Shell crawled down the talus slope and dropped flat behind a clump of brush. He could smell the water, and his throat seemed to close up.

"Christ," said Dusty hoarsely, "can't we get a drink before we start the evenin's killin'?"

Shell nodded. There seemed to be no one near the waterhole, but the animals might scent them and make a fuss. He wormed his way across the open flat ground, hoping to God the fire would not flare up. He kept his face turned away so that the firelight would not reflect from it, but it likely was so filthy that it couldn't reflect anything.

He crouched behind a pile of rock fifteen feet from the edge of the waterhole. There was no one in sight. He crawled over the rocks and bellied to the edge of the tank, feeling his way with his free hand until it struck the water. He thrust his face into the water and drank a little. He raised his head and looked toward the fire. The sergeant was on his feet, swaying a little, the bottle again at his mouth. He hurled the bottle aside, wiped his mouth, pulled up his slack trousers, and staggered toward the building he had been watching ever since Shell had first seen him.

The soldiers about the fire were laughing as they watched the staggering sergeant. "Watch her, my *sargento!*" one of them yelled. "She is a wildcat!"

Shell quickly skirted the tank and paused next to the canyon wall. Something moved at his feet. He leaped back and full-cocked the Spencer. A man lay at his feet, mumbling in a low voice. Shell stared at him. It was Victor. His contorted face looked at Shell. They had not unbound the *mozo*. Dusty came up behind Shell. "Cut him loose," he said. "We can use him."

Dusty covered Shell while Shell cut loose the *mozo*. The thongs had cut deeply into his flesh. He could not move his arms. He looked at the water, so close at hand. Shell picked up a battered tin cup and filled it for him, holding it to his lips. Victor slobbered at the water and Shell realized with horror that the Tarahumare did not have a tongue.

"Get movin'!" snapped Dusty.

Shell pulled the *mozo* to his feet and handed him the Colt. The *mozo* shook his head. He touched the handle of the heavy bowie knife. Shell sheathed the Colt and handed Victor the bowie. Something crashed at the front of the buildings. A woman screamed like frightened mare. Shell snatched up his Spencer and ran behind the buildings. He rounded the end building. The woman screamed from within it. Shell kicked open the partially closed door and ran in, Spencer at hip level. The sergeant's broad, sweaty back was in front of him. Rafaela stood with her back against the dingy wall, her hands covering her naked breasts. The tattered ruins of her thin shirt hung about her hips. The charro trousers had been ripped down to her shapely knees. Her dark unbound hair fell over her white shoulders. Her eyes were wide with terror, and a trickle of blood wormed down from the corners of her mouth. The sergeant lurched forward, muttering drunkenly. Shell struck once with the metal-shod butt of the Spencer. The sergeant staggered sideways. He stared at Shell, then ran for the door. A dark figure stood there, bowie knife in hand, staring at the Mexican with unblinking eyes. The Mexican screamed once. He drove past the *mozo*. The blade flicked out and blood flowed.

A Spencer cracked once, then again. A man yelled. The Spencer barked again. Shell ran to the door. A Mexican was raising a rifle, aiming it at Dusty. Shell fired from the hip and the Mexican whirled and fell into the fire. Shell looked back. The sergeant was making the biggest and probably the last mistake he would ever make in his suddenly shortened life. *He was trying to outrun a Tarahumare!* Already his life was leaking out as the bowie sliced skillfully at his fat rump or at his churning legs. Blood splattered as he ran as fast as he could. He vanished, screaming, into the velvety darkness, with silent death close behind him, almost like his shadow.

The shooting died away, letting the echoes slam back and forth in the canyon. They too died away. Dusty and Shell faced each other across the fire. The Mexicans had died where they had been drinking. The fire was licking hungrily at the clothing of the Mexican Shell had dropped into it. He gripped him by the ankles and pulled him free. The choking smoke from the burning cloth mingled with the acrid powder-smoke.

There was one final despairing scream like that of a mortally wounded animal. It echoed down the canyon and died away. In a little while Victor appeared, walking slowly, with the bloody knife in his right hand.

Shell looked at the two Mexicans who had been asleep or dead drunk. They'd never awaken again. Dusty was thorough, if nothing else.

"We get all of them?" said Dusty.

"You ought to know," said Shell.

The woman came to the doorway. She had wrapped herself in a serape. Her eyes were wide in her pale face. Shell walked to her and supported her. "Are you all right?" he said.

She nodded. There was a sickness deep within her. She looked at the bloody dead and then buried her face against Shell's chest with muffled sobbing rising and falling from her.

Dusty walked to the biggest building. He kicked open the door and walked in. A moment passed. "Hey, Shell!" he called out. "Look who's here!"

Shell helped Rafaela to a seat and walked to the building. He entered. A man sat at a rickety table. A candle guttered in the neck of a brandy bottle. His head lay on the table amidst the liquor slops. The candlelight reflected from his tarnished epaulets.

"Capitán Galeras, no doubt," said Dusty with ironic politeness. He raised his Spencer.

Shell knocked the Spencer aside. "You've done enough killing," he said.

Dusty eyed Shell. Slowly he lowered the repeater. "What are yuh goin' to do with him?" he said, jerking his head toward the officer.

Someone called from outside. They walked to the door. Padre Eusebio was leading two horses from up the barranca. Frank Harley swayed in the saddle of one of them. The padre stared at the dead. He crossed himself. "Mother of God," he said in a hoarse voice.

The quietness of the canyon was in direct contrast to the hell that had broken loose twenty minutes earlier. They had their supplies back and the woman as well. Shell shoved back his hat. There was no place for them to go but ever southward to hunt for La Barranca Escondida. If they found the silver, what could they do with it? They'd be hunted down in time. Shell shook his head. He cursed the day he and Dusty had found Frank Harley at Horno Tanks. It might have been better to let him die.

Chapter Fourteen

The canyon was filled with a cold searching wind as the sky lightened with the dawn. The fire had died down during the night but now and then a cat's-paw of wind would stir the thick bed of ashes and fan a red eye of life into them.

A film of ashes drifted on the waterhole and furred the blankets of the sleeping men.

Shell Burnett came down from his perch above the waterhole where he had stood last guard. He walked to the blanketed forms. "Rise and shine," he said. "Get up! Get up!"

Padre Eusebio was on his feet almost right away. He dressed simply by pulling on his moccasins and dropping the faded cowl of his robe. He quickly rolled his blankets and placed them near his saddle. Dusty thrust out a shaggy head and yawned. "Jee-sus," he said. "Killin' sure takes the starch out of a man." He grinned as the padre hurriedly crossed himself.

Frank Harley got up quietly. He shivered in the cold wind. "It will be cold up in those mountains," he said. "The fall will soon be here."

Victor appeared from where he had slept alone, near the door of the shack where his mistress had slept, and close to the barred door of the building that held Capitán Galeras prisoner. Actually he was more a prisoner of the brandy than of the men who had wiped out his little command.

Padre Eusebio busied himself about the fire, preparing breakfast. The smoke from the revived fire drifted down the canyon and wreathed itself over the piled Mexican dead who had been dragged by the horses away from the waterhole. Shell looked thoughtfully at the tumbled, dirty corpses. Once the rest of the Mexican soldiers saw those bodies, there would be no rest for the ill-assorted little band of treasure seekers.

Rafaela appeared in her doorway. Somehow she had contrived to patch up some of her clothing. Shell had given her one of his shirts, and she had managed to drape it fetchingly about herself. She had tied the serape about her slim waist to cover the ruins of the upper part of her charro trousers. Dusty looked up from his first cup of coffee and studied her as she spoke to Victor. He wet his lips, saw Shell looking at him, then slowly looked away. Shell himself remembered all too vividly how she had looked the night before, with her full breasts hardly covered by her slim hands, her lovely thighs and the cleft between them. He drove the thought from his mind.

They ate silently. It wasn't quite a festive mood, not with those blue-faced dead not fifty yards away. When they were done, Father Eusebio and Dusty gathered up the gear, saddled the horses, and filled the many canteens they had inherited. There were horses to spare now.

"What about Galeras?" said Dusty at last, jerking his head toward Galeras' prison.

"No more killing," said Frank Harley quietly.

"He is one of God's children," said Padre Eusebio.

Shell looked at Rafaela. She shook her head. "You cannot do it," she said quickly.

Dusty laughed. "All of a sudden we got mercy," he jeered. "What difference does it make?" He looked at Shell. "Yuh gettin' soft, *compañero?*"

Shell walked to the building and pulled away the bars. He placed his hand on the butt of his Colt and opened the door. Galeras sat at the table with his head supported in his hands. His body was shaking.

"Capitán Galeras?" said Shell.

The head slowly raised. "For the love of God," said the Mexican, "give me a drink, *amigo!*"

Shell rubbed his shaggy beard. "Victor!" he said. "Get a bottle."

The *mozo* brought a half-full bottle of the Baconora. Shell placed it on the table in front of the officer. He gripped it as though it was liquid gold and took a deep draught. He wiped his mouth and took another drink. His body shook spasmodically and for a moment Shell thought he'd spew the whole mess out over the filthy table, but Hernán Galeras was a first-class drinker. He knew his ability, if not his limitations.

Shell studied the flushed face of the officer. Galeras was handsome enough, in a rather evil-looking way. His rather narrow face did not detract from the handsomeness of it. Despite his heavy drinking there were not too many traces of the vice apparent in his features.

Galeras looked up at Shell. "You're one of the Americans, eh? I saw you in the barranca when we tried to halt you."

Shell nodded.

Galeras felt in his coat and came out with a tobacco pouch. He shakily began to fashion a cigarette. "You have captured my men, eh?"

Shell did not answer. He watched Galeras light the cigarette and draw the smoke deep into his lungs. Galeras looked at Shell. "You did not answer," he said.

Shell leaned against the side of the doorway. "You let them get out of control, *capitán,*" he said. "If we had not arrived the woman might have been dead from a mass raping."

"I know nothing of that."

"That's no excuse," said Shell. "As an officer of the

Army of the Republic of Mexico it was your duty to control your men."

"I . . .," said the Mexican. He gestured at the bottle and shrugged.

"You got stinking drunk," said Shell.

Galeras shrugged again. He looked up at Shell. "What is to become of me?" He looked down at Shell's holstered revolver.

Spurs chimed softly behind Shell. "We're all set to go," said Dusty. "What about them bodies?"

Galeras paled. He drank deeply again.

"Help yourself," said Dusty dryly.

The Mexican looked up at those two lean, sunbrowned faces, and at the cold Yanqui eyes, and he knew well enough what was going to happen to him. "You ride to the south?" he said.

"We do," said Shell.

Galeras wiped his mouth and puffed thoughtfully at his cigarette. "The man Frank Harley is with you, is he not?"

"He is," said Shell.

Galeras tilted his head a little. "To La Barranca Escondida, no?"

"To La Barranca Escondida, yes," said Dusty. He looked at Shell. "The whole damned country knows where we're goin'. Well, it won't matter to the *capitán* here."

Galeras raised his head. "Listen, *amigos,*" he said. "Let me make you a proposition. I do not want to die and you do not want me to die either."

Dusty grinned. "We *don't?*"

"Keep talking," said Shell. He had to admire the Mexican for his cool nerve despite the bitch of a hangover he was carrying.

Galeras held up a lean finger. *"Escuche!"* he said. "I planned to trap you at the bottom of the mesa. That was only partially successful, as you well know."

"Hear, hear," said Dusty.

Galeras ignored him. "Some of my men went back to Mesa del Campanero, with a message for my commanding officer at Hermosillo. In that message, I heroically stated that I, Capitán Hernán Antonio Federico Adolfo Bartolomé Panfilo Galeras y Castaneda, would stay on the trail of the Americanos until death stopped my quest."

"Viva, viva!" said Shell.

Galeras nodded. He sipped at the brandy and flipped his cigarette butt into the filthy fireplace. Quickly he rolled another.

"Get it over with," said Dusty. "It's a good day to die, greaser."

Galeras looked up. "So, my commanding officer thinks I am pursuing you. As long as he doesn't have to leave his women and his brandy in Hermosillo, why should he concern himself about Capitán Hernán Galeras and his brave men?"

Shell nodded. The Mexican was downright amusing, if nothing else.

"So," said the Mexican, "if the bodies of my men and myself are found it will be understood that we *did* die in our heroic quest, and therefore you Americanos managed to escape. But, if those bodies are not found, it would be assumed we are still on the quest."

Shell took the tobacco pouch from the table and began to shape a cigarette. "Get to the point," he said.

Galeras wiped the icy sweat from his pale face. Looking at those two pairs of cold Yanqui eyes was enough to unnerve any man, especially when he was pleading for his life. "Let me go with you," he said. "If I cannot be of value to you, you can kill me. I know this country. I am a fighting man as you are. You will need every gun you can get to fight off the Yaquis."

"What's your price?" said Shell.

"A share in the treasure if you find it. My life if you do not."

Dusty laughed. "A share in the treasure? What's your life to us?"

Shell lighted his cigarette and automatically handed the makings to Dusty. Galeras had made some sense. As long as his superiors thought he was hunting down the Americanos, they wouldn't bother to send out any more troops. It might just give them enough time to get the treasure and escape. It was a long shot. Everything they had done in this mad quest had been a long shot. Galeras knew well enough if he went back to Hermosillo with the story of the massacre of his men that he would not live to see the next day. His life would be forfeit to his superiors and he would be living on borrowed time while he was with the treasure hunters.

Galeras eyed Shell. "Well, *amigo?*" he said quietly.

Shell nodded. "It's a deal," he said.

"What the hell!" blurted Dusty.

Galeras grinned. He reached for the bottle and raised it to his lips. Shell drew and fired. The soft slug smashed the bottle, driving fragments of it against the wall. The strong odor of the spirits hung in the air. Hernán Galeras slowly and shakily wiped the brandy and blood from his face. There was green fear on his features as he glanced at Shell and Dusty.

Shell sheathed the smoking Colt. "You've had enough liquor," he said. "That was just a warning, Galeras. Remember it." He turned on a heel and walked into the growing light of the day.

It was almost noon by the time they had concealed the swelling bodies of the dead. Shell had sent Victor to get the body of the sergeant. His guts moiled when he saw what the Tarahumare had done to the man. They had tumbled the bodies into a hole a quarter of a mile up the canyon and heaved rocks in atop them. It had been Galeras who had thought of the idea of climbing a ledge just above the charnel pit to pry loose the scaling rock. Tons of it fell with a dusty crash into the pit to hide the bodies forever from the sight of men.

They rode south along the barranca as the heat of the day began to fill it. There was no sign left behind to indicate what had happened there except for a few dark stains upon the rocks. By late afternoon they climbed out of the barranca to the higher ground.

Frank Harley called to Shell. "There should be a landmark in sight, Shell," he said. "A knife-shaped peak almost due south."

All heads turned to look south. Sharp against the cloud-dotted sky stood the dark outline of a great peak shaped like the blade of a heavy knife. It was the one Shell had seen the day before.

"Cuchillo Peak," said Hernán Galeras as he bent his head to light a cigarette.

"That is it!" said Frank. "Head directly toward it."

"That won't be easy," said Shell. "This country is broken up into a hell's puzzle. Padre, can you get us there?"

The padre shrugged dubiously. "In time, perhaps," he said.

Galeras blew a smoke ring. "Already I am of value, *amigos,*" he said casually. "I know the way. We can be there in two days. Otherwise it would take a week, *if you got there at all.*"

Before the darkness came down Shell studied the country to the south. Those were huge mountains, towering thousands of feet into the dark sky, and between them were immense barrancas, thousands of feet deep. In all that vast, trackless country there was not one sign of human life. Not a building, a road, a trail, or a thin thread of smoke. Misgivings came over Shell. He did not trust Galeras. Padre Eusebio was already beyond the country he really knew. Rafaela Padilla had never been in there, although the story her grandfather had often told her had given her landmarks and signs that might help to lead to La Barranca Escondida. Dusty and Shell, of course, were utterly out of their element. Victor might know the country better than any of them, but if he did, there was no sign of it on his impassive face, and of course he could not speak.

Dusty looked at Shell. He was thinking the same as Shell. A man could get lost in that country and spend the rest of his life trying to find his way out of it, if he lived to do so. If once they entered that country they would be dependent on Hernán Galeras, whom they could not really trust, and on the memory of a blind man who might or might not know the location of the lost silver mines.

Minutes ticked past. It was rapidly getting darker.

"We must ride the trail to the lower ground now," said the officer, "while there is still enough light."

Shell rubbed his dirty beard. He looked at the shapely woman and her silent *mozo*. He looked at the patient, rather simple face of the padre. He looked at the hard lean face of his partner Dusty. Last of all he looked at the calm, patient face of Frank Harley. Harley seemed so sure of himself.

Now or never, thought Shell. "*Adelante!*" he said.

Galeras grinned. He flipped away the cigarette and set spurs to his horse, clattering over the loose rock into the thick brush to the south.

They would soon be committed. But there was no going back in any case. This time the die was surely cast.

Chapter Fifteen

Hernán Galeras had been as good as his word. They had reached the base of Cuchillo Peak in two days as he had said. Beyond that the route plunged deep into a barranca that almost made one faint of heart to look down into it and to see the vague trail that seemed to hang on the side of the barranca wall. From a sun-blasted mesa, heat shimmering in the late summer sun, they slowly descended the faint trace of the trail. To look down was to lose all courage, but there could be no going back. Halfway down, one of the riderless horses missed his footing and went over the side, turning end over end like a wooden replica of a hobby-horse, to strike far, far below. So far below, the sound of the heavy body striking the hard ground could not be heard by those who stood whitefaced on the crumbling trail.

It took the better part of a day to reach the bottom and here the world had changed. Instead of the sun-ravaged heights, swept by the dry wind, they saw a dense, lush tropical forest. Birds of many varieties flew through the woods and above them. Raucous guacamayo parrots greeted them fearlessly with outlandish noises. Water raced through deep-cut channels. Halfway across the bottom of the huge gash Padre Eusebio kicked his mare in the sides and raced ahead. In a few minutes he was back clutching two oranges in his hands. They rode ahead to find a small grove of the fruit trees beside a clear stream whose gravelly bottom was plain to be seen in the dying light. The bright fruit dropped from the overhanging trees and swirled in the furious current. Wild cotton trees thrust out thorn-studded trunks. *Urraca* jays screamed furiously at the strange intruders. High, high above the three-thousand-foot south wall of the incredibly huge barranca rose towering heights with drifting clouds swirling about them, hiding the tips of the mountains.

It was almost impossible to believe that such an area could exist in those mountains, after the days of travel through barren, almost waterless country, where sere vegetation could hardly survive. The air was quiet and heavy amidst the trees. It was a place where a man could idle many days away occupied with his thoughts.

Shell picked a campsite in a clearing not far from the edge of the stream. There was no sign of human life in the area, and yet he always had the uncanny feeling that they were being watched by someone who was never seen. This was the edge of the Tarahumare country. Those shy, wild people were seen only when they wanted to be seen. Rafaela had told Shell that they did not live in villages, but were nomadic, ranging through the pine-clad mountains in the summer, seeking refuge from the winter in the tropical canyon bottoms. It was not a country for the Yaquis. Their domain was farther west, and the quest for La Barranca Escondida would lead the little party in that direction once they passed the looming heights of Cuchillo Peak.

Shell looked thoughtfully at Victor. Rafaela had said he

had been outlawed from his tribe and left to die. Had his own people cut out his tongue?

Hernán Galeras strolled up to Shell, sucking on an orange. "We will be safe here for a time," he said. "The Yaquis do not come here and the Tarahumares will not bother us. We know, of course, that there will be no soldiers following us."

"You did a good job guiding us here, Galeras," said Shell.

The officer shrugged. "I had to," he said. He smiled. "One always does a good job when he seems to feel a pistol muzzle against his neck."

Rafaela disappeared into the lush growth. Victor sat down on a fallen tree between the place where she had disappeared and the camp. His dark eyes studied Dusty. Dusty sat down and pulled off his worn boots. He rolled a cigarette and glanced at the woods where she had gone. In a little while the sound of splashing came to them.

Shell and Hernán walked into the woods in the opposite direction, then stripped and went into the cold water of the swift stream, gasping and shuddering as they bathed. In a little while the padre came to watch them. His churchman's modesty would not permit him to strip in front of these two godless men.

A fire crackled in the clearing when Shell and Hernán returned to the campsite. Rafaela was seated on a log, combing out her thick, lustrous hair. Victor was nowhere to be seen.

It was the first time in many weeks that Shell had felt at ease, but he knew it was for only a little while. Somewhere south of them in that tangled, forbidding country was La Barranca Escondida and El Naranjal. It drew him and the others. There could be no denying its powerful attraction for them.

Victor came out of the woods. He had something in his hand. It was a stone and it had been shaped by nature or man into the shape of a tablet. The Tarahumare held it to the firelight and looked toward the blind man. Hernán jumped to his feet and hurriedly scanned the stone. *"Ojalá!"* he said. "See? Here is an inscription!"

Dusty stood up and walked quickly to them. He gripped the stone in his big hands and turned it closer to the fire. *"Departamento de Camino a Las. . . ."* His voice died away. "Part of the lettering has been worn away," he said.

"Wait," said Hernán. He scooped up a handful of ashes and wet them in the stream. He rubbed them into the weathered face of the rock until at last the ashes had penetrated into the inscription. He wiped the remainder of the stone clean. *"Departamento de Camino a Las Minas de La Barr. . . ."* He wiped the sweat from his face and peered at the lettering. *"Escondida y. . . .* That is all I can read, *amigos."*

It was very quiet around the camp. They all looked at Frank Harley. "Is it as close as that, Frank?" Shell said at last.

The blind man shook his head. "I don't understand it," he said quietly. "There was no *camino* to the mines through here."

"Maybe yuh just don't know," said Dusty.

Harley shook his head again. "Impossible," he said.

Hernán studied the stone. "I have seen stones like this elsewhere," he said. "Many years ago all the highways through the lower country were marked with such stones."

"There was no such highway in this area," insisted Frank.

"Mebbe you're just tellin' us that," said Dusty. He looked quickly about. "Maybe this is La Barranca Escondida."

"That is foolish," said Rafaela. "It is many leagues south of here. That I know."

"Then how is it this marker is here?" said Hernán.

Padre Eusebio pointed to the rushing stream. "In flood, such a stream could carry a stone like that for many miles. In the passage of many years the floods could carry it still further. The stream itself originates southeast of here. In a hundred years that stone could have been brought down here. See how worn it is?"

They all looked at the stone. There was little question but that the padre was right. "It proves one thing," said Shell. "If they put up highway markers in those days, they put them up to mark the route to real places, not myths or legends."

Dusty looked up into the darkness toward the towering peaks. "Yeh," he said slowly, "but how far did the stream carry it and where did it originally come from?"

No one had an answer. The stone was only a teaser. It could have been swept for miles and miles over a period of a hundred years or more, as the padre had so wisely said. But it whetted their appetites. Somewhere, in the velvety darkness to the south of them, beyond Cuchillo Peak, there must be an immense, hidden barranca holding a treasure in silver that would stagger the imagination.

"We'd better get some sleep," said Shell. "We climb up out of here tomorrow, and it should take us the best part of the day. We ride before dawn. We can reach the south wall of the barranca by first light."

Padre Eusebio extinguished the fire. In the darkness they all sought their blankets. Dusty had first guard that night. But there was little sleep at first for any of them with the exception of Victor. To him, the silver meant nothing; to the others, it meant everything.

Before the dawn they were up. A fire was built and a hurried meal was made and eaten. The horses and burros were rounded up, and Victor led the way through the darkness of the woods with the sure knowledge of the Indian.

By first dawnlight they sat their horses at the bottom of the three-thousand-foot wall and eyed the thin thread of trail that seemed lightly tacked onto the sheer side of the barranca. None of them spoke, but each of them remembered all too well the sight of the horse that had fallen from the trail on the north side of the barranca the day before. It was not a pleasant thought.

It was Victor who made the choice. He walked up the trail with sure-footed skill. Rafaela Padilla glanced at the taut faces of the others, then touched the flanks of her horse with the small spurs she wore. The horse started up the trail.

"Ladies first," said Hernán Galeras with a rueful smile. He followed Rafaela.

Padre Eusebio took the halter of Frank Harley's horse. He looked at Shell. "Perhaps it would be best if I followed with Señor Harley," he said. "Do you lead the burros, Señor Shell."

Dusty spurred his horse up after Galeras. Broken rock was cast aside from the hoofs. "He is in a hurry, that one," said the padre.

Shell followed Dusty. Now and then he glanced back and down to see the padre patiently leading Frank's horse. The burros trotted placidly along. They were used to this sort of thing and were as sure-footed as cats. Now and then a rock would tumble over the edge of the trail and the sound of it striking would come faintly from below, but as the sun rose and the party struggled higher and higher up the face of the barranca wall, the falling stones and rocks could not be heard when they struck.

Halfway up the trail everyone who was riding, with the exception of Frank Harley, dismounted. The horses were nervous, unsure of themselves. They shied in terror at the worst spots on the trail. It was all the party could do to keep on, dragging on the reins, gripping unsure handholds, ready at an instant to release the reins of a horse if the animal should make that last fatal step.

By noon they had reached three-quarters of the way up the barranca wall. They stopped for a rest and to regain control of their nerves. Far, far below them they could see the sunlight flashing from the ripples of the watercourse where it debouched from the cover of the semitropical trees. The bottom of the barranca was thickly covered with the trees, but the far side of the barranca stood naked in the bright sunlight. No one spoke. The sweat from near exhaustion and from the clinging fear of the terrible trail they had ascended ran down their dusty faces.

Victor was looking across the giddy depths of the barranca. He looked at Rafaela and then pointed across the canyon. Everyone looked in the direction to which he had pointed. Only Dusty, whose eyesight was excellent, saw anything. "Get the glasses, Shell," he said over his shoulder.

Shell got the fieldglasses. He raised them to his eyes and focused them on the far side of the barranca, about where the trail should be. For a long time he saw nothing but the cracked and riven rock of the barranca wall, and then he caught a movement. He refocused the glasses. Something was moving down the trail, although he could hardly distinguish the trail itself. Gradually he could make out what it was. A long file of hatless men leading horses. They were halfway down to the bottom of the barranca. Shell handed the glasses to Dusty. Dusty whistled softly as he saw what Shell had seen.

"What is it, Shell?" asked Rafaela.

"Yaquis, most likely," said Shell.

It was very quiet except for the sighing of the warm wind and the occasional blowing of a horse or burro. Rafaela looked up toward the top of the barranca wall, then down into the depths, and then toward the distant wall.

"It will take them hours," said Shell. "We can be long gone by then." He knew well enough they'd outdistance them that day, and perhaps the next, but in time they'd catch up. There was one other thing he was quite sure of, and that was the fact that the Yaquis would not quit. Too many of their kinsmen had died back at Tinajas Altas. They could not return to their people without having exacted vengeance. They were just as committed to their quest as were the people of the party watching them from across the huge barranca.

They started up the trail and none of them looked now across the barranca. Their full attention had to be on the crumbling trail. It was late afternoon when at last they reached the top of the trail and stopped again to rest. Shell scanned the far side of the canyon with the glasses. There was no sign of life on the other trail. He scanned the bottom of the barranca but nothing moved down there except the rushing stream and the wind-blown treetops. A hawk hung in the air midway between both sides of the canyon and level with the tops of the walls.

Shell lay bellyflat on the lip of the barranca. Dusty sat on Shell's legs as Shell hung the glasses over the crumbling brink and studied the bottom of the trail. He wasn't sure, but there seemed to be some movement down there. He spoke over his shoulder. "Pull me back, *amigo.*" Shell stood up and cased the glasses. "Padre, Galeras, Victor, Dusty, give me a hand." Shell gripped a bushel-basket-sized rock and rolled it over the edge. It struck the trail and bounded out into space, dropping far down into the wooded depths below. Rock crumbled from the trail. Rock after rock was rolled over the edge. They worked together to heave over a huge boulder. The roaring of the falling rock thundered from one side of the huge barranca to the other, and a veil of yellowish dust hung in the now windless air.

They sat back from the edge, with sweat running from every pore. Their action had driven some of the fear from their minds. Whether or not they had killed or injured some of their pursuers was of secondary importance. What mattered most was that the trail be ruined for anyone following them, but there was no way of knowing that.

Dusty wiped the sweat from his face. "Maybe it'll make 'em cautious, if nothing else," he said.

Galeras nodded. "Even so, *amigos,*" he said, "it would be best to push on. A Yaqui can go where a cat can go. Of this I assure you."

They rode to the south through the gathering shadows. Beyond them loomed the mountains, with their towering peaks still illuminated by the sinking sun. A chill wind swept the heights. Shell, Dusty, and Hernán rode ahead of the others, fanning out to keep track of the faint trail that crossed the mesa. The sun was nearly gone when the trace ran out. They sat their horses. Shell shaped a cigarette and passed the makings to Dusty.

"It is hopeless," said Hernán. "This is the wrong way, *amigos.*"

Shell nodded. He turned in his saddle to look back toward the others. The wind shifted and blew from the south. Dusty slowly took the cigarette from his mouth. "Listen!" he said. Faintly, ever so faintly, came the sound of a bell.

"By God!" said Shell. He looked at Dusty. "We've run into it by dumb luck!"

Hernán lighted his cigarette. "Impossible," he said.

Dusty shot him a hard glance. "Don't try to sidetrack us, Galeras, just as we're right on top of it!"

The rest of the party came up slowly. Padre Eusebio crossed himself when he heard the bell. There was a puzzled look on Frank Harley's face. They rode on through the gathering darkness. A mound showed ahead of them, with a tilted wooden cross, silvered by time, thrust into the top of it. Padre Eusebio, Hernán, and Rafaela tossed stones to add to the mound. It was the custom, in memory of the dead who were buried beneath the mound. The others? If Victor had a religion it was his secret. Frank Harley's religion was La Barranca Escondida. The two others? The tall, bearded Americans? Their only religion hung at their belts, sheathed in shaped leather, ready always to deal out sudden death.

"Look!" said Hernán. He pointed out rounded floors of paved rock. "*Arrastres!* To crush the ore from the mines!"

"Yes," said Frank Harley. "But *not* the mines of La Barranca Escondida. There were ancient workings in this area. *Minas reales*. A group of mines. El Refugio, El Santo Niño, El Yaqui, La Barbayena, La Urraca, and Los Dulces Nombres. All were once of good assay. I repeat! This is *not* La Barranca Escondida."

As though to give the lie to his words the bell rang softly.

Rafaela kneed her horse close to that of Frank. "It is possible that this is Guadalupe de Santa Ana," she said. "My grandfather spoke of it. At one time it was populous, but that was long ago."

They rode on. Ruins appeared on either hand. A large building stood at the end of the street, and the last of the light caught the outline of a cross atop a crumbling tile roof. A tall pole leaned away from the prevailing wind, and from the top of it hung a small bell with a frayed rope hanging a few feet below it. The wind blew harder. The pole swayed. The bell rang softly. It was as simple as that.

Hernán grinned. "The ghost bell," he said. "The sacristan has not rung that bell for a long time."

"He'd have to have damned long arms to reach *that* rope," said Dusty.

Hernán looked about. "Is this indeed Guadalupe de Santa Ana?"

"The bell might be marked," suggested the padre.

"There's one sure way of finding out," said Dusty. He

kneed his horse close to the pole. Three good blows of his bowie knife severed the pole. The bell clanged dismally as it shattered against a rock. Padre Eusebio crossed himself and squatted in front of the bell, fitting the pieces together. Shell lighted a match. The padre traced the worn letters with a finger. "The Church of Guadalupe de Santa Ana," said the padre quietly. He crossed himself again.

"We'll stay here tonight," said Shell. "Hernán! Find the water. Let's get these animals watered."

Father Eusebio carefully picked up the pieces of the bell and carried them into the dusty, echoing interior of the old church. In a little while the flickering light of a fire came from within the old church as the padre kindled a fire. The church afforded the best protection from the searching night wind which became a little more chill every night. Besides, the walls were thick and bulletproof. Padre Eusebio, as well as being devout, was also very practical.

Later, as Shell stood guard, he listened to the wind moaning across the mesa, whining about the old buildings and driving rolling brush through the empty streets. The wind did not like the return of humans to its playground.

Something howled out of the night. It was a long way off. Shell raised his head. There wouldn't be any coyotes at this altitude. Perhaps it was a wolf. The long-drawn-out howling came again. Shell shivered but it wasn't from the penetrating night wind. There was enough of his Celtic ancestry still in his veins to make him wonder if the howling came from a creature of flesh and blood.

Chapter Sixteen

The mesa top was still shrouded in the cold gray light of the early dawn. The great barranca south of the mesa was like the blow of an immense ax that had cut deeply into the earth. Rafaela sat her horse, muffled in her serape. "If that is truly Guadalupe de Santa Ana," she said to Shell, "then there is a trail at the bottom of this barranca. The Arisciachi Trail. Is that not so, Frank?"

"Yes," said the blind man. "The trail branches three ways. West to the Rio Mayo. East to the Rio de Haros."

"And the third way?" said Hernán Galeras.

"To the vicinity of Nayarit," said Rafaela, "and the Cerro de Huesos. Beyond that? Perhaps La Barranca Escondida. *Quién sabe?*"

The sky was lightening. Padre Eusebio looked back toward the empty village. "Look," he said quietly.

Twin streamers of smoke, perhaps two miles apart, stained the gray sky. "Those are not Tarahumares cooking their breakfast," said Hernán dryly. "I suggest we do not wait. We cannot go back. We must chance the trail that leads to the bottom of this barranca."

Victor led the way into the thick brush, searching for the trail. In a few minutes he halted, pointing wordlessly down into the dark depths. A wisp of a trail clung to the face of the wall.

"Santa Madre de Dios!" said Hernán. "Is that the only way?"

The Franciscan crossed himself. "We will make it with the favor of God, my son." He quirted his horse forward and then slid to the ground to lead the animal and one of the burros down into the barranca. The others followed him. Hernán and Dusty led the extra horses and the burro. Rafaela led her horse and that of Frank Harley. One blessing Frank had; he couldn't see that horror of a trail.

Two hundred yards from the bottom something struck the trail behind Shell. A rock bounced off into space. Rock after rock began to fall as the Yaquis pushed them over. Shell's horse whinnied pitifully as a rock struck his rump. A great rock fell with smashing force on the back of the bay. He fell sideways, dragging the reins through Shell's left hand. Shell opened his hand, flicking out bright droplets of blood from the furrow gouged by the reins. He heard the horse strike far below.

They led the horses and burros toward the far side of the canyon. Rifle fire crackled from the canyon brim, but the Yaquis were only wasting good cartridges. Dusty looked back. "They're starting down the trail, *compañero,*" he said. He ground-reined his horse and drew his Spencer from its scabbard. Casually he rested the heavy repeater on a boulder and looked at Shell. Shell joined him. Hernán smiled. These Yanquis and their conceit! Body of God! How did they expect to hit anything at *that* range?

The Yaquis were working their way down the trail. Dusty let them get two-thirds of the way down. "Bet a drink I get a hit, *amigo,*" he said out of the side of his mouth.

Shell nodded. He took up the slack in his trigger. "Take the lead man, *amigo,*" he said. "I'll take the last one."

There was no wind. The light was still vague. There was a moment's pause and then the two repeaters cracked almost at once. The lead Yaqui dropped on the trail. Dusty grinned at Shell. "Yuh owe me a drink, *amigo,*" he said.

Shell ejected the empty hull. It tinkled on the hard ground.

"Por Dios!" exclaimed Hernán. "Look!"

The last Yaqui swayed on the trail, pawing at the air with his hands, and then he fell from the trail, turning end over end to strike heavily far below.

"Even-up," said Shell. He levered a fresh round into the chamber. "Scratch one free drink, *amigo.*"

It was almost noon when they called a halt to rest the animals. They had long ago passed the place where the Arisciachi Trail had branched three ways. "We turn to the left here," said Frank, "following the barranca wall for a mile or so. There should be what looks like a box canyon right there. We follow that. The floor of it rises, and several miles from the mouth of the canyon we should reach the level of the mesa. Somewhere near there is a thicket of trees, eh, Rafaela?"

"Yes," she said. "Madroño trees."

"And beyond that?" said Shell.

Frank wet his lips. *"Cerritos chapos.* Three hills, or runt mountains. They are capped with red *topueste* dirt. One of them stands apart from the others."

"Cerro de Huesos?" said Rafaela.

"It should be," said Frank quietly.

"It better be," said Dusty meaningfully.

The afternoon came and began to wane as they forced their way through the choked canyon. It was indeed like a box canyon. Several miles from the barranca, as Frank had said, the floor of the canyon began to rise, and in the light of late afternoon they rode out upon the mesa top near a thick grove of madroño trees. Southwest of them, standing out boldly in the slanting rays of the sun, were two rugged-looking hills, or runt mountains. *They were capped with red topueste dirt!*

Dusty stood up in his stirrups. "There are only two of them," he said coldly.

"Impossible!" said Frank.

"Yuh can't see 'em!" snapped Dusty. "But *we* can! Damn you!"

Frank's face was dewed with sweat. He wiped it off.

Shell took out his fieldglasses and swept the terrain. Far to the left, crowning the flattened side of a ridge, he could pick out tumbled ruins. "Ruins to the left," he said. "Perhaps two miles off. Deep ravine between them and us."

"Nayarit?" said Rafaela.

"Don't you know?" said Dusty harshly.

"Be patient, my son," said the Franciscan.

"Shut that canting mouth of yours!" said Dusty angrily.

"If that is truly Nayarit," said Frank, "then there must be *three* hills."

"Damn you!" snarled Dusty. "There are only two of them!"

Shell spurred his horse and rode toward the hills. He did not look back. Let them come on or stay back, it didn't matter to him. He was getting sick of the whole business and especially of Dusty's constant carping.

The light was almost gone when he passed between the two hills. He looked to the right. A third hill stood there, capped with *topueste* dirt as the others were. It had been hidden from view by the two other hills. Some time in its past there had been a great landslide from the eastern face of the hill, revealing the naked subrock. It was shaped in broken ridges that looked exactly like a huge pile of gigantic bones! "The Hill of Bones," said Shell. He rode toward the lower slopes, looking back to see the others riding between the first two hills.

There would be a moon that night, but it had not arisen as yet. Shell reached the top of the hill and swung down from the horse. He took off his hat to feel the dry wind on his heated face. He could hear the others riding up the slopes below him. The wind shifted. He felt for the makings, and as he did so, the wind blew strongly, and he could have sworn he heard the faint sound of a bell. He slowly fashioned a smoke and was about to light it when he remembered that the Yaquis were somewhere behind them, pushing on, likely traveling faster than the party they were relentlessly pursuing.

They all dismounted at the top of the hills to look south into the clinging darkness. "My grandfather stood here many times," said Rafaela quietly. "To listen for the bell of El Naranjal."

Dusty laughed. "That's only a legend," he said. "How about that, Shell? Did you hear anything?"

Shell hesitated. "No," he said.

Frank Harley looked toward Shell with that uncanny sense of his. Shell knew Frank couldn't see him, but even so he turned his face away. "Let's get off this damned hill," said Shell. "It makes me uneasy."

They rode south of the three hills. The hoofbeats echoed hollowly in the thick darkness. "There is no water up here," said Hernán.

"We keep on," said Dusty.

"If we keep on much farther," said Hernán, "we will not be able to make it back to the last waterhole, with the little water we have left. Who knows? Perhaps the Yaquis are already there."

"Is there any water up here?" asked Padre Eusebio.

Frank looked toward the sound of the padre's voice. "Only at La Barranca Escondida," he said. His meaning was plain enough. They either found La Barranca Escondida, or they would die of thirst—if the Yaquis did not catch them first.

Shell looked back into the mysterious darkness. "I'll scout ahead. I'll be back by daylight."

"Alone?" said Dusty.

"Why?" said Shell. "Are you afraid I'll find the silver and run off with it?" He looked at Frank. "Any landmarks or any signs to show the way, Frank?"

"On a quiet night you're supposed to be able to hear the dogs barking at La Barranca Escondida. Yuh got a damned quiet night," said Dusty.

"There haven't been any dogs at La Barranca Escondida for a hundred years," said Frank.

"The bell then!" said Hernán.

Frank shrugged. "A legend. A myth. There is one landmark, Shell, that you might find. A thick grove of trees. The scientific name is *Populus wislizeni.* They are very rare. It is said that they grow only in two places in this country and few other places in Mexico. Here they are supposed to grow near Nayarit and La Barranca Escondida. The trail down into the barranca is masked by a grove of such trees."

"What do they look like?" said Shell.

"I don't know," said Frank.

Dusty spat viciously. "Great!" he snapped.

Padre Eusebio raised his head. "I know them," he said. "They are known in this country as *guerigo* trees. Furniture is made from them because the wood is tough and long lasting."

"Ride with me then," said Shell.

The padre mounted his horse. "There is said to be water at La Barranca Escondida. It will be of far greater value than silver."

"If you find it," said Hernán.

"It will be God's will," said the padre.

They rode off into the darkness. Hernán leaned against his horse. "Maybe they won't come back," he suggested.

"The padre is a servant of God," said Rafaela hotly.

"That is very true," said the *capitán*. "But Shell is not."

"Keep your thoughts to yourself, greaser," said Dusty thinly.

Hernán shrugged and smiled to himself in the darkness.

They rode for well over two hours through the darkness. There was a faint trace of moonlight in the eastern sky. "Wait!" said the padre. "My horse has picked up a stone in a hoof."

Shell dismounted. "We'd better lead them for a while," he said. It was much darker ahead of them. Shell looked back at the dim figure of the padre as he walked on. "Hurry up," said Shell. His right foot struck out into emptiness. He fell, grabbing onto the ground with his left hand while his right hand clung to the reins. He shouted once and the echo sounded far away. Strong hands gripped him and pulled him up. He let go of the reins. The horse reared and blew in terror. Shell crawled weakly onto solid ground.

Padre Eusebio tethered the horses to a scrub tree. "Wait here," he said.

Shell looked up weakly. "I wasn't thinking of going anywhere right now," he said with a sickly smile.

Father Eusebio padded off into the darkness, feeling his way with a long stick. In half an hour he was back. He pointed his stick at the scrub tree to which the horses were tethered. "That tree is *not* a *guerigo* tree," he said conversationally.

"I didn't expect it to be," said Shell dryly. "Did you?"

Padre Eusebio shook his head. "No. The grove of *guerigo* trees is a hundred yards beyond us."

Shell stared unbelievingly at him. "You're sure?"

"*Positive,*" said the padre.

The light grew. Twenty feet from them was a great swath of darkness, seemingly stretching on into infinity. Shell gingerly crawled forward. He stopped at the lip of an immense barranca. He dropped some rocks. He could not hear the sound of them striking far below. Padre Eusebio crawled up beside him.

The light grew. Gradually they realized they were looking down into the biggest barranca they had ever seen, so deep that the moonlight did not fully penetrate the darkness at the bottom. It was so vague and illusive they could not definitely make out any of the features.

They slept fitfully while the moon died and the darkness

came again. The morning sun warmed their backs as they lay there. The morning wind whispered over the mesa top. "Listen!" said the padre. Faintly, ever so faintly, came the sound of a bell from the depths of the barranca.

When the sun filled the barranca, Shell focused his glasses on the bottom. The sunlight sparkled from the waters of a running stream and shone on great groves of dark-leaved trees. Shell could just pick out globules of orange against the dark foliage. Beyond the stream, surrounded by the orange trees, he could make out white walls. A tower rose above the trees. Shell handed the glasses to the Franciscan.

"There is no question about it, my son," said the padre, after a few minutes. "This is La Barranca Escondida and El Naranjal."

"We'd better find the trail down into it," said Shell.

"I wonder," said the padre, almost as though to himself.

"What do you mean?" demanded Shell.

The soft brown eyes probed into Shell's hard gray eyes. "Is it a good thing?" said the Franciscan. "What will happen to you people when that silver is found?"

"That's why we fought to get here! It means *nothing* to you. It means *everything* to us!"

The padre looked down into the barranca. "Perhaps," he said reflectively. "Perhaps Satan himself placed that silver there as a trap for men. It is haunted, my son. Haunted by greed, sin, and possible murder."

"You sound almost like you wish it would happen."

The padre quickly crossed himself. "God forbid!" he said in horror.

The padre led the way to the grove of *guerigo* trees. Beyond the grove the trail appeared, tracing a faint line down the wall of the barranca. Shell felt a little sick as he looked down it. "Go back and bring up the others," he said to the padre. "I'll scout the trail."

Shell worked his way down on foot. The trail was crumbling, seemingly held to the side of the barranca by magnetism. Halfway down he found a place where the trail ended, to continue on fifteen feet further. A row of deep holes indicated that at one time poles had been inserted, to form supports for a crude bridge. He plodded wearily up the trail to the grove of trees. By the time the rest of the party arrived he had hacked enough poles and shorter pieces to use as supports and stringers.

It was late afternoon by the time they had bridged the gap. They carried the supplies across and then crossed the animals one by one. Just as Shell crossed the bridge he looked back up the trail. His blood ran cold as he saw a hatless figure move quickly into cover. "*Adelante!*" he called out. "Our friends are at the top of the trail! Get the horses and burros down! Dusty and Hernán! Drop behind to give me a hand holding them off!"

Frank Harley turned his blind eyes toward Shell. "No need for that," he said. "No Yaqui would ever come down here. To them the place is haunted. Remember the curse of the Jesuits."

"What about Victor?" said Shell.

"Look at him," Father Eusebio said.

The *mozo*'s face was a mask, but fear showed in his dark eyes. Only his loyalty and devotion to his mistress would get him to go down into the barranca.

Dusty looked up the trail. "Supposin' this *ain't* La Barranca Escondida?"

Frank smiled. "Then we'll find out soon enough, won't we, Dusty?"

Dusty stared at him, then spat over the side of the trail. "Stop," he said, "you're killin' me!"

It was dark by the time they reached the foot of the trail. They rode to the rushing stream and watered the animals and themselves. The night wind moaned softly through the great barranca. Every head was raised when the faint sound of the bell came through the darkness. Then it was quiet again.

Chapter Seventeen

The moonlight was flooding down into La Barranca Escondida. It glinted from the rushing stream and reflected from the white surfaces of the buildings. It shone fully on the ancient road that passed through the dark-leaved orange trees. At the far end of the road were the mysterious buildings. Shell glanced behind him as he walked the road. Dusty was fifty feet behind, followed by Hernán at an equal interval. Rafaela, Victor, and the padre followed, leading the animals. As Shell looked back he could clearly make out Frank Harley who was riding one of the lead horses. What was going on in Frank's mind now that he had found his dream? Would it crack if there were no buried treasure in the barranca?

The Yaquis had not appeared. Frank had been right. There was nothing to fear from them as long as one stayed in the haunted barranca. The Spaniards had left it a hundred years ago. Yet it seemed to Shell that someone, or *something,* was still there. There were times when he could have sworn he had seen a quick movement just out of the corner of an eye, but when he looked, there had been nothing there. Imagination of course. Or *was* it imagination?

He stopped in awe at the edge of the square. The old padres had built for the future, not realizing perhaps, that their handiwork would stand empty and echoing, lost for a hundred years. Facing Shell from across the empty square was a solid-looking church with a bell tower rising from the left hand side of it. A cross, still showing traces of giltwork, shone in the moonlight. A rounded dome covered with white cement rose at the rear of the church. To the right of the church stood an L-shaped building, the long leg of the L forming the side of the square. A colonnaded arcade extended the full length of the building. To Shell's left there were other smaller buildings and several narrow side streets faced by more buildings. A *carreta* leaned drunkenly in the center of one of the narrow streets as though waiting for its owner to come and hitch the oxen to it. All of the buildings were shuttered and lifeless-looking.

Shell waved an arm and walked across the square. Midway he stopped and picked up a little bundle of faded, rotting cloth. The stolid wooden face of a doll looked unblinkingly up at him, showing traces of the Indian ancestry of the woodcarver. The child who had dropped it had likely died as an old lady, years past.

Shell walked to the raised flagstoned *pavé* in front of the church. The shattered pieces of a bell were scattered beneath the bell tower. He looked up and saw that only one bell still hung in the tower. Anselmo's words came back to him. *"There were four bells in the church tower. One of them fell and was shattered when they attempted to lower it from the tower. Two had already been taken from the tower. The last of the four bells was left hanging in the tower."*

"So Anselmo was right after all," said Dusty from behind Shell.

Shell nodded. "So much for legend," he said. He stepped up onto the *pavé* and walked to the carved double doors of the church. He tried the wrought-iron handles. The doors creaked open. A musty odor drifted from the dark interior of the church.

"Go on in!" said Dusty eagerly. "Some of them church ornaments and stuff were made of solid gold or silver!"

Shell shook his head. "Let the padre go in first," he said.

Dusty walked toward the entrance, spurs chiming.

Shell stepped in front of his companion. "I said: *Let the padre go in first!*"

For a moment their eyes locked. Dusty shrugged. He smiled. "Have it your way, *amigo,*" he said carelessly. "There ought to be enough for all of us, even that stupid padre."

Hernán stood at the foot of the steps. He fashioned a cigarette. Some day, perhaps soon, those two cold-eyed gringos would have at each other, and with a little bit of luck they might just kill each other. He lighted his cigarette. That would leave all the more silver for Hernán Galeras, and the woman too, of course. With a little more luck, he might stumble onto the stores of wine that the Jesuits were sure to have left. He half-closed his eyes and smiled. It was such a beautiful thought!

Shell looked back across the square. There was a dreamlike quality about the place, as though it had a spell upon it. As though time no longer existed. It was so quiet and peaceful he almost felt as though the legendary and fabulous wealth of La Barranca Escondida was of little value compared to the peacefulness of the place.

The rest of the party came up. Rafaela was describing the place to the blind man. He kept nodding his head. "Yes! Yes! I can truly see it, Rafaela!"

The padre crossed himself as he came up the three wide steps to the *pavé.* He hesitated at the door. He looked at Shell. Shell nodded. "Go on in," he said. He handed Father Eusebio a block of lucifers. The padre threw back his cowl and walked in. A moment later a flicker of light came from within the cavernous interior. "Shell," said the padre in an awed tone, "they even left the candles!"

They walked in behind the padre. Rafaela held Frank by the arm, but the *mozo* stopped at the doorway and would not enter. He returned to the horses and burros.

The flaring light of the ancient candles revealed the untouched interior of the nave with the stations of the cross on either side. The adobe brick flooring was covered with dust which arose in a thin cloud and drifted toward the open doorway. The padre advanced to the sanctuary and lighted more candles and then he went down upon his knees before the bare altar.

Shell looked about. The flickering light revealed the intricate painted decorations on the walls and ceiling, done in black, red, green, yellow, orange, and indigo blue. Pictures of the Twelve Apostles still hung on the walls. Over the sanctuary altar was a dusty statue of the Madonna, and above it, close to the domed ceiling, was a statue of a saint with outspread arms as though in blessing. Under the white dome, seemingly suspended in space, were the crossed palms of martyrdom.

Rafaela walked forward and went down upon her knees behind the padre. Hernán looked back at Shell and Dusty with a faint, self-conscious grin, then trod out his cigarette, took off his hat, and went down upon his knees beside the woman. Dusty prowled about the nave looking for gold or silver ornaments, but the Jesuits had not left any, at least in the church. He snapped a lucifer on a thumbnail and lighted a cigarette, eyeing Shell as Shell took off his faded campaign hat. Dusty walked from the church, his spurs chiming softly. The echo came down from the vaulted roof of the nave.

"No one has been here in one hundred years," said the soft voice beside Shell. He looked at the calm face of Frank Harley. "One hundred years of peace and quiet, Shell," added the blind man. "Do you feel it, Shell?"

"No," lied Shell. Frank had an uncanny way of probing into a man's innermost thoughts.

The Franciscan stood up. He looked down on Rafaela and Hernán, placed a hand on each of their heads, then walked to Shell and Frank. There had always been a calm, reflective look on the padre's brown face, but if it was possible it seemed as though now it was even more so, as though a great weight had been lifted from him. "It is time to leave, my children," he said.

"Where is Dusty?" said Hernán.

They walked out onto the *pavé*. Father Eusebio had extinguished all the candles except one, which he left guttering in a red glass receptacle on the altar.

There was no sign of Dusty in the square. Victor pointed toward the massive L-shaped building that dominated one whole side of the square. A door hung open, and from within a faint flickering of light could be seen. Dusty wasn't wasting any time.

Shell walked to the building and into the colonnaded arcade that ran for many feet on either hand. He followed the sound that came from a room whose door hung open. A pale wash of light came from within. Shell stopped at the door. The room had dark, massive furniture in it, typical of many missions he had seen. Dusty had thrown back the lid of a heavy, iron-strapped chest. He was tossing out articles of clothing and cursing softly. "A lot of useless crap," he said over his shoulder.

"You're in one helluva hurry," said Shell.

Dusty looked at him. "*I* didn't come here for the good of *my* soul," he said.

"You might consider it, *amigo*."

Dusty laughed. He stood up and rubbed his dusty beard, watching Shell with amused eyes. "Yuh think you'll make time with the filly by actin' religious?"

"You've got a warped mind," said Shell coldly.

They could hear the others in the corridor. Shell walked to meet them. "This is evidently the old mission," he said.

Hernán nodded. "The old padres had the Indians digging for silver with one hand and lighting holy candles with the other."

"They left the candles," said Dusty from the doorway. "Let's hope, by God, they left some of the silver."

"They did," said Frank. "There was no possible way they could have removed it *all* before their expulsion. The padres here in La Barranca Escondida had more time to hide their bullion than most of the Jesuits did."

"There is a lovely old room here," said Rafaela from down the corridor. She beckoned to them with the lighted candle in her hand.

The room was low-ceiled, but very wide and quite long. A large beehive fireplace was in one corner, and a thick bed of ashes still coated the hearth. Dusty hangings were on the peeling whitewashed walls. Candle sconces of wrought iron were fastened to the walls, and a pair of solid-looking iron candelabra still stood on the massive table that dominated the center of the room. Hernán lighted more candles. As he touched the tablecloth, a thin film of dust arose from it and drifted toward the open door.

Dusty dropped into a chair and thrust his long legs up onto the table. One of his spurs caught in the ancient cloth and ripped it. "Where do we start looking, Frank?" he said as he formed a cigarette. His eyes were as hard as flint.

Shell made a cigarette and placed it between the blind man's lips. Rafaela took a candle from its holder and leaned over to light the cigarette. As she did so her full breasts swung against the thin material of her patched-up shirt. Dusty flicked a glance at her breasts. Shell watched her lovely face, ivory in the soft candlelight. She looked at him with her dark, lustrous eyes, and something caught at his heart.

"What about it, Frank?" repeated Dusty.

"He's very tired," said Rafaela. "Cannot we get some rest?"

"He ain't *that* tired," said Dusty.

Frank drew in the smoke and blew it out. The smoke wavered in the musty air, drifted toward the candles, then toward the door. "It's all right," he said. "I can't sleep right now. It's taken me twenty years of research and hunting to get here. Twenty years of death and defeat, of blood and sweat. *Twenty years. . . .*"

"Cut out the history crap," said Dusty. "We ain't interested."

Frank rested his thin hands on the table. "It is said that the bullion and other items were placed in one of the mines, the entrance of which is supposedly twenty-two hundred *varas* west of, and seven hundred *varas* south of the door of the church. A *vara* is thirty-three and one-third inches. This mine was then protected with a *patrón* and the entrance closed and carefully concealed."

"Patrón?" said Shell.

Frank nodded. "An Indian most likely. Killed on the spot and left there so that his ghost would always guard the mine until the true owners returned."

Father Eusebio crossed himself. "I have heard of such things," he said.

Dusty laughed. "What's supposed to be hidden there?"

Frank leaned back in his chair and blew a cloud of smoke. "I have read a copy of the inventory. Don't ask me how I found it. The man who I bribed to let me see it died quite mysteriously shortly thereafter. I memorized many of the items. *Item:* a baptismal font of carved cedar inlaid with silver. *Item:* a small cut-stone box filled with jewels. *Items:* a pair of processional candleholders, six golden incensories, three large golden communion plates, a pair of silver chalices, a shrine made of solid silver, and three candelabras of solid silver. *Item:* seventy-five *cargas,* or packloads of silver, each *carga* packed in cowhide bags, two bags to a wooden chest, each chest containing one-half of an *arroba*. These are from divers mines located in La Barranca Escondida. *Item:* ten *cargas* of gold, wrapped in cloth and cowhide, and stored in wooden chests. These from the placers of El Naranjal. *Item:* five *arrobas* of Castilla ore, twenty-two carats assay, clean and without mercury, from El Naranjal." Frank's voice died away.

There was a long pause. Tobacco smoke rose in rifted layers above the candles. Dusty leaned forward. His lean, scarred face reminded Shell of Mephistopheles. "How big is an *arroba?*" he asked in a hoarse voice.

"Two hundred and twelve pounds," said Frank calmly.

Dusty clapped a hard hand on the table. "Jesus God!" he said.

Father Eusebio hurriedly crossed himself. "The church items will be returned, in good faith, to the Church, of course."

Dusty flipped his cigarette butt into the fireplace. "Of course," he said. He grinned. "When do we start searching?"

"The moon will soon be gone," said Hernán. "It would be best to wait for daylight. The silver and gold do not have the legs. They cannot run away in fright from us."

Later, Shell lay in his room, hands locked behind his neck, staring up at the dim ceiling, blowing smoke rings up at it. He could not sleep. Here they were, as ill-assorted a bunch of adventurers as one might dream up, sitting on top of a fabulous fortune in silver and gold, and yet they could not leave the barranca. The Yaquis would wait. They had all the time and patience in the world.

Something moved near the open doorway. He raised his head. He sensed, rather than saw, who it was. "Rafaela?" he said.

She came quickly to him as he sat up. "I am afraid of this place, Shell," she said.

He drew her close to him. "It's only a legend," he said. "There is nothing to fear here."

She shook her head. "It isn't that," she said. "It's haunted by greed and by death. I feel it, Shell. I can't help it."

He slipped an arm about her slim waist. "Nothing will happen to you, Rafaela."

"It isn't me, Shell. It's you I'm thinking of. When Dusty and Hernán look at you I can see the greed and hate on their faces. Shell, don't ever turn your back on them!"

Something moved near the doorway. Shell placed his hand on the Colt lying on the small table beside the bed. He could see the dim outline of Victor. The dull sheen of a knife showed against the dark of his clothing. "Your watchdog, Rafaela," said Shell.

She turned her head. For a moment or two she looked at the Tarahumare. Shell could feel her heart beating against his chest. "Go, Victor," she said at last. "Get some sleep. I will be all right here with Shell. Go, I tell you!"

The Tarahumare hesitated. Slowly he sheathed the knife. They could hear his dragging footsteps as he walked away.

She looked at him in the darkness. "I am not afraid to be alone with you," she whispered.

"Are you sure?" he asked. "Perhaps it would be better for you to leave with Victor."

Her cool hands touched his flushed face. "I am not afraid, Shell. I want to be with you. I can't stand to be alone any longer."

He drew her back to him and dropped his head to the pillow, drawing her closer. There would be no going back now or ever. The wind whispered through the trees. The bell rang softly, just once, but neither of them heard it.

Chapter Eighteen

The steady ringing of the heavy bowie knives and the camp ax against the trees echoed from the towering barranca wall behind the church and mission buildings. A narrow path had been cut through the tangled growth of thorned brush and tough scrub trees that extended beyond the untended orange groves. Dusty, Hernán, Shell, and the padre had been at it since dawn. Nothing could force the *mozo* to come anywhere near the area. Perhaps he saw or felt something that they did not, but not even the threat of a bullet between the eyes from Dusty's cocked Colt had been able to move him. At last Shell had given him a rifle and told him to go hunting. The immense barranca abounded in deer and bear. The gobbling of wild turkeys had come to them on the dawn wind, and once during the night Shell had been aroused by what he thought was the screaming of a panther. But Rafaela had sleepily drawn him to her again. Shell wiped the dripping sweat from his face. He looked back toward the white buildings. She had gone before the dawn while he was still asleep.

Hernán again drove a stake into the ground they had so laboriously cleared and then stretched the knotted measuring-rope from it. He looked up at Shell. "Five hundred *varas* south of the east-west line of the church door," he said. "Two hundred to go."

Dusty leaned against a tree. He had stripped off his shirt

and his corded body was wet with sweat. He looked up at the sky. "Damned near midday," he said.

"We've got plenty of time," said Shell.

The padre worked his way into the brush. *"Dulce Madre de Dios!"* he exclaimed. He reappeared holding something up in the air. "It is a *zurrón,"* he said excitedly. "A rawhide bag that was fastened to the head to carry ore from the mines!"

No further time was wasted. The bowies and the ax cut steadily into the brush and trees. The padre hauled the cut material back to a clearing. Another hundred *varas* and Hernán found another *zurrón.* Dusty stumbled over a rusted miner's pick. Then the way seemed easier. Shell realized that they were now cutting growth that had come up in the past hundred years in what had once been the road to the mines. They broke through at last into a wide cleared space in the shape of a great crescent. Towering above them was the barranca wall, and at the foot of it a great talus slope. There was no sign of a mine entrance.

Dusty slammed his bowie into a tree, then made a cigarette as his eyes darted up and down the slope and to either side. "Jesus God," he said. "There's tons and tons of rock there."

"It would take months to dig into that," said Hernán.

Father Eusebio nodded. "I will get Señor Frank," he said.

Dusty watched the padre vanish down the laboriously cut trail. He lighted his cigarette. "Seems to me the ol' padre is sure interested in worldly goods," he said. "I thought he had taken vows of poverty, chastity, and obedience."

Hernán laughed. "They're all alike," he said cynically. "The old Jesuits were smarter than any of them. The Indians believe that the mountains are the masters of all riches. They think they can bargain with a mountain for something the mountain is master of, but they cannot bargain with a stranger to show him that something. The Indians likely began to believe this after the Conquest. The Jesuits took advantage of this. When Christianizing the Indians they taught them that if they showed precious metal to anybody but the representatives of God—the Jesuits themselves—that God would be wrathful and take vengeance." Hernán laughed. "The profane must not steal gold out of God's pocket. The fools believed the Jesuits."

The Franciscan reappeared leading Frank by the hand. Rapidly he explained the terrain to the blind man. There was a tense look on the blind man's face. "Look about on the rocks or trees," he said. "Look for strange markings. Anything!"

In twenty minutes Hernán raised a cry of triumph. "Here is a cross marked plainly on this rock!" he said exultantly. "What does it mean?"

Frank took his cigarette from his mouth. His hand trembled. "A cross can mean a number of things," he said. "Perhaps it means rich objects of the Church buried nearby. It might simply mean a Christian has passed this way."

"It is horizontal," said Hernán.

Frank's head snapped up. "Then the long part of the upright points toward the treasure!"

Four pairs of eyes swung quickly in the direction to which the upright pointed. It was a hopeless pile of tumbled rock, riven and shattered, thickly overgrown with thorny brush. Dusty led the way through the bright sunlight. In an hour Shell found another chiseled marking, partly obliterated by time. It was an arrow without heft inclining upward. Frank translated this into meaning that there would be other signs in the direction to which the arrow pointed.

There was no wind penetration of the jumble of rock and thorned growth. Sweat dripped from the four men as they worked their way through the tangle. It was midafternoon when Dusty stumbled over a rock and fell bellyflat atop another symbol carved into the flat rock upon which he had fallen. "The letter A!" he called out.

Frank was led to the spot by the padre. "It's a triangle," said the blind man. He raised his head, although he could not see. "Treasure is to be found within a triangle formed by trees or rocks."

"There are no trees," said Hernán. He looked at the piled-up masses of fallen rock and then up at the sheer barranca wall, golden-yellow in the sunlight. "Perhaps the rockfalls have covered everything."

Shell climbed atop a huge boulder. He scanned the area. Within a hundred yards to the east and to the west were boulders quite similar to the one upon which he stood. He was about to descend when he noticed part of a mark beneath a loose rock. He kicked the rock aside and saw yet another chiseled symbol. "There's a mark up here," he called down. "A triangle with a curved line projecting from the top."

Frank wiped the sweat from his face. "Wait a minute," he said. "Wait . . . ah, I have it! The treasure deposit is around a bend or curve formed by the rocks or trees."

"No trees," said Shell. "We'll have to settle for the rocks."

They pushed their way through the tangle, hacking with their knives and the ax. It was the padre who stumbled into the deep arroyo that was not apparent until one was almost on top of it. He crashed down through the growths with a clattering of rock and a rising cloud of thin and bitter yellow dust. His muffled voice came up to them. *"Gracias a Dios!* There is a mark here, Señor Frank It is the numeral three, but it is backward. . . ."

"Change direction," said the blind man.

"But there is no place to go!"

Shell slid down the slope. The concentrated heat of the windless arroyo nearly felled him. He saw the padre standing by the marked boulder. Beyond the padre was a thicket. Shell slashed into it. There was a natural passageway penetrating into the thicket of shattered rock and brush. "There's another mark here," he called out. "Like a U lying on its side."

"U hell!" said Frank excitedly. He laughed. "That's a *mule shoe!* It means that we're enroute to the treasure! Keep on, Shell! Keep on!"

Shell led the way down the stifling passageway with the padre close behind him. The padre's brown robe was in sad shape, torn and dirty, seemingly held together by the rope girdle from which was suspended the cross. Shell had to hand it to the padre; he was as hard a worker as any of them. The others followed them, and once when Shell looked back at them, he saw Rafaela. There was no shame on her face for what had passed between her and Shell. There was almost a look of pride, perhaps of possessiveness. She was no *puta,* who'd leap into the feathers with any man. It had troubled Shell at first as to why she had come to him, and then the realization had entered his mind that she must feel that they'd never leave the barranca except by the last trail out for any living soul. That was why she had come to him. She was grasping at what little life and love were left to her. For that surely God could not and would not condemn her!

It was Hernán who found the rusted mule shoe. Dusty looked at Frank. "I thought yuh said the mules were shod with silver?" he said.

"Part of the legend, Dusty," said Frank.

Dusty hurled the rusted shoe into the rocks. "The loot better not be part of the legend," he said truculently.

Rafaela stood beside Shell. She raised her eyes to look at his lean, sweat-glistening face. "Look!" she said. She pointed to the rock face above the piled talus. Faintly seen, and likely not visible if the sun was at any other angle, was a carved sunburst.

"What is it?" said Frank eagerly.

"A sunburst, Señor Frank," said Padre Eusebio.

For a moment the blind man did not speak, and then he smiled. "There are mines close by, my friends. Any symbol of the sun indicates the proximity of mineral wealth."

All eyes scanned the hopeless-looking tangle. Then the searchers plowed through the brush, stumbling over loose rock. Even as they searched, the sun moved on and the symbol seemed to fade away. Rafaela, by what seemed a miracle, had seen the sunburst at exactly the right time, during the few minutes the sun brought it out.

"Shadow writing," said Frank as he felt his way along the passageway. His blind face stared unseeingly up at the rock wall. "Only visible at the right time of day, perhaps even the month of the year. Look closely, my friends! It might be only a fraction of time!"

Shell wiped the sweat from his face and scanned the wall. Dusty ran a few feet along the passageway and stared at the wall. "Jesus! Oh Jesus!" he yelled. "I see somethin'! A bracket!"

"It means a tunnel is nearby!" cried Frank.

Padre Eusebio scrambled up on a rock. His robe split along the side, revealing his sweating flesh. He hurriedly drew it together and pinned it with a thorn. "There is something, my friends!" he said excitedly. "I am not sure. Yes! Yes! *Con el favor de Dios!* I see it!"

"Damn yuh!" roared Dusty. "Stop gibberin'! What *do* yuh see?"

The padre pointed. "Look there," he said. A mark showed clearly as the sun struck it. An arc with a dot beneath it. Even as they watched, it seemed to be fading back into the rock face. They all looked at Frank, who was shaping a cigarette with trembling hands. *"Treasure directly beneath this sign,"* he said. He closed his eyes. Sweat dripped from his face, and at last the trembling of his thin hands caused him to drop the tobacco and thin corn husk. Rafaela took the makings from Shell's shirt pocket and expertly fashioned a cigarette which she thrust into Frank's mouth and then lighted it.

"Look at it," said Dusty in disgust. "Tons of rock!"

Shell worked into a twisted offshoot of the main passage, with Rafaela close behind him. His bowie cut a way through the brush that choked the way. He broke into a comparatively clear area and looked up at the barranca wall. "Nothing," he said in disgust.

She touched his arm. "You are looking too high for your treasure."

He looked down at her. "You meant that *you* are truly my treasure?"

She stood on her toes and kissed him. "That is true, but I did not mean that, Shell. Look at that smooth-faced boulder behind you."

There was something cut into the surface, but it was partially covered by overhanging brush. Shell cut the tough stems of the brush to reveal another symbol. "Looks like a vertical mule shoe with three dots inside of it," he said. He could hear the others working their way into the clearing.

Frank Harley was led up to Shell by the padre. Frank took the cigarette from his mouth. "It means a flight of steps down into a mine or shaft, perhaps a cave," he said quietly.

"Where, damn yuh!" yelled Dusty. His harsh voice echoed loudly.

Frank looked toward him. "You loudmouthed jackass," he said pleasantly. *"You're likely standing right on top of it!"*

Dusty stared down at the hard earth beneath his feet, then dropped to his knees as though to tear at it with his big bare hands.

Shell looked about. "We'll need tools," he said. "We'll need the burros to help free the rocks that are piled here." He touched Frank on the shoulder. "You're sure of this, Frank?"

The blind man nodded. "I've kept my word. I've brought you to the place."

Dusty stood up and brushed his hands. "We ain't found any loot yet, mister," he said coldly.

Hernán rolled a cigarette. "It would be better to come back in daylight tomorrow," he said.

Dusty whirled on him. "Tonight!" he snapped. "There'll be enough light by the moon, *hombre!* We dig *tonight!"*

Hernán shrugged. "As you say, *amigo."*

They cleared more of the brush out of the way as they worked their way back to the passageway and then out of the deep arroyo. The sun was already gone and deep shadows filled the barranca. A cool wind blew through it. The church bell rang softly.

As they neared the mission they could smell roasting meat. Victor evidently had been successful in his hunt.

Padre Eusebio looked up at the dark towering walls. "A

man could find anything he needed here," he said reflectively. "There is water and fruit. Bear, deer, and turkeys. There is fine shelter from the winter winds and the cold. Above all, there is peace, wherein a man can examine his soul."

Dusty laughed. He took the cigarette from his lips and ground it beneath a heel. "For *you,* Eusebio," he said. "But not for *us!* There's enough loot buried back there to make us kings in the outside world, eh, *amigos?*"

No one answered. Each of them had their own thoughts. Who was right? The padre or Dusty? *Quién sabe?*

Chapter Nineteen

A drifting cloud of thin yellow dust hung in the deep arroyo. Ancient picks and spades tore at the loose rock near the boulder marked as the site of the shaft or tunnel. The bigger rocks were hauled off by the dusty burros and dumped to one side. There was no conversation as the four sweating men tried to rip their way into the tons of fallen rock behind the huge boulder. They had started to work by the light of sotol torches fashioned by Victor, but the *mozo* still would not come near the arroyo.

The moon was well up when at last Dusty's pick struck something that was not rock. He dropped the heavy pick and tore at the loose rock with his bare hands, heedless of the blood that dripped from the torn flesh. It was as though the man was possessed by a demon. The others stood back and let him work. To stand near him was to get struck by a flying rock. The rock clattered behind him until the moonlight shone on a heavy wooden door, well-strapped and studded with metal, which was set into a cleanly cut opening in the living rock. Dusty tried the door. The padres had not forgotten to lock it. Dusty snatched up the ax and slammed blow after blow near the thick bottom hinge until at last the blade broke through the door. It was a matter of minutes to hitch up the burros as a team. Meanwhile the ax broke through at the upper hinge and the door leaned outward a little. The ropes were made fast by Shell, and at a signal the burros were lashed by Hernán. The door sagged further and then fell with a resounding crash that echoed hollowly in the arroyo and then slammed back and forth between the canyon walls to die slowly away. Dusty leaped over the door to meet an onrush of bitter-smelling dust and something else that was mingled with it.

"Wait!" yelled Hernán. "The air might be poisonous!"

Dusty waved a hand back at Hernán. "To hell with that!" he yelled. He disappeared into the darkness of the tunnel. His boots thudded on the rock floor.

"Wait!" cried out Frank. "Don't go in!"

Shell started forward. The smell sickened him. "Dusty, you damned fool!" he yelled. His voice sounded hollowly in the tunnel.

"Shell! Shell!" said Dusty. Something fell heavily within the tunnel. Shell ran in, his guts heaving at the stench, and he stumbled over Dusty. He gripped him under the arms and dragged him back, over the fallen door. The padre and Hernán hauled Dusty into the fresh air beyond the tunnel. Shell swayed as he walked. He got violently sick in the brush.

The moon climbed higher as they waited. In an hour the air had cleared sufficiently enough to enter. Shell lighted a torch and walked in. Twenty feet from the entrance he stopped short. A skeleton sagged against a wall, the ghastly skull looking directly at him.

"The *patrón!*" said Padre Eusebio. He quickly crossed himself.

Shell grinned. He looked back at Dusty. "Is that what scared you, *amigo?*" he said.

"Get on!" snapped Dusty.

"Wait!" said Frank. Rafaela guided him to the three men. Frank sniffed the air. "Fresh enough," he said. "Watch for pitfalls, or traps of any kind. This has been a little too easy to suit me."

They lighted more torches and progressed slowly, finding more crumpled *zurrones* mingled with rusted picks and spades. Shell eyed the walls, ceiling, and floor. There was no sign of any sort of trap.

"Stop!" said Padre Eusebio. "Look down, Shell!"

The floor was studded with what looked like long dried shoots of some kind, with dark-colored thorny tips. Shell knelt and looked at them. The tips were as sharp as needles. He reached out a hand to touch one, and his hand was pulled back by Hernán. *"Madre de Dios!"* he said. "No! It is the maguey, tipped with poison. One prick from one of those and you die within the hour!"

The floor was studded with them for twenty feet. Hernán moved slowly along, burning the long dried plants with the flame from his sotol torch. The thick smoke drifted slowly from the tunnel past the coughing people. At last they could walk forward over the crackling and now harmless magueys.

"Look here," said Hernán. To one side a dark tunnel slanted steeply down into the depths. The Mexican held his torch over the mouth of it. A heavy log had been placed in the hole, and it had been notched like a gigantic chicken ladder. The wood was as smooth as glass and the notches had been deeply worn. "For the miners," said Hernán. "They carried the heavy ore in *zurrones* up these ladders from great depths."

"Only God knows how many of them died in these noisome holes," said Padre Eusebio, "for the glory of the Spanish Crown."

Dusty spat down into the hole. "For the glory of the Jesuits, you mean." He laughed. "God goes out the window when you padres smell gold or silver. Ain't that so, Eusebio?"

The padre did not answer Dusty. "There is more to be searched," he said.

The tunnel twisted and turned and at times was partially blocked by rockfalls. The old miners had not tunneled on a straight line or cut in cross drifts, but had evidently gophered in, following the rich vein in its meanderings. In an hour they reached an impassable rockfall. Dusty cursed as he tore at the loose rock.

"What do you think, Frank?" said Shell.

"The mine may be empty, Shell. They may have hidden the treasure elsewhere."

Hernán threw up his hands. "This is the end!" he said. "Mother of the Devil! It would take days to get through this, and to what end? Perhaps there is nothing after all."

"Have faith, my son," said the padre.

"I urinate on my faith!" spat out the *capitán*.

Frank raised his head. "There is still a draft in here," he said quietly. He placed his hand on the wall behind him and felt it. He struck it with his fist. Shell came beside the older man and worked his hands up and down on the solid wall. He stepped up on a rock and felt the cool draft work over his hands. Shell stepped back and raised his pick. He drove it hard at the wall. The sound seemed hollow. Again and again he struck. There was a cracking noise. A piece of rock fell. The inner side had traces of mortar on it. Shell drove the pick once more. A large piece of the wall fell heavily. Rock clattered on the dusty floor. The pick smashed hard into the rock, and there was a grating and crashing as the wall fell outward toward Shell. He had just time to clear it by a wild jump, bumping against the padre and driving him down.

The dust swirled through the passageway, half blinding them and causing them to choke. "Drop flat!" yelled Shell. They dropped to the floor below the thickest of the dust.

Dusty alone did not drop. He jumped over the prostrate body of Hernán and clambered over the rockfall. He held a torch in each hand. He hurled one ahead of him. Shell raised his head to see the torchlight reflect from something that glittered. He saw something else. A heavy vertical beam was moving slowly toward Dusty. "Get back!" yelled Shell hoarsely. Dusty jumped. The beam fell heavily exactly where Dusty had been standing. The crashing sound reverberated through the tunnel. As the beam was falling, Shell saw a triple row of murderous six-inch-long spikes protruding from it. If it had fallen on Dusty. . . .

The thickest of dust drifted down the tunnel. Dusty lighted more torches. Shell, the padre, and Hernán crowded behind him as he walked into a large, squared-off room. "Jesus God!" said Dusty.

"By the nails of Christ!" said Hernán breathlessly.

The padre crossed himself. *"Gracias a Dios!"* he said.

Shell was speechless. The rear wall of the room was completely concealed by the masses of material piled in front of it. Heavy wooden boxes, strapped with rust-scaled iron, were piled one atop the other. To one side was a pile of rawhide bags. One of them had split, and a pile of small silver ingots had fallen out onto the rock floor. There was a double tier of the wooden boxes in front of the back row, and atop them glittered a wealth of gold and silver objects.

"Look!" said the padre. He went to his knees even as he pointed out the ranked silver and gold vessels and other items of the church. There was, indeed, the baptismal font of carved cedar inlaid with silver. Two great silver candleholders were placed in front of six golden incensories. The torchlight shone brilliantly from the polished surfaces of three large communion plates. The display was dazzling.

Dusty strode forward and slammed his pick into one of the wooden chests. Half a dozen blows stove in the side, and a flow of small silver ingots fell to the floor in a tinkling cascade. Shell picked one up. It weighed about half a pound and was about four inches long, crudely cast. A cross was embossed on the surface as well as the name Carlos and the date 1766. He handed the ingot to Frank. Frank traced the embossing with his sensitive fingers. "Yes," he said, "Carlos the Third of Spain. It was he who in seventeen sixty-seven banished the Jesuits from all Spanish dominions."

Shell looked curiously at him. "But why would they mark the ingots with *his* name?"

Frank smiled. "They likely never intended for him to get his Royal Fifth, but if, by any chance, his officers *had* come into the barranca to check on the Jesuits, they would have showed them such ingots as evidence of their good intentions."

Dusty was smashing into other chests. Silver ingots clattered to the floor.

"Take it easy, Dusty!" said Shell. "It's all there!"

Dusty shot a wild glance at him. His face was so transfigured it was hard for Shell to recognize it. "I want to make sure those cheatin' bastards haven't cheated *us!*" he said.

"The chests can easily be opened," said the padre. He started back and stood behind Shell as Dusty moved toward him with the murderous point of the ancient pick aimed at his throat. For a moment, Dusty stared murderously at Shell, and then he slowly lowered the pick. He laughed, but there seemed to be no mirth in his eyes.

Shell slid an arm about Frank's thin shoulders. "You were as good as your word, Frank," he said.

The blind man shrugged. "It was you who got us here," he said.

Dusty turned quickly. "What about *me,* Harley?" he demanded.

"I meant that," said Frank. He smiled. "I meant all of you."

"There is plenty for all of us," said Hernán quickly. "*Madre mía!* I am rich! Rich beyond all my imaginings!"

"Yuh got no real right to any of this," said Dusty.

It was very quiet for a moment. An ingot slipped from the pile and clattered to the floor.

"But surely there is enough for all!" protested Hernán.

Dusty pointed a finger at Hernán. "We promised you nothin' but your life! Yuh want to lose *that* too, greaser?"

"Son of a whore!" yelled Hernán. He dropped his hand to his pistol. Dusty swung with the pick, but Shell drove it up with his right hand while he clamped a hand on Hernán's gun wrist. He slammed a shoulder against Dusty, driving him back over the tumbled pile of ingots. Dusty fell heavily, striking his mouth against one of the chests. He dropped onto his side and rolled over, shaking his head. Shell pulled up on Hernán's wrist and twisted hard. The pistol clattered to the floor. A backhander drove the Mexican against the wall.

He reached back for his knife. "You dung in human form!" he said between clenched teeth.

Shell stepped back and drew swiftly, cocking the heavy Colt. "Listen," he said in a flat voice. "Listen, all of you! By God, we haven't even got the damned loot out of here and already you're fighting about who gets what! No one is taking his share until we vote on what he gets! No one leaves here unless we all leave together! Agreed?" He looked at Hernán.

Hernán slowly dropped his hand. He smiled. "I agree, *amigo.*"

"Dusty?"

Dusty raised his head. He wiped a thin trickle of blood from his mouth. He nodded, but his eyes were as hard and cold as sapphires.

"Frank?" said Shell.

The blind man shrugged. "I have felt that way all along," he said.

"Rafaela?"

She looked quickly at him. "Is not your share between us, *mi corazón?*"

"We share alike," said Shell.

Dusty stood up. "Great," he said dryly. "Two shares for the pair of you." He laughed. "Are you not *one* in soul, *compañero?*"

"Padre?" said Shell.

Father Eusebio nodded.

"What share does *he* get?" said Hernán quickly. "He has taken the vow of poverty."

The padre raised his head and looked at the glittering treasure. "Let my share be that of the sacred vessels of the Church," he said. "That and no more."

Dusty laughed. "Listen to *him!* Poverty, eh? He asks for a fortune in gold and silver."

"We'll discuss that later," said Shell. "Let's get the sacred vessels out of here."

"Wait," said Dusty dryly. He dabbled at the blood that leaked from his mouth. His hard eyes flicked at Shell. "Yuh forgot the *mozo, compañero.* Don't he get a share as long as *all* of us are in on it? It ain't hardly fair to leave *him* out. Then you and the woman can have *three* shares."

It was very quiet for a moment. Shell slowly lowered his Colt. He let down the hammer and then sheathed the revolver. "Sometimes you try me, *compañero,*" he said quietly. Their eyes locked, and the hatred that had begun to sprout between them grew just a little bit more. "Don't try me too far, Dusty," added Shell. "You're wearing me a little too thin."

Dusty smiled. He picked up the two great processional candlesticks. "Let's get this stuff up to the church," he said. "Maybe God will let us get past the Yaquis if we return this to the church."

The padre crossed himself, bent his head in prayer, then reverently picked up the exquisite baptismal font. Each of them took some of the sacred objects and carried them through the echoing tunnel to the outside. They breathed deeply of the fresh night air.

Shell looked back at the tunnel. "This is almost too easy," he said. "There must be a joker somewhere in the deck."

Hernán silently pointed to the northern rim of the barranca. A thread of smoke rose high in the moonlit sky. To the east and west it was the same. Shell looked over his shoulder at the towering southern rim. Something warned him. "Run!" he yelled. He gripped Rafaela and half-pulled and half-dragged her toward the passageway. Hernán passed him, running like a goat. The padre dropped the baptismal font and grabbed Frank to drag him behind a boulder. Dusty jumped to one side, looked up, cursed savagely, and leaped across a rock ledge. The huge rock struck just above the mouth of the tunnel, shattering into bits that hurtled through the moonlit air like canister shot. A fragment struck Hernán between the shoulder blades driving him face-downward against the harsh ground.

The echo thundered through the canyon and died away. Dust drifted through the quiet air. Shell looked up at the rim. There was nothing to see. Had the rock dropped by itself or had the Yaquis pushed it over the edge?

Hernan sat up and felt between his shoulder blades. "Body of God!" he said lugubriously. "No mule ever kicked me *that* hard."

They walked back to where the sacred objects had been dropped. No one spoke. The baptismal font had been ruthlessly shattered. Several of the golden incensories had been dented. One of the large golden communion plates had bent almost double by the blow of a large rock fragment. The solid silver shrine had been damaged by being dropped to the hard ground.

Hernán wet his lips. He looked up at the barranca rim. "God in Heaven," he said, "this is an omen! We are cursed!"

Padre Eusebio went down on his knees and reverently touched the damaged articles. He bowed his head and prayed.

"A lot of superstitious crap!" said Dusty.

They gathered up the sacred objects and carried them from the arroyo to the mission. The moon was almost gone. Faintly seen along the barranca rim, near the top of the only known trail down into and *out* of the barranca, the glow of a fire was seen, while the thin smoke rose straight up into the darkening night.

Chapter Twenty

Weeks had passed during which the days were a medley of sweat, labor, and tension. Hour after hour they hauled the heavy chests from the mine and loaded them onto the patient burros. One of the burros almost died from exhaustion, and despite the protests of Dusty and Hernán, Shell turned the weakened little beast loose in the hopes that it would recover. The very night it was turned loose they heard the eerie screaming of a mountain lion, and the next day Victor found the horribly mangled remains of the burro. Somehow or other—it was impossible to figure out how—a zopilote appeared, the first one they had seen anywhere near the barranca, and by noon of that day, the pitiful little bones were already bleaching in the sun.

They stored the chests within a windowless room of the mission. There was no reason to guard it. The Yaquis would not come down into the barranca, but even if they had come down, they would not have bothered with the gold and silver. Padre Eusebio saw to it that the sacred objects were placed in the dusty, echoing church, and then patiently began to piece together the baptismal font. To replace the objects and see to it that they at least were partially repaired became almost an obsession with the Franciscan.

Only the *mozo* Victor and Frank Harley did not work to take the treasure from the mine. When the *mozo* was not hunting, as he usually did every day, he would sit with Frank, and in time, although the *mozo* could not speak, there seemed to be a communion between the two of them. Frank would talk in his quiet voice, telling the *mozo* of the wonders of the world, of history and philosophy, of science, and of religion. It must have been to Victor more like a fanciful tale than the truth, but even so, he seemed content. The treasure meant nothing to him. Now and then his dark eyes would raise to the barranca rim. He knew what the Yaquis would do to him if they caught him. The loss of his tongue would be as nothing compared to what they would do to him.

Once the treasure was secure in the mission, Shell saddled one of the horses and explored the huge chasm. The place was self-contained. An inexhaustible source of water flowed from one end to the other, appearing from beneath the barranca wall and flowing under the opposite wall. Deer, bear, and turkeys abounded and there were many birds. The orange trees bore heavily and there was grass in abundance for the horses and the lone burro. There was, indeed, just about everything a man could wish, except for a safe way out to the rest of the world. As long as the Yaquis held the top of the trail, there was no possible way to escape from La Barranca Escondida.

It was not uncomfortable. The mission was well built and roomy. There was plenty of firewood for the many fireplaces, and there was a plentiful supply of bedding and other articles stored within the mission.

"It is almost as though they fully intended to come back, Shell," Rafaela said one evening as she worked in the kitchen.

Shell rolled a cigarette and lighted it. "They likely did," he said. "They certainly didn't plan to leave their treasure for people like us. Somehow they must have believed they would be allowed to come back. Frank says the Tarahumares, Opatas, and Yaquis firmly believe they will come back. That is why they still guard this country."

She nodded. "They knew no one could take the silver and gold from here without a great deal of trouble." She laughed. "I would have been content with the little cut-stone box of jewels."

Shell slowly took the cigarette from his mouth. He had no recollection of seeing such a box. It certainly wasn't in the church or in the mission storeroom. "Did you see the box?" he said.

She looked quickly at him. "Yes. It was behind the silver shrine. I distinctly saw it. Why do you ask?"

Shell rubbed his beard. He looked toward the open door. "I don't remember seeing it in the mine or on the way here," he said. "Nor is it here, Rafaela."

"But I saw it, Shell!"

He placed a finger to his lips. "I believe you," he said softly. "But whoever took it from the mine didn't place it with the rest of the treasure or in the church."

She looked toward the door. "Padre Eusebio?" she said.

Shell nodded. "He evidently thinks they were part of the church property. Dusty would kill him if he found out."

"You had better warn the padre," she said.

Shell nodded. He kissed her and left the kitchen. The moon was not up as yet. There was no sign of the others. He walked softly across to the church. It was where the padre spent most of his time now that the beloved sacred objects had been replaced in the church. The front door was closed. Shell eased it open and looked back across his shoulder. No one was in sight. Dusty and Hernán had begun to spend a great deal of time together. Hernán had rooted out some ancient bottles of brandy from one of the outbuildings, and they would suffice until his thirst grew again and he'd have to find more. Shell softly closed the door behind him. He glanced into the baptistry as he walked up the nave toward the sanctuary. The magnificent ornaments and sacred objects had been placed in the church by the padre after he had done his best to repair them. A candle guttered in a red glass on the altar, and several other candles flickered and guttered in the draft. There was no sign of the padre.

Shell walked to the altar and looked up at the figure of the Madonna and the saint. He was not a Catholic. In fact he had no religion, but something made him remove his hat and put out his cigarette. Where was that blasted padre? He walked into the dim sacristy. A candle had burned almost to nothingness in a dish. The light flickered, forming grotesque shadows on the stained walls.

Shell crossed the sacristy. Beyond it was a row of rooms, formerly used as storage places and workshops in the ancient days. Here it was that Padre Eusebio stayed, rather than in the mission. He had become silent and withdrawn since the treasure had been discovered and brought out of the mine.

A chink of light showed between the heavy shutter of one of the smaller buildings. Shell looked about. It was very quiet. No one was within sight or hearing. Metal struck against wood within the building. Shell tried the door but it was barred from within. He peered in through the chink but could see nothing. He walked to the rear of the building and tried one of the shutters. It swung open easily. He thrust a long leg into the room and closed the shutter behind him. He walked into the main room. His boots grated on the dirty floor. The padre was bent over something on his cot, hammering steadily. He had stripped to the waist, and across his muscular, bare back were healed welts, many of them, crossing and recrossing each other. Shell narrowed his eyes.

Those welts had been administered with the full force of the lash. Those were more than penitential stripes. He moved closer and accidentally kicked aside a tin cup that lay on the floor. The padre whirled. His eyes narrowed as he saw Shell. He snatched up a long-bladed knife and crouched a little as he came toward Shell. His face had utterly changed. As he moved, Shell saw something else. There was a letter branded on his left shoulder. The letter M. Deeply burned into the flesh so that it could never be eradicated. He knew well enough what that was. He had seen such brands before on Mexican prisoners. *M stood for murderer.*

The candlelight glittered from a pile of jewels that lay on the coarse bedding of the cot, and beside them was the small cut-stone box, and beyond that was the heavy wooden cross always carried at the Franciscan's belt. A hole had been bored into the upright of the cross.

Shell dropped his hand to draw his Colt and then realized he had left his gunbelt in the mission kitchen.

Padre Eusebio, if he was *Padre* Eusebio, hefted the knife. "I can have this in your throat or belly before you can pull a stingy gun on me," he said in a low, threatening voice. "Keep quiet!" he warned.

"What's the game, padre?" said Shell quietly.

"Padre?" The man laughed. "I carried it off pretty well, but I didn't think I'd keep on getting away with it."

"An escaped criminal, a murderer," said Shell. "Is that it?"

Eusebio nodded. "I would have made my way to Mazatlán if it hadn't been for the Yaquis. I was in a bad way when I ran into you. I could hardly resist keeping on with the Franciscan role once you accepted me as such."

"You did very well," said Shell dryly.

Eusebio smiled, revealing his fine white teeth. "As a boy I served at the altar. My father was sacristan of the church. I wanted to be an actor and ran away from home." He shrugged. "As you see, other things came up. Thanks to the revolution I managed to escape. It was easy to don the robe. Who would suspect a humble Franciscan of being an escaped murderer?"

"Who indeed, padre?" murmured Shell. "And now what?"

Eusebio gestured toward the cot. "The jewels are enough for me. I planned to secrete them in the cross. Now you have found out." His voice died away. He smiled apologetically. "I had grown to admire and like you, *amigo*."

"And now you must kill me," said Shell.

"That is so," said the Mexican.

"And when the others find I am gone?"

Eusebio laughed. "You think that drunken officer would care? You mean nothing to Victor."

"There is my *compañero,*" said Shell.

Eusebio laughed again. "Him? Even now he and Galeras are plotting to take everything for themselves. I have overheard them. They would leave the *mozo* and the blind man here. They would kill you and me. The woman?" Eusebio shrugged. "She would be shared between them until such time as they found their way out of these accursed mountains with a fortune in treasure."

"If they don't kill each other," said Shell.

Eusebio tested the edge of his knife against his thumb. "Exactly," he said. "I am not an unkind man. It will be swift, *amigo.*"

Shell shook his head. "You'd never get away with it. Besides, what will happen to you? As a supposed man of God you might give them away to the authorities. They'd never let you live to get out of these mountains, Eusebio."

The Mexican narrowed his eyes. "¿So?"

"Keep the jewels in the cross. I'll keep my mouth shut. The others need never know you are a fake."

"You want me to side with you, eh?"

Shell looked down at the glittering knife. "For a while, at least. I'm not sure you can be trusted."

"That is mutual, my friend." Eusebio smiled. "But then we have no choice, do we?"

"Put on that robe. I would have never known about you if you hadn't taken it off. You could have killed me easily if you had kept up the act, *amigo.*"

Voices sounded outside of the building. Eusebio hastily pulled on his robe. He scooped up the jewels and dropped them into the cut-stone box. "Take the bar off the door," he said over his shoulder. When Shell turned from removing the bar, the cut-stone box had vanished. The heavy cross hung from the rope belt. The padre smiled and made the sign of blessing to Shell. It was amazing how the man could take on the role of the humble Franciscan.

"Shell! Shell! Where the hell are yuh?" yelled Dusty.

Shell opened the door. "In here," he said dryly. "Making a confession."

Hernán laughed. His dark eyes scanned the room. "It might be good for me as well."

Dusty looked quickly about the room. "What's going on here?"

Shell leaned against the wall and shaped a cigarette. "We were discussing the prospect of getting out of here," he said.

"That's why we came to see yuh. We'd better have a council of war. The sooner we make a break out of the barranca the better."

"Hopeless," said Shell. "You can't get up that trail."

Dusty grinned. "The *mozo* found another way."

Shell shrugged. "That's more than I could do. Let's go."

They met in the big room within the mission. A fire crackled on the hearth against the chill of the evening. Frank Harley sat in a chair beside the fire with Rafaela standing beside him, while Victor sat at his feet.

Dusty had the floor. Heretofore, whether he liked it or not, he had let Shell do the leading. But now, with the treasure in their hands, and the world waiting for it to be dispensed by Dusty, he had taken over the leadership. "The *mozo* can show us the way," he said. "We can take enough of the silver or gold with us to keep us in style for a long time. When we can arrange an expedition, we can come back here and get the rest of it."

"How much do you figure on taking out?" said Shell.

"We can load the extra horses and the burro. I'd say an *arroba* apiece for them, and we can carry more with us."

"Too much," said Shell. "If the Yaquis chase us, provided we can get clear of them at the barranca top, you'd never get away loaded down like that."

"It's a chance we've got to take," said Hernán.

Shell looked at Frank. "What about him and Rafaela?"

Frank raised his head. "Forget about me," he said. "I'm staying here."

"We might not get back to the barranca," said Shell. "You know the odds, Frank."

"I'll take that chance," said the blind man.

"You loco?" said Dusty. "Yuh got the wealth of Mexico in your hands!"

Frank turned toward the fire. "Somehow," he said quietly, "it just doesn't matter any more. A man could find a worse place to live out his life. Besides, I'd only hold you back. No, I am not going with you."

"You can't stay here alone, blind as you are," said Shell.

"I will not be alone," said Frank.

Shell looked quickly at Rafaela. She shook her lovely head. "It is Victor," she said. "He will lead us out of the barranca and then return. It is what he wants, Shell."

"Supposing he doesn't return?" said Shell.

Frank raised his head. "He will return, if he can. If not, there is food for a long time. At that, I'll probably live longer down here than you will up there."

It was very quiet after his words. A log snapped in the fireplace. Dusty lighted a cigarette and eyed Shell.

"Why don't you stay with me, Shell?" said Frank.

Dusty laughed. "With the main part of the loot still here? No chance, Frank. Shell goes with us. We need every gun we can get."

"And if I decide not to?" said Shell.

There was no answer, but the intent was plain enough on the faces of Dusty and Hernán.

"When do we leave?" said Shell.

"Tonight," said Dusty. "The moon will give us light. We've got enough time to reach the top of the barranca and be well on our way by dawn."

Shell felt for the makings. He began to fashion a cigarette. He looked at Rafaela. "And you?" he said.

"I go with you, Shell."

"Very touching," said Dusty. He grinned. "If Shell doesn't make it, lady, you'll still have ol' Dusty here."

She looked at him. *"Bazofia!"* she said with all the venom she could muster. "I'd kill myself first."

Hernán spat into the fireplace. "The Yaquis might take care of that for you," he said. He grinned evilly. "After they have had their pleasure of you, of course, *querida*."

"We're wasting time," said Shell. "Hernán, Dusty, get the loot ready." He walked from the room. He had no choice. The padre trotted after him and stopped him near the corral. "What do you think?" he said.

Shell shrugged. "If we ever mean to get out of here we'll have to do it before the winter comes on."

"And the Yaquis?"

Shell looked up at the barranca rim. "They'll be waiting, padre. *They'll always be waiting.*"

Eusebio plucked the makings from Shell's pocket and expertly fashioned a cigarette. Shell grinned as he lighted the cigarette. Eusebio drew the smoke in deeply. *"Madre de Dios!"* he said. "I needed that!"

"You don't seem enthusiastic about leaving, padre."

The Mexican shook his head. He looked down at the heavy cross. "Within the holy cross I have a fortune. Enough to take me anywhere I wish to go. But, *amigo*, it cannot take me away from my conscience."

"A conscience is not a good thing for a thief and a murderer."

Eusebio waved his cigarette. "That is so." He looked about. "I like it here," he said simply. "I have acted the part of a padre for so long I am accustomed to it. Perhaps, when I escape from this great natural prison, I could turn over the jewels to the Church and take holy orders, eh, my friend?"

Shell touched the Mexican's branded shoulder. "With *that* on your hide? And the stripes on your back? No, Eusebio."

The Mexican nodded. The weight of his crimes and his conscience weighed heavily upon him. He looked up at the barranca rim. "I will go with you," he said quietly. He looked at Shell. "Perhaps I can help you to escape."

"And then?"

Eusebio held out his hands, palms upward. "Señor Frank is right. If Victor dies, the blind man will need help. I realize now there is no place in the outside world for me. Here I will have peace and the care of the old church. I do not need a woman. They mean nothing to me. To live outside of Mexico would be too hard to bear. Here, at least, deep in this forgotten barranca, I will live in Sweet Mother Mexico."

"You don't have to go with us, Eusebio," said Shell.

The Mexican raised his head. "It is my duty to help you," he said quietly. "Say no more about it."

"And the jewels?" said Shell quietly.

Eusebio looked down at the belted cross. "They will be of no value to me here. If anything happens to me, take the cross with my blessing."

Shell did not speak. There was an irony in the words of the criminal turned pseudo-padre. Shell walked to the corral and began saddling the horses they would need. Now that Eusebio did not intend to escape with them, they would have another horse to load with the treasure, but Shell decided not to say anything about it. They might desperately need an unloaded horse with which to aid their escape. Shell had no illusions. All the gold and silver in La Barranca Escondida could not pay their way past those vengeful and grim-faced Yaquis, but a fast horse might save someone's life.

Hernán and Dusty dragged out the heavy cowhide bags that had been packed in the wooden chests. They were lashed onto the spare horses and the patient burro. The moon began to rise as they finished. They led the animals into the shelter of the trees and got their gear. Each rifle and pistol was checked and rechecked. Anything that would make a noise was either discarded or silenced by being wrapped in rags.

Shell and Rafaela said good-by to Frank and left him alone in the great room of the mission. Shell had looked back at the calm and patient face of the man who had spent twenty years of his life dreaming about La Barranca

Escondida, prowling through the back country of Mexico gathering bits of information here and there. He had haunted the old missions and churches to read the dusty, crackling records of the Jesuits, until at last no man knew better than he where La Barranca Escondida was hidden. But, when he had reached his dream, it no longer seemed to matter to him. Of what use was the fabulous wealth to a blind man who had committed himself to life imprisonment in the great barranca? Strange thoughts raced through Shell's mind as he walked with Rafaela to meet the others. The barranca had cast a spell upon Frank Harley and the *mozo* and Eusebio as well. None of them wanted to leave.

Chapter Twenty-One

The silent *mozo* had led them through the thick orange groves and then through a bosque that grew from the edge of the stream, right where it vanished beneath the forbidding western wall of the barranca. He followed the barranca wall within the shelter of the trees and pushed his way through a thicket of brush to stop before a place where great shards of rock hung against the wall, seemingly ready to drop at the sound of an echo. Victor pointed toward the rock wall illuminated by the moonlight.

"He's loco," said Dusty. "There ain't no trail there."

The *mozo* walked ahead and seemed to vanish into the solid rock. Shell walked after him and then saw what appeared to be a darker line against the pale yellowish rock. A draft played about his face. Victor stood above him, perhaps twenty feet, looking up the narrow, precipitous cleft that seemed to sheer deep into the barranca wall. There was just about enough room for the laden horses to pass through. Victor looked down at Shell and motioned him to come on.

Shell went back to get his horse. He fastened the lead rope from a loaded horse to the saddle of his own mount and then led it up the steep passageway, followed by Rafaela who led her horse. "Padre" Eusebio led his horse and the burro. Behind him came Hernán and Dusty, each leading his riding horse and one of the laden horses. Dust arose from the crumbling rock as they pushed their way up the narrow, twisting slot. If the Yaquis heard them they could fill that trail with tons of rock, sealing the whole party, their animals, and a fortune in treasure forever from the sight of man.

Now and then a shaft of pale moonlight struck into the cleft when the angle of it was right, but most of the time they felt their way up in the dimness. Now and then a loose rock would slither and clatter down the cleft, and the progress would be halted while every ear strained to hear any alien sound from above. It seemed to Shell that they'd never reach the top. The horses were blowing heavily. If one of them slipped and broke a leg they'd never get the others past him.

Victor turned a shoulder of rock, and as Shell came up behind him, dripping sweat despite the coolness of the night and the steady draft down the cleft, he saw that the *mozo* had stopped. There was no telling how far they were from the top of the cleft, but Victor held a hand to his mouth and pointed upward. It was close, then.

Shell withdrew his Spencer from its sheath and carried it in his left hand as he pulled on the reins of his horse. The sorrel's eyes were wide in his head and Shell could swear that the harsh sound of his breathing and blowing would carry for hundreds of yards.

Victor stopped again. Shell worked his way up behind him. Just beyond the *mozo* was the top of the cleft, shrouded with thorned brush. Victor motioned Shell on. Together they bellied up the cruel rock surface and lay flat in the brush. There was plenty of moonlight now. The *mozo* vanished silently into the brush without stirring any of it. He was like a snake.

Shell lay flat, cuddling his Spencer, wetting his dry lips and wishing to God his heart would stop pounding so that he could hear better.

Victor came back as silently as he had vanished. He nodded to Shell. Shell brought up his horse and the lead horse. The brush was thick enough to conceal them. One by one the others reached the top of the trail and halted for a breather. Shell padded after Victor. Beyond the brush there was a naked, saw-edged ridge of rock that ran east-west, paralleling the edge of the barranca. Victor pointed to the west. There was a notch in the ridge. He held Shell by the shoulder and indicated the notch. That was evidently the way.

Shell went back for the others. He felt as though he was leading them into a deadly trap, but there was no going back now. If the Yaquis spotted them, they'd never let the *yori* escape down that deathtrap of a cleft. Victor led the way to the base of the notch. He looked at Shell and then at Rafaela, as though to say good-by. He walked past them. Dusty casually raised his pistol and placed the muzzle against the *mozo*'s broad chest. "Yuh ain't goin' anywhere," he said. "Don't play dumb. Yuh understand me, all right."

"But he must go back!" said Rafaela. "Frank depends on him!"

Dusty looked at her. "To hell with Frank," he said thinly. "We need every man we can get, and this clod can help us. He knows this country. He knows the waterholes. It's us or Frank, and right now Frank is strictly on his own."

"You're pronouncing a death sentence on him, my son," said the padre.

Dusty laughed. "Listen to him," he said.

"I will go back," said the padre.

The pistol swung to cover him. "I said we need every man we can get, Eusebio, and that even includes *you,*" said Dusty. His eyes flicked at Shell. "Don't get noble, *compañero,*" he added.

Victor led the way up through the echoing notch. Shell looked back as they reached the crest of the ridge. Far across the great void of the barranca he saw a faint glow of fire. To his left, a quarter of a mile beyond the notch, he was almost sure he could see a faint light as well. Perhaps Victor had truly found the way.

The moon was almost gone when they passed beyond the western end of the ridge. The way was clear enough. The ground was as hard and clear as pavement. The muffled hoofbeats echoed faintly. When the moon at last was gone they could not continue because of the dense, velvety blackness that surrounded them; but they must be well clear of the barranca. They halted in a great bowl of rock. Shell stood first guard. He looked back through the darkness. Frank's words came back to him on the faint night breeze. *"He will return, if he can. If not, there is food here for a long time. At that, I'll probably live longer down here than you will up there."*

There was little sleep for Shell that night. Rafaela lay close to him for warmth, but there was no comfort in it for Shell. The thought of what might possibly happen to her if the Yaquis found them was too sickening to consider. At last he fell asleep with her snuggled up against him, and his last thought was of the first time she had come to him that night in the mission when she had been afraid. *"I am not afraid now, Shell,"* she said. *"I want to be with you. I can't stand to be alone any longer."*

A hard hand gripped Shell by the shoulder and another

hard hand was clamped over his mouth. He awoke with a wild start to look up into the shadowy bearded face of Dusty. "That sonofabitch Galeras pulled out when he was on guard," said Dusty. "Took two of the loaded horses with him. Come on! He can't get far!"

"Let him have the damned stuff," said Shell. "There's still more than enough for us."

"Come on, damn you!" Dusty's voice sounded like that of a stranger.

Shell got up and picked up his Spencer. Rafaela had awakened and stood up. She clung to him. "Don't go with him," she said. "I am afraid!"

"He hasn't gone far," said Eusebio from the darkness at the lip of the bowl.

"That damned *mozo* here?" said Dusty.

"Yes," said the padre. "He will not leave Rafaela."

They climbed up to the lip of the bowl. "Stay here," said Shell to Eusebio. "Dusty and I will go after Hernán."

It was almost dawn. The faintest of gray light showed in the eastern sky. Shell thanked God that they had managed to get away from the barranca before daylight. The Yaquis would still be there looking down into the barranca, where a blind man sat all alone, patiently waiting for a tongueless Tarahumare to return.

Dusty trotted along with his carbine at the trail. "I'll kill that Mex sonofabitch," he'd say every now and then.

Shell was higher on the slope than Dusty. "There he is," he said. He could see the Mexican riding one of the horses and leading the other two. Dusty sprinted ahead. The Mexican did not see the two Americans closing in on him until Dusty was within fifty feet of the last horse. Hernán ripped his Henry rifle from its sheath. Dusty darted to one side and raised his Spencer for a killing shot. As he did so he tripped heavily and went down on his hands and knees, dropping the Spencer, butt first. The Spencer reacted with its main weakness. Nestled in the butt stock were six rounds of .56.50, bullet-tip to primer, with spring tension holding them against each other. As Dusty fell, the buttplate struck the hard ground and the shock set off one of the cartridges. There was a shattering explosion as the other five rounds let go, splintering the stock. A shard of wood struck Dusty on the left cheek, and the spurt of blood blinded him. Hernán grinned. He swung the Henry rifle to fire on the helpless American.

Shell fired through the swirling smoke raised by the explosion of the Spencer. Hernán set spurs to his horse. The horse reared and plunged and tried to run, but Hernán hung onto the lead rope of the pack horses. Shell could hardly see the Mexican through the swirling smoke. Hernán aimed at Dusty again but Shell fired first. Hernán shook spasmodically. He dragged on the lead rope, and the first pack horse plunged sideways as the rope cut his mouth. Hernán was dragged from the saddle. He dropped heavily and tried to raise his repeater, but Shell fired first again. The Mexican jerked as the heavy slug ripped into his chest. His head dropped and he lay still.

Shell walked slowly through the rifted smoke. The crashing explosion of the Spencer and the other shooting could have been heard a long way off. Dusty got to his feet and wiped the blood from his face. "The sonofabitch," he said. He grinned. "He could have got away easily enough if he had let go of that lead rope."

Shell nodded. He picked up Hernán's Henry rifle and handed it to Dusty. He hooked a boot toe under the dead man and rolled him over. He unbuckled the cartridge belt and handed it to Dusty. "You'll need this," he said.

"Get the horses," said Dusty.

"To hell with the horses!" said Shell. "The Yaquis are sure to have heard that shooting. I'm going back for Rafaela."

Dusty spat. He looked at the loaded horses. "A load apiece," he said in disgust, "and you want to go back for a filly who can be bought for a handful of pesos."

Shell turned. "I ought to kill you for that," he said coldly.

Dusty spat again. "Go get her," he said. "I should'a knowed better."

Shell loaded several fresh rounds into the butt plate opening of the Spencer to replace those he had expended. He started back to where the others waited.

"Shell!" said Dusty.

Shell turned and looked at his *compañero*. "Yes?" he said.

Dusty grinned. "Thanks for just savin' my life, *amigo.*"

"De nada," said Shell. He resumed his swift walking. He heard Dusty laughing to himself.

Eusebio waved him on. "We heard the shooting," he called. "Where are the others?"

"Hernán is dead. Dusty is with the horses. Have you seen any Yaquis?"

"Not as yet. Perhaps we are too far from the barranca."

"Let's hope so," said Shell fervently.

They mounted and led the pack horses and the burro to where Dusty waited for them. Dusty spurred Hernán's horse and dragged on the lead rope of the pack horses, riding into a broken-up area of shattered rock stippled heavily with brush. "Come on gawddammit!" he yelled.

They could see no Yaquis, but the very thought of those predatory bronze humans was enough to spur them on. Victor trotted on foot beside Rafaela's horse. "Is this the right way?" asked Shell. The *mozo* nodded.

The sky was much lighter now. Every now and then one or the other of them would look back over his shoulder, half expecting to see those fearsome humans in pursuit. The packs bounced about on the backs of the horses and the burro. One of them broke loose and fell, scattering silver ingots on the ground. "Forget it!" said Shell. "It isn't worth our lives!"

The sky was lightening rapidly. Dusty suddenly reined in his horse. "Jesus God!" he yelled. "This can't be the way! I can see the barranca!"

Shell's blood ran cold. He spurred his horse and rode up behind Dusty. Sure enough, the western end of the barranca was ahead of them.

"It's that damned *mozo!*" yelled Dusty. He looked wild-eyed at Rafaela. "You put him up to this!" He swung down from his horse and ran toward the edge of the barranca. He looked back at Shell. "There's still time for me and you to get out of here, *compañero!* What do you say?"

Shell shook his head. He slid from his horse. They could not go back the way they had come. There was only one way to go, and that was west, and they had already lost too much precious time.

"It's that damned woman!" yelled Dusty.

Shell whirled. "Damn you! Enough!" he spat out. He dropped his hand to his Colt. Shell had always been fast on the draw, as fast or perhaps faster than Dusty, or so he always thought, but Dusty's gun seemed to leap into his hand. Just as it cracked, Victor's knife hurtled end over end through the air and struck deeply into Dusty's corded neck. The Colt slung whipped past Shell's face. Dusty staggered, dropping the smoking pistol. He reached up to grip the knife. He looked at Shell with staring eyes. *"Compañero! Compañero!* Help me!" he said pitifully. He walked unseeingly toward the brink of the barranca.

"Dusty!" yelled Shell.

Dusty did not turn. He hesitated for a moment at the very lip of the barranca. "Done in by a damned Indian," he grunted. A spate of thick blood poured from his slack mouth. He stepped off the rim and fell end over end. They did not hear his body strike far below.

"We must run!" said Eusebio. "There is no time to save the treasure! Look!"

Shadowy figures were moving in swiftly on foot. There was no question about who *they* were.

"Too late," said Shell. He raised his Spencer.

Eusebio looked back at Shell. "You can't hold them off, *amigo,*" he said. "Let me try and stop them. They might be Christians."

"Don't take a chance!" said Shell.

Eusebio turned. "Once they listened to the robed men of this country," he said quietly. "Perhaps they have not forgotten."

"No!" said Rafaela.

Eusebio did not seem to hear her. He walked toward the approaching Yaquis. He held up his heavy wooden cross. "My children," he called out in Spanish. "Stop! Listen to me!"

It was very quiet as the pseudo-padre walked toward the Yaquis. The sun was tipping the giant peaks of the eastern ranges and flooding down onto the western slopes.

"They'll kill him!" said Rafaela.

"Perhaps not," said Shell. "There was a time, as the padre said, when they would listen to the robed men."

Victor pointed urgently to the very edge of the barranca.

"What does he want?" said Shell.

"He wants us to take advantage of what little time we have," she said.

Shell looked at Eusebio. "I can't leave him," he said.

"We can't hold them off here!" said Rafaela. "Shell, we need every second we can get!"

"I can't desert him," said Shell.

The Yaquis had halted. They stood there motionless, watching Eusebio as he approached them, holding high his cross and making the sign of blessing toward them. It was very quiet. Victor took Rafaela by the arm and led her to the very lip of the barranca. "Shell!" she cried.

"Go on," he said. He slowly raised his Spencer. The wind shifted and blew the padre's ragged robe about his bare legs.

"Shell!" she screamed hysterically. "Don't waste time!"

"Go on, dammit!" he snapped.

Victor pulled her to the very edge of the barranca and lowered her to a ledge. The last thing Shell saw was her great agonized eyes looking at him.

Eusebio halted twenty feet from the silent Yaquis. Shell could hear him speaking, but the words were not distinguishable. The pseudo-padre moved closer to the Yaquis. A burly-chested buck walked forward to meet him. Eusebio spoke to him. For a moment they stood there facing each other like figures in a tableau. The Yaqui's hand suddenly dropped to his knife. The heavy blade whipped up, glittering in the sun. The wooden cross was cleanly severed, scattering jewels about like brilliant droplets of colored liquid. Eusebio did not move. The blade swept up and then down, driving deeply into the Mexican's flesh. Blood flew as brightly as the scattered jewels. There was no sound from the pseudo-padre as he went down on his knees. The rest of the Yaquis moved in with unsheathed knives.

Shell wasted no more time. Eusebio was far beyond any mortal help. Shell sprinted to the edge of the barranca. For a moment he sickened as he looked down into that vast void. He saw Victor's brown face below him. Shell sat down and dropped his legs over the edge. Strong hands gripped his thighs, and Victor guided Shell down to a narrow ledge.

Victor led the way, at times with his face close to the wall and his outstretched hands digging into hardly discernible crevices, while his moccasined heels protruded over the edge. Shell had to follow him. It was that or face the Yaquis, and it would be better to fall cleanly to his death than to face their bloody knives.

Rafaela crouched beneath a rock overhang a quarter of the way down the face of the barranca wall. Shell drew her into his arms. A rock fell past them, a foot or so away. One after another, rocks fell, some of them rebounding from protuberances of the wall to soar out into the bright sunlight and then drop far, far below. The low thunder of their striking echoed from one side of the great barranca to the other. After a time the rocks stopped falling. There was a pause, and then something else dropped. The headless body of Eusebio turned end over end as it fell.

"He saved our lives," said Rafaela. She crossed herself. "He was indeed a true son of the Church."

Shell nodded. There was no need to tell her about Eusebio. Whatever else he had been in his life, he had redeemed himself at the very end. *Greater love hath no man. . . .*

Victor guided them until at last they reached the cleft by which they had ascended the barranca wall the night before. They had just reached the bottom when the first rock fell. Rock after rock crashed down into the cleft. Overhanging masses of loosened rock poured down into the cleft until it was completely impassable.

They walked through the woods in the dappled sunlight. The clear waters of the stream glinted sharply. Somewhere in the shadows turkeys gobbled. A deer bounded out of sight. A bear waddled slowly away. Victor trotted ahead to the mission and to Frank Harley.

Shell looked up at the barranca rim. "There is no way out of here now," he said. "Perhaps never, Rafaela."

She rested her head against his shoulder and then looked up into his face. "We came looking for treasure," she said. "Have we not found it in each other?"

"Yes," he said. He bent and kissed her. They walked toward the mission.

Perhaps some day they could escape from La Barranca Escondida, but would it really be an escape? Perhaps they had really escaped from the outer world. There was a spell in the barranca that had captivated them far more than the towering, impassable walls. Perhaps they never would leave La Barranca Escondida. *Quién sabe?*